Body Language

Netra Antionette

Netra Antionette

Contents

Special Thanks

To Angela Murphy (@angelareadstheblock) — **thank you.**
I'll never forget the day I was weighed down by grief, stress, and more than I could carry, and I posted a simple thread saying all I wanted was for my heart to rest. You didn't know me well, but you still reached out via email. You took the time to send the sweetest message. Words that reminded me I wasn't alone, words that touched me when I needed it most.

It was such an honor to have you Beta read this story. Your support, your encouragement, and your genuine heart means more than I can ever put into words. I adore you, Angela. Thank you for reminding me that even in chaos, there is kindness.

Special Thanks

To Aleeka — better known as **@leekasbookishbehavior.**

What started as a few casual back-and-forth conversations on Threads turned into a friendship that I treasure. Friend, thank you for every early read, every thoughtful note, every feedback message that kept me pushing when the story got heavy. You've cheered me on in ways you'll never fully know.
I see the space you're building in this bookish community & the creativity, the consistency, the love you pour into helping readers and authors find each other.
I'm so proud of everything you're accomplishing and I know this is just the beginning for you. Keep shining and keep creating.

Dedication

For the girls who had to grow up too fast.

For the ones who became mothers before their time. Whether that was rocking siblings to sleep, cooking dinners, paying bills with prayers, or holding together worlds that should've been held for you.

Life is not a romance novel. It's messy, unfair, and complicated in ways no child should have to know. But what is a great reward without great risk? You are the risk-takers. The survivors. The keepers of broken homes who still managed to bloom.

I see you. We see you. And whether you believe it or not, the world admires your strength. You've carried everyone else's storms on your back, but hear me when I say: you too are deserving. Deserving of peace. Of rest. Of softness. Of a love so raw, unfiltered, and unconditional that it reminds you that

You Were Never Meant To Be A Savior Alone.

This book is for you.

May you never forget that your scars are proof of your survival, not the limit of your worth.

-Netra Antionette

Author's Note

Alright, let's get one thing straight before you dive in. This book is not just sex on pages with a plot thrown in like parsley on top of takeout. This story has layers, baby. Layers like an onion, a croissant, or that wig your cousin swears is "natural."

Yes, there is sex in here. Yes, it's good sex. But too much sex would've been irresponsible of me. Why? Because these characters are literally going through hell. And if your world was ending, would you really be worried about getting ate from the rooter to the tooter? I think not. And if you would... therapy is calling your name, sweetheart. Loudly.

Now, don't get me wrong. Sex is a stress reliever. Amen. Hallelujah. But in real life, when shit is crumbling? You're not busting a nut while Rome burns. You're crying in the bathroom, pacing the floor, or plotting revenge. Let's keep it real. That's why in this story, intimacy doesn't show up as a band-aid. It shows up as a release after the storm, when hearts are cracked wide open and the smoke starts to clear.

So if you came here thinking this was gonna be "pornhub with pretty sentences"—**surprise**! This is a love story. A raw, layered, messy, complicated, wild ass love story. The kind that makes you stop mid-page like, "Wait... do I even believe what I thought I believed about love, loyalty, and survival?" By the end, I guarantee you'll be questioning yourself. And probably me too.

I say all that to say... sorry in advance. Sorry for the chaos. Sorry for the heartbreak. Sorry for the moments that will make you want to throw your Ereader or book across the room and then go dig it out of the couch cushions two minutes later because you have to know what happens next.

But also, you're welcome. Because you're about to experience a story that will stretch you, shake you, and maybe even heal you in places you didn't know needed healing.

Now buckle up and let's get into it.

With love,

Netra Antionette

Trigger Warnings
(Read This, Baby)

This book is not a soft stroll through wildflowers. It's heavy. It's messy. It's real. Inside these pages you'll find **substance abuse, abandonment, grief, trauma, sex, survival, the ending of a pregnancy, fighting, depression, heartbreak, and the kind of love that will heal you just to break you open again.**

If you've ever had to raise yourself, raise your siblings, or raise hell just to survive. You might see pieces of your reflection here. Please take care of yourself. Step away when it's too much. Breathe. Cry. Throw the book across the room and then pick it back up when you're ready.

But let me be clear: this story also holds joy. It holds survival turned into art. It holds the proof that even cracked foundations can grow roses. And yeah... it holds some great sex. (Sorry, Ma&Pops and my church fam. Or maybe not sorry because yal be doing it too, but nvm)

In these pages, you're gonna get both: the gut punches and the glitter, the heartbreak and the healing, the pain and the poems.

So this is your warning. Protect your heart, pour a drink, and maybe stretch first—because this ride will leave you sore, seen, and maybe a little in love with people you had no business rooting for.

Playlist

1. Bag Lady – Erykah Badu

2. Ghetto Girls – DaBaby

3. Do Not Distub – Teyana Taylor ft. Chris Brown

4. So Sexy – Twista

5. Love Language – SZA

6. Bed of Roses – Teyana Taylor

7. Exchange – Bryson Tiller

8. Rocket – Beyonce

9. Speechless – Beyonce

10. Lady – D'Angelo

Scan the QR code for more....

BODY LANGUAGE

1

Prologue

Mama hadn't moved in hours.

She laid there, curled on her side, hair matted to her face, lips dry, eyes somewhere far away. My baby brother whimpered in my arms, and I rocked him the way I'd seen her do before she stopped doing it all together. The box fan blew hot air from one side of the room to the other, and our empty fridge hummed in the background.

I was twelve.

And life had knocked my mama out cold.

"Mama," I said, "we outta food. I think Huxley needs milk or somethin'. You gotta get up now."

She blinked once. Slowly.

Then turned her face to the wall like I wasn't even there.

"He just ate." she whispered. "He just needs to sleep it off."

Her voice didn't sound like hers. It sounded borrowed and lost.

I looked down at Huxley.

He was almost one, and I was all he had.

Mama finally sat up and looked around like the walls were pressing in.

"I just need some air," she mumbled. "Watch your brother."

She walked out in a faded robe and house shoes. She was gone for a while, so I put Hux down, tucking him in with a towel since she hadn't washed our sheets.

I peeked through the dusty window and that's when I saw him.

He looked too clean to be from around the projects. Gold chain. Fresh cut. Smooth voice. A man who smiled like pain was a product he could package.

"I ain't tryna get in your business," I heard him say. "Just saying it gets better."

Mama shook her head, crying with her whole body.

"I can't sleep. I can't think. I just—my husband left me. My oldest is being more of a parent than I am. I got a baby that won't stop crying and no money to even keep the lights on."

He nodded slowly, like he understood.

Then he reached in his pocket.

"You can't pour from an empty cup, sweetheart. You gotta numb the hurt just a lil', so you can be there for your kids."

He handed her something wrapped in foil.

She hesitated. Just a second.

Then took it with shaky hands.

And that was it.

The moment that man thought he gave my mama relief...he gave her ruin instead.

Three days later, the power shut off.

I opened a bill tucked in her drawer.

Final notice. Due last week.

When I asked Mama what happened, she said:

"I had to trade somethin' to get somethin'. That's grown folks' business."

She said it like it was logical. Like it made sense.

Like she hadn't chosen a high over heat.

So I rocked Huxley that night in the dark, holding him tight, while I cried into his onesie and whispered:

"I got you. I got us. I swear."

That was the day I stopped being a kid.

That was the day I became my mother's keeper.

My brother's mother.

And my own damn savior.

2

Niveah

They always say a woman's body is her biggest weapon.

Nah.

Mine is my mouth.

And not in the way men fantasize about in group chats with their homeboys who'd fold over a wink and a lipgloss smirk.

I'm talkin' conversation, strategy, and vibe.

That influence you lay down with words so soft, he doesn't even feel it lifting his pockets.

It's 2:13 p.m. on a Tuesday.

I was on an island where the sun touched my skin like it's in love with me.

My hair was still damp from the ocean and the man I came with had just left to get me another frozen drink with two cherries like I asked.

And while his absence is temporary, the other man on my phone was a permanent confusion.

His voice was in my ear. Deep. Low. That fake-deep where you can tell he's never been heard, just tolerated.

And that's where I slide in.

"Are you close with your mom?" I asked.

He paused. That kind of pause men do when they're not used to being asked real shit unless it's a trap.

Then he said, "She tried. But she was always tired."

Mmm. There it is.

"Did she ever tell you she was proud of you?"

Silence. Breath. Then a soft, "Not really."

I leaned back in the chair, let the salt breeze hit my skin, and whispered,

"That's probably why you work so hard. You're still trying to earn something you should've been given."

He didn't say a word. So I kept going.

"You ever wonder what version of you would've existed if you were just... loved without expectation?"

That man exhaled like I'd just baptized him.

And when I said,

"You were a little boy who wanted to be enough for a tired woman,"

I swear I heard his trauma unzip itself and take a seat next to him.

I don't flirt. I listen.

And every "Mmm," every "I get it," every "Have you ever told anybody that before?" wrapped around him like warm bandages over wounds he forgot he had.

He started telling me things. About how he used to sit on the porch, waiting for his dad to come back. About how he used to show his mom his report cards, hoping it would make her smile. About how every woman since then has felt like a test he was trying to pass.

And I just felt like a safe place.

But inside, I was focused, strategic, but still on my vacation.

Because here's the truth:

I don't care. Not like that.

I mean, I care enough to make him think I do.

Enough to let him be the vulnerable version of himself no other woman gets to see.

But I'm not here to fix him. I'm here to finesse him.

Men like that... the ones with scars they dress in designer and trauma they mistake for drive.... They just want to be seen.

So I look. Not at his body, but at the parts of him that never got held right.

And I hold them. With words. With tone. With silence.

He said, "You're so different."

I said, "Baby, I'm just paying attention."

Then he asked if I needed anything.

Anything.

So I smiled and said, "You know, I'm working on something. Something for women like me. Taking care of siblings and an addict mom is hard... and sometimes the funding feels like a fight."

I wasn't working on shit, but that man wired me $5,000 before our call ended.

No titty pic.

No sexy voice.

No emotional manipulation.

Just my mouthpiece and a mission statement.

I hung up and turned back to my view like nothing happened.

Because right on time, my favorite man walked up shirtless, with the drink I asked for, two cherries and all.

"Miss me?" he said, handing it over.

"Of course," I lied, sipping slowly.

And that's the thing y'all don't get...

I don't do mess.

I do math.

I don't steal. I strategize.

God gave you a mouth and a mind before He gave you hips.

So, why lead with your ass when your intellect clears checks too?

Let these men think your superpower is sex.

Let them underestimate the art of your voice.

Let them believe the only time you're dangerous is when you're naked.

Then smile, speak, and finesse the house deed from under their name.

These men have money they don't even know how to manage.

Too many commas. Too much ego. Too much desire to be "understood."

And I major in understanding with a minor in getting what I want without giving what they think they need.

So no, I didn't touch him. I didn't kiss him. I didn't promise a damn thing.

I just reminded him that he was human.

None of this is for me.

It's for the little brother who still sleeps with the light on because we can finally pay the bill.

For my baby sister who deserves to see a different kind of womanhood than I did growing up.

For the version of me that used to wish to get the new shoes and pray food into empty fridges.

I had to learn how to hustle.

How to stretch charm like rent money.

How to use what I had—my mouth, my mind—to build what I needed.

Because life didn't hand me shit but struggle and a strong back.

Do I feel bad about it? Not really.

I don't scam.

I don't sell dreams.

I just know my worth and invoice accordingly.

I never lie.

I might not tell the whole truth, but I still don't lie.

God dealt me this hand because He knew I could play it.

Bad cards and all.

Still win.

Still smile.

I still leave the table with a full plate and my dignity intact.

So, if a man wants to feel seen? I'll look.

If he wants to feel heard? I'll listen.

And if he wants to feel needed?

Well...

There's always a price for that.

3

Niveah

My phone was tucked between my cheek and shoulder as I stood in front of the mirror, dragging a chestnut brown liner across my bottom lip with precision. My skin glowed like melted chocolate. The kind of skin they write poems about but never get to touch.

"Mmm," I hummed, slow and syrupy. "That's the thing about you. You walk like the world owes you something, but your heart still folds when nobody's looking. I know that type."

The man on the other end of the line didn't speak at first. Just a breath. Deep. Raspy. Soft, like he was sitting somewhere expensive, finally feeling seen.

"I've never had anyone say that to me before," he said. "Like... really see me. Your mind is just so beautiful."

They always said that. Because It is.

"You've been holding so much in," I whispered. "The family. The business. The pressure to always have the answers. Who holds you when it's heavy, baby?"

His breath caught.

Hook set.

"Niv..." He sounded undone. "No one understands how hard it gets."

I had a strategy. A price list disguised as poetry.

He cleared his throat. "What you got going today?"

I adjusted the straps on my bodysuit and gave my reflection a slow once-over. Waist snatched. Hair long and thick. Gold hoops. Diamond jewelry on my wrist and ankles.

"About to run to the bank," I lied. "Gotta get some cash out. My sister's nanny has been holding us down, and I couldn't pay her last week."

Another pause on his end. Then, like clockwork—

"You should've said something. I'll wire something now. What's her name?"

My smile was slow and smooth.

"Mine."

He laughed. "Say less. Check your account in ten."

And just like that, rent, utilities, a new perfume, and brunch with my best-friend Ty was handled. From a conversation. No panties removed. No moans performed. Just a mouth and a man who hadn't been listened to in too long.

"When can I see you again?" he asked.

I slid my feet into gold slide-ins and glanced at the phone.

"Soon," I said, then smirked. "We'll talk."

Translation? On my time. Never his.

"NIIIIIV!" my brother called from the hallway. "You said we were leaving twenty minutes ago!"

Thank you, God. Saved by the kids.

"Sorry, baby," I said quickly, grabbing my bag and slinging it over my shoulder. "My babies are calling. Duty calls."

"Aight," he said, reluctant. "You gon' hit me later?"

"Mhm. We'll talk."

Click.

I tucked my phone into my purse and stepped out into the hallway where my brother stood, all 6'2" of him leaning against the wall with an attitude.

I walked straight up and kissed him on the cheek.

"Man, what the hell—"

"You used to suck your thumb and piss on yourself," I smirked, pushing past him. "And I was the one changing your little pamper with your tiny penis. Don't ever act too grown for my kisses."

"Yo, stop. Nah, forreal," he groaned, wiping his face with the back of his hand. "You gotta chill."

I laughed, grabbing my keys off the side table. "You ready?"

"Yeah. I'm headin' to the car now."

"Okay," I nodded, glancing at the time. "Ima run in the kitchen to see Heidi real quick and then I'm comin'."

"Aight. Bet." He opened the front door and walked out, his tall frame moving like he knew he had a little muscle now. I watched him for a second, heart heavy and full.

He used to barely reach my hip. Now he was taller than me, voice deep, thinking he grown.

We came so far.

I walked into the kitchen and was hit with the scent of cinnamon and warm toast. Rita stood at the sink, hands deep in soap bubbles, cleaning the dishes from breakfast. Her hair was wrapped up in a scarf, and she was humming the same song she always sang when she was in a good mood.

"Buenos días, hermosa," I called.

"Buenos días, mi amor," she replied over her shoulder. "La comida está en el horno si tienes hambre."

I walked past the counter and kissed the crown of Heidi's head. She was sitting at the bar in her pink leotard, feet swinging as she worked on her coloring book.

"Morning, superstar," I whispered.

Rita turned and said, "She has ballet class in an hour."

"I know, I know," I smiled, turning to my little sister. I grabbed her soft cheeks and kissed them all over. "You keep practicing like this, and you're gonna be the best ballerina in all of Antionette."

Heidi giggled. "Promise?"

"I pinky promise." I stuck my pinky out and she locked hers with mine, sealing the deal like it meant everything.

I kissed her one last time, straightened up, and looked at Rita. "I'm headed to take Hux to basketball. Gracias por todo."

"Claro, mi reina," she said with a soft smile. "Be careful."

Rita had been with us for the last three years. What started as a part-time gig to help with Heidi became a full-time presence in our lives. She cooked. She cleaned. She braided hair and reminded me when my own appointments were. She mothered when I couldn't.

At first, it had just been me and Hux. Years of just us—me figuring out school drop-offs and lights turned off. But at twenty, everything shifted. Mama showed up talking about how she was clean, how she was different, how she met a man in rehab who was gonna change everything.

His name didn't matter. What mattered was the newborn baby she came home with.

Heidi.

And for a second—just a second—I thought maybe we had a chance at being normal again.

But six weeks after Heidi was born, her dad relapsed and two weeks after that, he died.

Mama followed him right back into the darkness. No fight. No farewell. Just disappeared into herself again.

Getting full custody of my siblings wasn't even a question.

And I did what I had to do to keep them straight.

Rita was a gift. She lived with us free of charge—my decision—and I made sure she was paid well enough to send money home to take care of her kids and grandkids. Because when someone loves your family like their own, you don't just pay them. You bless them.

"Love y'all," I called over my shoulder, heading for the door.

"¡Te amo también!" Rita yelled back.

"Love you toooo!" Heidi shouted.

And with that, I stepped back into the world, keys in hand, body snatched, bank account freshly blessed, and a teenager waiting in the car like I didn't wipe his ass fifteen years ago.

NETRAANTIONETTE

The projects still smelled like fried bologna and busted dreams, but somehow, it felt like home.

I pulled my car up to the curb slowly, letting the speakers fade as I threw it in park. The heat hit different out there. Doors wide open, box fans in windows, somebody's auntie out on the stoop still in her nightgown yelling about stolen hot chips and kids doing too damn much.

As soon as I stepped out, the madness started.

"Well, look who decided to come back to the trenches!"

"Damn, Niv! That you?! Lemme hold somethin'!"

"Girl, you too fine to be walkin' out here wit' all that! We need a warning bell or somethin'!"

I laughed, locking my door and tossing my keys in my purse. "Y'all still loud as hell and still broke. Some things never change."

"Don't act brand new now!" Old Man Roosevelt hollered from his plastic lawn chair. He'd been sitting there since I was thirteen. Swore he once dated Aretha Franklin.

"New? Baby, I'm luxury with a hood refund policy. Don't play with me," I called over my shoulder.

The whole sidewalk laughed.

"Luxury with a refund policy" was gonna have them talking for weeks.

I made my way toward the back stairwell. The building looked the same. Paint chipped, doors off hinges, some little kid's bike abandoned by the dumpster. The ghosts of who I used to be hung in the air like summer sweat.

A group of girls stood near the second railing, all crop tops, lashes, and rolled eyes. I spotted Zejah. Fourteen. Smart mouth. Too grown for her own good.

I walked over and tapped her shoulder. "Lemme holla at you."

Her friends melted away like they knew the drill.

Zejah folded her arms. "She in there."

I raised an eyebrow. "How's she been?"

She shrugged, eyes dropping to the ground. "Not too good. Some dude came by last night. Tall, tattoos, talkin' real low. He was in there a while. She came out after he left and just... sat on the porch. Got high. Fell asleep. I went in around midnight. She was still out there."

"And this morning?"

"She was gone. So I guess she made it inside."

I exhaled through my nose. Same cycle. Same slide.

"Thanks, baby," I said, slipping her a folded fifty.

She took it without a word, tucking it quick like we were passing contraband.

"You call me if something looks weird or off, you hear me?"

Zejah nodded. "I already know."

That's why I trusted her. Not with everything. But with enough.

She wasn't just nosy. She was watchful like I used to be.

I gave her one last look and turned toward the stairs—the same ones I used to run up two at a time with a toddler on my hip and groceries balanced on one arm.

The spare key was still hidden under the busted flowerpot by the door. Same fake-ass ceramic rose glued to the top, chipped and leaning like it had been through one too many storms. Everybody in the hood knew that was the hiding spot.

The door creaked open and the minute I stepped in, it hit me.

It smelled like somebody lit a blunt, busted a nut, and never opened a window. It smelled like a can of *Bounce That Ass* was left in the microwave on high.

"Jesus," I coughed, waving my hand in front of my face. "I know crack smells like regret, but this is just disrespectful."

The living room looked like chaos had signed a lease. Blankets thrown everywhere. Ashes on the table. Takeout containers. The kind of mess that made your skin crawl.

Growing up, I used to clean the place religiously just to feel like I had some control. Since I left with Hux and Heidi, the house had clearly given up. And so had she.

I walked down the hall and knocked once on the bedroom door before pushing it open.

"Mama."

She was sprawled on the bed, mouth half open, wig on sideways. The cheap fan in the corner was rattling like it had asthma. A bottle of brown liquor sat on the nightstand, sweating in the heat just like she was.

I stepped in fully. "Ma."

She blinked, slowly. Took her a minute to come back into her body. When her eyes finally focused on me, she smiled like she saw a memory instead of a person.

"Where Heidi?" she croaked.

"At ballet," I said, crossing my arms. "And I just dropped Hux off at practice."

She blinked again, like I'd just told her the news of the century. "Oh... right. That's good. That's good."

She reached for the bottle and took a long swig, straight to the head like it was Gatorade.

"You should come stay at the house," I offered, already knowing the answer. "You got a room there. A real bed. A clean kitchen. Air conditioning that doesn't sound like it's fighting demons."

She sucked her teeth and sat up on one elbow, wobbly and proud. "I ain't coming to your house, Niveah. This is my motherfuckin' house. I'm grown. Independent. I don't live off my child."

I tilted my head and blinked. "You live off gas station wine and expired ego."

She squinted at me. "You tryna be smart?"

I leaned on the dresser. "No, just trying not to light a match in here and accidentally cause a funk explosion. You really in here simmering in sex and sour everything?"

She flipped me off without looking. "Fuck you."

"Really, Ma?" I said, pulling the curtain back to let some light in. "Maybe if you'd let the sun in once in a while, you wouldn't be acting like a depressed vampire."

She sat up, squinting into the brightness like it offended her personally.

"I ain't coming to your little house with all your little rules. You got a drug-free sign on the fridge like you a probation officer."

I smiled. Big. Sweet. Petty.

"I'm glad you know."

She shook her head and reached for her lighter. "You always think you better than me."

"Nah," I said, walking back to the door. "I just think I shouldn't be like you."

Right on cue, my phone started ringing from inside my purse.

I held up a finger at my mama. "Hold on. It's Tyceona."

She rolled her eyes like I'd just told her Jesus was calling and I needed a minute.

"What, heathen?" I said, answering the phone.

"Bitch, I had a dream last night that you got rich and left me for some bald nigga with a yacht and a British accent."

I wheezed. "Not British. He sounds like tea and trust funds?"

"Yes, bitch. He had an accent and a yacht and wore linen pants with no drawers. That man had no worries."

I laughed, turning away from the window to hide my smile. "You need to stop eating oxtails before bed."

"Whatever, hoe. Look, I know you don't normally work Mondays, but that new club, GivGold? They're looking for dancers tonight for their soft opening. Apparently, some of their girls got sick."

I blinked. "Girl, what?"

"It's some last-minute shit. We already missed auditions 'cause you swear you're too legendary to audition for anything, but they said they need bodies and I am a body."

"Ty," I said, dragging her name. "I've been dancing at '*Her Majesty*' for six years. Me and my regulars—and their wallets—are paying my bills just fine. I'm not out here trying to prove I can make somebody nut off a pirouette."

"First of all," she snapped, "that's why you THAT bitch and not a bitch. Second, PLEASE. Ugh. I'm not saying quit our club. I'm saying we hit this one-night lick and be out. It's woman-owned. New crowd. Bougie clientele. We ain't gotta pull nothin' but a look and a vibe. Just imagine the money."

Money.

See, Ty knew the magic word. With my life, you could never have too much. Somebody always needed something. Groceries. Tuition. Bail. Therapy. Bail again.

"I don't know..." I said.

"Please?" she begged. "Just come through. I really wanna check it out. We might end up with new clients—hell, new sugar daddies. Upgrade the roster. New meat."

I rolled my eyes but smirked.

Me and Tyceona had been best friends since elementary. She grew up in the next building over. Her mom was an alcoholic who couldn't put the bottle down—not as bad off as mine, but just enough to raise a survivor. Me and her both knew what it felt like to walk home without a parent waiting for you and cook dinner at eight.

We learned early how to laugh through pain, how to read a room, and how to get a dollar without getting undressed. Our bond was trauma-born, but grown on loyalty and stupid jokes.

"Come onnnn," she begged. "Please. If you do this, I swear I'll never say nothing again when you bring that weak-ass salmon dip to girls' night."

I gasped. "My salmon dip is elite."

"It's an Elite Disappointment. That shit tastes like fish regret."

I sucked my teeth. "What time do they need us?"

"Uhhh... in like 45 minutes."

"Bitch."

"It's okay!" she rushed. "I already got everything you need. Fit, shoes, even your hoop earrings I borrowed last month and 'forgot' to give back."

I paused. Tight-lipped. "Bitch."

"You love me. Now hurry up, hoe. And I'll let you pick whatever song you want.. first round."

"Mmhm." I unlocked my car and slid into the seat. "I want some of your cut too."

"Done. I owe you anyway."

"I'm on the way," I said, hanging up.

I wasn't planning to dance, but when life called ...I knew how to answer.

4

Niveah

I pulled up slow, windows down, lashes longer than my patience, music bumpin' just enough to let them know THE problem had arrived.

GivGold looked like a baby daddy with good credit opened a club.

Black and gold everything. Velvet ropes. The smell of hookah, Black Ice air freshener, and broken dreams swirling in the air.

Ty was already outside, leaned on her car, eating Flamin' Hots with a pickle stuck in the bag. Red dust on her fingers, bonnet tied around her purse strap.

When she saw me, she laughed and said,

"Bitch, finally! You tryna dance or you waiting on Jesus to do your makeup?"

"First of all, you're lucky I came. I was three seconds from putting on my robe and watching reruns of *Girlfriends*."

She looked me up and down and nodded. "Okay...you look good. Waist sittin'. Lace tight. I see you gave them thighs a lil coconut oil baptism."

I posed. "Soft but slippery, baby."

We turned toward the line of girls outside the club. All types: long wigs, no wigs, barely-there outfits, fishnets fighting for their lives. One girl was doing squats in stilettos, another was hyping herself up in the mirror of a compact.

Ty sucked her teeth. "Why shorty got on her cousin's prom dress?"

"Why that one look like she just clocked outta Popeyes and kept the shoes on?"

"She did! That's grease in them socks. I know that smell."

Another girl walked by smelling like straight Bath & Body Works.

I whispered, "She got on A Thousand Wishes and desperation."

We passed a group of girls side-eyeing us heavily. One of them had a BBL so fresh, her walk had a loading screen.

Ty leaned over and whispered, "Why does her ass look like it's still buffering?"

I choked. "Bitch, I don't feel like fighting today."

A girl in line rolled her eyes at us and mumbled, "They not even all that."

Ty turned around like a principal catching a student texting. "And YOU are not even in the club yet. Talk to me after your name on the flyer, boo."

I hit a lil spin. "God don't like haters with cheap heels."

We finally made it to the front. Ty looked up at the GivGold sign and said,

"Okay, it's givin' money. It's givin' somewhere you meet a rich uncle who got a pacemaker and a pension."

I nodded. "It's giving maybe this was a good idea."

She turned to me seriously. "You ready?"

I adjusted my hoops. "I was born ready."

"Let's go in here and make 'em forget every bitch they ever loved."

The room smelled like fresh perfume, baby oil, and competition.

After we finished dressing, girls were already inside a room, heels high and bodies glistening.

Me and Ty walked in like a damn announcement. We wore matching all-black fits. Mine was a velvet two-piece with cutouts on the hips and just enough shimmer to catch light when I moved. Ty had on a black mesh one-piece with silver piping and a deep V-cut.

Different styles, but same energy on purpose. When two dark-skinned women walk in with intention and symmetry, men go stupid and women go silent. We both had our hair slicked back into matching ponytails, not a single strand flying.

No frizz, no flyaways. Just finesse. That was our signature for years.

Twin energy.

Not because we were trying to be the same, but because that's how you shake a room without touching a damn thing.

One woman with confidence is a statement. Two? That's a damn conspiracy.

We stood against the back wall, quietly watching the other girls talk and stretch. You could smell nerves in the room. One girl kept pacing. Another was bent over, adjusting her fishnets like it was gonna fix her choreography.

And then—

CLAP. CLAP. CLAP.

A thick, light-skinned woman with a pixie cut, full lips, and a voice you could feel in your chest walked in like she ran the whole damn place. She wore all white, with gold bangles stacked on both wrists and a clipboard tucked under her arm.

"Alright ladies," she said, "I'm Miss Arlette. I'm the CEO and Creative Director here at GivGold, and I've divided y'all up into groups of ten."

She smiled wide, her eyes scanning the room with confidence. "We're gonna go group by group. One at a time or two in a row—it's up to y'all how you wanna move."

I looked at Ty. Ty looked at me.

I whispered, "She done fucked up now."

Ty grinned. "She doesn't even know."

"Together?" I asked, already knowing the answer.

Ty nodded. "Always."

"Who wants to go first?" Miss Arlette asked, flipping her clipboard and sitting down.

Every girl in the room damn near threw their hand in the air. Probably just trying to get it over with before their kneecaps started shaking from nerves. I get it. That's normal.

Me and Ty sat back because see.. when you know you got it, you don't rush to prove it.

You let everyone else go first, and then you erase their memory.

Girl after girl hit the stage. There was twerking. Hair flips. A lot of heavy breathing. One girl even did a cartwheel that ended in a split.

We clapped, cheered, and smiled just enough not to be haters.

Arlette looked up from her clipboard and called out, "Last two—let's go."

Me and Ty stood at the same time, slow and in sync like it was rehearsed. It wasn't. That's just how we moved. We stepped onto the stage, black on black, slick ponies bouncing, and paused in front of her.

She tilted her head. "Names?"

Ty gave me a side-eye smirk before stepping forward and saying out loud, "My name is MissBehavior."

Without missing a beat, I leaned in and said, "And I'm MissCommunication."

She raised an eyebrow, blinked once and said, "You know what... I don't even need to know why. Just show me."

She turned to the DJ and threw her hand up, signaling to start the music. The DJ cracked his knuckles and pressed play like he knew what was about to happen.

"Ghetto Girls" by DaBaby dropped.

Same beat as *Project Bitch* by Cash Money. When that beat plays, you already know it's not a performance. It's a warning.

Me and Ty looked at each other and smiled. We were raised in Sunrise Court, but nobody calls it that. It's Gun Hill to the world, and the name speaks for itself.

We didn't come from money. We came from cracked sidewalks, power outages, and arguments that echoed through paper-thin walls.

Everything about us was made from struggle, but our stage presence? That came from God. Natural. Raw. Country-fed and chaos-raised.

No surgery. No shortcuts. Just ass, aura, and an attitude.

As soon as the beat hit, I gripped the pole with both hands and swung my body around it like I was born spinning.

Ty dropped low in front of me and started doing what only she can do: Twerking. In Waves. Ripples. Shakes that made gravity question itself.

That cornbread-and-collard-green fed booty of hers was talking and had the room silent. Not a word. Just the sound of bass and disbelief. MeganTheStallion could never. Jell-O should sue.

That ass didn't bounce, it floated. Like it had rhythm insurance.

I swung myself up the pole with one leg hooked, spinning sideways before I hit a split so clean, you'd think I was Elastigirl off *The Incredibles.*

Upside down, heels in the air, I made them stilettos clap like I was cheering for all my naysayers.

And at the same exact time, Ty was on the ground making her ass clap. That natural percussion God gave her syncing perfectly with my heels.

Same sound. Same time. Same power.

We didn't even have to look at each other because we already knew. She hit the floor and flipped her hair back as she bounced and couchie-popped like her rent was due and the water bill was waiting. She climbed the pole with all thighs and legs gripping like it was personal. She hit a full upside-down split. And as she did, I dropped too.

Split to split. Symmetrical sin. We landed couchie-to-couchie, still clapping, still locked in.

The other girls stopped breathing. Arlette's pen dropped. The DJ damn near screamed.

When we move together, it's more than entertainment. We're proof that survival has choreography.

She bounced. I popped. She swirled. I flipped. And when that final bass dropped, I landed and flipped into a handstand, and started walking on my hands in a circle around Ty, heels clapping like gunshots.

Ty arched into a full bridge on the floor—legs wide, head tilted back, tongue out and started throwing ass.

CLAP. CLAP. CLAP. CLAP.

My heels. Her cheeks. Perfect. Fucking. Sync.

The sound hit the walls like thunder and temptation had a baby. When the beat gave us that final drop, we jumped up at the same time, backs to the crowd, and hit our final pose.

One hand on our hip, the other to the ceiling like we were collecting tips straight from heaven.

Unbothered. Untouchable. And we didn't say a word because when you end a performance like that, **the silence is the applause.**

Arlette was still sitting with her mouth open like she'd just seen Jesus do the cha-cha in red bottoms.

She blinked and adjusted her bangles. Then slowly stood up, fanning herself with the clipboard like the Holy Ghost had crept into her spirit.

"I—"

She paused. Looked around. Then looked back at us.

"I don't need to see another DAMN thing."

The whole room turned. Arlette turned to the girl holding a second clipboard off to the side and snapped,

"Go ahead and tell the girls in Rooms B and C to head out. They can go home, rehearse, and try again next time."

Gasps. The girls in the room snapped their necks like they'd just heard their man say he don't like weave.

"Wait, WHAT?"

"I know tf not."

"Hell naw. This some bullshit—"

She raised a finger like she was pressing pause on the mess.

"Instead of talkin' all that shit, maybe practice more and y'all will make the cut next time," she said coolly. "Matter of fact, you should be paying MissBehavior and MissCommunication for lessons."

The room erupted with under-the-breath mumbles and side-eyes. That's when Ty leaned forward with a big smile and no filter.

"Hit up PoleItUp Fitness! Lanette will get you right, baby."

I snorted on the low. One girl stomped out, heels loud and raggedy. Another muttered, "Ain't even all that..."

Arlette didn't flinch. She just waved the rest of them off like background noise and walked straight toward us with a smile that said business was booming.

"I'm hosting a private poker event here tonight," she said, stopping just in front of us. Her eyes were sharp, smile unbothered. "I want to keep it sexy but classy. Champagne. Big wallets. Celebs. A few regulars with money and too much ego."

Then she turned to me and said,

"MissCommunication, I want you in the private room. The VIP. That flexibility of yours is something crazy. Baby, you stretch and spin on that pole like you were born on a turntable. You belong in that private room. The minute you hang upside down, they gon' hand over their whole 401K."

Then she turned to Ty and grinned.

"And MissBehavior, I need you headlining. Dead center. That ass moves like water. I ain't never seen no natural body float like that.. You could clear the stage and empty pockets with a two-step."

Ty bowed like a princess at a petty pageant. "You already know."

Arlette leaned back and added,

"And after everything... I want y'all to close out the night together. Side by side. The final set. The finale of the century. The soft opening people talk about for years."

She took a step towards us, hands on her hips.

"So. What y'all say?"

Me and Ty looked at each other, smirking like the setup was already ours. At the same time, we said,

"Sounds like a motherfuckin' plan."

5

Niveah

If pressure had a location, it was **GivGold.**

From the second you stepped on the black marble, you could feel it—sex appeal with security clearance. It wasn't a regular club. It was a curated experience... and broke was not on the guest list.

At the door, security didn't play. Big men in black with voices that didn't rise, just cut straight through the noise. If you looked like you weren't there to spend heavy or lose big, you weren't getting in. Men. Women. Didn't matter.

They weren't letting any dusty, clout-chasing, screenshot-taking, section-hopping folks mess up the vibe. If you didn't come to drop a bag or risk your last check at the blackjack table, security would look you up and down and hit you with a polite:

"Not tonight."

And baby, I respected it. You could smell money in the air mixed with Cuban cigars, coconut body oil, and the faintest whiff of jealousy. There were no lines inside. No pushing. No yelling. Everything moved like somebody planned it down to the last bottle sparkler.

Arlette had the shit figured out. She didn't just build a club. She built a damn economy. She had bottle girls in rotation looking like art pieces. Some of them were real servers. Some were just... plants. Pretty girls paid to flirt and fish for high rollers. Dressed like guests but really surveillance with lashes. Their job was to find the men and women with money and make sure that money never left the building unless it was on a tip.

I'll give her that. She thought of everything. I knew right then that it wouldn't be long before GivGold became the spot in all of Antionette.

Not the biggest. Not the loudest. But the most intentional, and intentional is where the real money lives. The cherry on top was that she set me and Ty up real proper with our own dressing room. Private and away from the rest of the girls. Full-length mirrors. Plush white chairs. Scented candles burning. A little fridge with champagne and pre-cut fruit. Even our names taped to the door:

MissBehavior & MissCommunication — Private Suite.

That's the type of shit I'm talking about. It wasn't a broom closet, but a space. A reminder that we weren't just there to shake ass and disappear. We were assets. And Arlette earned herself some extra brownie points in my book for that. What started as a quick money grab, A lil "lemme slide through, hit a lick, and go home" type deal? Turned to something permanent real quick...

NETRAANTIONETTE

I walked into the VIP room where the poker tables were already set up—green velvet, gold trim, and enough silence to hear your thoughts. Nobody else had been allowed in yet, which was exactly how I wanted it. I needed the room to myself. Time to stretch. Time to breathe. Time to slip into another world, the one I always go to before I perform.

When I dance, I don't just move. I escape. I have to because I've always loved dance. Specifically ballet.

It was one of the only things offered at my raggedy public school growing up, so I clung to it like my life depended on it. It became my peace, my prayer, my portal.

People used to say I was born to be a star. That I'd make it big one day. That I had the discipline, the lines, the stage presence.

And maybe I would've...But life had other plans. Bills don't wait on auditions. And my siblings couldn't raise themselves.

So, the pole became my Plan B that paid like Plan A.

Still movement. Still beautiful. Still me, just under different lights.

The room had a small stage tucked in the corner, but it was everything I needed.

One single pole standing tall under a spotlight. Elegant and intimidating, like it was watching me back.

I stepped closer, running my hand up the cool metal.

It wasn't just a stage, it was where women like me turned survival into art.

Arlette told me to keep it classy, and that's always been my preferred lane anyway.

I've never had to get naked to get paid. I sold fantasy. I sold control. I sold softness with boundaries. And I stayed booked.

I wore a nude leotard that hugged every curve like it was made for my melanin. Paired it with nude stiletto heels so sharp, they could slice a man's intentions in half. Honestly, what's better than nude on chocolate?

Glistening under the lights like God made me for that moment and whispered, *"Take everything."*

I sat at the edge of the stage, took a deep breath, and began to stretch—slowly, deliberately, letting my muscles remember who the hell I was.

Not just a dancer.

Not just a sister.

Not just a hustler.

But a woman who could bend without breaking.

The lights were low enough to make my body glisten under the spotlight. I had already slipped into my flow, already disappeared into that headspace where nothing mattered but breath, movement, and control.

A soft R&B beat floated through the sound system. I hung from the pole by my ankle, slowly spinning, watching my world tilt and come back to center.

Men started filing in. They came in loud, like all men do when they're trying too hard to make each other believe they're not afraid to lose.

"Y'all already know I'm taking everything tonight," one said, laughing as he clapped his friend on the back. "Whoever sits across from me? Just donate your stack now, 'cause I'm feelin' lucky as fuck."

They kept talking, joking, flexing, slapping hands, and still found time to watch me.

I shifted into a superman hold, body extended out mid-air, heels slicing the air slow and deliberate.

I heard one of them mumble, "Damn, she's sexy as hell..."

I didn't say a word. Just turned my head, locked eyes with him, then looked away like he never existed. **I don't talk when I dance. My body does all the speaking.**

Another man chuckled. "Aight, she one of those. Don't say anything. Just make you feel it."

They kept watching, and I kept moving. Smooth, sensual, like I was made of syrup. Every swing, every hold, every grind down that pole.

Then maybe it was the lighting. Maybe it was the sway of my body.

But something broke open in them. Like they forgot I was there at all. Like I was the music. The light. The background of their boldness.

"That fool still coming tonight?" one asked, low but not low enough.

"Yeah," the other one said, sliding into his seat. "His ass thinks he's slick. Don't even know we already onto his play. Soon as he flash that bet, I'm baitin' him and we cleanin' him out."

"Oh, he getting tricked tonight. Believe that."

I kept dancing. But my ears? Wide open. My body rolled down the pole, back arched, knees bent, heels landing softly. I hit the floor in a slow crawl, flipping my hair like I couldn't hear a thing. More men came in, dap'd up their friends, grabbed drinks, whispered side bets.

The dealer walked in next. Buttoned up, sharp as hell, "We ready to start?"

And then...

That voice.

Deep. Smooth. Calm like danger that doesn't raise its tone.

"The most important player hasn't even made it in the room yet."

I was mid-spin, upside down again, but I felt it in my spine. The way that voice slid into the room and laid itself down like power.

I lifted my head, curious, because if your voice sounded like that—your face better match.

And Lord...It did.

He wasn't flashy like the rest. No chains swinging. No loud colors. No diamonds fighting for attention. Just a crisp black suit. Tailored to the body of a man who worked out but didn't brag about it. A fresh fade. And a beard that looked like God shaped it Himself.

What got me was .... He didn't walk to the table first. He walked to me.

Direct. Intentional. Quietly arrogant in that way that rich, fine men who don't need attention always are.

He stopped a few feet from the stage and just looked at me. Not hungry. Not thirsty. Just... curious. Present.

I never had a man look at me like that. Or maybe I just never wanted one bad enough to notice.

He didn't throw money. Instead, he nodded to the man standing behind him. The man knelt down, opened a leather briefcase, and pulled out a thick stack. Fine ass mystery man bent down and placed it gently at the base of my stage. Didn't say a word. Just rubbed his beard, smirked slightly...

And that's when I saw it. The Shamballa bracelet.

Real ones know. 18k beads. Diamond-encrusted. Retail price is every bit of forty bands.

He rubbed his hand across his beard again, and I couldn't help but follow the motion of his wrist. That bracelet glittered like it had secrets. And I wanted to know all of them.

My hips moved slower. My lock on him deepened. I didn't even know his name...

But I already knew, **I wanted him.**

6

Kendrix

I made my rounds. Gripped every palm at the table with that same firm shake that said "Yeah, I'm him."

Eye contact. Nod. Small smile, but nothing extra. Just enough to remind these niggas I wasn't pressed to be here. They were pressed to play me.

Half the room had been begging for this game for months. Always talking shit. Always claiming they were "up next."

I was in a good mood too, so I said fuck it. Let's play.

I pulled out my chair, unbuttoned my jacket, and took my seat like I owned it. Because in a lot of ways, I did.

I own cigar lounges, underground clubs, and high-end nightlife.

I built experiences, rooms that men like them paid to sit in.

I came in with my mind clear, fully focused. Ready to flip egos and stacks like I always do.

But the minute I stepped through that door, something shifted.

She caught my attention and didn't even have to try.

Every room I walk into had dancers. Bottle girls. Strippers. Models.

Half-naked women who'll do a back bend just to get close enough to ask what I do for a living.

So trust me when I say—I'm used to pretty. But she didn't move like she was performing. She moved like she was at peace. Like the pole was a prayer and her body was the scripture.

All rhythm. All grace. And her skin was smooth and deep like brown sugar under candlelight.

The way she spun—slow, sensual, with intention. It didn't just catch my eye. It locked it, and I kept trying to refocus.

The dealer sat down, cards got shuffled, chips started getting stacked, and the boys were already running their mouths. But my gaze drifted back to her.

She was hanging upside down, arms extended, heels pointed, body stretching like temptation itself.

Fuck.

I shifted in my seat.

She was beautiful as fuck. The kind of beautiful that doesn't ask for attention—it just owns the air. Her face was unbothered. Her body was speaking in a language I didn't know but suddenly wanted to learn.

I leaned back, tossed in my first bet, and nodded at the dealer to keep the game moving.

But truth be told, I wasn't thinking about the damn cards anymore.

The dealer slid the next hand across the table. I looked down at my cards. Solid. Not perfect, but enough to run with. I tossed in another stack, leaned back, and tried to pull my focus in, but her body kept dancing on the edge of my vision like it had a goddamn magnet in it.

Every slow twirl... every glide down that pole...

Shit was witchcraft.

I lost the next hand. Then the one after that. I squinted at the cards, then at the men across from me, then right back at myself like—

"Nigga... get your head back in the motherfuckin' game. You down two hands behind somebody doing aerial yoga in heels."

I leaned forward, whispered under my breath like I was about to slap myself.

"You acting like you ain't seen ass before. Focus, Kendrix. That pussy is not yours. That stack is. Stop thinking with your dick and play your damn cards."

The man next to me chuckled. "Something funny?"

"Nah," I said, cracking my neck. "Just talking to myself. He's the only one in this room I trust."

But right when I tried to zone back in, she cleared her throat.

My eyes snapped back to her. She wasn't dancing like before. The rhythm had changed. It was subtle, but different.

Her eyes were locked on *me*. Not flirty, but focused, intentional, and sharp. Her body was swaying side to side, but there was a pattern like she was moving to a beat only I could hear.

She glided across the pole, spun once, then bent low, her body still rolling like waves.

Then she did something that made my gut tighten. She lifted her right leg slow and deliberate, toes pointed toward the floor... **and then flexed it to the left. Directly at two men across the table.**

A soft pivot. A dancer's move. But her eyes never left mine.

That was a signal.

I didn't even blink. I adjusted my wrist, leaned back in my chair, and started watching the two she pointed at. One was already counting his chips like he won the round. The other kept looking at him... like they knew something I didn't.

Until I did.

A bluff. A tag team. They were playing me. The little head tilt. The too-casual glance. The way their hands moved in sync, betting and folding on a rhythm like it was rehearsed.

Got you, bitches.

I matched the bet. Then raised and watched them fold like they had never played a hand in their life.

They tried to hide it, but that split second of surprise gave them away.

Both of them looked at each other like how the fuck did he know?

And I just smiled. Real slow.

Then I looked back at her.

She was still dancing, back to looking like nothing happened.

But her lips curved just enough for me to see it.

She knew I caught the message.

I wanted her even more. I wanted to know everything she wasn't saying.

The poker game was over. Stacks cleared. Chips collected. Men shaking hands like it hadn't just been a room full of quiet betrayal and fake math.

"Good game, Ken."

"Next time, I'm coming for you."

"We headed out to the main floor. More fine ass girls about to hit the stage."

I nodded, dapped a few of them up, smirked like I hadn't just taken their money and a little pride too. They left in packs, ego limping behind them.

Meanwhile, I sat there, sipping my drink like I hadn't been staring at the reason I won all night.

Her.

She was finishing her last set. The music slowed. Her body still rolled like smoke.

And when that spotlight dimmed and the bass faded out, she stood tall, wiped her hands on a towel, and grabbed her robe off the stage bench like it was just another day.

She was about to leave, all unbothered and goddess-like, but I wasn't done.

I stepped in front of her before she could pass, close but not too close, and dipped my head low so only she could hear me.

"You always warn strangers mid-spin? Or was I just your charity case for the night?" I whispered.

She blinked at me once. I expected something sweet. Cute. A little *"just looking out"* moment.

But no.

"You looked like you was either about to cry… or piss on yourself."

She shrugged. "I help the needy."

I choked on a laugh. Caught off guard, but in the best way. Most women try to flirt soft. Pretty. Passive. She threw punches and smiled while doing it. I liked that shit.

I leaned in closer. "You talk to all your heroes like that?"

She didn't flinch. "You think you're a hero because you finally stopped getting your ass handed to you?"

I raised a brow. "I think I'm the reason they built this private room for you to dance in and not have a GoFundMe link in your bio."

She smiled, slow and wicked. "That the same mouth you use in business meetings?"

I grinned, "Nah, this the one I use to get women who think they're immune to men like me."

She laughed and didn't cover her mouth or giggle all fake like most girls who want to be chosen. She just let the sound hit the air like she wasn't afraid of shit.

Damn.

We stood there, quiet for a second, just looking. Her arms crossed. My drink in hand. Staring like we were both trying to figure out what the other person's deal was.

I licked my lips out of instinct and caught her watching when I did.

She smiled. Real soft like *"Careful. That's the road to hell."*

And I was about to say something slick, probably inappropriate when Arlette burst through the door like the building was on fire.

"Y'all still in here?" she said, eyes bouncing between us like she'd walked in on something she didn't exactly expect. "We got a whole damn club full of money waiting and y'all back here playing."

She started to step away from me, but Arlette narrowed her eyes. Not at her, but at me. Like she just felt the shift in the room. She knew energy, and something wasn't sitting right.

"MissCommunication, why are you still in here?" she asked, squinting. "You got another set in twenty, baby."

"I was just heading out," she said, straightening up and smoothing her robe.

I never took my eyes off her, so Arlette made sure to walk around me slow and placed her hand flat on my back—real familiar. Real marked territory.

It was light. But it was loud. And it pissed me the fuck off.

I stiffened. Let it linger just long enough for her to think it meant something, then stepped out of her reach like she had a bad scent.

She clocked it. Eyes narrowed. Jaw tight.

That little move back was me saying, *Don't pull that shit with me.*

She looked at me like, "Really?" But didn't say it.

Instead, she cleared her throat like she was still in control and said,

"MissCommunication, go get ready, please."

Then turned back to me and smiled wide and fake.

"And give me and this fine-ass man of mine a little privacy."

I blinked.

Then smacked my lips so hard it echoed.

"Man of who?" I muttered under my breath, but not low enough.

She didn't say a word. She just walked out the room slow, hips calm, face unreadable. As soon as the door clicked shut behind her, Arlette crossed her arms.

"Really, motherfucker? You just gon' flirt in my face?"

I looked at her, unbothered, then I dropped my voice and said it straight so she could really get it through her fucking head.

"Man, chill the fuck out. You not my girl."

She blinked, trying to hold her composure, but her eyes said everything her mouth wanted to scream.

"Stop doing that shit every time you see me with somebody," I said, stepping back, giving her space like she needed it. "Touchin' me. Claimin' me. That shit's dead. Been dead."

"What the fuck ever, Kendrix," she snapped, brushing her hair out her face like she needed something to do with her hands. "I got a club to run."

She turned, heels already clicking toward the door.

But right before she walked out, she paused just long enough to say:

"I'll find you when it's over, so you can take me home."

She didn't even wait for a response. Just slammed the door behind her like that meant something. I stood there for a second, shaking my head.

"Take you home? You lucky I still hold the door open for you, the fuck."

7

Niveah

I don't know what type of shit Arlette and that man from the VIP room had going on, but the way he curved her ass was so effortless and boldly disrespectful. He did it right in front of me, so yeah, that told me everything I needed to know. That man ain't give a damn about her being there. His eyes were locked on me like I was his next investment.

I wasn't looking for anything serious, though—let's be clear. But that nigga was paid. And I had plenty of bills that needed to be paid too.

If the math is mathing and the eye contact is communicating... Who am I block my blessings?

I was sitting in our dressing room chair, legs crossed, robe half open, sipping ginger ale like champagne while Ty finished curling the last section of my hair.

I had already changed into my final outfit. The red one-piece hugged me like it had a vendetta and glittered like money. My heels were laced tight and vicious, blood red with gold tips.

It was the final dance of the night. The main event with Ty and I.

She knew putting us as the closer was genius. We were gonna walk out there and empty every wallet like a damn tax collector.

"When you say fine," Ty said behind me, comb in one hand, edge control in the other, "was he fine? Or was he fine fine?"

I smirked. "Girl. Fine as fuck. And you know I don't say that about just anybody."

Ty clicked her tongue. "Yeah, 'cause a nigga pockets will make him look better to me. But you be needing the face to match."

"Nah. He could be the richest man on Earth, but if he look like Shrek?" I looked at her in the mirror. "That motherfucker still a big green booger to me."

We both screamed laughing.

She flicked the comb, laid my last baby hair with a flourish, and said, "Alright, you done. And bitch... you look like a homewrecker in a romance novel. 10 outta 10."

"Good. That's exactly what I was going for."

The door swung open and Arlette walked in.

She had changed into an all-white sparkling dress that screamed boss bitch, hugged every curve, and dragged the floor like royalty.

"Okay then," I said, raising a brow. "Pop yo shit, Ice Queen."

Ty whistled. "You look expensive and untouchable."

Arlette smiled. "I know. Y'all look good too. I love the red outfits. Whew. That red about to murder under the lights."

She eyed us up and down like we were merchandise guaranteed to sell out.

"You ladies ready?" she asked.

I stood and adjusted my straps. Ty was already standing, applying one last swipe of gloss.

"Ready ain't even the word," I said.

The lights dimmed. Spotlights spun before snapping center stage. Arlette stood dead center, back straight, mic in hand, with that all-white glittering gown flowing behind her like she floated to the stage instead of walked.

The crowd was loud. Applause. Whistles. Claps over drinks. Somebody even screamed, "THAT'S MY GIRL!"

She smiled, then raised one hand with the kind of calm only a woman in full control could hold.

"First of all... thank you."

She looked out over the crowd like she'd handpicked every person in the room.

"This soft opening was bigger than a dream. It was a damn statement."

Cheers again.

"Now... Antionette has never seen a place like this. And I promise, this is only the beginning."

She took a beat and let that settle.

"But before we close out this legendary night... I got one last surprise for all my ballers and shot callers."

"Two women. Both dangerous. Both unforgettable."

She smiled, licking her bottom lip before continuing.

"One's a silent assassin who speaks with her body and shuts down rooms without saying a word."

"The other? A rebel with rhythm. Disrespectful with the hips and mesmerizing with the face."

Laughter and gasps came from the crowd.

"Together?" Arlette paused, raising one brow. "They don't just dance. They start wars."

The crowd screamed.

"So, get loud for the future of GivGold. The future of Antionette nightlife. The duo you'll never forget..."

She threw her hand in the air, voice rising:

"Give it up for MISSBEHAVIOR & MISSCOMMUNICATION!"

She walked off stage saying,

"I need a hot girl... "

BOOM.

I Need A Hot Girl by the Hot Boys exploded through the speakers.

The bass rattled the floor. Red lights bathed the stage like warning sirens. The crowd lost their shit and dudes were throwing money before anybody even walked out.

Ty and I hit the stage together, flipping in heels like Olympic gymnasts. Not a stumble and not a hair out of place. Just the click of stilettos on stage and the gasps from grown-ass men.

We landed at the pole in a split. Hips grounded and tongues out. We humped the floor like it was our favorite dude, and just like that, the mood shifted. Ty popped up first, grinning like a felon with a full ride. She turned around and bent over slow, giving the crowd that cornbread-fed, shake-like-sin ass routine she was famous for.

She didn't twerk. She served ass like it was on the dinner menu and the captain's special came with dessert. She backed it up to the beat like her ass had its own body. Meanwhile, I spun around the pole in sensual circles, letting the room heat up. I let the lights bounce off my skin, catching the soft gold glow in every glide.

Then I saw him. Center of the room. VIP section. Glass in hand. Unbothered by the screaming. The chaos. The storm of bills flying around him. Eyes only on me.

We locked eyes like we'd planned the whole performance together. He sipped his drink, slow and calm, like he had nowhere else to be but watching me. Unfazed and undressing me with his eyes like he had a right to.

The way he licked his lips made my heart jumped and maybe... my pussy did too.

Damn.

What was he doing to me?

Who gave him that kind of power?

That's when I snapped out of it. HELL NAW!

I'm the one who does the seducing. I'm the one who talks with my body and makes men twitch in places they didn't know could feel. So, I hit the pole harder. It was damn near acrobatic. A spinning fireman drop straight into a locked eagle split. Painful, perfect, and damn near illegal in five states.

He sat up in his seat.

Checkmate.

Money rained down like confetti at a New Year's Eve party. The floor was covered with cash, but I didn't care.

My eyes stayed on him. And his never left mine.

He took another sip of his drink, slow again, like I wasn't flipping and fucking gravity.

Then Arlette walked up behind him like she was approaching something that *belonged* to her. She slid her hands onto his shoulders—territorial, smug, but too damn late.

He just leaned forward a little, cool as ever, letting her hands fall like they were crumbs on his suit.

And he never looked away.

I almost laughed. I wanted to yell from the damn stage—

"Step your pussy up, baby girl. The game changed the minute I walked in."

But I didn't say a word.

I just twirled on that pole like I was speaking another language.

A dialect of seduction only the real ones could understand.

Right on cue, Ty and I strutted to the edge of the stage, hips swaying like we were walking through wet dreams.

We picked the two closest men and pulled them onto the stage. Flat on their backs. We swung a leg over each one and lowered slowly, making it look like we were riding their faces while keeping the rhythm locked in.

I didn't blink. I didn't break. I kept my eyes on him.

And that's when he smiled. Slow and dangerous like he'd just been claimed.

But I wasn't done. Not yet.

The pole was my weapon, so I climbed. Body tight, arms firm, thighs locked. And then I did the Pegasus. One of my signature variations.

Upside down, one leg split and pointed toward the ceiling like I was about to take off midair. The other leg bent sharp, flexed just behind the pole, holding me like a damn bird in flight.

But I didn't stop there. I added the a slow, body-controlled grind mid-air, while I arched my back and threw my head so far back, it looked like a surrender.

Every angle was divine. Sweat glistened like honey on my skin, and the crowd was screaming like a church altar call.

And he straightened his spine like he'd just seen something biblical.

Then I stood without using my hands and I looked at him one last time. Dead in his eyes. He was still leaned forward, staring like I had him in a trance. He licked his lips again, like he was starving and I was the only thing on the menu.

I gave him a small smirk, turned around, and walked off stage with my hips swaying like they had their own agenda.

I didn't look back because I didn't need to.

He was already mine and as I disappeared behind the curtain, I thought to myself:

"That's how you get a man to beg for your energy without opening your mouth, or your legs. Just move like you know he doesn't deserve a damn piece of you... but he might earn the fantasy."

NETRAANTIONETTE

Our dressing room was quiet with just the low hum of the music from the main floor fading into the walls. Ty was halfway out her outfit, one stiletto kicked to the corner and the other still on like she couldn't decide if she was clocked out or not.

"Bitch," she said, flopping into the chair with the most dramatic sigh, "we just made this club ours, bitch."

I laughed, taking off my bodysuit, letting the soft cotton of my sweatsuit touch my skin. "Hell yeah. That pole still smoking."

Ty grabbed a makeup wipe and cleaned her face. "One of them ballers I gave a private dance to asked if I like seafood. I told him I'm allergic to bullshit, but I might let him take me out for shrimp anyway."

I looked up from my bag, squinting. "Ain't nothing good open this time of night but Waffle House and legs. Tell him to wait until tomorrow to see just how bad he want it."

Ty tossed the wipe in the trash. "You right. But maybe I did want my legs open. I mean, they was already stretched out earlier on the stage."

We both hollered, and Arlette busted in holding two fat bags of money like Santa Claus, if he only sent gifts in fives, tens, and sweaty hundred-dollar bills.

"Okay!" she said, face glowing. "Y'all did that shit."

She dropped one bag in front of me, the other in front of Ty, and stepped back like she was giving offerings at the church.

"That's y'all cut. Y'all made the night what it was. The crowd is still talking. I ain't gonna hold you, this place wouldn't have hit like it did without you two. So... what I'm sayin' is..."

She paused.

"Come work for me."

Ty and I looked at each other. She raised one brow, smirked, and said, "Bout damn time you asked."

She laughed, tossing her hair. "I got both of your numbers. This was the soft opening, but we'll do the grand opening *for real, for real* in a few days. I'll be in touch. Just keep practicing your sets... or don't. Hell, y'all already perfect."

She turned and left.

Ty stood up and stretched. "You gonna tell our old club *'Her Majesty'* we leveled up?"

I zipped my bag and pulled my hoodie over my head. "Nah. That club held us down for years. When we ain't have shit, they gave us something. Ima let him know wassup, though. But I'll still slide through on the slow days or when this place is closed. Loyalty still is everything to us."

Ty nodded. "Bet. That's real. That sound like a plan."

We walked out, headed towards the back door. I didn't expect anything else tonight. I was satisfied, tired, and full in every way that counted. But the moment we opened that back door to leave, he was standing there.

Leaning against the side of a matte black Escalade, talking on the phone like he was mid-conversation.

But I knew he wasn't. He looked too casual to be caught off-guard. One hand in his pocket, the other holding his phone up to his ear, but his eyes locked right on me.

He knew I'd come through that door. I didn't stop walking. I didn't blink, speak, or smile. But inside, my chest was thumping. I walked right past him and let my shoulder graze his chest just enough for him to feel me.

He didn't flinch or move, but I heard him hang up that fake-ass phone call, and I smiled to myself.

8

Kendrix

She walked past me like she didn't feel the heat I was throwing. She didn't slow down or bat a lash. That type of self-control only comes from someone who chooses not to give in. I liked that.

"'Excuse me, pretty…" I said, my voice smooth and slow.

She turned halfway, one brow raised, wearing a sweatsuit like she didn't just make the entire club forget their mother's names.

Before she could say anything, her homegirl started laughing.

"Oh yeah, sis… I see he's tryna be poetic. I'm going to my car to make a call. Handle that."

She laughed. "I'm good, Ty. Love you. I'll be right behind you leaving, sis."

She turned back to me and I tilted my head, my eyes never leaving hers. "You sure about that?"

She squinted a little. "Sure about what?"

"That you'll be leaving right behind her."

She smiled, already folding her arms like she was setting up the chessboard in her head. "Yeah, I'm pretty positive."

I smiled. "I'd love to have a little of your time."

I stepped in just a little closer, close enough to smell the soft vanilla on her skin. She looked down at her wrist—where a watch would've been—and tapped her bare skin. "Well, time is money. And it takes money to get my time."

Arms still folded. Chin slightly tilted. Waiting.

Shit.

I laughed a little under my breath. "Aight, you got it. That's fair."

Then I looked her straight in her eyes, "So what's your name?"

She gave me a smile that hit harder than any punch I ever took in my life.

"You never ask a dancer her real name," she said. "You have to earn that. So, for now..."

She leaned forward just enough for me to feel the whisper on her lips.

"...all you get is MissCommunication."

Damn.

I felt that shit in my bones. Not just the way she said it, but the fact that she meant it. No thirst. No flinch. She was holding her own, and she knew she was the one with the power in this exchange.

I nodded once, that grin creeping up slow.

"MissCommunication, huh?"

She stood tall again and didn't blink.

I rubbed my beard, eyes still locked on hers.

"Aight. I can respect that. I like a woman who makes a man work for his answers... especially when he's got the money to keep asking."

She didn't have to respond because that smirk of hers told me everything.

"You got time to sit somewhere and talk?" I asked.

She tilted her head, thinking. Then she slid her hand under her chin, like she was weighing the pros and cons.

"Hmm," she said, lips curling just a little. "Let me think about it..."

A dramatic pause.

"Probably not."

I blinked. "Damn."

"I don't know you," she added, shoulder shrugging. "You could be anybody and could do anything to me. So until I know you a little better, we can only speak outside, in the open, with my gun close enough to shoot you if you try me."

I couldn't even be mad at it. That was the sexiest shutdown I ever got in my life.

"Shit," I chuckled, rubbing my chin, "I was hoping for a different response..."

Then I looked her right in the eyes.

"...but I like that one even more."

A woman like that didn't just walk home with any rich man who whispered something sweet. She was smart and cautious.

She reached into the side of her bag and pulled out a small black card with no name, no number, just a QR code on it. She handed it to me.

"What's this? A booking card?"

She laughed.

I held it up and shook my head. "I ain't tryna book you for a party or no private dance, MissCommunication."

I stepped a little closer, lowering my voice just enough.

"I'm tryna spend some time with you. That's it. I seen how you dance... Now I wanna see how you think."

She smiled big and just when I thought I might've been saying the right shit for once, the back door busted open like the SWAT team had just pulled up.

"Baaaby!" Arlette slurred, stumbling out with a hand over her chest like she was shocked to see me outside. "I been looking everywhere for you. What are you doing out here?"

She made her way toward me, wobbling like a toddler in church shoes. "I'm so drunk. The bartender had me taking shots to celebrate. Are you ready to go home?"

I didn't even get to answer cursing her ass out. MissCommunication took one look at the whole performance and laughed.

She tilted her head at me, eyes still full of fire.

"Well," she said. "Looks like you have other responsibilities."

And just like that, she turned and walked off toward her car, hips swaying like she knew they were the last thing I'd be dreaming about tonight.

I was so fucking pissed, I could feel my blood pressure in my teeth. Arlette wasn't drunk. She was jealous. And I was two seconds from forgetting every ounce of home training and making her feel that shit.

She pressed her body up against me like I was supposed to melt.

"I told you to stop doing that shit," I said, stepping back like her presence was contagious.

She blinked, confused. "I told you I wanna get back together. Look how good the club did tonight. That's us, baby. We could be Antionette's next power couple like Jay and Bey."

She slid in closer, kissed my neck like the shit still worked. "I'm horny too. You know no one can make me cum like you."

I wiped her kiss off like it was bad news. "Too bad. Go masturbate to our memories."

She blinked fast, lips parting like I just hit her with a frying pan.

"Chill the fuck out, Arlette," I said, real calm but loud. "You not my girl. Stop poppin' up every time you see me with a woman like this is your dick. It isn't."

She crossed her arms like a toddler in time out. "Wow. So you tryna talk to a bottom-of-the-barrel-ass bitch? A pole-dancin' nobody?"

"Bottom of the barrel?" I stepped in closer, eyes locked. "Arlette, you were the barrel. Full of expired ass and delusions."

Her jaw dropped.

"And let's get this straight while we're on topic," I added. "You're not competition. You're not even a consideration."

I started to walk to my truck, but stopped and turned back one more time.

"Oh, and cut that 'go home' bullshit," I said laughing. "We never lived together. You just had a drawer and a dream."

"Whatever, Kendrix! You gone want this again. And when you do, I'll be unavailable."

I opened my truck door, climbed in, and rolled the window down.

"Unavailable?" I smirked. "Perfect. Be unavailable, undelivered, uninstalled. I don't give a fuck. Just be gone."

NETRAANTIONETTE

By the time I made it home, it was already past four.

The silence hit me like a wave. Just me, the marble floors, and a whole lot of damn space I didn't feel like being in.

I kicked off my shoes and unbuttoned my shirt while I walked through the kitchen, thinking I'd grab some of the leftover lamb chops my chef made earlier. I didn't even have the energy to reheat.

I opened the fridge, looked at 'em, and closed that shit. I went and pulled out some dog food instead. At least somebody was eating tonight.

"Come eat, Pharaoh," I called out.

He came running in like he owned the place. He ate. I watched. Then I gave him a pat on the head and took my tired ass upstairs.

I loved my house. Paid for every brick in full. But I ain't gonna lie, I was a little delulu when I bought it. Too much space, too many rooms. That's why I stayed at my clubs so much.

I only wanted one person there with me. The woman who danced without speaking, warned me without words, and got my attention without even trying.

When I finally laid down, the cool silk sheets didn't even comfort me like they usually did. All I could think about was that damn card she gave me. I reached over to my nightstand, grabbed it, and scanned it with my phone.

It pulled up a photo of her looking fine as hell and underneath it were her social handles, a business number, and an email.

Damn.

I stared at that screen longer than I should've. Then said fuck it and hit the number.

It rang once.

Twice.

Three times.

By the seventh ring, I was already annoyed.

Was she sleep? Ignoring me? Did I just get curved with a QR code?

"Hello?"

Her voice was low. Sleepy. But still soft as satin and just as dangerous.

I didn't give her time to say another word.

"Pretty," I said, voice rougher than I meant. "This Kendrix. From the club."

I paused, smirking to myself.

"I know this is your business phone but ain't nothing about this call business. So Ima hang up... and let you call me back from your personal line."

Then I hung up. I didn't wait for no reply. I knew I was taking a risk. But oh fucking well. She'd already taken too much control anyway. Hanging up in her face, demanding she call me from her personal line like I was paying her bills and laying pipe was crazy. Maybe I overplayed that one. But hell... I couldn't be no regular nigga in her eyes, so I had to move different.

I needed a distraction, so I grabbed the remote and threw on The Chi to keep from overthinking. Fifteen minutes in, my eyes started drooping. I was halfway into a dream about ass and oxtails when my phone started ringing. Unknown number. I damn near dislocated my wrist trying to grab it fast.

"Hello?" I said, voice halfway sleep.

"UNBLOCK ME RIGHT NOW, KENDRIX!"

I sat up like I saw a ghost.

"Man, what the—?!"

"Yes, nigga! You got me out here looking crazy like I ain't still a part of your life. We still go together real bad!"

I closed my eyes, gripping my temples. I was too tired for this Tyler Perry-ass monologue.

"Arlette, get the fuck off my line. I thought you was someone important."

"Oh, so I'm not important now?! Wow. That's crazy. You acting like I ain't been down. Like I ain't help you when your little brother went to jail. Like I wasn't the one helping you stack all that money on the side so he could come home to more than he left with."

"What the fuck did you just say?"

"I said what I said, Kendrix. I was THERE. Not these other bitches."

"Shut the fuck up, Arlette."

"I'm just saying."

"NO. The fuck you not. You're not just saying nothing. You're weaponizing some shit that broke my family just to make yourself feel important."

She went quiet.

"You know my brother didn't even do what they locked him up for. You KNOW how hard that time hit my mama. My pops. Me. And you got the fucking audacity to bring up his situation like you were part of the healing? You just watched the hurt and made sure you was close enough to get credit if we all survived it."

"... I didn't mean it like that, Kendrix."

"Man, fuck this whole conversation. You toxic. You selfish. And you got this weird-ass fantasy that you still got access to me when really, I shoulda cut you off when you crossed that first line."

"I say one thing about your family and you going off."

"Don't you ever bring up my family again." My voice dropped low because I was so aggravated and done with her shit. "I know you wish you had a family like mine. Loving. Supportive. Actually gives a fuck about you. Get off my line."

Click.

I hung up before she could even say anything back. I turned the TV off and tossed the remote across the bed. At that point, I needed to take my ass to sleep before I got in the car, drove to wherever Arlette was, and choked her ass out with one of her own wigs.

I laid back, took a deep breath, and said a little prayer.

"Lord, please don't let me catch a case tonight."

I closed my eyes and tried to drift, but my phone started ringing again. I snatched it off the charger.

"What the FUCK do you want now, Arlette?!" I barked.

"EXCUSE ME?! This ain't no damn Arlette?!"

That voice stopped me dead.

"Oh—shit. My bad. My bad, Pretty—"

"Uh-uh! I don't play that messy shit! You told me to call your phone and you got it blowing up with angry hoes like it's Love & Hip Hop Season. I'll hang up this motherfucking phone and go do my sugar scrub in peace."

I blinked, stunned.

"You quiet now, huh?" she said, voice getting sassier. "Tell whoever got access to your line and yo dick to go take that up with God 'cause I ain't the one to be caught in the middle of your drama."

"Nah, Pretty, I swear—"

"Don't 'Pretty' me unless you got peace in your life and boundaries set with your hoes."

I couldn't help it, so I laughed.

"Damn," I said. "You really like that, huh?"

"I'm like that, like this, and a lil' bit of whatever else your last girl was missing. You still wanna talk or you wanna keep playing Ring Around the Toxic Rosie?"

I laid back. My whole mood flipped.

"Yeah... I wanna talk."

"Then talk. But say the wrong shit and I will ghost your ass before you blink twice. Start with your full name and a fun fact. Let's go."

"Alright. My name is Kendrix Givelle."

I laughed. "A fun fact is, the first time I ever had sex was in a church parking lot, and I made the girl catch the Holy Ghost for real."

She snorted. "You play too much. Tell me something real."

"Aight. Real? My brother got locked up a few years ago. Whole family been tryna keep it together ever since. Shit changed me. Made me different."

She got quiet. Like she was listening for real.

"Look," she said. "I don't do drama. Arlette is gone be around the club. And I'm not about to mess up my bag putting pleasure before business."

"You ain't gotta worry about that," I said. "Arlette doesn't have any dealing with me."

"That's what niggas always say before somebody get to fighting over them."

I laughed. "Ain't nothing coming in between this connection I'm tryna build, Pretty."

She didn't say anything at first, so I decided to just keep it all the way real.

"Truthfully, we kicked it heavy back in the day," I said. "Then my brother got locked. I didn't realize how much I leaned on him until he wasn't there. And around that same time, she was just always there. Checking in. Bringing me food. Keeping me company. She has a brother in the system too, so we trauma bonded off that. That was my first fuck-up. The red flag I ignored is that she don't talk to her folks. At all. Her mama, her sisters—they all see each other in the store and act like strangers. My mama ain't never even met her, and that's for a reason."

"She ever wanted to meet your mom?"

"She did. But I knew better. My mama is the type that if you tell her you're beefing with the woman who birthed you, for no real reason outside of jealousy, she immediately doesn't trust you. She feel like if you don't respect the one who brought you in this world, you don't give a fuck about nobody."

"Whew. Your mama sounds like she doesn't play."

"Nah, she just real. But, I shoulda let Arlette go a long time ago. But she made shit easy. Comfortable. I could disappear for a week, and when I came back around, she'd be right there like nothing happened."

She let out a breath. "That's not a woman, that's a DoorDash order."

"Exactly."

She laughed again. "She doing all this extra shit like she still hurt over everything."

"I told her the truth. Invited her over, made dinner, and she thought I was about to propose or some shit. Nah. I told her I was done. She went nuts. Screaming, crying, throwing shit. Then she throws a box at me... and it's a pregnancy test and an ultrasound."

"Wait—"

"Yeah. She said she was tryna surprise me."

"Oh my God."

"I ain't know what to say. I froze. She left, flying down the street like Fast & Furious. Wrecked her car. Broke her arm and leg... and lost the baby."

"Damn."

"I felt like shit and guilty. Like even though we wasn't together, I owed her. That was my kid. I couldn't just act like she didn't exist after that, so I stuck around. But when she got better? That's when the real Arlette showed up. All over my homeboy, tryna make me jealous."

"And you didn't beat his ass?"

"Hell nah. He called me and told me what was up. I said, 'Go ahead and smash. Treat her like a Lyft ride. Get in, get out, don't speak on it. She thought she was being slick. Tryna make me jealous. He smashed. Then she went and fucked my other homeboy."

She hollered.

"I swear. So nah. I don't give a fuck about Arlette. She for the streets, the alleys, the potholes... all that."

She wheezed laughing.

"I'm serious. She thought she was playing chess. Didn't know the whole crew was in a group chat clowning her."

"Okay," she said, catching her breath. "I get it now. Y'all history is toxic-tales level tragic. But why you tell me all this?"

"Because I ain't tryna lie to you," I said. "And I'd rather you know the mess than hear it from somebody else."

She got quiet again.

"Well. I still don't know about this between us. But... you're interesting. And I like how you tell stories."

"That's just my voice, Pretty. Wait till I really start telling you shit."

"Oh Lord."

There was a pause. The kind of pause that isn't awkward. Then she hummed, low and sweet.

"Where are your hands at right now?" she whispered.

I swallowed. "Huh?"

"You heard me," she said. "Where are your hands, Kendrix?"

I smirked, dragging a hand across my chest under the sheets. "One on the phone. The other... wondering where it should be."

"Mmm." She moaned softly, and I swear that shit went straight through my body like current.

"And yours?"

She giggled, breathy. "You already know."

That sound had my whole body tightening.

"Let me FaceTime you," I said quick, already reaching for the button.

"No," she said, firm but playful. "I want you to use your imagination. Let me speak to your mind."

"Pretty..." I groaned, running my hand lower.

"Shhh." She hushed me like she had the right. "Tell me what you'd be doing if I was there."

I closed my eyes, giving in. "I'd lay you on your stomach first. Spread you out on these sheets. Hands full of your ass while I kiss down your spine."

She gasped. "Mm. And then?"

"I'd flip you over... slide between your thighs and take my time. Have you begging before I even—"

"Fuck," she cut in, moaning like I was already there. "Keep talking."

I cursed under my breath. "Pretty..."

Her moan was soft, but deliberate. "You hear that? You hear how wet I am just thinking about you?"

I gripped myself hard, biting back a groan. "Goddamn."

"Answer me something," she whispered.

"What?"

"You like it sloppy... or you like to take your time?"

I groaned. "Both. Start slow, finish messy."

She giggled, breath uneven. "Exactly how I like it."

Her breathing picked up. My grip tightened. She whispered every detail like she was choreographing my thoughts. How she'd arch her back, how she'd grab my shoulders, how she'd make me lose every ounce of control I swore I had.

Her voice painted every picture so clear, I didn't even need the FaceTime. She had me right there with her.

"Say my name," I muttered.

"Kendrix," she moaned, drawing it out like a melody.

That was it. That was the breaking point.

Her voice quickened. My hand did too. The sound of her gasps had me losing it. And just like that—together, breathless, separate beds but the same rhythm—we came.

"...Damn," I said, still trying to catch air. "You really just... did that through a phone."

She laughed softly. "And you let me. Mr. Control, became undone by a voice."

I laughed, shaking my head. "You're dangerous, Pretty."

"You're just now figuring that out?"

I cleared my throat and leaned back against the headboard like I wasn't already ten toes in over a woman I just met.

"So... you gone let me take you out for breakfast?" I asked.

"Nigga... breakfast is in a few hours."

"Perfect," I said. "Just enough time for you to take a nap and get dressed. Hell, if you need a midday nap, we can take one together. I'm a gentleman. I'll let you pick the side of the bed and everything."

"Boy, please," she laughed. "I'll think about it."

I smirked. "See, that 'I'll think about it' already sounds like a soft yes. Just text me your address. I'll scoop you around 9."

"Mm-mm. You can send the location. I'll Uber. You don't need to know where I stay... just like my name, you gotta earn that too."

I nodded like she could see me. "Damn. Fair enough."

"Goodnight, Kendrix."

"Goodnight, MissCommunication."

The call ended, but my brain didn't. I set the phone down on my chest and stared at the ceiling like a certified simp-ass nigga. Had me smiling and shit. Thinking about brunch spots and mimosas and if she'd like the playlist I'd make just for her ride.

9

Niveah

I couldn't stop smiling to myself. The night before, I had Kendrix Givelle coming undone through a goddamn phone. No hands on him, no FaceTime, not even a skin pic. Just my voice.

That's always been my gift. Making love to a man's mind before I ever touch his body. Most of them don't even realize they gave me the keys to the whole car until I'm halfway down the highway.

And the crazy part is that it had been years since I was even interested in a man for real. But he wasn't surface-level. He wasn't giving corny lines or fake deep. And once he explained that whole circus with Arlette, I was even more on gang to get a taste of his pockets.

And if I was being honest with myself?

I wanted to see what he was about.

Even though I swore I was gon' behave and play hard to get, I already knew that was a lie. He was too damn fine, and the bottomless mimosas weren't gonna help my case.

I showed up to the brunch spot looking like a soft-spoken problem. Brown sugar body wrapped in a black two-piece set with my navel piercing peeking out, hoop earrings, and a face that said expensive taste but emotionally unavailable.

Kendrix Givelle.

The man looked good enough to piss me off. White tee under a designer denim jacket, beard trimmed just right, gold chain resting like it was hand-placed by God himself. That same calm confidence like nothing could shake him, but I was determined to try.

"So, what you ordering?" he asked, sitting across from me with that little smirk that made my knees lock under the table.

"Chicken and waffles," I said, sipping my mimosa. "Because I'm sweet, but savory."

He chuckled. "Oh, you a food philosopher now?"

"I'm a lot of things," I said, licking fruit from my drink off my thumb like I wasn't already being disrespectful on purpose. "You just getting to know the top layer."

"Oh yeah?" He leaned in. "What's under that?"

I took another sip. "Therapy. Childhood trauma. And a mouth that's gotten me into and out of some crazy shit."

He laughed. The food came out and we both damn near moaned when the plates hit the table. We started eating, talking about everything and nothing at all. Like two kids skipping school, high off life and each other.

He asked what my dream job was.

"I wanna open a dance studio," I said with my mouth full. "Not just pole, either. Ballet, jazz, hip hop, heels—all of it. A space for girls who need an outlet, not judgment. I want it to feel like freedom when you walk in."

That made him look at me different. Like he saw me in a light nobody else had even flipped on yet.

He leaned back, smiling. "That's dope as fuck. Pretty face and mind to match it."

That's when I started blushing and talking more shit.

"You got all these compliments lined up like you practice them in the mirror."

"I do," he said without missing a beat. "Wanna see the mirror?"

I gasped and grabbed my mimosa. "See, and here I was thinking you were respectful."

He winked. "I am. Unless you want otherwise."

One more sip and I was gon' be sitting on the man's lap.

"Okay, random," I said, biting into my waffle. "If you could be any animal, what would you be?"

He wiped syrup from his lip, thinking. "A panther. Smooth but deadly when needed. What about you?"

"A raccoon."

He blinked. "Wait, what the fuck?"

I grinned. "Because they be minding their business until they're not. They're nocturnal like me, always got a snack in hand, and survive in chaos with a full face mask on."

He laughed so hard he dropped his fork. He leaned across the table again, his eyes locking on mine like he could see straight through the sass and right into the softness.

"So, what would it take for me to get your real name?" he asked, voice low and smooth like butter melting on the edge of a stack of pancakes.

"Just keep making me laugh like this. And don't be weird."

He raised his glass to toast. "To not being weird."

I clinked mine against his. "And not fucking this up."

"You know what," he said, wiping his mouth with his napkin. "Come ride with me."

I damn near choked on my drink. "Ride where?"

"Nowhere crazy. Just... ride with me. Get some fresh air and chill."

I squinted, setting my glass down slow. "Nigga... you could be a whole serial killer. You think Ima just hop in your car like this ain't how those missing documentaries start?"

He smirked, unbothered. "If I was a serial killer, you'd be the last one I killed."

I gasped. "Excuse me?!"

"I mean... look at you." He shrugged. "Why would I take you out the game when you the most entertaining thing I got going?"

I had to laugh, even though I tried not to. "You're sick."

"Only for you," he said, grinning like he knew exactly what he was doing.

I leaned back, arms crossed. "So what you tryna lure me with, huh? Candy? A puppy? A fake Netflix password?"

"Nah," he said, leaning closer. "Gas tank on full, music you gon' like, and a man who drives with one hand."

I blinked. "Mmm. Okay, Mr. Drive-With-One-Hand. You know that's the national symbol for 'I got good dick,' right?"

"Exactly," he said, not even blinking.

I shook my head, sipping my mimosa. "You're too confident for me."

He smiled slow. "And you too curious not to find out."

NETRAANTIONETTE

I wasn't supposed to get in his damn car. And yet, there I was, leaned back in the passenger seat, a blunt in my hand, R&B sliding through the speakers like the whole night had been curated by God Himself.

"Hit that again," Kendrix said, his one hand on the wheel, the other resting lazy on his thigh.

I took a pull, exhaled slow, and looked at him sideways. "You know you the reason I'ma end up texting my bestfriend talking about, 'I think I love this man.'"

He smirked, not looking away from the road. "Damn. That quick?"

"Don't flatter yourself," I said, passing the blunt back. "It's just the weed talking"

He hit it, blew the smoke smooth out the corner of his mouth, then looked over at me. "Or maybe it's the way I got you singing every word like you auditioning for my personal band."

"Boy, shut up." I laughed, but I didn't stop singing. Summer Walker was pouring out the speakers, and the both of us were singing like we were the background vocals.

He shook his head. "This some simp-ass shit."

"Facts," I agreed, still laughing. "But I love it."

"Nah, you love me," he teased, giving me that side grin like he knew he had me.

I rolled my eyes, hiding my smile. "What the Fuck? You obviously don't know who I am."

He laughed so hard he almost missed the turn. "See, that's that shit. You be talking crazy but got the nerve to blush when I look at you."

"I ain't blushing" I said quickly, flipping my hair. "That's just the weed."

"Mmhm." He handed the blunt back, his fingers brushing mine slow on purpose.

I pulled on it just to keep from saying something stupid. The way my stomach flipped, I had to remind myself who I was. Niveah 'Don't-Fall-For-No-Nigga'. I been fine without 'em and I could keep being fine. But damn. He smelled good. He made me laugh easily. And the way he gripped that steering wheel with one hand had my thighs damn near clapping.

He glanced over at me again. "What you thinkin' about?"

I exhaled slow, passed the blunt back, and smirked. "You."

He raised an eyebrow, that grin tugging at the corner of his mouth. "Oh yeah?"

"Don't get cocky," I teased, shifting in the seat. "I mean it in a way of... where does this whole connection take us?"

The way his jaw flexed when I said it had me second-guessing if I'd gone too far, but I have a reason for everything I do and say.

"Since you wanna be all deep and mental," he said, "let me say this... when I lock in, I lock the fuck in. So keep that in mind, Pretty."

I turned my head back toward the window, hiding my smirk behind another pull from the blunt.

Yeah. I got him right where I wanted him.

But the way he said it didn't feel like a game. It felt like a promise. A warning.

I blew the smoke out slowly, turning back to him with a lazy grin. "That supposed to scare me?"

"Nah. Supposed to prepare you."

"Mm." I tilted my head, acting like I wasn't two seconds from melting into his passenger seat. "You're the one that should be prepared. I don't come with a warning label. I come with a survival kit."

He laughed, shaking his head. "See, that's what I like. You talk that shit but keep blushing."

"I don't blush," I shot back quick.

"Pretty," he said. "You damn near pink right now."

I smirked and leaned back in the seat. "I had you moaning through the phone last night. I'll take that over a simple blush any day."

He damn near choked on his own laugh. "Oh, so you just gone throw that back in my face?"

"You started it," I said.

He shook his head, grinning hard. "That's crazy. You really bragging about that?"

"Im not bragging. Just reminding you that if I can make you fold over the phone, imagine what I can do in person."

His grip on the wheel tightened, and I caught it.

"Dangerous," he muttered, almost to himself.

"Mmhm. And you like dangerous, remember?" I teased.

"You gone be the death of me."

I smirked, turning my head toward the window like I didn't feel my thighs pressing together. "Better pick out a nice casket then."

We both burst out laughing and by the time the laughter stopped, the car slowed. We were pulling up to a big beautiful home.

We rolled up slow, and my eyes got wide. The driveway alone looked like it cost more than everything in my neighborhood put together.

I sat up straight. "I know you're not taking me to your damn house."

Kendrix burst out laughing. "Nah, Pretty. Not yet."

"Not yet?!" I whipped my head at him. "Nigga, what you mean not yet? You got a five-year plan already?"

He smirked, easing the car to a stop. "Relax. This ain't mine. It's my parents' house."

I blinked at him. Then blinked again like he'd lost his damn mind. "So you mean to tell me... we went from brunch, to blunt, to 'surprise, meet my mama' in less than four hours?"

He grinned softer that time. "She's the most important woman in my life. And I just want her to meet someone who I feel could be just as important. And yeah... I figured that out in less than four hours."

The way my stomach flipped, I had to laugh just to keep from showing it. "Boy, that phone sex really got you whipped."

He grinned, licking his lips. "You're not completely wrong."

"Mmhm," I said, rolling my eyes. "Well, don't think Ima play along. If she ask, I'm telling her I just met your ass yesterday and I don't even know you."

"Say what you want, Pretty."

"Don't test me," I warned. "I'll call you the wrong name on purpose in front of your mama."

"You crazy as hell."

I smirked, but deep down, my chest was tight. Talking to niggas is easy. Playing in their pockets is like second nature. But families and meeting mamas was territory I didn't touch. Ever.

Maybe he caught the hesitation in my face, because he leaned over, voice low and certain. "Get your ass out the car, Pretty. Come on."

I blinked and he smirked. "Don't worry. I'll make sure she likes you."

"And if she doesn't?"

He grinned. "Then she's wrong. But that has never happened before."

I sucked my teeth and grabbed my bag, mumbling under my breath, "This nigga got me out here breaking all my damn rules."

NETRA ANTIONETTE

The second my shoes hit the marble, I realized I had underestimated the hell out of Kendrix Givelle. I knew he had money. You could see it in the way he dressed. But that house was next-level. It was obvious that he was born into money. The kind of money that didn't ask for a receipt and sure as hell didn't check the price tag.

The foyer alone looked like the kind of shit you only see in movies. Ceiling so high and paintings on the wall that probably cost more than my entire house.

My mind wanted to slide my pussy across his face right after he slid his card through every register at Saks, Neiman's, and Chanel for me.

"Damn," I whispered under my breath.

He smirked, holding the door for me like he ain't just walked me into the Black Excellence version of Hogwarts.

We made it to the kitchen, and I saw a lady sitting at the table, posture straight, eyes sharp but warm. Next to her, a girl that looked about fifteen, but sitting there with an attitude like the world owed her something.

I blinked, biting back a laugh. I didn't even know her, but the way she was rolling her eyes at the woman made me wanna slap her ass on the spot. Reminded me of my brother when he thought he was too grown for his own good.

I leaned closer to Kendrix and whispered, "You better tell me she's not one of yours, because if she roll her eyes at me like that, we gone have our first family feud."

He chuckled under his breath, shaking his head. "Chill, Pretty. That's my niece."

"Mhm." I narrowed my eyes, crossing my arms. "Better tell lil' mama I fight kids too."

That earned me the deepest laugh out of him, one hand coming up to rub his beard as he tried to hide his grin.

"You wild," he said.

"Wild enough to keep her in check," I shot back, giving the girl one of them auntie stares that said *don't play with me today.*

The girl blinked, sat up a little straighter, and turned her eyes back to the table.

Yeah. That's what I thought.

The woman at the table hadn't even turned around when we walked in. She was too busy fussing at the girl like she'd said the same thing three times already.

Kendrix leaned down, grinning, and kissed the girl on the cheek. "What you in here getting in trouble about now?"

She rolled her eyes so hard I thought they might get stuck. "You know Mama is extra."

I almost laughed right there. Same tone Hux hit me with every damn time I told him about some dumbass shit he thought made sense.

The woman huffed, still not turning toward us. "She acts just like your brother. You can't tell her nothing. I swear, I'm sick of it."

Kendrix rubbed his niece's shoulder. "Well... I want y'all to meet someone."

That made the woman finally glance over her shoulder. "Who you got up in here, Kendrix?"

He started, "This is my niece and my sister-in-law—"

"Khloe," I blurted out before he could even finish.

The woman's eyes went wide.

I grinned, stepping forward. "I know not!"

Khloe's chair flew back, and before I knew it we were wrapped up in each other's arms.

"Girl!" she squealed, squeezing me tight. "I thought I'd never see your crazy ass again!"

Kendrix just stood there, brows raised, looking between us like he'd walked in on a plot twist he didn't see coming.

"You two... know each other?" he asked.

Me and Khloe pulled back, grinning like fools.

"Know each other?" Khloe said, laughing. "Boy, please. We been knew each other. Crown and Covered, remember that, girl?"

I laughed. "Girl, yes! Senae used to hook us up every time."

Khloe threw her head back. "Man, I need to take that drive again. No one has touched my hair like her since. I miss those Saturdays. Just sitting in there with the girls, sipping drinks and talking shit."

I smirked. "Well, you know she remodeled the shop, right?"

Khloe's eyes lit up. "For real?!"

"Yeah. They say it's top tier. I heard you damn near gotta book a month out just to get a spot."

Khloe fanned herself dramatically. "Oh, we gotta make a trip then."

Kendrix stood there watching us like we were speaking a whole different language. His mouth curved into the faintest smile, like he was both amused and curious as hell.

I smirked, brushing my hair out my face. "Told you, I don't need no introductions."

Kendrix blinked, then looked at me, then back at Khloe, then back at me again.

"Oh... this just got interesting," he said under his breath.

10

Kendrix

Man... I ain't gon' lie. I was shocked as hell watching them two damn near knock the kitchen table over hugging like long-lost sisters. Her knowing Khloe was a good thing. Real good. Khloe was solid. Always been a good girl, straight shooter, and could see right through people's bullshit like she had X-ray vision. If she fucked with you, you was good people. If she didn't... well, lets just say you didn't last long.

The fact she lit up had me feeling like maybe I wasn't crazy for thinking what I was thinking about that woman.

I leaned against the counter, watching them go on about some salon called Crown and Covered like they was back in high school. I ain't even realize I was smiling till Khloe looked over at me and smirked like she knew something.

"Alright," my niece piped up, grabbing her phone off the table. "Ima let the old folks do their thing. I'm going to the pool."

I blinked, straightening up. "Old folks?"

She shrugged, unfazed, already halfway down the hall. "If you over twenty-five, you old. Sorry, Uncle Ken. Rules are rules."

I shook my head, smirking. "Keep talking slick. Imma show you old when you need a new phone and your parents say no."

"Whatever!" she yelled back.

I turned back to Khloe. "Where is mama at?"

She pointed down the hallway. "In the sunroom with her tea and her plants. You already know."

I rubbed my hands together.

"Aight," I said, clearing my throat. "Hate to break this up, but I wanna take her to go meet Ma. I'll bring her back."

"Go ahead. I got a call with a client anyway." She turned to her. "And don't play, girl. You got my new number now. Make sure you use it. You're family now."

Pretty snorted.. "Girl, please. I don't even know this man."

Khloe pointed a finger at her, grinning. "Mhm. That's what you say."

I shook my head, laughing, then reached out and took her hand. "C'mon, Pretty."

We stepped into the sunroom, and my mama was sitting in her favorite chair, sun spilling through the glass walls like God ordered the lighting just for her. Pearls on her neck, hair wrapped, flawless. She had a book in one hand, a teacup in the other, and an expression that said *I already know half the shit you gon' say before you say it.*

Her eyes cut to me first, then slid straight to Pretty. It was slow but calculated. Smile on her face, scalpel in her tone.

"Well, Kendrix," she said, setting her cup down. "You finally decided to bring someone worth introducing. Didn't think this day would come before I expired."

Pretty blinked, then smirked, head tilted just enough. "Well damn. You sure know how to make a girl feel welcome."

Ma's lips twitched like she was trying not to laugh. "I'm just honest, sweetheart. Honesty keeps the world from wasting time."

"Oh, don't worry," she said, easing into the chair across from her. "I don't let anyone waste my time. And if they try, I charge them for it."

Ma raised one perfect brow, clearly impressed but refusing to say it out loud.

"Well, at least you know your value," she replied. "That's... refreshing."

They sat there looking at each other, energy bouncing like a tennis match I wasn't about to referee. I leaned on the doorframe, watching, biting back a smile.

Finally, Ma folded her hands. "So. What's your name, dear?"

Pretty glanced at me, her eyes aggravated when she caught my grin. I knew what I was doing. I didn't even try to hide it. Hell, this was my slick way of getting what I wanted. She wasn't about to play games with Ma.

She leaned back, smirk tugging at her lips, and said it. "Niveah. But everyone calls me Niv."

My mama repeated it slowly, like she was tasting the sound. "Niveah. Beautiful name."

I just smiled, sitting back like I'd won. *Gotcha, Pretty Niv.*

11

Niveah

Kendrix's phone buzzed. He glanced down, sighed, and said, "Excuse me for a minute. Gotta take this call." He kissed his mama on the cheek, then looked at me with that little grin like, *You'll be fine.*

She set her tea down, folded her hands, and looked at me dead-on. "So. Niveah." She said my name like she was testing it. "Tell me what you do."

I leaned back, crossing my legs slow. "I communicate."

Her brow arched. "Communicate?"

"Yes, ma'am," I said, meeting her stare head-on. "Some people use their bodies. Some use their money. I use my mouth and my mind. Done right, it'll get you everything you want... and then some."

Her lips curved. Not quite a smile, but more like amusement. "You sound like trouble."

"Only to people who try to waste my time."

That made her laugh, a quick sharp one. "Good answer." She leaned in slightly. "You're a pretty girl. But pretty don't last long if it's all you bringing. So I'll ask plain: what's your endgame?"

I didn't blink. "My family. My little brother. My baby sister. They've been my world since the day my mama stopped showing up for hers. I don't need a man to save me. I save myself and them. But I'm not dumb enough to think I can't build more if I got the right person by my side."

For a second, she just looked at me. And in that pause, I swear I saw a sign of respect.

"You know," she said softly, "most girls sit in that chair and tell me what they think I want to hear. You said what I needed to hear."

I smirked. "I don't lie. I may not tell the whole truth, but I never lie."

That earned me a full smile. "Mhm. Sharp."

I leaned in a little, matching her tone. "Sharp enough that your son better be ready."

She laughed, shaking her head. "I like that." She picked her cup back up and sipped. "Don't break his heart, and don't let him break yours."

I smiled slow. "Don't worry."

"So you dance?" she asked.

I didn't blink. "I do. Ballet was first. Pole came later. People assume that makes me less, but it's the opposite. It made me more."

"That's bold."

I tilted my head. "Only looks bold when you watching from the sidelines. When you living it, it's survival."

Her brows rose slightly. "Mhm. You talk like you know exactly who you are."

"Because I do," I shot back. "And I don't need anyone's permission to be her."

"Careful, baby. Men like my son love a woman who knows herself. But they'll test if you can keep knowing yourself once they're in the picture."

I smirked. "Then it's his test to fail, not mine."

She studied me for a long second, like she was peeling my skin back just to see what I was made of.

"You remind me of myself when I was your age. Full of fire. And let me tell you something, the moment I stopped pouring all of me into everyone else and started pouring into myself first?" She tapped the rim of her teacup for emphasis. "That's when my marriage turned. That's when my husband stopped running my world and started eating out of my hand."

I raised a brow. "Sounds like power to me."

"Damn right it is," she said smoothly. "And don't let anybody tell you different. But—" Her eyes sharpened like a knife. "I love my son. He's a good man with a good heart. If you ever break that heart intentionally, I will come for you myself. And I don't fight fair."

Instead of flinching, I leaned forward, a slow grin pulling at my lips. "Good. Because I don't fight fair, either. So I guess we'll never have to find out what that means."

She stared. Then... she laughed.

"Just promise me something, baby girl."

I nodded once. "What's that?"

"Don't lose yourself. My son is strong and steady, yes. But men like him can be consuming. You forget to feed yourself, you'll starve while feeding him. And then you'll resent him for a hunger you created yourself."

That one cut deeper than I wanted to admit. I swallowed, kept my eyes on hers, and said, "Don't worry. I never forget to eat."

"Good answer."

The door clicked open behind me. Just as Kendrix stepped back into the sunroom, his mama leaned forward one last time.

"I like you. Not because you're pretty. That's stupid. I like you because you didn't fold."

She sipped her tea once again. "Now keep it that way. Because the minute you start shrinking to make a man comfortable, you'll lose the very thing that made him want you."

Then, with a sweet little smile for Kendrix as he sat back down, she added, "You picked a beautiful handful, son."

I smirked, crossing my legs slowly. "Ain't that the truth."

NETRAANTIONETTE

We stepped out of the sunroom, and before I knew it, Kendrix had my hand in his, leading me down a stone path through the estate like we were in some damn movie. The grounds stretched forever.

"You really grew up like this?" I asked, giving him a side-eye. "This ain't no regular house."

He smirked, watching me more than the scenery. "Are you impressed?"

I shrugged, pretending not to be. "It's cute."

"Cute, huh?"

"Mhm." I smirked. "But don't think money makes you special. A lotta of niggas rich, but still lame though."

He stopped, turned to face me, that grin dangerous as hell. "Good thing I'm not one of those niggas."

I bit my lip, heat sliding up my neck, even though I tried to keep my face straight. The scent of chlorine hit me instantly. His niece was in the pool, floating around on a unicorn floatie, phone in one hand like she wasn't worried about electrocution.

She spotted us and grinned. "Don't let him bore you!"

I laughed, waving back. "Girl, he's trying!"

Kendrix shot her a look. "Keep playing. You gone want something."

She rolled her eyes like a true teenager. I was still laughing when Kendrix's hand slid from mine to the small of my back, guiding me toward the pool house. The heat from his palm sent a shiver down my spine.

The door clicked shut behind us, the sound of splashing fading as he locked it. I glanced around. Leather lounge chairs. Towels folded neatly on the counter. Big windows letting the sun pour in.

"Mm," I teased, leaning against the counter. "You really bringing me to the pool house like we in some secret high school hookup?"

He stepped closer, his eyes low and hungry, beard shadowing that slow grin. "Nah. High school niggas don't know what to do with you."

I opened my mouth to fire back, but he was already crowding me, his hand gripping my thigh and pulling me up onto the counter like I weighed nothing.

"Hold on—" I laughed breathlessly, my palms pressing against his chest. "You been letting me talk all this big shit, and now you—"

"Taking over," he cut me off, lips brushing my ear. "You had control long enough. Time for me to drive."

My stomach flipped. "Oh, so now you're Mr. Take Control?"

His thumb pressed slow circles into my inner thigh, making it impossible to keep my voice steady.

"You better be quiet," he said, teeth grazing my neck. "Unless you want my niece out there asking why you sound like you seen the Lord."

I smirked, ready to clown him back until his lips touched mine. And Lord... I don't kiss niggas. Its too intimate and personal. But that kiss was so good. He tasted like bourbon and danger, and the way he took his time with my bottom lip had me helping him tug at my own clothes.

"You got me trippin'," I murmured, breathless. "I don't kiss niggas."

He pulled back just long enough to smirk. "That's because I ain't no nigga. I'm Kendrix."

Then he spread my thighs wide, sliding me down the counter, and lowered his head.

The first lick had me gasping, my hand flying to cover my mouth. "Kendrix—"

"Mmm," he hummed against me. "Taste just like I knew you would. Sweet. Messy. Mine."

I tried to close my legs, but he pushed them wider, his big hands pinning my thighs down. His tongue swirled slow, teasing, before he sucked so hard I damn near saw stars.

"Fuck—" I whimpered, biting my hand.

He pulled back just enough to growl, "Nah. Don't hide from me, Pretty. I want all them sounds. I want this pussy bragging about me."

Then, dead serious, he leaned closer, eyes locked on my core.

"You hear me, Pretty? You're mine now." He slid his fingers inside me and licked his lips. "Ain't that right, baby?"

I let out a shaky laugh. "You... you talking to my pussy, right?"

He smirked, lips brushing my inner thigh. "I'm talking to her too. She listening better than you." He tapped my clit with his tongue like punctuation. "Ain't that right, Pretty's pussy? You gon' let me take care of you, huh?"

I threw my head back, half laughing, half moaning. "You crazy."

"Crazy about you," he cut in, sliding two fingers in and out so slow it had me arching off the counter. "Shit, she's greedy already. Clenching like she ain't ate in weeks."

"Kendrix," I gasped, toes curling.

"That's it," he murmured, tongue circling my clit while his fingers stroked deep. "Don't fight it. Give it to me. I want every drop."

I was shaking so bad I could barely breathe. He was licking, sucking, and talking shit the whole time.

"Yeah, baby. Moan for me."

"Shit, she so damn wet I could drown in it."

"Go ahead and cum, Pretty. Make her thank me."

When the orgasm hit, it slammed into me so hard, tears formed in my eyes as my body jerked. He groaned against me, eating up everything like he was starving.

When I finally collapsed back against the counter, chest heaving, he kissed my thigh and looked up with that smug-ass grin, beard shining.

"She said thank you."

I burst out laughing, slapping his chest. "You're so stupid."

He licked his lips slow. "Nah. Just fluent in Pretty's pussy."

NETRAANTIONETTE

By the time we made it back into the kitchen, I still felt weak in the knees. My damn soul was probably still laid out on the counter in that pool house.

How the hell I go from telling a man I don't kiss niggas to letting him eat my insides like Sunday dinner... and then stroll up in his mama's kitchen smiling like nothing happened?

Weird. As. Hell.

But there I was, posted up at the island with a glass of sweet tea, laughing like I'd been part of the family for years.

Kendrix had three brothers. Kairo, Kross, and Kordai. And Lord have mercy, they were all fine as hell. It was like the Lord said, *copy, paste, add a little seasoning each time.* And the personalities were loud, unhinged, petty, and perfect.

Khloe was across from me, rolling her eyes so hard I thought she'd sprain something while her husband Kairo kept poking at her.

"I'm just saying. Khloe always talking about how I don't make time," he said, scooping a spoonful of red beans and rice, "but she never forgets to swipe that black card. New shoes. New wigs. Chefs for dinner because she's 'too tired to cook.' Time don't matter when the bills stay paid."

Khloe's head turned so slow I thought she might break her neck.

"Excuse me?" she said, voice flat.

The kitchen got quiet like everybody braced for impact.

"I'm saying," Kairo continued like he didn't just dig a grave, "you can't yell 'quality time' and still be at the spa every Friday. That's what Pops taught us. Be a provider first. Maybe that means I can't always be present."

Khloe dropped her fork on her plate. "Money ain't everything to me. And that logic is your real problem."

You could tell that wasn't the first time they'd had that argument.

Kordai blinked slow. "Nigga... what?"

Kross started laughing so hard he damn near dropped his spoon. "Why would you even say some dumb shit like that out loud? Do you hear yourself?"

His mama side-eyed them both and turned to Kairo with zero patience. "You sound dumb as hell. Money ain't never raised no child or fixed a marriage. You wanna be your daddy so bad, try being better than he was."

"Y'all don't get it," Kairo snapped.

I had to cover my mouth to hide my laugh, but Khloe wasn't hiding shit.

"You keep talking, Kairo," she said sweetly, "and I'll season your food with rat poison."

Their mama side-eyed Kairo, and cut him down with one line. "Provider, huh? Where your daddy at now?"

Kairo blinked. "...At a work trip."

"Exactly," she snapped. "On a fucking work trip. And you in here repeating the same bullshit that left me raising four boys half the time by myself. He realized how dumb that was when it was too fucking late. Stop being a dumb ass before I knock some sense into you."

Kairo just shook his head like he was used to it. Khloe grinned like she won the lottery. That's when my phone lit up on the counter.

Zejah.

"Hey Zejah, what's up?"

Her voice came through fast, panicked. "Niv, where you at?"

The laughter froze in my throat. "Why?"

"You need to get to your mama's house now."

My chest tightened. "What happened?"

"She's outside, screaming at some man. They been arguing for almost an hour. He tried to leave, but she keeps trying to fight him. Ms. Messy Beth done called the police."

My stomach dropped to the floor and the kitchen noise blurred behind me.

The second I hung up the phone, I guess my face said it all, because Kendrix's eyes locked on me. That calm, cocky grin he'd been wearing was gone.

"What's wrong, Pretty?" he asked low, leaning in like it was just us in the room.

My chest was tight, my mind already racing. I didn't even sugarcoat it. "I need you to take me somewhere. Right now. A Uber gone take too long."

"Where?"

"Don't ask questions," I cut in. "Just get me there."

For a second, we just stared at each other. Then he stood, sliding his chair back slow, his eyes never leaving mine. "Bet," he said simply. "Let's go."

I exhaled a shaky breath I didn't even realize I was holding.

He didn't press me. Didn't make me explain in front of his family. Just reached for my hand, pulled me up from the chair, and walked me straight out like it was already handled.

12

Kendrix

The second she told me to drive, I didn't ask questions. I just grabbed the keys and we were gone. But when she directed me toward *Gun Hill*?

Man. I tightened my grip on the wheel, staring out the windshield as the scenery got rougher. Streetlights busted. Graffiti covering brick walls. Kids still outside, even though it was late, posted up like they ain't had a bedtime in years.

Why the fuck Niv, of all women, needed to be over there? I didn't know, but I wasn't about to ask yet.

I kept one hand on the wheel, the other resting close enough to reach the Glock tucked under my seat if shit popped off. I had a couple more in the truck too. Old habits. My pops always said: *Better to have it and not need it than need it and not have it.*

"Park there," she said, pointing to a busted-ass spot in front of a building that looked like it was one cough away from collapsing.

I pulled in, cut the engine. She hopped out fast, like she'd done this walk a hundred times. I slid out right behind her, shutting the door.

That's when I saw a woman, thin and jittery, face marked by every bad decision life ever handed her, standing toe-to-toe with a dude. She was yelling, shoving at his chest like she didn't give a fuck. He was gripping her wrists, jaw tight.

"If you don't stop pushing me," he barked, "Ima beat yo ass, I swear to God."

My jaw flexed. Niv didn't even hesitate. She stormed right up like she'd been born for that shit.

"Touch her," she snapped, "and you gone be laid out on this concrete before you blink, nigga."

The whole block went, "Ooooh!" like somebody just threw gas on a fire.

"Girl, shut up," some lady on the steps hollered. "You always acting like you better than everybody 'round here."

Niv spun around so fast. "Bitch, don't get dropped in them fake-ass Uggs! If I was better, I wouldn't even be out here breathing the same broke air as you."

Another dude chimed in, "Man, y'all too loud. It's kids out here."

She cut him down without blinking. "Then take your ass inside and parent them, since you clearly not doing it now."

I tried not to laugh.

The man threw his hands up. "Man, I ain't even on that with her. She said she was gone have my money for them rocks, but she didn't. So I took my shit and I'm tryna leave."

The woman whipped around, eyes glassy but her mouth sharp. "He a lying-ass nigga. I might not know much, but I know how to count, motherfuck-er!"

"Ma!" she snapped.

I froze. *Ma?* My head turned so fast I almost gave myself whiplash. The jittery, loud, strung-out woman throwing her whole life into the street... was her mama? I looked from the woman back to Niv. Same fire in their eyes. Same don't-back-down stance. Only difference was Niv wore it polished and controlled.

Her mama whipped toward her. "Don't you 'Ma' me like you the boss!"

"You damn right I am!" Niv shot back, eyes blazing. "'Cause you sure as hell ain't acting like one! Go the fuck upstairs!"

Everyone around yelled "Damn!"

That's when the flashing lights hit the block. Two cops stepped out, hands on belts, scanning the mess. "What's going on here?"

Before anybody else could speak, Niv stepped up, calm.. "It's a misunder-standing. It's handled."

Her mama, loud as ever, pointed at the dealer. "Ain't no misunderstanding! I want my fix! He tryna play me!"

The cops froze, eyes wide. And that's when I knew I had to step in.

I moved forward, dropping my voice low so only she could hear. "Come with me," I told her mama. "I got something for you."

She blinked, eyes flicking me up and down, her face softening like I'd just walked straight out of her daydream. "Now this somebody I'll go with."

Behind me, I could feel Niv rolling her eyes so hard the earth tilted.

"Yeah," I said smooth. "I got you. Let's just get outta here. No more scenes."

She huffed but started shuffling toward the stairs, her eyes still on me like she couldn't believe a man that fine was talking to her.

I followed close behind, every sense on alert, while Niv stayed back, sliding right in front of the cops with that sweet smile she wore like armor.

"Look," I heard her say, "I don't know why they called y'all. It's handled. She good. I'm good. And trust me, this neighborhood don't need no more chaos today."

Meanwhile, I was trailing her mama upstairs, already wondering how the hell I got myself in the shit.

Walking into that apartment was like stepping straight into hell with no AC. The second the door creaked open, the smell hit me. Weed, old grease, and something sour I couldn't place. The carpet looked like it had seen the Civil Rights Movement. The couch was leaning like it had arthritis. I damn near wanted to stand in the doorway with my shirt over my nose.

But I sat down anyway because if I didn't, she was gone think I was too good to be there. And even though I was, I needed to play it cool until I talked to Niv.

Her mama plopped down across from me, lit a cigarette, and blew the smoke straight into the air. Nails chipped,clothes half falling off her shoulder.

"So, who are you?" she asked, squinting at me through the smoke. "And what you doing with my daughter?"

I leaned back, resting an arm on the armrest like I was comfortable when I wasn't. "Just a friend."

She smirked like she didn't believe a damn word. "Mmhmm. Y'all always start off as 'just a friend.'" She took another drag, exhaled slow. "You hitting it?"

I raised an eyebrow, but I kept my face straight. "That's between me and her."

She laughed, this dry, raspy cackle that made my skin crawl. "So you special, huh? You must be. She don't bring nobody around here."

I didn't give her shit. Just shrugged, calm.

Her eyes narrowed. "Where that shit you said you had for me?"

I slid my phone out, typing quick.

> Dirt. Bring it to my lo. ASAP.

My boy texted back almost instantly.

> Bet. 10 minutes.

I looked up at her, cool as hell. "It's on the way."

She grinned, ash dropping off her cigarette onto the carpet like it was an ashtray. "See? Now you talkin'."

Niv stormed through the door.

"What the fuck is wrong with you?!" she yelled, slamming her purse down so hard the whole table shook.

Her mama didn't even flinch. She just leaned back, blowing smoke out her nose like a dragon. "Don't come in my place of peace with all that yelling, girl. You already loud as hell."

Niv's eyes damn near bugged out her head. "Peace?! Mama, you was outside tryna fight a grown-ass man over some rocks!"

Her mama laughed. "Shit. He was gone give 'em to me until you showed up acting like you my parole officer." She waved her cigarette toward the door. "Go on back to your house with all that bullshit. Don't nobody need it here."

I sat back, watching Niv and her mama go at it. I could tell Niv was trying hard to keep that respect in her voice. But you could see it in her eyes that every nerve in her body wanted to snap.

"Ma," she said through gritted teeth. "You out here acting like a damn fool."

Her mama smirked, tapping ashes. "Better a fool than a fake. You out here acting like you're perfect."

Niv inhaled, deep, like she was counting to ten. I knew that count. That was the *don't cuss your mama out even though she deserve it* count.

Before she could let loose, my phone buzzed.

> Outside. By your truck.

"Be right back," I said, standing up.

I headed downstairs, grabbed the bag from my boy without a word, and jogged back up. I ain't know if I was helping or making shit worse, but fuck it. I wasn't about to let that circus drag out with cops around.

I walked in, set the weed on the table, and her mama lit up like Christmas.

"Well damn," she grinned, sliding a tray out from under the table with papers already laid out. "Now you speaking my language."

She started rolling like she'd been waiting all day.

Niv's eyes burning a hole in the side of my head. She didn't have to say it. Her whole body screamed *Nigga, I should beat the fuck outta you right now.*

I shifted in my chair. "It's handled."

"It's not handled," she snapped, finally looking at me. "You just fed the problem."

Her mama chuckled low, licking the paper closed. "You can go now, sugar," she said to me like she was queen of the damn projects. "She'll get someone to take her home."

"I'm not leaving her here."

"I don't need a babysitter," Niv said, voice sharp. "This used to be my home. I'm fine here."

I leaned forward, locking eyes with her, even when she tried to look away. "I don't care. If you need to get home, I'm taking you. Point blank."

Her mama sparked the blunt, laid back like she ain't just set the whole night on fire. "Go on, Niv," she said, smoke curling around her words. "Let that man take you home. I'm tryna get high and relax. I don't need you here all in my face, telling me what I need to do and not do."

Niv snatched her purse off the chair, saying something under her breath, and walked out.

We hit the stairwell, and I could feel the steam rolling off Niv. She wasn't even looking at me. Then this little voice came from nowhere.

"Niv... can I talk to you?"

We both turned.

Shorty couldn't have been more than fifteen, sixteen. Pretty little face, nervous eyes.

Niv sucked her teeth, annoyed as hell. I knew she wanted to keep walking, but she stopped. "What you need, Zejah?"

The girl twisted her hands. "I, um... I need to go to the doctor tomorrow. And I need some money."

Niv tilted her head. "I know your mama got Medicaid. Appointments should be free."

Zejah looked down, shaking her head. "Niv, please. I don't need a sermon right now. I just... I just need what I need."

I saw Niv's jaw flex, but she didn't argue. She dug into her purse, pulled out three twenties, and handed them over.

The girl's eyes got glassy, but she nodded quickly, clutching the bills like they were gold. "Thank you, Niv."

Niv turned, heading for the truck.

While her back was turned, I slipped a folded hundred out my pocket, slid it into the girl's palm. She looked up at me, shocked, lips moving in a silent thank you.

I winked and tapped my lips, mouthing, *Keep it quiet.*

She tucked it fast, and just as Niv turned, I stepped back like nothing happened.

"If she does anything else, call me, Zejah!" Niv called over her shoulder.

"I will!" the girl said quickly, nodding.

The second her ass hit the passenger seat and I pulled off, I knew it was coming.

"You got me fucked up, Kendrix. Don't ever think you can pull some shit like that again! I don't need your charity, I don't need your rescues. You don't know my mama like that."

I kept my eyes on the road, letting her vent.

"You ain't slick. That whole smooth, calm, unbothered shit might work on them other hoes, but not me. You think just because you fine and drive with one hand I'm supposed to shut up and let you do whatever? Nah. Your ass is good as blocked after tonight. Don't even pray for me, because I'll block God from telling me you prayed!"

"You done?" I asked, real calm.

She whipped her head toward me so fast. "Am I done?! Boy, if you don't—"

And just like that, she was right back at it. Going the hell off.

I let her ride for a minute, then I cut in with a grin. "You gone need throat lozenges after all that yelling, Pretty. Want me to stop at Walgreens?"

She sucked her teeth and turned toward the window.

I let the silence sit in the truck for a bit before I said, "I gave your mama some dirt."

"Dirt?! The fuck you mean, dirt? You tryna kill my mama?!"

"No, Pretty. Not dirt dirt. It's the worst weed known to man. People would rather stay sober than smoke that shit."

Her eyes narrowed. "You lying."

"Nah," I said, chuckling. "She gone smoke it, get a headache, probably be throwing up. Might even catch the shits if she overdo it. That kinda smoke make you reconsider life choices real quick. After that, she ain't gone want to touch nothing."

Her mouth dropped open before she burst out laughing. "I know the fuck you didn't!"

"Shit, I did." I grinned, proud of myself. "Call it tough love with a side of quality control."

"Good. She need the shits, but you're still blocked."

"Yeah, yeah," I smirked. "We both know you lying."

"Yeah, whatever," she said, snatching my phone and typing her address into the GPS.

We rode in silence for a minute. I glanced over and she was staring out the window.

I cleared my throat. "Pretty..."

She hummed without looking at me.

"How long your mom been on it?"

"Since I was about twelve" she said softly.

"Damn."

"She used to be... different," she said, voice lower now, like she was scared to say it out loud. "Braided my hair every morning. Showed up to school activities. Cooked dinner. Then one day, it was like somebody unplugged her. And she never came back the same."

I stayed quiet, letting her talk.

"That's why I have custody of my brother and sister. The court didn't even fight me on it. It was either me or foster care." She let out a bitter laugh. "So I grew up real fast. Learned how to pay bills before I knew how to drive."

She finally turned to me. "So yeah. That used to be my home. Now it's just where I come to clean up messes I didn't make."

I swallowed, nodding slow. "You a soldier for that. Real talk."

She rolled her eyes, trying to brush it off. "Don't gas me up, Kendrix."

"I ain't gassing shit," I said, eyes cutting over to her. "I mean that. A lotta people fold under less. You didn't fold. You're still standing. Shit... and still glowing."

"Thank you," she said. "But not just for saying that. For everything. Today was..." She let out a little laugh. "One of the most eventful days I've had in a long time."

"Glad I was the event."

She rolled her eyes, but she didn't argue.

The GPS spoke up just in time, and I eased the truck into her driveway. The house sat back a little from the street, warm porch lights glowing against the night. Cozy. Family vibes. The kind of place you could actually breathe peacefully in.

"That's you?" I asked, putting it in park.

"Yeah." She glanced at the house, pride written all over her face. "I didn't want anything too far from my mom. Just in case. But I wanted better for my siblings, so I'm renting it right now. Hopefully, the owner decides to sell."

I took a good look. "It's nice, Pretty. Real nice."

"Big come-up from Gun Hill, huh?"

"Big one," I agreed.

I hopped out before she could say anything and rounded the truck to walk her to the door. She fished her keys from her purse, glancing at me sideways.

"I'd let you in," she said, slipping the key into the lock, "but I've been gone all day. Time for me to give my nanny a break."

"I understand." I slid my hands into my pockets, leaning a little. "But when can I see you again?"

She smiled, unlocking the door. "Your bitch, Arlette, said the club opens back up in two days. That gives you time to think about me and miss me."

I laughed, shaking my head. "That's not my bitch."

"Mhm. That's what you better say."

"Well," I said, stepping closer, lowering my voice, "I got business out of town for a couple days. Handle some things. But just so you know, this is the last time I'm leaving without you. Next time, pack up the kids, the nanny, whatever. You riding with me."

She tilted her head, trying to hide her smile. "We'll see, Kendrix."

I grinned. "Yeah, we will."

She pulled me in quick, arms soft around my neck and kissed me. Sweet but with enough tongue to have me wanting more.

She whispered, "Goodnight," before slipping inside, leaving me standing there like a simp-ass nigga, smiling at her closed door. And I didn't even care.

13

Niveah

I woke up smiling like somebody had dropped a stack of hundreds under my pillow. Not because of a dream, but because I fell asleep with Kendrix in my ear.

That man had me on the phone all damn night, talking about everything and nothing. The type of shit that make you forget the time. By the time I looked up, the sun was peeking through my blinds and his ass was boarding his flight back.

I found myself wishing time would speed the hell up so I could see him at the club later. But first, family.

I stretched, pulled my bonnet off, and rolled out the bed. Heidi was already in the kitchen, legs swinging at the bar stool, eating cereal. Hux was sitting across from her with that same sour ass look he'd been rocking the last two days.

I leaned against the counter, arms crossed. "What's the problem now?"

He just shrugged, stabbing at his eggs.

I raised an eyebrow. "Don't play with me, Hux. You got two options. Fix your face, or I fix it for you."

He sucked his teeth. "I'm straight."

"Mhm." I grabbed a mug and poured some coffee. "Keep on with that attitude, and Ima call Coach. Have you running suicides until you throwing up at practice."

His fork froze mid-air. He cut his eyes at me, then muttered, "That's foul."

"That's sisterhood," I shot back, sipping my coffee. "Now finish your food."

Over the last few days, I'd taken them to the movies, let them loose in the mall, even let Heidi spend a good thirty minutes in Claire's shopping. I loved every minute, but Lord, Hux's mood swings were about to test my salvation.

Heidi, on the other hand, was grinning at me with milk on her chin. "Can we get ice cream after school and my practice today?"

I slid my keys into my bag. "Rita's taking you to practice today, superstar. I gotta go practice with Ms. Ty."

Her little face lit up. "Tell Ty I miss her! And tell her I want her to come paint my nails again."

I leaned down and kissed her forehead. "I will. And I'll tell her to bring the sparkly polish, because I know what you like."

She giggled, swinging her legs.

I glanced over at Hux, who was slouched in his chair, eyes glued to his phone. Same blank look he'd had all week.

I walked over, slipped my arms around his tall-ass shoulders, even though I knew he didn't want it. He stiffened for a second, then let out a sigh.

"You love annoying me," he muttered.

"Yup," I whispered against his ear. "And I'm never gonna stop. Now, tell me what's really up."

He set his phone down slow, finally looking at me. And just for a second, that hard shell cracked.

"I'm good, sis," he said quietly. "I'm sorry. I just... got a lot on my mind. Trying to balance school, practice, games... everything."

I cupped his cheek, forcing him to look me dead in the eye. "Listen to me. You got this. And you got me. You hear?"

His lips curved into the smallest smile. "Yeah. I hear you."

"Good." I straightened up, grabbing my bag. "Now eat, baby boy."

He groaned, rolling his eyes, but his smile stayed.

As I headed for the door, I called back, "I'm going to check on Ma since it's been a few days."

"Keep me updated," Hux said, finally sounding like himself.

"I will." I blew them both a kiss. "Love y'all!"

"Love you too!" they yelled in unison.

I pulled up to Gun Hill slow, and the porch politicians were everywhere. Old heads and hustlers, sitting around like they ran the block when all they really ran was their mouths.

"Well, well, well," one of them yelled out. "Look who decided to grace us with her fine ass today."

"Boy, shut up before I call yo wife and tell her where you at," I shot back, locking my car.

Another one squinted, pointing. "Hey, Niv... who was that you brought 'round here the other day in that big-ass truck? Nigga looked like a steak dinner in the middle of the projects. Had us ready to run down on him until we saw you hop out."

I smirked, tilting my head. "Yeah, he good. Touch him and I'll kill you myself."

The whole porch cracked up, one old head slapping his knee.

"See, that's why don't nobody mess with you, Niv. You got that mean pretty. Fine as hell but dangerous as a pit bull."

"Better believe it," I said, stepping past them. "Now stay out my business before y'all end up on a t-shirt."

"Girl, you still savage as hell," one called after me.

"Savage pays the bills," I tossed over my shoulder.

I made it to Ma's stairwell and Zejah was sitting on the bottom step, bag of Hot Cheetos in her lap, earphones in, phone propped up on her knee while she scrolled through YouTube.

"Zejah," I called.

She looked up quick, wiping her fingers on her shorts. "Hey, Niv."

I dropped down on the step next to her. "How's Ma been?"

She shrugged. "Haven't really seen her. She ain't came out... unless she did when I was sleep." She popped another Cheeto in her mouth. "My mama started making me come in early though. Says I gotta clean up before she heads out."

"Head out where?" I asked, already knowing I wasn't gonna like the answer.

"The casino," she said, rolling her eyes. "Talking about she gone catch her a man. Whatever that means."

"It means she out here looking for somebody old enough to get an AARP check but dumb enough to give her all of it."

Zejah covered her mouth, trying not to laugh with a mouth full of chips.

I reached over and rubbed her knee. "Thank you, baby. For always keeping an eye out."

She looked at me like she wanted to argue that it wasn't a big deal, but I cut her off. "If you need anything, call me. I don't care what time it is."

"Thank you. I will."

"Good girl." I kissed the top of her head before standing.

I adjusted my bag on my shoulder, took a deep breath, and started climbing the stairs. I didn't know which version of Ma I was about to get. The wild one ready to curse me out, or the ghost who barely remembered I existed.

When I pushed the door open, I almost turned right back around.

"This can't be the right house," I said under my breath.

The smell of old smoke and yesterday's liquor was gone. Instead, I caught a faint whiff of... Febreze. The carpet was clean, vacuum lines still fresh like somebody gave a damn. A brand-new couch sat where the lumpy, cigarette-burned one used to be. A flat-screen TV was on the wall, still with the little sticker in the corner to show that it was new.

I set my bag down slow and started moving through the living room. My eyes scanned everything. The new couch, spotless carpet, even the damn TV remote neatly sitting on the armrest.

"Hell no," I said, opening the kitchen cabinets. Stocked. The fridge was full. I damn near wanted to cry, seeing milk that wasn't expired and fruit that didn't look like it had been through slavery.

It wasn't adding up. Did the city sneak somebody else in here behind my back and ship my mama's ass off? I was halfway ready to cuss the housing authority out when I walked down the hall toward the bathroom. Just as I reached the door, it cracked open and my mama stepped out

She looked... clean.

Hair brushed, skin still damp like she just showered, wearing one of her old satin robes. Not a full transformation, but compared to what I was used to? Shit, it was the glow up of the decade.

Her hand was pressed against her stomach.

"What are you doing?" I asked, brow raised.

She smirked faintly, leaning against the doorframe. "Layin' down. Been a few days, I wasn't feeling too hot. Head hurting. Stomach been actin' up." She gave a short laugh. "Shittin' all over myself too. Child, I ain't took this many baths in years."

I had to bite my lip to keep from laughing. A new bed. Clean sheets. Even some wall decor.

"Ma..." I said slowly, stepping inside. "Where the hell all this come from?"

She smiled, proud like she'd done it herself. "Couple days ago, somebody came knocking. Said they was sent here to do all this for me. Next thing I know, whole place spotless. New furniture, groceries, everything."

I narrowed my eyes. "And who exactly is this mysterious somebody?"

Her grin widened, and she leaned closer like she had a secret. "That fine young man you brought through here the other day. Mmm." She shook her head like she was replaying it in her mind. "Baby, I ain't wanted to leave since. And this TV?" She pointed. "I been sitting here watching old movies back-to-back. Forgot how much I missed that."

I shook my head, staring around at the house again, my mind spinning. Kendrix. I knew it.

"How Hux and Heidi been doing?"

I leaned against the doorframe, crossing my arms. "They good. Heidi has ballet after school today. Hux acting like the world on his shoulders, but he handling it."

Her lips trembled into a soft smile. "When can I see Heidi? Hux said... she starting to look more and more like her daddy."

I smiled to myself. "Yeah... she is."

Ma blinked, and tears started sliding down her cheeks. "I miss him so much." She sniffled. "When can I see Heidi?"

I locked eyes with her. "When you clean yourself up."

Her face crumpled. "But... Hux comes by sometimes." Her voice broke. "He comes and sees me."

I inhaled through my nose, steadying myself. "Hux is older, Ma. He lived through a lot of this. And whether you realize it or not, it scarred him in ways you still don't understand. I'm not doing that to Heidi."

She covered her mouth with her hand, tears streaming harder now.

"As far as Heidi knows, her mom is sick. Sick, and getting help. That's the story I gave her. The rest is on you." My throat tightened, but I pushed through it. "It's up to you to get the help."

"I'm trying..." she sobbed. "I swear, I'm trying."

"Then try harder." My voice cracked on the words, and before I could stop myself, a tear slid down my cheek.

I stepped closer and pulled her into a hug, my arms wrapping around her fragile frame. She smelled like soap and smoke, and for a second, I felt like I was holding the woman I used to know.

"This is a good step, Ma," I whispered against her hair. "Don't stop here."

She nodded weakly against my shoulder.

I pulled back, wiping my face fast. "I gotta go to practice. Let Zejah know if you need me, okay?"

She sniffled again and nodded, clutching her robe tighter.

I kissed her temple before heading for the door, swallowing hard. No matter how tough I tried to be, it never got easier walking away.

By the time I made it back down the stairs, my chest felt so damn heavy. I kept my chin high as I walked past the old heads on the porch, even managed to toss out a quick, "Kiss my ass, fools," when one of them called after me.

The minute I shut the door to my car, the world went quiet and I broke. Hot tears slid down my face before I even knew they were coming. I pressed my forehead against the steering wheel, trying to breathe through it, but the sobs came anyway. The kind of crying you pray nobody ever hears. I hated that shit. I hated crying. I hated feeling like that little girl again, standing in the middle of a messy-ass living room while my mama chose a high over me.

I wiped at my cheeks with the back of my hand, but more tears kept coming. I thought about Hux trying to be strong when he shouldn't have to. About Heidi smiling, not knowing the half of it. About Ma saying she was trying. Trying?? How many times had I heard that before?

I slammed my fist against the steering wheel. I was so damn tired of being the one holding everyone together when I barely had the pieces of myself in place. And still... I couldn't stop because if I let go, who would catch them?

"God... why?!" I yelled, pounding the wheel once, twice, three times. Tears blurred my vision. "Why you give me this life?"

"I don't deserve this shit! I been good to people who didn't deserve it, I been strong when I was breaking inside, I been raising babies that ain't even mine like they mine." My throat burned as the words tumbled out, messy and desperate.

"I'm tired, God. I'm so tired."

I screamed until my voice was raw, tears streaming down so heavy I could barely see. I wiped them with the heel of my hand, but they just kept coming. The more I fought, the harder they fell.

My phone lit up on the passenger seat.

Kendrix.

I stared at it. No. I couldn't answer. Not with my face streaked in tears and my soul hanging out raw. It stopped ringing. Then it lit up again.

I sniffled, swiped my sleeve across my face, and hit answer. "Hello?"

"Pretty... what's wrong?"

That question broke me all over again. My lips trembled. "I don't know... I just... I feel like..."

The tears started harder, almost choking me. I could hear the panic in my own breathing.

"Hey," he said softly.. "Breathe. You hear me? In... and out. That's it. Don't fight it. Let it out. I got you."

I did what he said. His voice wrapped around me like a blanket I didn't know I needed.

"That's it," he murmured. "I'm right here. You safe, Pretty. Ain't nobody watching but me. Let it go."

I cried harder. Ugly, snotty, soul-deep cries. The kind I never let anyone see. But I couldn't hold it with him.

He didn't flinch, rush me, or tell me to "be strong." He just... listened.

"I don't ever... I don't ever do this. Not with anyone."

"I know," he said. "And I ain't anyone."

"But listen, if them tears don't stop falling, Pretty, I'm gone need that pussy to start raining down on me the same way."

Through my tears, a laugh slipped out. "You are stupid as hell."

"Stupid and serious," he shot back, playful. "So go ahead and cry it out. Ima collect later."

I shook my head, half laughing, half crying, wiping my face. "You're really something else."

I leaned back against the seat. "Thank you. For... for everything. And not just this." My voice softened. "I know it was you. The house. Ma's house."

He was quiet, then said, "You can't expect somebody to get clean living in filth. She'll get there when she ready, but her surroundings matter. I just wanted to lighten your load a little."

"Thank you."

"Don't thank me," he said. "Just let me keep doing it."

I let out a shaky breath.

"Can I pick you up tonight?" he asked. "I'm going to the club and I want you riding with me."

I snorted. "You know your bitch, Arlette, gonna have a heart attack."

"I don't give a fuck about Arlette," he said. "The ambulance will come get her when she passes out."

"I got practice now, but... yeah. You can come get me later."

"Bet," he said.

"Alright. I gotta go."

"Pretty?"

"Yeah?"

"Don't ever feel like you have to hide that side from me again."

I didn't respond right away, but the smile on my face said enough.

"See you later, Pretty," he said.

"See you later, Kendrix."

14

Kendrix

I shot her a quick text. ***Pulling up, Pretty.***

By the time I parked outside her place, I stepped out, straightened my jacket, and walked up the drive.

The front door cracked open. Sweatsuit hugging her like she was doing me a favor just existing. She turned, about to lock the door, and when she spun back around, she damn near jumped out her skin.

"Shit, Kendrix!" she clutched her chest. "Don't do that! I know everybody in this area. They not stupid enough to try me. I can walk to the truck just fine."

"Kids home?" I asked, nodding toward the door.

She blinked, slow. "Uhh... nooooo." She dragged the word out, confused. "Rita took them to get hibachi since they begged for it for dinner. Why?"

I pointed toward the door behind her. "Can I?"

Her brows shot up. "Can you... what?"

"Go in." My smirk widened. "I'm coming to collect."

The look she gave me said she knew exactly what the hell I meant.

Her lips twitched. "Boy, please." She shook her head, laughing under her breath. "I gotta get to the club, horny man."

I stepped closer, tilting my head down until I could feel her breath on my lips. "Yeah, and I need to eat."

Before she could smart-mouth me again, I kissed her. She tried to laugh against my mouth, but it turned into a soft moan that damn near had me losing my mind.

Without breaking the kiss, I pushed the door open. She backed up step by step, guiding me inside, her hand catching the edge of my jacket like she didn't wanna let go.

We stumbled down the hall, her leading, me following, lips never parting.

By the time we hit her bedroom door, I had one hand on her hip, the other sliding up her back.

The second we made it into her bedroom, she spun on me, eyes low and wicked, lips glistening like trouble.

"You said you came to eat, huh?" she whispered, tilting her head.

"Damn right."

She slid her hoodie off her shoulders, and let it fall to the floor.

"Then lay back, Mr. Ken."

I didn't even argue. I sat on her bed, kicked off my shoes, and leaned back against her headboard.

She climbed up slow, one knee on each side of my chest, and looked down at me.

"You wanted this so bad," she said. "now you gone listen to every word my body has to say."

My dick jumped just from the way she said it. She tugged her sweats down, revealing that nude lace I'd been imagining since earlier. My mouth watered. She caught it and smirked like she'd won.

"Keep your hands where I can see 'em," she ordered.

"Yes, ma'am," I said, already hard as fuck.

She lowered herself slow, pressing that heat against my mouth. I groaned, lips parting to taste her, tongue sliding up and down.

"Ohhh..." Her head tipped back, a soft laugh tumbling out of her mouth. "Yeah... that's it. Hungry ass."

I wrapped my lips around her clit, sucking slow, and she gripped the headboard behind me for balance. Then she started moving. Grinding. Riding.

Gliding up and down my face like I was the damn pole and she was showing off a new routine. Her voice dripped poetry with every moan. "See... this how you get fed without ever cooking. This how you make a man beg without saying a word." She rolled her hips, slow and deliberate, smearing her wetness across my lips and beard.

I groaned against her pussy, the vibration making her buck. I slid my tongue deep inside her, and she cried out, nails clawing. She didn't hold back. Didn't move timid. She rode my face like she owned it.

"Yessss," she moaned. "Don't stop... eat it like you mean it."

I buried my tongue back in her, sucking and teasing until she was dripping down my chin. She rocked faster, body trembling, and every time she gasped, I swore I'd never want to hear another sound in my life.

"You hear me, Kendrix?" she panted. "This is how I speak. My body tells the truth. My lips just talk shit."

I groaned again, tongue circling her clit, and she damn near screamed, her thighs squeezing tight around my head.

"Fuuuuck..." she moaned, hips grinding harder. "You wanted this... so take all of it. Every drop."

She came undone on my face, her body jerking as she moaned loud enough to wake her whole block. And she didn't even stop. She kept rocking, slower, milking every last ounce of pleasure until she collapsed forward, breathless, resting her forehead against the headboard.

"Pretty... you just made me see the Lord twice."

She laughed, still trembling, and slid off me, her legs weak. "Good. That's what happens when you beg for the sermon."

NETRA ANTIONETTE

By the time I pulled up in front of GivGold, Pretty was glowing. Before she went inside, she grabbed my blunt off the console, lit that bitch, and took a long pull like it was her oxygen. She winked at me, then jogged into the building.

I sat there for a second, shaking my head. "This motherfucker."

When I finally walked in behind her, I wasn't even fully in the door before I felt it. That hot-ass death stare from Arlette. Posted up by the bar in a dress that probably cost too much for it to be doing that little. Her eyes locked on me like she'd caught me sneaking out of her damn mama's house.

I didn't even give her the satisfaction. I cut through the main floor crowd, dapped up a couple familiar faces, then ducked into one of the private lounges in the back. Closed the door, lit another blunt, and leaned back on the couch like I had peace in my life.

That shit didn't last long when the door flew open.

"So you just gone stroll up in here with that bitch like I'm invisible?!"

I took a slow drag and exhaled right in her direction. Didn't move a muscle.

"Kendrix, are you deadass right now? You really gone embarrass me like that? After everything we been through?!"

I was calm as ever. "Arlette, lower your voice. Ain't nobody in here but me, you, and my patience."

She threw her hands up. "Oh, so now I'm crazy? That's what you doing? I been calling you all day and now I see why you ain't pick up. She had her mouth on your phone and your dick probably, didn't she?"

I leaned back further, lips twitching. "Sound like you picturing it too hard. You jealous or turned on?"

"Nigga, I will—"

"You will what?" I asked. "Cuss me out in a private room you weren't even invited in? Make yourself look even more pressed than you already do?"

Her mouth opened, then closed. She glared, chest heaving.

"You out here playing in my face, Kendrix. Like I'm some random bitch you just stumbled across," she snapped. "You really think I'm about to let you embarrass me like this?"

"Arlette, let me be real with you one time."

She folded her arms, chin tilted high. "Please. Enlighten me."

I leaned forward, resting my elbows on my knees. "The only thing embarrassing in this room is you. You're still acting like you hold a place in my life when truth is... the only place you hold is in the past. And you stuck there, running your mouth, while I'm over here building a future you'll never be a part of."

Her mouth opened, but I wasn't done.

"You keep saying you know your worth," I said. "but you're begging for a man that don't want you. That's desperation, and it's loud as fuck."

She took a step closer, jabbing her finger at me. "Oh, I can show you better than I can tell you."

"The last time you said that that shit, all you showed me was why I left your ass where you at now."

NETRA ANTIONETTE

I had just finished flicking the last bit of ash into the tray when a dancer strolled, swinging her hips like she was auditioning for my attention. She leaned on the doorframe, licking her lip gloss like it was supposed to hypnotize me.

"Well, well," she purred. "The famous Kendrix Givelle. I was wondering when you'd let me keep you company."

I didn't even look up all the way, just side-eyed her. "You wondering wrong, sweetheart."

She fake pouted, walking closer, tits damn near spilling out her top.

"Aw, come on, baby. Just one dance. I promise I'm worth it."

I leaned back, lips twitching into a smirk. "Nah. You gorgeous, but you're not my flavor." I slid a few hundreds from my pocket and held them out. "Go buy yourself something nice and tell MissCommunication to come see me."

Her eyes lit up at the money even while her ego took a hit. She snatched the cash with a grin, "Sure thing, Big Daddy."

"Don't call me that again," I said smoothly.

She laughed nervously and bounced out the room.

Two minutes later, the door opened again and *fuck.*

Pretty walked in. Leather hugging every curve and ass sitting. She had her hair pulled back, hoop earrings glinting under the dim lights, and a look on her face like she knew she was the baddest thing breathing. My jaw tightened. The way that outfit was squeezing her had every nigga out there wanting her.

She laughed as soon as she saw my face. "What you want?"

Before I could even answer, she climbed right into my lap, facing me like she owned my throne. Her arms wrapped around my neck, lips just inches from mine.

I gripped her thighs tight, leather creaking under my hands, and smirked. "What I want, Pretty? Hell, you sitting on it."

I licked my lips, staring at her. "Nah. But I got something for you that'll shut you up for at least five minutes."

She leaned back a little, biting her lip like Christmas came early. "Oh, so we doing gifts now? You tryna spoil me already, Givelle?"

"Not trying," I corrected, sliding my hand into my jacket pocket. "I am."

I pulled out a small velvet box and set it in her palm. The second she felt the weight of it, her whole demeanor shifted. She loved gifts. I could see it in the way her smile softened, like she was already picturing herself wearing it. Not because it screamed money, but because it screamed thoughtfulness.

"Go ahead," I said.

She opened it slow, like her body couldn't decide between playing it cool and squealing. Inside was a delicate bracelet. White gold with a line of small amethyst stones, deep purple and gleaming under the light.

Her lips parted. "Kendrix..."

I smirked. "You like it?"

"I... yeah," she whispered, eyes glued to it. "This is... shit. It's beautiful."

I took the bracelet from the box, holding her wrist gently as I slid it on. "Purple's my favorite color on a woman," I told her, fastening the clasp.

She raised an eyebrow. "Why? Because it makes us look like royalty or some shit?"

I grinned, leaning closer so my lips brushed her ear. "Exactly. Purple stands for power. Passion. Mystery. And every time I see it on a woman... it reminds me she's dangerous enough to make a king kneel without lifting a finger."

She laughed, shaking her head. "Boy, you smooth as hell. Talking about kneeling like you ain't the one tryna have me bent backwards somewhere."

"Don't get it twisted. I'll do both."

She looked down at the bracelet, then kissed me. When she pulled back, her lips were shining, and that smirk of hers was lethal. "I gotta go," she said, sliding off my lap, leather creaking as she moved. "Your bitch, Arlette, has me entertaining some men before a meeting."

I leaned back, smirking. "You gone stop calling that hoe, my bitch. But yeah, Pretty. That meeting's with me."

She froze mid-step, glancing over her shoulder with a look of fire. "Figures."

Then she started walking, hips swinging like she knew I was watching.

"Don't be late, Givelle. I like my men punctual... and hard."

NETRAANTIONETTE

The lounge was thick with smoke and money. Two men sat across from me, Derrick and Sosa. Suits, gold watches, and the kind of smiles that looked good but meant you needed to count your fingers after shaking hands. We'd been talking numbers for weeks, and it was supposed to be the final sit-down.

But the second I stepped in, I damn near lost my train of thought. Pretty was on the pole. Leather still painted to her ass, body glistening under the soft lights. She moved like the music was built for her spine, her hair brushing her shoulders as she spun.

Derrick leaned back with a grin. "The dancer already made us real comfortable, Kendrix. Hell of a show while we waited on you."

Sosa laughed, sipping his drink. "She had us forgetting why we came here."

I lit a cigar, forced my smirk to stay calm. "Good to hear," I said, like she wasn't the reason my chest was tight too.

I exhaled smoke slow, leaning back in my chair. "So... where we at?"

Derrick tapped the table. "We like your idea. The expansion on the cigar lounges. We bring in our liquor, your cigars, and use the poker rooms as the front. Money circulates clean. Everybody eats."

Sosa nodded. "We're ready to move forward. Just needed to look you in the eye before we shake on it."

On the surface, it sounded good. Too good. But I'd been in this game long enough to know when a nigga was selling me water in the middle of a rainstorm.

And right then... I noticed Pretty.

The way she moved. She wasn't just dancing anymore. She was communicating with me.

Her spin slowed, her body swaying side to side instead of front to back. Then, she hooked her ankle high on the pole and stretched, pointing that heel in the direction of Derrick and Sosa.

I raised my brow behind a cloud of smoke. Message received. Something's off.

I leaned forward, cigar between my fingers. "So, let's talk numbers one more time."

They started running the play again, but my ears weren't on the math. They were on the way Pretty's eyes cut toward them every time they overpromised. On the way her body slowed when they lied, the same way it picked up when they told the truth.

The table was covered with neat stacks of paper, contracts typed up real professional, pens sitting on top like they just knew I was about to sign.

Derrick leaned in, tapping the first page. "All we need is your signature here, Kendrix. You're about to triple your profits in less than six months."

Sosa nodded, flashing all them teeth. "Easy money. We handle distribution. You just keep doing what you do best. Nobody loses."

I rolled the cigar slow between my fingers, my eyes on the paperwork but my mind on Pretty.

She was still moving on that pole. At first, she looked like she was just vibing with the music, but I knew better. I'd been watching her too long not to recognize the pattern.

Her hips swayed side to side like a no. Her eyes cut quick at Derrick when he said nobody loses.

Then she spun around, arching her back, legs splitting wide in the air, toes pointed right at the papers in front of me.

I raised an eyebrow. *Don't sign that shit.*

Derrick leaned closer. "What's the hesitation, Kendrix? You asked for a smooth move, we delivered. This is it."

I smirked, leaning back. "Smooth ain't always smart. Sometimes it's just slick."

Sosa's grin faded, but Derrick laughed like I cracked a joke. "You don't trust us?"

Pretty's pace changed again. She spun up the pole, gripped tight, then leaned back into an upside-down hang. Her legs scissored before she stretched one out pointing straight down at the bottom of the contract like a damn arrow.

The fine print.

I reached over, flipping the pages without breaking eye contact with her. "Nah, it ain't about trust. It's about detail. And something in here don't smell right."

Derrick shifted in his seat. "Everything's clean, Kendrix."

I smirked, looking dead at him. "Maybe for y'all. But for me? This clause right here," I tapped the bottom paragraph with my cigar, "means you walk away owning half of what I built while I cover all the risk."

Silence.

Pretty dropped down the pole slow, knees bent, arching her back like she was sealing the deal, and I knew I said exactly what she wanted me to.

Derrick cleared his throat. "We can adjust the terms."

"Yeah, you will," I said smoothly, leaning back and blowing out a stream of smoke. "Or this conversation's over."

Out the corner of my eye, Pretty smiled faintly, swinging around the pole. I leaned forward, stubbed my cigar out on the ashtray, and said,

"So, what's it gon' be? Adjust the terms... or watch me walk out with every dollar you thought you were about to eat?"

15

Niveah

I was halfway through touching up my lip gloss when the door flew open without a knock. I didn't even need to look up to know it was trouble. The smell of too much perfume and not enough class gave it away.

Arlette strutted in, heels clicking like she was sending SOS signals to her insecurities. She tossed a bag onto the vanity in front of me, stacks of cash peeking out.

"There," she said, flipping her hair. "That's all I need from you today."

I blinked slow, leaned back in my chair, and crossed my legs. "Excuse me?"

She smiled, but it was that tight, fake-ass smile. "I don't need you for the finale tonight. I'll call you if I need you again."

For a split second, I just stared at her. My chest rose slow, my nails tapped the armrest, and I had to count to three in my head because the old me would've flipped the damn vanity table over and beat her ass.

Instead, I smiled.

"So let me get this straight. You're so busy being jealous that your nigga — who, by the way, ain't even your nigga — gave somebody else a little attention, that you decided to mess with my bag? Baby, your beef is with him, not me. Don't get mad at me because your position is weak."

Her jaw ticked. I leaned forward, grabbed the bag, and pushed it right back toward her.

"Here's the thing, sweetheart," I said, gloss shining under the lights. "I don't need your money. I make my own. You can't cut me out of a bag that already has my name on it. And just so we're clear, I don't wait for your calls. You wait for mine."

Arlette smirked, leaning one manicured hand on the vanity. "That's my man you're running behind."

I laughed so loud it echoed off the mirrors.

"Let me let you in on a secret. Play your part because here's the thing, these niggas gone play theirs. You keep putting your faith in a man, setting yourself up. The minute he gets bored or sees another pretty face, he gone sprint toward it like it's the finish line. Don't matter how good you look, how smart you are, or how well you ride — if he don't give you a title, don't you dare stress over him. You get your bag, get your power, and keep it moving. Stop acting like one nigga is the finish line when you're the whole damn race."

I leaned back in my chair, crossed my legs, and gave her a slow once-over.

"Arlette, let's be real. Instead of checking him, you're bold enough to come for my bag? That's some bitch shit."

Her nostrils flared, but I kept going.

"See, the difference between me and you? I never had to give a man my pussy to get what I wanted. Not once. My mind and my mouth been cashing checks before I ever thought about spreading my legs. So, let me really fuck your head up. Kendrix has never even stuck his dick in me. Not once. So ask yourself why are you really pressed. Matter fact, ask yourself what I'm doing that has him moving different... because maybe you can learn something. "

I leaned forward, dropped my voice just enough to cut deeper.

"You don't stop any bags of mine, sweetheart. I am the bag. Men throw money just to breathe the same air as me. You mad? Be mad at him. But don't ever think you have the power to block my shine because I shine regardless."

I smoothed my hair back, stood up slow, and looked her dead in the face.

"The money's good here, but I can sit up and talk with a man and make better. I'll be out your hair tonight."

I let a smirk curl at the corner of my mouth.

"But do me a favor, Arlette. Let me know how much money you make without me when it's all over."

Her face cracked just a little. Not enough for her to admit I hit a nerve, but enough for me to see the truth. I reached for my purse, unbothered, when my phone buzzed against the vanity.

I glanced down. The name lit up the screen, and I smiled slow. *My favorite man.*

God really knew how to replace a loss with a blessing.

> **My Favorite Man:** Landed in town for the weekend. Got a seat waiting for you at dinner. You free?

Arlette thought she could rattle me? Please. God doesn't close doors on me without opening up a penthouse suite.

I grabbed my jacket, looked in the mirror one last time, and typed back a quick

> Always free for you

NETRAANTIONETTE

I pushed through the back door, the night air kissing my skin like freedom itself.

"Niv!"

Kendrix' had the type of voice that could make a weaker woman stop in her tracks. But I wasn't weaker.

I turned just enough for him to see my smile then slowly lifted my middle finger. "Handle your business, Mr. Givelle."

Ty was parked right where I knew she'd be, leaning on her steering wheel with that grin that always showed up when I did something bold. I climbed in, slamming the door behind me.

"You ready?" she cackled. "You really flipped that man off."

"Hell yeah," I said, adjusting my jacket. "If Arlette wanna play petty and pull me off the finale, cool. Her dumbass doesn't even realize that we are a package deal. "

Before Ty could respond, Kendrix stormed up to the car, knocking on the window.

I rolled it down, leaning my elbow on the frame.

"What do you want?" I asked, my voice sweet as poison.

"Where you going?" he demanded.

I tilted my head. "Didn't I already tell you? My pleasure better not fuck up my business. But since you can't keep your bitches in check, Arlette pulled me off the final set. So congratulations, you let your mess cost me money."

His brows furrowed, like he didn't know whether to get mad or apologize. That was my cue to keep pressing.

"You wanna know something, Kendrix?" I leaned forward so he could see the fire in my eyes. "The men I deal with would never let anything sabotage what I have going on. Not one. Because real men don't create chaos between women. They control the room so that shit like that never can happen."

I paused, letting that sink in before I continued giving him the cutthroat truth.

"You think that chaos between women is cute, Kendrix? It's not. It's weak. It's sloppy. Real men don't let women crash out over them like it's a contest. They shut the circus down before the clowns even touch the stage. I don't deal with men who let women crash out over them like they have the last dick on earth. I fight too good for that. And I got kids to raise. Jail ain't on my vision board, Pretty Boy."

Ty snorted beside me, trying to hide her laugh. Kendrix just stood there, chest rising and falling heavy.

"Where are you going, Pretty?"

"On a date."

The way his jaw ticked? Whew. It was like I slapped him without lifting a hand. "The fuck you not. You not going out with nobody but me."

That's when I smiled. The type of smile that said *bless your delusional little heart.*

I lifted my hand slow, pretending to study my finger. "Hmmm... no ring here." I tilted it back and forth like I was checking for diamonds in a bad light.

Then I pulled out my phone, scrolling fake fast. "Let's see... pictures of an engagement? Nope. A little video of you asking me to be your girlfriend? Nada. Huh. Crazy. Must've missed that memo."

Ty damn near choked laughing in the driver's seat. I smirked, sliding my phone back in my purse.

"Sorry, Kendrix," I said, sweet and sharp. "You don't own me. I do what I want."

His lips parted like he was about to check me, but I wasn't done.

"That's the problem with men now," I continued, voice rising. "Y'all think just because you're handsome and got some money that you're automatically the only option. News flash, baby. Your bitch in there losing her marbles over you while another man has a plate of grapes ready to feed me on a private island. Which one sounds insane to you?"

He licked his lips, smirking like he was tryna stay calm. "You really think I'm about to let you go out with some other nigga?"

I leaned forward, unbothered. "Aren't you tired of me clocking your tea, Kendrix?" I ran my tongue over my teeth, real slow. "The fact you said 'let you' proves my point. You don't let me do shit. I choose. And right now, I'm choosing what's best for me. Not your ego. Not your mess. Me. Men like you think the world runs on your time. You really believe we just supposed to sit pretty, quiet, and wait for you to decide when we deserve effort. Like our lives are on pause until you ready to press play."

"Pretty—"

"Uh uh," I cut him off, holding up my hand. "Don't 'Pretty' me like that nickname make you different. You can puff your chest all you want. You want me to only go out with you? Put a title on it. You want me to wait around while you handle your chaos? Clean that shit up FIRST. You want me loyal? Give me loyalty I can actually touch. Because what you not about to do is play king while I sit here acting like I ain't the whole damn kingdom. Right now, you're just noise. And noise don't pay bills."

Ty whistled low, shaking her head like she was watching a show.

He leaned both hands on the window frame, staring at me like he was two seconds from snatching me out the truck. "Come with me and I'll figure all this out."

I grinned. "Uhhh, how about...NO! I'll never be the woman who puts her life on hold waiting for a man to figure out anything. Either claim me or stay the hell out my way. Because I promise you, there's a line of men ready to give me everything you're still debating and figuring out."

His mouth opened like he had more to say, but I was done giving him the stage. I leaned back in my seat, grabbed Ty's arm and smiled sweet enough to sting.

"Byeeeee, Kendrix," I said. "Oh, I might call you tomorrow... depending on how my night goes."

Ty burst out laughing as she pulled off, tires rolling over his pride nice and slow.

NETRAANTIONETTE

The restaurant smelled like spice and money. Not that fake "let me impress you with a flashy chain" money, but old, quiet, generational money. The kind you could hear in the way people carried themselves when they walked past your table.

Sitting across from me was Sincere. Sincere with the accent that melted panties faster than candle wax. Sincere with the smile that could convince a nun to sin.

"Likkle gyal," he said, leaning back in his chair, his voice smooth as aged rum. "You look more beautiful every time I see you. What's the secret?"

I smirked over the rim of my wine glass. "Dancing, bills, and mimosas. Keeps the skin tight."

He laughed so loud the older couple two tables over glanced our way. That deep Jamaican laugh that rolled through his chest and always made me feel like home, even when I knew better.

Sincere wasn't new. Sincere was the *foundation*. He'd been teaching me the game since I was eighteen, when I didn't know finesse from faith. He taught me how to make men feel seen without giving them shit but a smile. How to take control of a room without ever raising my voice. How to get what I wanted without ever laying on my back—unless I wanted to.

"Tell me, Niv," he said, as he poured more wine into my glass. "Yuh still breaking hearts wid just a look?"

"Of course," I said, licking my lips slow. "Some habits just don't die."

Truth was, Sincere was the habit I never really wanted to quit. We had a love that wasn't built on possession or fairy tales. He didn't lie to me. Never pretended I was the only one. Hell, half the time we talked about the other women he entertained, and I respected him more for the honesty.

Sincere gave me something better than false promises. Options.

He'd always say, *"I'll never chain you, baby girl. Stay if yuh want. Leave if yuh must. Just know when yuh here, yuh treated like a queen."*

And he meant that shit. Every time.

I leaned closer, dropping my voice so only he could hear. "You know I missed you, right?"

His smirk curved wicked. "Yuh miss mi, or yuh miss what mi carry?"

"Both," I said, shameless.

He laughed again, shaking his head. "My Niv. Brutal with the mouth, soft with the eyes."

And the truth? I did love him. Not in the fairy tale, *build a home and grow old together* way. That wasn't Sincere. Sincere loved women too much to belong to one. And I respected that.

But the friendship? The loyalty? The fact that whenever I needed him, he was one phone call and flight away? That was priceless.

And the dick? Well, that was just the bonus plan.

Sincere leaned back in his chair. His eyes stayed locked on me, that slow Jamaican smirk spreading wider as I told him about Kendrix.

"So let mi get dis straight," he said, tapping his glass like he was trying not to laugh. "Di man tink he own yuh, but him nuh even lock yuh down? Yuh serious?"

I rolled my eyes, stabbing a piece of jerk shrimp with my fork. "Deadass. Acting like he branded me or something. I had to let him know."

Sincere slapped the table so hard the waiter jumped. He laughed that deep, belly-shaking laugh that always got me. "Lawd Jesus. Yuh dangerous, Niv. Man probably sweating bullets right now."

"He was," I said, popping the shrimp in my mouth slow, making him watch my lips. "And he gone keep sweating, because I don't do that 'waiting for a man to figure it out' shit."

Sincere whistled low, shaking his head. "Cha. Poor man tink him in control, and di whole time yuh di one driving di car. Yuh nuh easy."

I smirked, leaning closer. "And you love that about me."

He grinned, leaning in too. "I do and I live fi dat. Mi proud of yuh, baby girl. Yuh never let no man tek yuh shine. Kendrix lucky yuh even give him di time of day."

His words made something warm spread in my chest, but I kept it playful. "You calling me a blessing?"

"More like a hurricane," he said, sipping his wine. "Beautiful, an' when yuh done, nothing is ever di same."

I laughed so loud heads turned. "You're so damn dramatic."

"Mi only speak di truth," he said smoothly. Then he raised a brow. "So tell mi, yuh like him?"

I paused, swirling the wine in my glass. "More than I want to."

"Mhm." He studied me with that knowing look. "Dat why yuh vex. Him gettin' under yuh skin."

I squinted at him. "I'm not vexed. I'm... mildly annoyed."

He chuckled. "Same thing. Yuh heart beating for him, an' yuh mind don't like it."

I sighed. "Maybe. But he gon' learn quick—if he can't handle me, somebody else can."

Sincere leaned in, eyes gleaming. "Yuh sure yuh ready fi dat game, Niv? Cause from di way yuh talkin', dis one might not play wid yuh. Him might flip di whole board."

I raised my brow, lips curving. "Good. I like competition."

He burst out laughing again, shaking his head. "Di man nuh stand a chance."

I smirked, stabbing another shrimp. "That's his problem, not mine."

Sincere hand brushed against my thigh under the table. That damn smirk played across his lips, like he knew exactly how much heat he was stirring.

"Relax, mami," he said. "Mi just miss di feel of yuh."

I tilted my head, pretending I wasn't already squeezing my thighs together. "Oh, so now you touching on me like you forgot the last time?"

He laughed low, his hand squeezing a little higher. "Yuh tink mi could ever forget? Woman, mi dream 'bout dat night. Still waiting fi the encore."

I smirked, swirling my wine slow. "You stay dreaming."

He leaned in closer, voice dropping. "Dreaming... an' paying."

That got me. My brows lifted, but my lips curved. "Since when did we start transactional dinners?"

"Nah," he said, sliding a small black card across the table so smooth, nobody around would notice. "This is appreciation. Because yuh worth it. And mi don't want yuh worrying 'bout a damn ting except enjoying yuhself."

I looked down at the card, knowing damn well the limit on it was higher than most people's yearly salary. My chest felt warm, but I kept my face cool. "You trying to buy me?"

He smirked. "Yuh can't be bought. But mi can make sure yuh never lack."

My lips tugged into a smile I tried to hide behind my glass. "Dangerous man."

"Only dangerous 'cause mi give yuh options," he said, eyes locked on mine. "Yuh don't need me. But yuh want me. An' dat make di difference."

My thighs clenched when his thumb traced slow circles, and I damn near melted when he whispered, "Tell mi yuh don't feel dis, Niv. Go 'head an' lie to mi face."

I leaned forward, letting my lips graze the rim of my glass, giving him a look so sharp it could cut glass. "I could lie. But I like how honest my body is when you touch me."

His grin spread wicked. "Dat's what mi love. Yuh mouth talk tough, but yuh body always confess."

I chuckled, setting my glass down. "Keep playing, Sincere. You gon' mess around and get a whole performance."

"Say di word, baby girl," he murmured, thumb pressing a little firmer on my thigh. "We don't even need di stage."

I laughed, shaking my head. "You crazy."

"And yuh love it," he shot back without missing a beat.

"Mi done wid dis," he said smoothly, snapping his fingers once. Two men in tailored suits slid up like shadows.

"Handle the bill. Make sure mi suite ready."

"Yes, sir," one said, already pulling a card from his pocket.

I raised a brow. "You really out here snapping like you in The Lion King?"

He grinned. "Mi king everywhere mi go. Tonight mi just want my queen beside mi."

I shook my head, but the warmth in my chest said different. "Careful. You start talking like that, I might get used to it."

He leaned in close, lips brushing my ear. "Dat's di plan."

The suite was too damn pretty for the filth we were about to do in it. Silk sheets. Dim lighting. Floor-to-ceiling windows that looked out over the city like it was waiting for a show.

"You know this isn't a good idea," I whispered, leaning back against the door as he crowded me with his body.

He smirked, brushing his lips across mine without kissing me yet. "Mi don't do good ideas, princess. Mi do unforgettable ones."

I tried to roll my eyes, but my body betrayed me, already melting against him. "You always got a line, huh?"

His hand slid down, gripping the curve of my ass like it belonged to him. "No lines tonight. Just truth. And truth is... yuh been on mi mind too long."

The kiss was greedy. Hot. The kind that made me forget who the hell I was for a second. His tongue slid against mine, slow and sure, and I swore my knees buckled.

"Sincere..." I breathed when he pulled back.

"Say mi name softer, baby," he teased, trailing his mouth down my neck. "Make it sound like a prayer."

"You don't need prayers," I said, gasping when his hands tugged my top over my head. "You need therapy."

He laughed against my chest, sucking one of my nipples into his mouth. "Then mi your therapist tonight. Now tell mi what you need."

I bit my lip, tilting my head back as his hands slid under the band of my skirt. "You already know."

"Say it."

"I need you to eat this pussy."

That's all he needed. One second I was teasing, the next, I was on my back on those silk sheets with his head between my thighs.

The first lick had my toes curling.

"Fuck, Sincere."

He groaned against me, the vibration making me arch up. "That's it. Give mi all of it. Don't hold back."

His tongue was slow, then fast, then deep—like he was trying to write his name inside me.

I grabbed the sheets, head tossing back. "Shit... don't stop."

"Mi nah stop till yuh run," he said, voice muffled but cocky as hell.

"Sincere... oh my God."

He pulled back just long enough to smirk up at me, lips glistening. "Don't call Him now, baby. Call mi."

By the time Sincere finally pulled back, my thighs were trembling like I just finished running suicides in a gym.

And let me go ahead and say this—

As you can see, I love an eater.

Yeah, Kendrix had me all intrigued with his smooth talk and "big dick energy," but let's be real, he wasn't stopping shit. I wanted a nut, and Sincere was the cheat code.

Why not get it from a man who's always been there delivering exactly what the fuck was needed?

See, me and Sincere had a different kind of thing. We didn't always have to be intimate, but when we did? Whew. It was always what it needed to be. He knew the assignment before I even gave out the syllabus.

And yeah, I could've given him more tonight. Could've let him flip me over, dig deep, and put me to sleep the other way. But sometimes, all a girl wants is to get that bread, get that head, then leave.

Instead, we laid there, laughing and talking because we'd been best friends forever. Venting about life. About stress. About how both of us stayed booked and busy.

Somewhere between his laugh and him saying, *"Niv, yuh know yuh mi peace, right?"*

...I knocked the hell out.

When I finally woke up, the room was quiet. He was gone.

But on the edge of the bed sat a purple Chanel bag and a fat stack of bills tucked inside.

And also a note, written in his handwriting:

Niv, You know I love venting and spending time with my favorite woman. But duty calls, and I had to go see someone. Can't wait to do this again.

I laid back against the pillows, smirking. Arlette swore she stopped my bag. Baby, she just helped me get more.

16

Kendrix

I ain't even gon' lie. Since the moment Pretty left that damn club, flipping me the bird like I was some weak ass man, she'd been stuck in my head like my favorite hook.

I tried to bury myself in work. Meetings. Calls. Even hit the gym like I had demons to sweat out. It didn't matter. Shorty was in every thought.

And the wildest part was that she was probably somewhere laughing, legs crossed, sipping on champagne somebody else bought, like I wasn't still tasting her on my tongue.

That shit had me tight. It wasn't even about the sex. Hell, we ain't even fucked yet. My dumb ass. It was the way she moved. That confidence. That cutthroat feminism that made me feel like I had to step my game up just to stand next to her.

But at the same time, it pissed me the fuck off.

I knew she was the type to remind you every five minutes that you didn't own her. That she could walk away whenever the fuck she felt like it. And that was cute... until I realized I wanted her walking to me, not away from me.

I leaned back in my chair, staring at my phone like I could force her name to pop up.

Nothing.

Not a text. Not a missed call. Not even one of them little "wyd" joints.

"Aight, Pretty. Bet."

I told myself I wasn't about to chase her. I wasn't that nigga. But the way my chest felt heavy as hell when I imagined her with somebody else... Yeah, I was lying like shit.

I already knew I was gone call her. Matter fact, I was two seconds from pulling up unannounced. I try not to get like that but when I lock in, I lock in.

The bar was so quiet that it made a man sit in his thoughts too long. I looked over at my brother, Kross.

He leaned back, smirking. "You been off your game, bro."

I chuckled low, shaking my head. "Damn, can't I just sit and chill with my brother without an interrogation?"

"Nah," he said, sipping his drink slow. "Not when you look like you fighting with yourself. That's not business stress. That's woman stress. Spill it."

I stared at the glass in front of me before I picked it up. "She different, Kross."

His eyebrow shot up. "Different how?"

I exhaled, feeling stupid as hell for even saying it out loud. "She want titles. Without them, she says she moves how she wanna move. At first, I thought she was just running game... but she stands on it. And the wild part is that I respect it. Shit, I like it. But it's messing with me because I ain't gon' lie. I want more than what she's offering right now."

Kross's smirk faded. He studied me for a second, his usual playboy grin wasn't there. "That sound like me and Rivah."

I looked up. "You serious about her?"

He nodded, eyes distant like he was picturing her. "Dead serious. She got this way of making me want to be still. Like I don't gotta run nowhere, don't gotta prove shit. She calls me out, makes me better, and don't even realize she doing it."

For a second, we just sat there in silence. Two niggas who spent most their lives dodging feelings, now confessing like we was at Sunday service.

"You know it's crazy?" I said finally. "I thought Kairo would be the only one to fold. Married at eighteen, swore he had it figured out. Fifteen years later, he out here risking everything for some dumb shit."

Kross shook his head. "Yeah, he's putting everything else above what's really important. I never wanted anyone in my space longer than a weekend. Rivah changed that. Got me thinking about shit I used to laugh at. Sunday mornings. Family dinners. Shit, even a future."

I let out a dry laugh, rubbing the back of my neck. "Sound like you in deep."

He shot me a look. "Sound like you are too, bro. You ain't talked like this since..."

He didn't finish. He didn't have to.

I ain't never told nobody this. Not my brothers. Not my pops. Not even my mama. But fuck it, you gone know, because maybe if I say it out loud, it'll stop eating me alive.

Her name was Megan.

I met her when we were kids, running around while our dads did business. At first, her old man wasn't with it. Me hanging around his daughter like I had a chance in hell. But you can't stop what's meant. We grew up together. Laughed together. Then one day, I looked at her and realized she wasn't just the girl with the big smile and louder laugh and I wanted her. Senior year of highschool, we were in deep. No games. Just me and her. She got pregnant, but only we knew. She was scared as hell that her daddy would've lost his fucking mind. I was ready to man up. Ready to give her everything, ready to protect them both.

Then one rainy-ass night... she was driving home from cheer practice. Lost control. They said she went quick. That she didn't feel anything. But I don't believe that. I believe she was scared. And I wasn't there.

I lost her. And the baby.

That shit changed me. Broke me. I swore then that I'd never love a woman again.

So yeah, when Arlette came along later... it wasn't love. Never was. But when she pulled that pregnancy test out and she lost that baby after that accident, it fucked with my head. Triggered everything I buried. I felt like I owed her, like if I walked away, I'd be betraying Megan all over again.

So, I stayed. Even when I didn't want her. Even when she started showing me who she really was. It wasn't about her. It was about my guilt.

And the fucked-up part? My family never knew and still don't. People who knew I dealt with Arlette thought it was because it was something to do. Nah. It was trauma. It was me trying to fix something I couldn't.

Niv is the first woman since Megan that made me even want to breathe love again. First one I wanted to risk being around my family. First one that got me thinking about futures I said I ain't want no more.

And that's the scariest shit of all. Because I already know what it feels like to lose it all in one night.

NETRAANTIONETTE

The drive to her place felt longer than it really was. Truth was, I could've closed my eyes and made the trip blindfolded. I gripped the wheel tighter than I needed to. It wasn't nerves. Nah, I don't get nervous. I'd been with many women. Dated 'em, spoiled 'em, fucked 'em, and left 'em. None of it ever shook me. But she did.

Hell, I still remembered the way she looked at me across that poker table. She didn't say a word, but told me everything I needed to know with a little sway of her hips. Like she spoke a language only I could hear.

I ran a hand over my beard.

That stunt Arlette pulled at the club was uncalled for. Niv had every right to be pissed. I knew she was probably looking at me sideways, like I couldn't keep my house in order. And I'd be damned if she lumped me in with them weak-ass niggas who thrive off chaos and let their women war for sport.

That wasn't me. And I wanted her to know that wasn't me.

I was driving through quiet streets, headlights bouncing off houses until I hit hers. You could tell she'd picked it for her people, not herself. That right there made me respect her more. She wasn't living for show. She was living for her siblings that she carried on her back every damn day.

I pulled up to the curb and just sat there for a second. That was the part where most men would back off, give her space, and wait for things to blow over.

But I wasn't about to let her slip.

Pretty, you up?

Her reply came fast:

> Nope. Just texting you telepathically in my sleep.

I smirked, shaking my head. Smart ass.

> Come outside.

Couple minutes later, the door cracked open. Then she stepped out in sweats and a bonnet, looking like temptation dipped in cocoa and comfort. Damn. She was the only woman I knew who could look like that and still make a nigga wanna risk it all.

She folded her arms. "What do you want? I got Netflix waiting on me."

I leaned on my truck, eyes running down her frame like I paid the mortgage on it. "How was your time last night?"

Her face softened for a second, then she sighed. "Really good. And even ended very well."

The way she said it... calm, real, no performance. I had to tell myself not to read or think too deep into her response. Otherwise, I would've been ready to put a bullet in somebody for being a part of her "ended very well."

I cleared my throat. "Look, Pretty... I like you."

She tilted her head, that bonnet catching the porch light. "Kendrix, a lot of men like me. That's nothing new. But I don't give them my attention."

She took a step closer. "So what do you have that sets you apart? Because I thought it was something... but when you had your bitch doing reckless shit, I realized you aren't worth my attention."

Then she turned back towards the door like I was already dismissed, but I followed her.

"Goodnight."

"Wait." My voice came out rougher than I planned. "Give me a minute to prove what makes me different."

She turned back slow, arms crossed, one eyebrow raised. "You got sixty seconds, Mr. Givelle."

I nodded, pulled my phone out, scrolled to one contact that I'd just un-blocked, and hit call.

"Hello?" Her voice popped up fast. Arlette.

Arlette picked up on the first ring, loud already.

"Arlette, listen to me and listen to be closely."

Niv tilted her head like she didn't expect that tone.

"Excuse me?!"

"You heard me. I just canceled every card you had tied to me. Every last one."

Her breath hitched through the speaker. "What the fuck you mean—"

"I mean I wired thirty thousand to your account. That's more than you're owed. More than enough for you to move on, maybe move away, and start a life without using my name as your crutch."

She started going off again, voice rising like static, but I didn't let her finish.

"You've been overdue, Arlette. I let guilt keep you around. But that shit ends tonight."

She screamed, "You can't just erase me! And move away? GivGold is mine! If I'm not the face, then who the fuck is?!"

I locked eyes with Niv. Her arms dropped, just a little, like she was caught between disbelief and wanting to cuss me out herself.

I leaned back, phone to my mouth.

"It's Niveah's club now."

Arlette lost it on the other end. She was cursing, screaming, and threatening. I didn't even blink.

"If you pull up there again," I said, still staring at Niv, "I'll have you arrested before your heels can step out and hit the ground. Don't test me."

Click.

The silence was thick, heavy. I slid the phone into my pocket and stepped up on her porch, close enough to smell the faint coconut oil in her hair.

Her eyes were wide, lips parted. Shock written all over her face.

I tilted my head, voice dropping.

"You said I don't set myself apart. That I'm just another nigga who 'likes' you. But tell me, how many men you know gone drop racks and cut off dead weight just to show you where you stand? GivGold? That's my shit. I built and created it. I just knew if I put my face on it, half the city's greed and jealousy would've tried to tear it down. So I made it look like it was woman-owned. Let Arlette play the role. Because no man disrespects a woman's business the way they'd come for mine."

She blinked, but her mouth stayed shut.

Good.

"You wanted proof that I'm not like the rest?" My chest brushed hers now. "There you go, Pretty."

Her laugh came out sharp, sarcastic.

"Oh, so now you think doing that just made you special? Kendrix, it doesn't"

I smirked. "Then why you shaking right now?"

She scoffed, but her arms folded tighter across her chest, defensive. Her body was telling me what her mouth wouldn't.

I leaned down, whispering just enough for her to feel my breath on her neck.

"I know you want me just as bad as I want you, Pretty."

For a second, she didn't move. Didn't breathe. Then she tilted her head back, met my eyes with that same fire she always had, and smirked.

"Cute speech," she said, dragging the words out slow, sarcastic as hell. "But you gon' have to try harder, Mr. Givelle."

She reached for her door, ready to end the little porch performance, but before her hand could pull the knob, my palm slapped flat against the glass screen door, pushing it shut.

"Kendrix—"

My chest pressed to her back, my breath hot against my ear. "Stop playing like you don't like it, Pretty," I whispered. "You already tore my guard down. Its time to drop yours."

Then my lips found her neck.

She gasped. "Kendrix, stop—"

But the way it slipped out, half-moan, half-plea, betrayed the hell out of her

"Mm. What happens if I don't stop?"

She turned, grabbed my face, and kissed me like she'd been starving for it. She walked us backward into the house, giving me that look like, *follow me if you bold*. And I was bold as fuck.

By the time we hit her bedroom, we weren't thinking about shit but each other. Her clothes were off, my shirt half unbuttoned. My hands roamed, learning every curve I'd been imagining since the first night I saw her.

I kissed down her chest, sucked her nipple into my mouth, flicking it with my tongue until she moaned loud enough to make my dick ache. My hand teased the other, fingers pinching, pulling.

The second her lips crashed against mine, I knew that night wasn't ending like all the others.

I'd tasted her before. Had her grinding on my face, moaning my name, damn near breaking me with nothing but her body and that slick ass mouth. But I hadn't been inside her yet. And the way she was looking at me, I knew her body was begging, even though her mouth would never admit it.

She pulled me toward her bed.

"You sure you ready for this?" she whispered, smirking like she was daring me.

I laughed, pressing her back into the mattress. "Pretty, I've been ready since the night you walked into that club."

I kissed down her neck, slow but hungry. She spread her legs without even thinking, and I groaned when I saw how wet she was.

"Damn," I said, touching her. "You ready for me, huh?"

She bit her lip, lifting her hips into my hand. "Nigga, shut up and fuck me."

I stroked myself, letting the tip tease her entrance.

"You gonna let me in, Pretty?" I whispered, rubbing circles on her clit with my thumb. "Or you still pretending you don't want me?"

She moaned, rolling her hips. I pushed in. Slow, deep, steady. Her gasp hit my chest, and I damn near lost it right then.

"Fuck," I growled, burying myself in her tight, wet pussy. "You feel like heaven, Pretty. Wrapped around me like you're mine already."

Her nails dug into my back as she whimpered, "Kendrix... oh my God..."

I pulled out almost all the way, then slammed back in, hard enough to make the headboard shake. She cried out, legs locking around me.

"Yeah, that's it," I groaned, driving deep. "Take this dick. Don't run from me."

She tried to smirk through her moans. "Who said I was running?"

"Oh, you not?" I flipped her onto her stomach, yanking her ass up. "We gone test that."

I slid back in from behind, gripping her hair to pull her head back. The sound she made went straight to my dick.

"Say my name," I demanded, thrusting slow and deep.

"Kendrix—fuck!"

"Louder."

"KENDRIX!"

I slapped her ass, watching it jiggle. "Good girl. Keep that same energy."

She pushed back against me, throwing it back so good I had to close my eyes and catch myself. She looked back with that wicked smile.

I flipped her back over, hooking her legs over my shoulders, going so deep her eyes rolled back.

"That's it," I groaned, sweat dripping. "Clench around me like that again and Ima lose my shit."

Her body tightened, and she gasped, "Then lose it. Give it to me, Kendrix."

I growled low, fucking her harder, faster, while kissing her like I couldn't get enough. She came first, legs shaking, pussy gripping me so tight, I had to bite her shoulder to keep from cussing too loud.

"That's my Pretty," I whispered against her skin. "Everything about you. So perfect."

I pulled out just enough to watch her take every inch again, her body trembling as I gave her everything I had. And when I finally came, it was with her screaming my name, holding me like she didn't ever wanna let go.

We collapsed together, sweaty, breathless, hearts racing in sync. I kissed her forehead, still inside her, refusing to move.

"Told you," I whispered with a smirk. "Don't play with me."

She rolled off me, bonnet hanging on for dear life. I kissed her shoulder and was about to crack another joke when she smirked and said, "Boy, please."

"Oh shit!! The kids."

She put her hand flat on my chest before I could even sit up, looking at me like I was slow.

"You really think I woulda let this happen with them here? Hell no."

I relaxed.

"My brother's at a tournament. One of the team moms is bringing him home. My sister is at a playdate with her classmate. Rita wanted to take her so I could get some rest."

I smirked, brushing her thigh. "You call this rest?"

She laughed, biting her lip. "I've done everything but rest."

We both cracked up but when it finally died down, she turned to me.

"Why me, Kendrix?"

I frowned. "What you mean?"

"Why make me the face of GivGold? Why let me meet your family so early? You barely know me."

I laid back, staring at her for a second, deciding how real I wanted to get. Then I reached over, cupping her cheek so she had to look at me.

"When I know, I know," I said simply. "It doesn't always make sense, but it doesn't have to. Not with you. The first time I saw you dance, I wasn't just looking at a body. I was watching how you moved a room without saying a damn word. That's rare. That's power."

Her lips parted, but she didn't say anything.

"Pretty, I've been around this game my whole life. Money. Businesses. Women who wanted the status more than me. But you... you walk in with nothing but confidence and presence, and the whole place shifts. You don't need a man to carry anything for you, but I want to. I want you on my team. Business-wise, romantically... both. We'd be unstoppable."

She raised an eyebrow, half skeptical, half amused. "Unstoppable, huh?"

"Hell yeah," I said, leaning closer, voice low. "You got the brains, the beauty, and the hustle. I got the resources, the reach, and the drive. Together? Ain't nobody touching us."

She smirked, rolling onto her back, staring at the ceiling. "You sound real sure of yourself."

"That's 'cause I am," I said, tracing circles on her thigh. "But it ain't just business for me. I like you, Pretty. Like, really like you. More than I've wanted to like anyone."

She stayed quiet, but I saw the way her chest rose, like I'd just knocked the wind out of her. Then she finally turned her head and looked at me, eyes glinting.

"You talk good, Kendrix. I might like you too."

That was all I needed. I kissed her and my hand slid up her thigh, ready to pull her back under me when her phone started on the ringing nightstand.

She pulled back. "Hold on. This might be Rita or Huxley."

I sat up, licking my lips, watching her grab it. The second she saw the screen, her whole expression shifted.

"Zejah..." she said out loud, already answering.

The second the line clicked, I could hear screaming, crying, and chaos bleeding through the speaker.

"Zejah, calm down," Niv said, voice sharp but trembling. "Baby, slow down. Tell me what's wrong."

But the girl was talking too fast, hiccupping through sobs. Whatever it was, it wasn't good.

"Breathe," Niv demanded. "What happened?"

More muffled crying, and I saw Niv's face pale.

"Fuck." She pressed her hand to her forehead. "I'm on my way!" she shouted into the phone before hanging up.

She jumped out the bed so fast. She was already yanking on her sweats, grabbing her bag.

"I don't know what's going on. I have to go see check on my mom."

I was already on my feet, pulling on my jeans. "Ima take you."

She opened her mouth to argue, but nothing came out. She just nodded, eyes glossy, and headed for the door.

I followed her out the house, heart pounding for reasons I couldn't even name. She jumped in the passenger seat, breathing hard. I slid behind the wheel, started the engine, and glanced at her.

Her leg was bouncing, hand gripping the phone like she was waiting for it to ring again. I reached over, resting a hand on her knee.

"Pretty," I said low, steady. "Whatever it is, we'll handle it."

She turned her head, eyes full of fear but still hard as steel. "You don't even know what you just signed up for."

I squeezed her knee once. "I don't have to. I signed up for you."

17

Niveah

The whole ride felt like my chest was caving in, but I kept my face turned toward the window, jaw locked so tight it hurt.

Zejah had called me a hundred times before. To tell me Ma was yelling. To tell me some random nigga was in the house. To let me know the lights had been cut off again. And every time, her voice was calm, steady. Like a soldier giving a report.

But that night... her voice cracked.

She wasn't calm. She wasn't steady. She was sobbing so hard I could barely make out words. I'd never heard her sound so... scared. And it bothered me in a way that I wasn't ready for.

I pressed my hands against my thigh, forcing the tremble out. *Don't break. Not here. Not now.*

It was the call I'd been preparing for my whole damn life.

The one that said my mama finally went too far.

That she overdosed.

That she pissed off the wrong person.

That she was gone for real this time.

I'd played that scenario in my head so many nights I lost count.

Imagined the funeral.

Imagined me explaining to Heidi why her mom's sickness got worse and she died.

Imagined holding Huxley while he tried to act strong but I knew it still ruined him.

My throat burned, tears slipping before I could stop them. I scrubbed at my face quick, talking to myself under my breath.

"Fuck. Get it the fuck together, Niv. You don't cry. You don't break."

My chest heaved, but I forced the tears back. "You always knew this could happen. You've been ready. Shake that shit off."

I bit down on my lip, trying to anchor myself.

But inside, I wanted to scream. To fall apart. To curl into a ball and admit that holding it all together for everyone else all the damn time was breaking me down piece by piece.

The silence in the truck felt louder than my own heartbeat. My fingers were digging crescents into my thigh when suddenly his hand covered mine.

They were warm like he knew I was seconds away from shattering.

I turned, and Kendrix was watching the road, one hand on the wheel, the other holding mine like he wasn't letting go, even if I tried to snatch away.

"If you ever need a moment to break," he said, not even looking at me, "you can. I'll be right here holding it all up until you're ready to stand again."

My eyes blurred again, no matter how much I tried to fight it.

Because he didn't say *be strong*.

Didn't say *you'll get through it.*

Didn't tell me to *man up* like life hadn't already forced me to.

He said I could break. And he'd hold me through it.

That one sentence hit harder than every tough-love lecture I'd ever given myself.

I turned away fast, biting my lip so the sob didn't crawl out my throat. But I couldn't hide the truth. Not from him. Not from myself.

And in that moment, I knew....

I was falling for Kendrix Givelle.

No matter how much I swore I wouldn't.

No matter how dangerous it was to want someone like him.

Because finally, the strong one wanted to be held.

When Kendrix turned onto the cracked street of Gun Hill, my heart started beating so hard I swore it shook the whole truck. I was bracing myself for chaos. Blue lights bouncing off brick walls, sirens screaming, neighbors hanging out on porches whispering but still loud as hell. An ambulance door swinging open, ready to take my mama's body out under a white sheet.

I was ready for it or at least I thought I was.

But when we pulled up...

Nothing.

No police cars. No flashing lights. No chaos.

Just the same neighborhood I grew up in. Same dudes on the corner posted up, same old heads sitting on milk crates watching the night crawl by, same smell of cheap weed and fried chicken in the air.

For a second, I thought maybe Zejah overreacted. Maybe I got myself worked up for nothing.

Then I saw her on the staircase that led up to my mama's apartment.

My mama sitting on the steps with Zejah curled up in her lap like a baby.

The sight damn near knocked the wind out of me.

My mama. The woman who lost every nurturing bone in her body. Holding that little girl like she didn't want her to feel alone.

Zejah's face was buried in her chest, her thin shoulders trembling so hard.

My stomach twisted because that's when I knew. It wasn't about my mama. It was about Zejah. Maybe she just lost someone or she just lost everything.

I froze on the sidewalk, staring. My relief came first and as fucked up as it sounded... it wasn't my mama. I hated myself for it, but it was the truth. I wasn't staring at a lifeless body. I wasn't about to hear "she's gone." And that guilt ate me alive before I even made it to the steps.

I took a breath so deep it hurt and whispered under it, "Pull it together, Niv. She needs you right now."

Me and Kendrix walked up the steps slow. The closer we got, the clearer I could see Zejah's face. She was all blotchy, eyes swollen, snot spilling out of her nose. She was curled against my mama, shaking like a leaf.

I leaned down in front of her, putting myself eye level.

"Zejah, baby... what's wrong?"

She looked at me like she was too scared to say, lips trembling, eyes darting everywhere but mine. My patience was thin, but I wasn't about to press her and make it worse. Before I could open my mouth again, my mama leaned her head down, whispering something soft in her ear.

And that right there stopped me dead. Because, who the fuck was this woman?

This wasn't the mama I grew up with. This woman had on clean clothes. Hair brushed back. Even a little gloss on her lips. Her arms wrapped around Zejah like she actually gave a damn. It felt foreign and like I was watching a stranger play dress-up as my mother.

Zejah sniffled hard and finally started talking through her tears.

"Me and my mama... we got into a fight."

My eyes scanned her knees. Skin torn up. Fists scraped like she'd been swinging with everything in her.

My stomach twisted.

"Why?" I asked softly, even though I was already pissed at the thought of her mamma throwing hands with her daughter.

Zejah's face crumpled all over again. Tears spilled faster. "Because... because she found out that I'm pregnant."

"Oh... shit," I said under my breath. I knew it wasn't some simple little girl mistake. That was life-changing. I swallowed hard, forcing myself to keep my face calm, even though my insides were screaming.

Before I could even get another word out, my mama stood up fast, brushing off her jeans.

"Well, I gotta go smoke. Y'all got this."

Typical.

She didn't even wait for me to respond before walking back up the stairs to her apartment like she didn't just drop me in the middle of a bomb going off. I rolled my eyes so hard I swear I saw the back of my brain. That was my mama all day. Dipping out when shit got too heavy. Apart of me wanted to snatch Zejah up and tell her to be grateful she even got those few minutes of comfort, because that was more than I ever got.

But watching her cry harder broke me a little. I sat down next to her and hugged her.

"Look, Zejah," I said firmly, "your life is about to change. For real. A baby isn't a small thing. And you have to stop being hot out here before you ruin yourself completely. You hear me?"

She just cried harder. Shoulders shaking, chest heaving.

I sighed, rubbing my temples. "I'm not trying to be mean, baby. But this.... This is family business. I'll help you where I can, but this don't really have anything to do with me."

The look she gave me could've cut through steel. She whipped her head toward me, eyes blazing through all those tears.

"It has everything to do with you," she snapped, her voice cracking but loud enough to slice through the air.

My brow arched. "What the hell you mean?"

Zejah sat up straighter, wiping her face with the back of her hand. Her lip trembled.

"Because I'm pregnant with your niece or nephew."

The air left my lungs.

"...What?" My voice barely came out.

Her eyes locked on mine, watery but steady.

"It's Huxley's baby."

18

Niveah

My whole body went cold.

Huxley???

The name hit me harder than a slap. My little brother. My responsibility. My baby that I raised like he was mine when our mama couldn't get her shit together. I was staring at the girl carrying his child, which meant I wasn't just raising Hux and Heidi anymore. Now I had to make sure his baby... and Zejah... didn't crumble under the same shit I'd spent my whole life trying to escape.

I felt my stomach twist, rage and heartbreak doing somersaults inside me.

Responsible for two kids and a newborn. How the fuck did I get here?

No. Four. Because like it or not, Zejah was just a kid herself. And the way she was looking at me... scared and reaching for something stable.. told me I couldn't just leave her to figure her life out alone.

Then, like a puzzle slamming into place, everything about Hux made sense.

The late-night walks. The random mood swings. The way he'd been quiet lately, looking like he was carrying a mountain on his back but too damn stubborn to ask for help. The smart-mouthed responses followed by quick apologies. I thought it was just ball practice, grades, being a teenager. But nah... he'd been holding this. Holding her. Holding a secret so heavy, and all the while I was clueless.

God, why him? He's still a baby himself...

Zejah's voice broke through my storm.

"I been telling him to tell you," she cried, her words stumbling over hic-cupped breaths. "I told him we needed to figure out a plan before my mama found out, before things got this bad. But he kept saying... he kept saying he was gonna handle it."

I swallowed hard. Handle it? Hux thought he could handle *this*? A baby? At his age?

"Lord have mercy," I whispered, more to myself than to her.

I just sat there and listened. That's all I could do. I sat there on that busted-up stairwell with the sound of babies crying in the distance, dice shaking in some old head's cup, and Zejah pouring her whole little heart.

"I tried to call Hux before I called you," she said, sniffling. "But he didn't answer. Hasn't called me back, either."

My chest tightened. *Of course, he didn't answer. His ass was at that tourna-ment.*

"Yeah," I managed, keeping my voice steady even though my insides weren't. "He's at a tournament. That's why."

She nodded, wiping her face, but the words kept spilling.

"My little sister... she saw Hux give me some money yesterday for lunch."

That made my stomach flip. Yesterday? In Gun Hill? How the hell did Hux even get there and back without me knowing? My mind started racing, but I bit my tongue. It wasn't the time for those type of questions.

Zejah's voice dropped lower. "Then... my mom went in my drawer. She thought it was where I kept my stash."

I felt my jaw clench.

"She found the ultrasound picture." Zejah's face crumbled. "She started cursing me out, calling me stupid. Saying I was just throwing my life away. She knew I was talking to Hux because she came home early one day from the casino and saw him here. She told me... she told me it was fine, as long as I made sure he gave me money so I could get the things I needed."

That's when the rage in me snapped. My fists curled so tight my nails dug into my palms.

Zejah's tears fell harder. "And then she said..." Her lips trembled. "She said I was stupid for getting pregnant by him because my baby would just be a drug addict like its grandmother. Said it wouldn't be long before Hux was the same way. That he's just as fucked up as his mom."

The words sliced me open.

"She said..." Zejah's voice broke. "She said my baby would be a hoe because that's what you are, Niv. She said that's how you got out the hood."

I swear to God I felt my blood boil. *Bitch, you got some nerve...?*

Zejah's shoulders shook as she sobbed. "I snapped, Niv. I cursed her out. I couldn't take it no more. And then she—" Her voice cracked as she lifted her sleeve to show the bruises blooming on her arms. "She started swinging on me. My mom fought me, knowing I'm pregnant. She said anytime I feel like walking back in her house, I better be ready to fight since I wanna be grown."

She crumbled then, full-on breaking down in front of me, her words barely a whisper:

"I didn't have anyone else to call."

I leaned in, wiped a tear from her cheek with my thumb, and said softly, "It's okay. I'm gonna handle everything."

Then I looked up. Kendrix was already watching me, eyes locked on mine like he knew exactly what "handle" meant.

"Baby," he said carefully, like he was trying to talk me off a ledge. "Let's talk about this for a minute—"

"No." I cut him off before he could even finish. My mind was already made up, and nothing in the world could change it. I turned back to Zejah.

"Zejah, you know Kendrix, right?"

She sniffled, nodded. "Yes."

"Good." I sat up straighter. "Do you have a few duffle bags or anything in your room?"

"Yes," she whispered.

I nodded once, decisive. "Okay. Kendrix is gonna go with you in there and pack your things. Only grab what you want, what's valuable. Don't try to bring any extra shit. If you need more clothes, I'll make sure you got that and more."

Her eyes darted between us, wide, like she wasn't sure if I was dead serious. I tilted her chin up so she had no choice but to look me in my eyes.

"Zejah," I said, my voice low and dangerous. "Are you sure you want me to handle this?"

Her lips trembled, but she nodded. "Yes."

I searched her face for hesitation, for any sign she wasn't ready. There wasn't one. Just a girl who'd had enough.

"Good." I leaned closer. "But I'm warning you. When I go in there, I'm not taking it easy on her. Not after the shit she said. Not after she disrespected my whole family and laid hands on you. Which, in my book, means she put her hands on my family since you're carrying him or her. That's blood now. So don't you dare try to tell me to stop or feel sorry for her. Because I won't stop. Not until I'm good and ready."

For a second, I thought she might cry harder. But then a shaky little laugh slipped out instead. She wiped her face, grinning through the tears.

"I know," she said, breathless. "And I'm ready, Niv. It's been long overdue."

I stood slow. My blood boiling but my body calm. I looked up at Kendrix, and he was still watching me. I straightened my shoulders and squared my stance with a steady calm that sent chills through my own damn spine—

"Ok. Let's go."

NETRAANTIONETTE

Zejah pushed the door open first, and the second her mama laid eyes on her, the bullshit started.

"Oh, you back? So you ready to throw hands again?" Her mama leaned back in her chair, legs crossed like she was daring her own daughter to swing first. Then her eyes slid past Zejah and landed on Kendrix, and her mouth curved into this nasty little grin.

"Ohhh," she purred. "So you brought some fine man with you. Mmm. And here I thought for sure little Hux, crackhead Jr., was the daddy."

I stepped through the doorway right then. Her eyes went wide like she just saw the Grim Reaper in heels.

"Zejah," I said calmly, not taking my eyes off her mama. "Go get your things."

She hesitated.

"Now."

She nodded quick and disappeared down the hall with Kendrix trailing behind her, leaving me and that woman face-to-face.

I crossed my arms, cocked my head. "So. What's that shit you been saying?"

She smirked, lighting a cigarette like this was casual. "Yeah, I said it. I don't know why she wanna go get pregnant like I already ain't got enough damn kids for her to take care of. If she wanna do something, she need to go downtown, find her a job, pay some of these bills."

I let out a sharp laugh. Not because it was funny, but because it kept me from putting my foot through her chest right then and there.

"You got a lotta nerve," I said, voice calm. "Maybe instead of running your mouth about me and my family, you should've been a better mama so your daughter isn't out here doing everything you should be doing for your kids."

She blew smoke in my direction, squinting like she was unimpressed. "Oh, here you go. Miss Savior Complex. Miss Perfect. Girl, please. You out here swinging around poles, talking bout being better. Don't get too high on your little pedestal."

I smiled slow. "Funny. I don't need a pedestal. I stand ten toes on the same ground as you. The difference is, I don't need a blunt or a bottle to keep me standing."

That one hit. I saw it in the way her jaw tightened.

"Whatever," she muttered. "You don't know what it's like. You don't know the pressure, the pain—"

"Oh, I know," I cut her off, stepping closer. "I know because I lived through your mess. I raised my siblings like Zejah has been doing. I carried weight mothers like you cared less to hold. Don't you ever think I don't know what it's like."

Her eyes narrowed, that little smirk creeping back. "And look at you now. Still mad. Still bitter. You think you better than me because you found a nigga to bankroll you?"

"Everything I have," I said, stepping closer, "I got on my own. Don't get it twisted. I got a few paid niggas on my roster, but I never had to lay on my back to get what I want or need. Unlike you—" I dragged my eyes up and down her like she wasn't even worth a second glance, "—I'm self-made. I depend on no one. What a nigga adds is a luxury."

She tilted her head, sucked her teeth, then laughed like she had won. "Self-made, huh? That's what you call it? Baby, you still a hoe. Just like my daughter. Pregnant by a lil crackhead in training. Pssh. Take her. She can help you screw a few men while you at it."

Something in me snapped clean in half.

"I realllllllly try to be nice, but Bitch, you got me so fucked up."

Before she could breathe another word, my fist connected with her jaw. The sound echoed off those thin walls, her cigarette flying across the floor.

"Ohhh bitch, you thought this was a game?" I said, grabbing her by her shirt before she could fall.

I slammed her against the wall so hard the whole damn wall of picture frames slid crooked.

"You think I'm one of your little boyfriends you can talk crazy to?" *BAM!* I popped her in the mouth again.

She tried to swing back with a weak-ass hit, and I laughed in her face while dodging it. "That's all you got? Girl, my little sister slap harder than that when she mad she can't get ice cream."

Then I hit her again right in the gut. She folded like fresh laundry.

"You been running your mouth for YEARS," I said, shaking her by her collar like a ragdoll. "Talking down on your own kids like you wasn't the first failure they ever met."

"Stop—" she gasped, holding her stomach.

"Nah, bitch. Don't say stop now." I kneed her in the thigh. "You wasn't saying stop when you had Zejah cleaning this dusty-ass apartment and taking care of kids while you was at the casino spreading your legs for free drinks."

She tried crawling toward the couch, but I yanked her back by her ankle. "Get your ass back here! You gon' take this ass whooping standing like a woman."

"Niv, please—" she started crying, mascara streaking down her face like a Lifetime movie extra.

"Please what?" I mocked, hitting her with another quick jab to the ribs. "Please stop telling the truth?"

She covered her face, whining, "I can't take no more!"

I leaned down, my voice low and mean in her ear. "Aww. Poor baby! Well, you gone take it because you earned it."

Then I popped her again in the same spot.

Her bad wig had slid halfway off, her shirt was twisted around like a damn pretzel, and she was begging.

"Okay! Okay! I'm sorry! Please, Niv, stop!" she cried, crawling back against the wall.

I stood over her, chest rising, knuckles stinging, and smirked. "See how easy that was? Coulda just kept my family's name out your mouth and saved yourself this ass whooping."

I wiped my fist on her shirt and pointed down at her. "Say one more thing about Hux or that baby, and I'll beat yo ass every Tuesday like clockwork."

She nodded quick, eyes wide, lip bleeding.

Behind me, I heard Kendrix mutter, low and proud, "God damn..." like he just witnessed history.

I stood tall, adjusting my bra strap like nothing happened. Then looked down at her again and said, "Matter fact, thank me. Because this ass whooping is the first real love you've had in years."

I looked down at her and for the first time in years, she was shut the fuck up.

I bent down, grabbed her chin so she had no choice but to look at me, and said slow and clear, "Zejah is moving in with me."

Her eyes widened. "W-what?"

"You heard me. And don't even *think* about running your mouth or I'll call DHS right now and have your Section 8, food stamps, and every little child support dollar snatched up so quick you won't even have bus fare to take your dirty ass to the damn clinic."

She tried to jerk her face back, but I gripped tighter.

"And don't test me. I'll do it tonight. The only reason I won't is because I refuse to make those other kids pay for the mess you created. But you got 60 days." I let her go and stood tall.

"Sixty. Days. To get your shit together. Or I will personally come back in here and beat your ass every single day until you do."

Her lip trembled. She opened her mouth, and I snapped, "Say something. I dare you."

She shut it. Just like I knew she would.

I turned, pointing toward the door where Kendrix was watching.

"And let's get one thing straight," I added, looking back down at her. "Zejah is not your concern anymore. She's mine. If she decides one day she wants to rebuild a relationship with you, I won't stand in the way. But until then, fix yourself up for the rest of your kids."

Her tears fell silent, and for once, she didn't have shit slick to say.

I smirked and looked at Kendrix. "I'm done, handsome."

He looked at me like I'd just declared war and won. "Let's go, baby."

I glanced at her mom one last time. "Sixty days, ma. After that? Pray Jesus get to you before I do."

NETRA ANTIONETTE

We pulled up in front of my house. I felt like my body was running off pure adrenaline and my brain hadn't caught up yet. Kendrix parked, cut the engine, and the sound of the world finally came back.

I turned in the seat, looking at Zejah, who was staring out the window like she'd aged five years in one night.

"How old is your sister?" I asked, my voice low, steady.

She blinked, then looked at me. "Yanna? She's twelve."

"Does she got a phone?"

Zejah nodded. "Yeah. I've been texting her."

I leaned back against the headrest, letting out a slow breath. "Good. Tell her to keep an eye on my mamma... the way you used to. And I'll make sure she stays with money and whatever else she needs."

Her lips parted, surprise flashing in her eyes before tears started forming again. She pulled her phone out quick, thumbs flying. "Thank you."

"You're welcome. Can you go wait on the porch for me?" I asked her. "Kendrix and I will bring your bags."

She sniffled, grabbed her purse, and slid out the truck.

As soon as the door shut behind her, I finally let my chest collapse. Leaned back in the seat, closed my eyes, ran my hands down my face and whispered, "What in the entire fuck?"

Kendrix leaned back in the driver's seat, watching me with that same calm look he'd had since all hell broke loose earlier. Not once did he flinch. I stared out the windshield at Zejah sitting on my porch, kicking at the concrete with the toe of her shoe like a kid that didn't know whether to cry again or breathe easy.

I finally let the words slip out. "I don't even know if I handled that right."

Kendrix laughed low, shaking his head. "Pretty... you didn't just handle it, you body-slammed it, drop-kicked it, then put it in a chokehold until it tapped out."

I shot him a side-eye, trying not to laugh. "You so damn stupid."

He grinned. "Nah, for real. I don't think I ever seen nobody mama get her ass beat and get a TED Talk at the same time. You the first."

I couldn't help it, so I laughed.

I shook my head. "You always know what to say, don't you?"

He smirked. "Nah. Half the time I just be winging it and praying I don't sound like a dumbass."

That made me laugh again.

I sighed, letting his hand go, but not before squeezing it. "You know... I would let you meet the kids."

His whole body stilled, like I'd just handed him a key to something he didn't expect yet.

"Yeah?"

"Yeah," I nodded. "But... I got some important things to talk about with my brother first."

"I can only imagine," he said softly. Then he leaned in, brushing a kiss against my lips.

"When you're done with him," he added, "Call me."

"I will."

I kissed him once more, a little longer, before pushing the door open.

"Goodnight, Kendrix."

"Goodnight, Pretty."

I stepped up beside Zejah on the porch. She looked nervous, twisting her phone in her hands.

"You talked to Hux yet?" I asked.

She shook her head quick. "No... but he's been calling and texting me, though."

"Good," I said, unlocking the door. "Because he's gone be surprised the same way I was."

Her throat bobbed like she wanted to say something else, but instead, she just nodded. Together, we walked into the house.

I headed straight for Hux's room. I didn't even bother knocking. I pushed the door open, and he was slouched on the edge of his bed with his phone in his hand.

The second he saw me, his eyes darted away. Guilt written all over him.

I crossed my arms. "What's going on, Hux?"

"Nothing," he said, too quick.

"Boy, don't play with me." I stepped further in, shutting the door behind me. "You been walking around here stressed, snapping at folks, acting like the whole world got you bent. I ain't stupid."

He sighed heavy, rubbing the back of his neck. "It's just... school. Basketball. You know how it is."

I tilted my head, studying him. "Mm. That's cute. But it must be Zejah, huh?"

The way his head snapped toward me told me everything I needed to know. His eyes went wide, mouth falling open like he forgot how to form words.

"How... how you know about that?" he whispered, voice cracking.

Before I could even answer, the door creaked behind me. I turned, and Zejah came in. Eyes red, cheeks wet, tears spilling all over again.

"Hux..." she choked out, voice trembling.

He stood up so fast the bed squeaked, his face went pale as he looked between me and her. I just crossed my arms tighter, locking eyes with him.

"Looks like it's time for everyone to stop lying."

Hux didn't say a word. He just moved. Fast.

Like his legs didn't even ask permission from his brain. Like something in him broke loose when he saw her.

He rushed over and pulled Zejah into his arms with a force that made my throat tighten. She collapsed against his chest like her whole body had been waiting for that one second of safety.

And it hit me, just how deep it really was. Hux doesn't like physical touch. Never has. He's been that way since he was little. I used to have to bribe him for hugs with cookies and money to let me twist his hair. So to see him hold her like that?

It wasn't just some messy high school fling that accidentally turned into a baby.

My little brother loved that girl.

He pulled back just enough to look at her face, scanning every scratch, every tear.

"I read your message," he said, voice trembling. "You fought your mama? For real?"

Zejah nodded, biting her bottom lip like she was still scared of what he'd think.

He leaned down, kissed her forehead softly, and asked, "You okay?"

It was quiet and so gentle that I barely heard it.

She just nodded again, holding him tighter.

I stood there just watching. Processing. Feeling every version of myself collide.

I cleared my throat, and they both jumped slightly. Like they forgot I was there.

"Okay," I said. "Let's get something real clear right now."

They both turned toward me like two kids waiting to find out if they were about to be grounded or spared. Still clinging to each other.

"I'm not gone yell," I started. "I'm not gonna fuss. What's done is done. Y'all grown enough to make a baby, so now y'all gone have to grow up faster than you thought."

They looked down at the floor.

"But," I added, my tone softening, "you're not doing it alone. I got y'all. However you need me. Emotionally. Financially. Whatever."

I watched their shoulders drop in relief.

"But," I raised a brow. "There are rules."

Zejah nodded first. Then Hux.

I folded my arms. "You live in my house. You follow my rules. There will be no sneaking around, no late-night linkups, and no smart-ass mouths. You wanna be grown? Cool. But you gone respect my roof."

"Understood," they said in unison, like it was a damn drill sergeant talking.

"Alright," I said, standing up straighter. "First things first, y'all are not sharing a damn room. Zejah you can have the room down the hall."

Zejah blinked. "Okay."

"But that's Mama room," he said. "You said that room—"

"I said," I cut him off, pointing, "your mama had that room for years. YEARS, Huxley! When's the last time she stayed in it for longer than a cigarette break and a Xanax nap?"

He looked down and mumbled, "Never."

"Exactly. That room belongs to whoever actually sleeps in it now," I said. Then I turned to Zejah. "It's yours. Hux is staying in his own room."

Zejah nodded respectfully, but Hux looked like he wanted to protest again.

"Yes, the damage is done. Yes, y'all made a baby. But the only people who will be knowingly fucking under this roof..." I smiled sweetly and pointed at my chest, "... is me. Got it?"

Their faces were PRICELESS.

"You wanna cuddle? Chill? Hold hands and watch Netflix? Great," I continued. "Living room only. If I walk past that hallway and your grown-ass is in her room, that door better be wide open like it's expecting the Lord to walk through."

I tilted my head and added with a smile, "And if I catch that door closed? I will politely invade your privacy, go full FBI, and install cameras in both rooms. Don't play with me."

They both nodded like soldiers who just got drafted.

"Now," I said, clapping my hands together like an HR director at orientation, "school is still in session. Neither one of y'all are dropping out or slacking off. Hux, you already know what time it is."

He nodded.

"Zejah, I'm pulling you out of that damn public school. You're coming to the magnet academy with Hux and Heidi."

Her mouth fell open. "Wait... you serious?"

"Very. You're too damn smart to be trapped in that school with no A/C and a principal that smell like depression and backwoods. I'm getting your transcripts sent this week."

She blinked like she was about to cry again, but in a good way.

"Also," I continued, walking toward the kitchen like I didn't just drop another bomb, "I'm calling Talynn Baldwin. She's a top notch OB/GYN."

Zejah looked stunned. "But that probably costs—"

"It costs what I'm willing to pay," I cut her off again. "You gone carry this baby like royalty, not like a burden. That child will have a mother that's cared for, not dismissed."

Hux sat down like the whole future just hit him in the chest. I saw his head drop into his hands and I just... let it sit there.

Because it is real. This is what life does when it starts life'ing too damn fast.

"I'll be tough on y'all," I said, softening my tone. "But I'll always be here. You hear me?"

They both nodded.

I crossed my arms and looked dead at both of them, making sure every word stuck.

"And lastly, let me break this down real simple before y'all start thinking life is about to stay cute. Zejah, unnecessary mood swings? Yeah, I'm not having it. You cry, you laugh, you throw an attitude. Whatever you do, that baby's gonna feel it and reflect it."

She sniffled, trying not to smile, and I pointed at Hux.

"And you. Don't think you gone get off easy. This ain't no one-sided parenthood. You wanted to shoot the club up, congratulations, you now own the whole building."

Zejah choked on a laugh.

"Y'all are both going to parenting classes. Matter fact, I'll sit in the back with snacks just to make sure y'all pay attention. And Rita? She cooks her ass off, so on some days, Zejah, I want you in that kitchen watching her. You ain't babysitting anymore, baby girl. This is your child. Step into it."

I turned back to Hux, smirking.

"And on the days Zejah gets her girl time, guess who's on daddy duty? Spoiler alert, it's you. Full responsibility. Don't even call me unless the house is on fire."

They both stared at me like I had cursed them with a lifetime sentence.

"Oh, and one more thing."

"What?" they said together.

"You both are about to start watching Heidi, too. Rita deserves a damn break, and I can't wait to see the looks on y'all's faces the first time she says she wants McDonald's but really means Chick-fil-A. Good luck."

I clapped my hands together with a fake-ass cheerful smile.

"Welcome to parenthood. I hope this teaches you both the importance of condoms next time."

19

Kendrix

It had been two weeks since I told Arlette her run was over, and since Niv became the new face of GivGold.

And in just fourteen days, the club was louder than it had ever been before the doors even opened.

Her face was on every damn flyer, billboard, and IG story. Phones going crazy, men trying to book tables weeks out like they knew her personally. It was scheduled to be our first big Friday with her front and center, and I already knew it was gonna be a movie. People were lined up outside at six, knowing we didn't open the doors until nine.

All because of her.

I leaned back in the office chair with the contracts and financial reports spread out on the desk. Shit didn't just look good. It looked different. Cleaner. Smarter. Like she'd been born to run this shit. She'd already pulled in a few sponsors from her own connections, tightened up bottle service so nobody could skim off the top, and made sure our dancers felt more like assets than replaceable bodies.

I'd been in the game a long time, but I'd never seen someone walk in and move like they'd been built for this. And the craziest part was that she'd done all of it without even needing me to hold her hand.

Damn, Pretty. You proving me right every step of the way.

My phone buzzed on the desk. My sibling group chat was going crazy

> **Kross:** Y'all better get down here early. Club gone be shoulder to shoulder tonight. Tell Niv I said don't

have these niggas out here catching heart attacks over her.

I smirked and shook my head. They already knew.

What made me laugh was thinking back to when Niv and Rivah finally met. Two smart-mouthed women with the same sharp humor and the kind of confidence you can't buy. They clicked so fast, it was like they'd been sisters their whole lives. Watching them together, I knew me and Kross were in for a ride. A dangerous, beautiful, loud-ass ride.

I ran my hand over my beard, staring at the flyer on my desk like I hadn't seen it a hundred times.

Her brown skin glowing under the lights, and that smile that said she knew exactly how much power she had.

What fucked me up the most was how easy it felt to let her lead. Normally, I didn't trust anybody with my business. But with her, I wasn't worried. I just sat back and let her make moves because I knew she'd make the right ones.

Damn, Pretty. What the hell you doing to me?

8:45 p.m. on the dot.

I told myself I wasn't watching the clock, but that was a damn lie. The minute she walked in, every head in the club turned.

She wore all black everything. Her hair was pinned up, edges laid so clean it looked like art, with a diamond chain that caught the light every time she moved.

Men stared. Women whispered. Even the staff stopped moving just to catch a glimpse. I sat my ass back in the chair like I wasn't ready to stand up and meet her halfway.

"Damn," I said under my breath. "Pretty done turned this bitch into her runway."

She walked up slowly into the office, taking her time, making me sweat on purpose.

"Club looks good," she said, eyes scanning the floor like she wasn't the reason it looked like heaven on earth.

"Correction," I said, leaning forward in my chair. "You look good. Club just catching up."

She rolled her eyes but couldn't hide the blush in her cheeks.

"Boy, please," she said. "Save that slick shit for the girls you're lying to on IG."

"Funny. You're the only one I'm thinking about lying to right now."

She leaned on the desk, close enough for me to smell her perfume. "What would you even lie about?"

"That I haven't been waiting on you all damn night," I said.

Her smile cracked, quick, before she straightened back up. "You better hope this night go smooth. I done worked too hard for your little jealous hoe to mess up anything."

I smirked. "Don't even put her in the same sentence as you. She doesn't have that power."

"Mm-hm," she hummed, then smirked. "That's what you better say."

NETRA ANTIONETTE

I knew Niv was gonna show out, but what she put into play was on some other shit.

The lights dipped low, whole room painted in red like lust itself had rented the spot for the night. First beat of *Do Not Disturb* dropped, and the place got so damn quiet you could hear a dollar bill unfold.

Two of Niv's girls came out—ones she pulled from her old spot. I remember her saying they were solid, but "solid" ain't even scratch the surface. They moved like they ain't have bones, just silk and sin holding them together.

One of them hooked an ankle on the pole, leaning back so her hair kissed the floor, while the other slid down in a wave so slow it had half the room forgetting to breathe. I leaned back in my chair, cigar lit, watching all the niggas around me try not to choke on their own thirst.

See, they expected twerk anthems. Fast money, fast ass, same shit every other club in Antionette fed them. But Niv flipped the script. She set a vibe. The kind that made men think about touching, not just fucking. The kind that had women straightening their spines, wondering if their men would pay attention to them like that after they left.

I looked around the room, smirk tugging at my mouth. Niggas gripping glasses like lifelines. Women biting lips. Couples leaning close, whispering in each other's ears while their hands slid under tables.

I caught one dude in the corner whisper, "Goddamn," and his girl elbowed him without ever looking away from the stage.

That's when I knew, Niv didn't just put on a show. She built a damn spell.

And I'll admit, sitting there, watching her vision come alive, I felt something I don't let myself feel too often: pride. Not the kind you get from money or power. I have that already. It was different. I was watching somebody create an entire world out of their mind and body and making everybody else beg for access.

By the time Chris Brown's verse hit, the whole room was leaning forward like they'd been hypnotized. Applause shook the walls when the lights cut.

And all I could think was...

Damn. My Pretty just turned GivGold into the most dangerous spot in Antionette.

Niv walked out on the stage and the crowd went stupid. Phones up, hands clapping, voices shouting her name like they'd been waiting all night just to see her. She didn't even flinch. Just raised the mic slow, lips curling into that smile that said she was about to own every soul in the room.

"First off," she started, voice smooth, "thank y'all for coming out tonight. GivGold isn't just a club—it's a true experience."

Cheers exploded. I puffed on my cigar, eyes locked on her.

"But let me make one thing clear," she went on, slicing through the noise like a blade. "Pole dancing, ballet, hip hop, whatever the style .. isn't just ass and glitter. It's art. It's storytelling. It's a body speaking without words."

The crowd screamed. She smirked, looking dead in the camera some girl had pointed at her like she was daring the whole world to say different.

"This stage isn't about shame. It's about power. About body positivity. About women deciding when, where, and how we get seen. So if you came looking for just a show, you're gonna leave knowing you've been touched by art."

My chest tightened, watching her own the hell out of every syllable. Niggas in the front row looked like they wanted to propose. Women were nodding hard enough to break their necks.

She lowered the mic, leaned on one hip, and dropped her last line with a smirk that nearly had me ready to climb up there and snatch her off the stage.

"And don't get too comfortable. I'll be back."

The whole room went wild because everybody knew exactly what that meant. She wasn't just the face of GivGold. She was the soul. And she was about to remind every single one of them why they called her MissCommunication.

I leaned back in the VIP watching chaos unfold around me. My brothers and their women were always like watching reality tv.

Kross is so in damn love with Rivah, and I swear she been running her mouth since she sat down. Funny as hell, though. Every two minutes, she was saying some off-the-wall shit that had the whole table crying laughing. My moms always said a woman with a quick tongue was dangerous. Rivah was living proof.

Across from me, was Kairo and his wife Khloe. She had that "fuck it" glow, throwing back drinks like water, finally letting loose like stress was all her life consisted of. The DJ dropped a track she liked and she damn near broke her neck bopping to it. Meanwhile, her loud-ass husband, Kairo, was damn near breaking the sound system yelling over the music.

"Aye, Kordai," Kairo hollered, pointing across the floor at a group of women, "that one right there thick as hell. Go pull her."

Kordai side-eyed him so hard, I almost choked on my drink. "Nigga, I might be fresh out. Not desperate."

We all cracked up, and Kairo sat back upset that he couldn't play matchmaker.

Pretty slid past the section wearing an all black, long-sleeve leotard, pink tutu sitting high enough for a front-row view of chocolate perfection. Black heels clicking like music all on their own.

My dick twitched. My cigar damn near went out.

And, of course, Rivah noticed. Loud as hell.

"Lawd have mercy," she drawled, leaning forward for a better view. "That ass need its own zip code."

Khloe wasn't no better, fanning herself with her hand like she was in church. "Mm-mm. She too damn sexy. Kendrix, that ass sit up better than two bunk beds."

Kairo choked on his drink, shaking his head. "See, y'all doing too much."

"Nah," Rivah grinned, sipping her drink slow. "We just letting him know she fine enough to have his credit score jump fifty points just for touching that ass."

The whole table burst out laughing while I sat there trying to play it cool, smoke curling from my cigar like I wasn't two seconds from excusing myself to drag her ass in the office and handle my damn business.

Then, out of nowhere, I saw a tall, dark suit that screamed "old money," surrounded by security like he owned the block. Nigga walked in like the air belonged to him. Accent heavy as hell when he spoke to the man on his left, like he was giving orders instead of conversation.

I sat back, puffing on my cigar, watching the scene unfold.

The host walked up to him all smiles. "Good evening, sir. Do you have a reservation?"

"Yes," he said. "Private room. Code is 2442."

She glanced down at her tablet, eyes widening just a little before she plastered on her professional face again. "Yes, sir. Right this way."

Cool. Rich niggas in town. Happens all the time.

Until he opened his mouth again.

"And can I get MissCommunication?"

My entire chest went still.

MissCommunication.

I kept it cool. Real cool. Sat back like my ass wasn't ready to leap across this whole damn section.

The host hesitated. "Oh... um, I'm sorry, sir. She's not doing private dances tonight."

He leaned down just a little, smiling. "Tell Niveah that Sincere is here for her."

The host damn near stuttered, eyes flashing shock before she nodded. "O-okay, sir. One moment."

Sincere?

Who the fuck is Sincere?

And more importantly, why the fuck did he know her real name like that?

I kept my face cool while my stomach turned. Across the table, Rivah leaned forward with wide eyes. "Oop. Not the government name."

The host came back with Niv, and the way she lit up when she saw him pissed me the fuck off. She walked straight up to him, no hesitation, hugged him tight like they had history. Not the church hug. Not the polite two-pat hug. Nah, this one had comfort in it. Familiarity. She whispered something in his ear, he smiled, kissed her cheek, and followed the host out like it was routine.

I sat back in my seat with my face calm. Couldn't let my brothers see me tripping.

She came gliding over to our table like she hadn't just had me ready to set the whole building on fire.

"Y'all good over here?" she asked, smiling.

"Yeah, girl, but you fine as hell," Rivah cut in, drunk giggles spilling out of her like she didn't know she was pouring gasoline on the wrong flame.

"Fine ain't even the word," Khloe added, already swaying to the music, glass in hand.

I felt my molars grinding.

Niv laughed, leaned down, and rubbed my beard.

"What's wrong? Your posture's off."

I smirked, leaning back, acting like my blood wasn't boiling. "Is that something I need to worry about?"

She tilted her head, that slick ass smile still on her lips. "You should always worry..."

She paused, letting that shit hang before adding,

"...but nah. He's just an old friend."

An old friend.

I don't like old friends. Especially ones that walk in dropping her real name like they own the rights to it.

I kept my face straight, but inside, I was ready to drag her "old friend" out that private room.

20

Niveah

I felt Kendrix's eyes burning holes in my back as I walked away, but I didn't speed up or slow down. I just let my hips talk for me.

I knew Kendrix was pissed. That little rub on his beard told me all I needed. But here's the thing ...

I didn't give a fuck.

Yeah, I liked him. I love the way he touched me, the way he looked at me like I was a whole universe he was just discovering. But let's be clear, he wasn't my man officially.

And since he wasn't my man, I didn't owe him a damn explanation.

Not about where I was going. Not about who Sincere was. Not about a damn thing.

Men kill me. They want you tied down like a dog on a leash while they run the streets like strays. They give you crumbs and expect loyalty.

Nah. Fuck that.

All I ever asked Kendrix for was simple:

Keep your shit tight. Keep the drama far away from my money. Don't let your mess spill into my life. I never told him it was mandatory to give up his line-up because, technically, I was never given the title of his girlfriend.

That's the problem with men. They want you to hand over your freedom while they give you nothing but vibes and excuses. They want you to prove you're different while they still out here doing the same shit.

I'd rather starve than settle for crumbs.

So yeah, I knew he was mad as hell, probably plotting a hundred ways to stake his claim. But until he figured out how to give me what I needed—titles, honesty, security, peace—his little mean mug didn't mean shit.

I don't chase. I collect.

The private lounge door closed behind me with a soft click, and just like that, the noise from the floor dulled to a low hum. The lights were dim, candles flickering on the side tables.

Sincere sat with the same smooth skin and cocky-ass grin. He hadn't aged a day since I met him at eighteen. If anything, he looked richer. Broader. Like time had only sharpened him up.

"Well, look at you," He said. "Still know how to stop a room dead, eh?"

I smirked, sliding into the seat across from him. "And you still know how to make an entrance, huh? Had security looking like you're the Prime Minister."

He laughed, teeth flashing. "Gyal, when you walk with money, people walk behind you."

"Mm. I see you haven't changed."

"Neither have you." His eyes trailed over me slow, taking his time. Not thirsty, just... appreciating. Like I was fine art and he'd bought the whole gallery. "Though I like the new shine. You finally letting the world see what I always told you. You're dangerous when you're in your element."

I crossed my legs, leaning back, unbothered. "Being dangerous pays bills."

"And then some," he said, sliding a glass across the table to me. Expensive wine. He already knew my taste. "Tell me, how you been, mami?"

I took the glass, sipped slow. "Better. Busier. But that's not saying much. You know I've always been good."

He chuckled low. "Confident as ever. I love that."

We talked, laughed, slipping back into that rhythm like no time had passed. But every so often, I felt Kendrix's presence like a ghost behind that door. I knew he was out there somewhere, watching the minutes tick, probably burning a hole through the club floor just imagining what was happening.

And maybe that's why I leaned in, voice dropping lower. "You know, Sincere, there's a man here tonight who thinks he can keep up with me."

His brow arched. "Think? Poor soul. He don't know you don't do easy."

"Exactly." I swirled my glass, smiling. "And the more he tries to cage me, the more I'm tempted to remind him... I don't get caged. I own the whole damn jungle."

Sincere laughed. "That's why I always loved you, Niv. You don't beg. You don't bend. You bend men."

I slid my heels across the polished floor, hips swaying, every movement deliberate. Sincere leaned back on the velvet couch, legs spread, one arm draped over the backrest, eyes locked on me.

"Lawd have mercy," he said with that thick Jamaican accent. "Yuh still move like yuh bones playing the riddim."

I smirked, rolling down the pole with a slow body wave until I was squatting in front of him, one hand trailing up his chest without even touching him. "Guess the rhythm never left me."

His grin was wide, those dimples deep enough to swim in. "An mi glad fi dat. How many man yuh done mash up wid that waist since me?"

I laughed, turning around to grind the air, tossing a look over my shoulder. "Wouldn't you like to know?"

He chuckled, shaking his head, eyes glued to the way my ass swayed in the tutu skirt. "Yuh wicked. Pure wickedness. If I was a fool, mi woulda lock yuh away long time."

"But you're not a fool." I hooked my heel on the arm of the couch, dropping into a split slow, arching my back until my hair brushed the floor.

His tongue slid across his bottom lip. "No... mi smart. Smart enough to know yuh cyan lock fire in a box. Yuh born fi blaze, gyal."

That sent a shiver through me. Because Sincere always had a way of speaking life into me, even when he was half-joking.

I rose back up, twirling around the pole, letting my legs hook as I swung, then slid down slow until I was face to face with him again. He didn't throw a dollar. Didn't reach for me. Just watched with that calm, confident stare.

I knew when my private dance ended, I'd walk away with more than enough. Not in just bills scattered across the floor, but in something bigger. Respect, adoration, and a fat deposit later that I wouldn't even have to ask for.

"Yuh know what mi really want?" He sat up. "Fi have yuh sit right down on mi face 'til yuh cyan stand it no more. Watch yuh shake while mi drown."

My breath caught, and before I could respond, the door clicked.

Kendrix closed it behind him, calm as hell. Leaning against the doorframe, with his arms crossed.

"She don't need an old friend to do that," Kendrix said. "I already do it. Better than you could dream."

Sincere didn't flinch. He leaned back, letting a slow grin creep across his face as his eyes cut to me, then back to Kendrix.

"So this the man?" His tone was playful, not a hint of intimidation. "The one bold enough fi believe he own yuh... but still foolish enough not fi lock yuh down and make yuh him wife?"

Kendrix didn't blink. He stepped in closer, all broad shoulders and calm danger, the kind that made even the air nervous. "You real comfortable talking about my woman like that."

I raised an eyebrow, because last I checked, I was nobody's woman. But I let him continue.

Sincere chuckled, smooth as his accent. "If she was your woman, yuh wouldn't be in here marking territory, big man. She'd be home in yuh bed."

Kendrix tilted his head, tugging at his beard. "She was in my bed. You're just late to the party."

Oooooh. I had to fight the grin pulling at my lips

Sincere leaned forward, elbows on his knees, eyes on me the whole time. "So tell mi, Niv, this the kinda man yuh want? One who think claimin' yuh with words is enough? Or one who give yuh the world without asking yuh to beg?"

I finally slid off the pole, slow, letting both of them choke on the view. My heels clicked against the floor as I walked over, leaned down, and whispered in Sincere's ear. "You still talk too damn much."

Then I turned to Kendrix, brushing past him, close enough for my perfume to slap him in the face. "Kendrix, can you please meet me in the office?"

Kendrix didn't even argue. He just clenched his jaw, gave Sincere one last look, and walked out the room.

I turned back to Sincere, crossing my arms with a little smirk. "You just had to do it, huh? Couldn't let me have five minutes without you trying to light the room on fire."

He smiled, slow and cocky. "C'mon, Niv. Yuh know mi couldn't resist. Let's see how bad di man want it."

I tilted my head, lips curving. "You play too much."

He leaned back, grin growing wider. "And you love it."

I grabbed my phone off the chair, giving him a look over my shoulder. "Don't get too comfortable. I'll be back."

"I know."

I rolled my eyes but couldn't hide the smile tugging at my mouth as I pushed the door open and stepped out.

Kendrix was leaned against the wall, arms crossed, a cigar between his lips. I hated how fine he was when he was mad.

"You good?" I asked, brushing past him like my pulse wasn't jumping.

He didn't move. Just let his eyes trail down my body. "You tell me."

I laughed. "Don't start acting like you got ownership papers on me, Kendrix. I told you—"

He pushed off the wall, stepping into my space before I could finish. His cologne wrapped around me. "Pretty, I don't need no papers to know when something's mine."

I smirked, tilting my chin up. "Mmm. Funny, because last I checked, I was just a free agent making power moves."

He licked his lips, close enough that I felt the heat of his breath. "Keep talking. You gone talk yourself right onto this desk."

I raised a brow. "Thats supposed to scare me or tempt me?"

"Both," he said, no hesitation.

That's when I knew I had him. His posture screamed control, but his eyes were begging for me to test every inch of it.

I slid into the office, and dropped into the chair behind the desk. He shut the door behind him.

"You coming to argue or to listen?" I asked, crossing my legs slow.

Kendrix leaned forward, resting his palms on the edge of the desk like he was staking his claim.

"You need to drop him. Matter fact, you need to drop any nigga who think he's playing that position in your life. From the sounds of it, Mr. Sincere makes sure you stay with paper. Cool. Any other man on your little roster like that? Cut them too. If you need anything—money, bills, trips, hell, a pack of gum—you come to me. Period."

I bit down on my lip, hard, to keep from laughing. His face was so serious I almost felt bad. Almost.

"I like you," he continued, eyes locked on mine like I was oxygen. "Like, really like you. And I don't play about that shit. So I'm letting you know right now, whatever the fuck y'all had going on in that private room? That shit ends today. You don't need no heroes. You don't need no sponsors. You don't need nobody. You have me."

He meant every single word. I could see it all over him.

I let a slow smile spread across my face before I stood, closing the space between us.

"You done?" I asked softly.

His silence said he thought he'd just dropped a mic.

"Okay. Here's the thing," I said, tilting my head like I was explaining something simple to a stubborn child. "Kendrix... I am not your girlfriend. You've never made that a thing. Sooo, technically..." I drew the word out, dragging my nails lightly over his chest. "...I don't have to do a damn thing you say."

I stepped back, smirking at the flicker in his eyes. "I'm not telling you to cut your women off. All I've ever asked is that they stay respectful. Who am I to throw around demands when I don't belong to you... and you don't belong to me?"

I crossed my arms, every inch of me calm but sharp. "Let's be clear, I can get a bag from anyone without ever opening my legs. So yes, there's a list, baby. A list of men I could call right now, hold a simple ass conversation, and have a direct deposit hit before I finish my wine. That's not me bragging. That's me reminding you who the fuck I am."

I leaned in, close enough to let my lips ghost his ear. "So unless you ready to make me yours for real... don't throw around demands like you own MY place. I like you too, Kendrix. But without a title? You don't have a say in shit I do, love."

I pulled back with the sweetest smile, like I hadn't just snatched the rug out from under him.

Kendrix's eyes never leaving mine. "I can't do this," he said finally. "Not if I know there's other niggas out here providing for you like I'm not enough."

I blinked slow, then tilted my head.

"Then don't," I said simply. "Because I'm not risking security for romance. Cute dates and deep talks don't keep lights on, Kendrix. Money does. Stability does."

His jaw flexed, the muscle ticking like he was trying to keep his temper on a leash. "You didn't want me fucking with Arlette."

"And you right," I cut in, my tone just as calm as it was cold. "Because she messed with my money and brought drama where I don't allow it. Trust, if any nigga even *thought* about doing the same? He'd be dropped and worse. Don't confuse him with her."

He leaned closer, heat radiating off him. "So what, you just gone keep playing puppet master with other men's pockets?"

I smiled. "See, that's the difference, love. You never have to worry about me having a man like your Arlette. **I don't let any man think he's bigger than the motherfucking program because I am the program**."

His nostrils flared, his chest rising like he was ready to argue, but I didn't care. I wanted him to understand that not one syllable I'd said was up for negotiation.

He stared at me, eyes dark with a mix of anger and want, then finally let out a humorless laugh. He turned for the door.

"Say less," he said before walking out the door without another word.

21

Kendrix

Niv was on stage, closing the night out. The crowd was screaming, bills flying in the air like confetti, and I swear every nigga in the place was drooling over her.

I sat back, trying my hardest not to even blink her way. I was pissed. Not the type of pissed you shake off after a drink. Nah. The kind that sat in your chest heavy, that made you want to punch a wall just so you ain't say something you couldn't take back.

I pulled out my phone, scrolling just to distract myself. Arlette's name popped up.

I should've blocked her ass back after the last time. Should've done it weeks ago.

> Can we talk?

I stared at it, thumb hovering, doing absolutely nothing.

On one shoulder, that little angel voice whispering, *Don't be stupid. Don't text her back. You don't even fuck with her like that.*

But then the devil on the other shoulder grinned and said, *So she can grind on niggas, let them throw money on her like you don't got it, but you can't even answer a damn text?*

Before I could overthink it, the phone buzzed again.

> Can we talk please?

I tilted the phone, staring at it like it might give me the answer.

I felt somebody watching me. I glanced up, and Ty was standing there. Not smiling. Not saying shit. Just looking at my phone.

"Fuck," I muttered under my breath.

Her silence said everything. I knew she was about to run straight to Niv with it, but fuck it. I wasn't about to start explaining myself like some weak-ass nigga.

"What you need, Ty?" I asked, voice flat.

She hesitated, then said, "Niv told me to tell you... you can go. She's got a ride home."

That shit hit different. Like a sucker punch straight to the gut.

I clenched my jaw. "Aight."

I looked back down at my phone.

My thumb moved without hesitation this time.

Bet. When?

I sat in my truck, engine off, seat reclined just enough to stay low, eyes locked on the front of GivGold like I wasn't the one who built it.

She had Ty to come deliver a message. I already knew that was her way of saying "fuck you" without using her mouth.

My phone buzzed but I didn't even look at it right away. I was too busy watching the door swing open.

She came out in that black lace robe over a barely-there bodysuit, walking like the damn ground should thank her for stepping on it. But it wasn't just her. Her arm was linked with Sincere's.

I shifted in my seat, watching them stroll toward his car like I wasn't in the building twenty minutes ago, asking her to drop everyone else and choose me.

Choose me.

But nah.

She chose her moment. Her mood. Her little power play.

Sincere was soaking it up too, looking like he already knew how soft her moans sounded.

If my brothers were still around, this would've been a whole other scene. Kross would've popped off just outta loyalty. Kordai would've offered to handle it for me. Kairo probably would've pulled me to the side like, *"You gone let that shit slide, bro?"*

My phone buzzed again.

> I'm home now. If you wanna come.

I stared at the message. Angel on one shoulder telling me to block her. Devil on the other grinning like, *"Since she want to act single, act single."*

Niv slid into Sincere's passenger seat like she wasn't breaking every unspoken rule between us.

That was the final straw.

I unlocked my screen, hit *Reply* on Arlette's text.

> On the way.

NETRA ANTIONETTE

By the time I pulled up to Arlette's house, she was already outside leaned against the front door like she'd been rehearsing whatever she planned to say.

Her posture screamed "ready," but her eyes... they were softer. Not wide with rage like usual. Just tired.

She opened the door without a word. I walked up slow, hands in my pockets, the weight of too much bullshit pressing on my back.

As soon as I stepped in, I said it straight.

"I ain't got time to argue. You wanna talk? Talk."

She closed the door behind us.

No yelling. No neck rolls. No dramatics.

Instead, she walked to the couch, sat down, and looked up at me like she was trying to unlearn how to cry.

"I love you, Kendrix," she said softly. "I've loved you for years. We've always been solid... so I don't understand how one girl in the club just shows up and flips everything upside down."

Her voice cracked, and I realized I hadn't heard her sound like that in so long.

It didn't sound like Arlette. It sounded like the girl I used to laugh with on slow Sundays.

I exhaled and sat down across from her.

"You always been cool, Arlette," I said. "I liked the way we used to kick it... years back. When you weren't being wild. When you weren't trying to be the loudest one in the room."

She blinked, fast.

"But somewhere between my brother getting locked up and me tryna keep shit from falling apart, you changed. You got good with business. I'll never take that from you but everything else turned to chaos."

She opened her mouth, but I kept going.

"It started being about shitting on your family. About what you had, what you wore, who was watching. Like everything was a damn competition. Meanwhile, I'm tryna survive and you can't even pack a lunch."

Her mouth twitched like she wanted to defend herself, but I leaned forward.

"I made sure you didn't go without. I did that because I cared. But you couldn't even return the favor with peace. And after a while, I stopped fucking with you for real. Yeah, we had sex. Yeah, we ran business. But I didn't see you as no wife. That was long gone."

She sniffled, and just when I thought the softness would turn back into fire—

"I was loyal," she whispered.

I laughed.

"I know you fucked my homeboys."

Her head snapped up like I'd slapped her.

"Stop this loyalty act. I knew. I been knew. But I didn't say shit, because truth is... the only reason I kept anything going after that wreck was because you lost the baby."

That broke her. Her lips quivered, and the tears came heavy. "If I hadn't sped off... if I wasn't acting so damn crazy that day..."

She couldn't finish it.

And even though I should've stayed cold, I felt it in my chest too. That accident wrecked more than a car. Two wrecks took two kids from me before I could even meet them. I thought about Megan. Pieces of me I would never get back.

I stood and walked over to her. I sat beside her and let her fall into me.

She was sobbing and shaking. Snot and tears soaking into my shirt.

I didn't love her or even like her, but I wasn't heartless.

Sometimes grief doesn't let you be the villain. Sometimes you just sit in the wreckage with someone who remembers the same pain you do.

"I just wanna be under you one last time," she whispered against my chest, breath shaky.

I didn't say anything.

Because I wasn't sure if she meant under emotionally...

...or under me in the way I knew I'd regret.

She looked up at me, eyes glassy, lips trembling.

"Can you make me feel something else?"

I didn't answer. Her eyes were already filling in the blanks, and mine were running wild with visions I didn't want.

Visions of Niv pressed up against velvet, lips parted, head thrown back in laughter while Sincere whispered some slick shit in her ear. That smug smile he gave me at the club still gripped the back of my mind like a claw. I could see his hand on her waist. His mouth too close to hers. The way she leaned into him.

I hated how much that shit bothered me. Hated how I was gripping the fabric of Arlette's damn couch like it owed me answers.

I stood up, pacing the floor like I was trying to outrun the thought of Niv getting soft for another man.

I knew what Arlette wanted. She wanted to disappear inside the version of me I used to be. The man who touched her without overthinking it. The man who didn't flinch when she begged, who didn't have a whole new woman under his skin.

Maybe for one night, I could give that to her. Or maybe I just wanted to punish someone... and she was the only one dumb enough to hand me the weapon.

She reached for me, and I didn't stop her.

Her hands slid under my shirt like she still had the right. She was busy talking. Words I wasn't hearing, promises I didn't believe. My jaw locked when she kissed my neck, but I didn't push her away.

I could feel myself spiraling, but I let her keep going.

She guided me down onto the couch, crawling over me like memory. Like manipulation.

I stared at the ceiling while she straddled me, whispering, "You remember how I used to make you feel?"

Yeah. I remembered, but I wasn't trying to feel anything. I was trying to forget.

Forget the way Niv smiled at Sincere. Forget the softness in her voice when she said, "he's just an old friend." Forget how I wasn't even officially her man, but felt like she just cheated on me anyway.

Arlette was touching me like I was hers, and I let her.

I let her take her time, let her say things that used to mean something. Let her kiss my scars and pretend like she had the right. But I didn't kiss her back. I didn't make it sweet. I didn't even close my eyes.

Because I wasn't there, I was at Niv's door.

I was watching her walk away from me without hesitation.

When I finally touched Arlette, I mean really touched her, I wasn't gentle.

I didn't go slow. I didn't care what she needed. I gave her what I had left.

Rough. Mindless. The kind of fuck that feels more like revenge than pleasure. She was moaning, clawing at me, calling me by name like it meant something. Like she was winning.

But the whole time, I couldn't stop thinking—

I wish this was her.

And that was the worst part.

Because no matter how deep I went...

No matter how loud Arlette got...

She would never be Niv.

I was still sweating. Still inside my own damn head.

She curled up next to me, trying to act like what we did meant something, all I felt was fucking hollow.

Regret burned at the back of my throat like cheap liquor.

She asked me to stay real soft, like it wasn't her who just got through crying about how she messed up everything and still turned around and let me fuck her like a disposable itch I needed to scratch.

"You can stay if you want..." she said, fingers brushing over my chest like her touch could anchor me. "Just lay down. Be here with me tonight."

I sat up.

"I'm not staying. And I'm damn sure not cuddling with you," I said, pulling my pants back on and trying to shake the fog in my head.

I was tipsy, high, and mad as hell at myself. I didn't even wanna be in her damn house, breathing recycled air that smelled like old perfume and desperation.

My head was spinning. I could still see Niv's damn smile. Her hand locked into Sincere's arm like he had the right to guide her anywhere.

Fuck.

I ran a hand down my face and sat back down on the couch.

"Ima just sit here. Close my eyes for a minute."

She lit a candle like she was setting the vibe, and I damn near rolled my eyes out my skull.

It wasn't a vibe. It was a mistake with throw pillows.

And just like clockwork, like she couldn't help her damn self, she started talking again.

"You didn't have to say it like that... like I didn't mean shit. Like everything we've done just ain't matter to you—"

"Man, shut the fuck up."

I didn't even raise my voice. Just said it calm and slow.

She froze and I kept going.

"You always do this. Always kill the moment. We already fucked. You cried. You got your nut. Let me relax in peace before I lose my shit in here."

She went quiet, flipping through the channels like her pride had taken the hit it needed.

I leaned back, head hitting the cushion, eyes closed, fists clenched.

I should've been anywhere else.

But I was....

In the home of a woman I didn't even like.

Trying to forget a woman I couldn't stop wanting.

22

Niveah

It had been seven days since I heard his voice and seven days since he'd been blowing my phone up like I was the one who fucked up.

Missed calls. Double texts. Triple texts. And that long ass "I guess this how it is now" paragraph nobody asked for.

I laughed every time my phone lit up. Not because I didn't miss him, but because men really be thinking they invented the game.

Yes, I left with Sincere.

Yes, I let him walk me to his car, real cozy like.

But no, I didn't stay.

Baby, I hopped right in Ty's car and told her to keep it cute but keep up. And when I say this man didn't even notice someone was following him? That's how you know he was gone. Mind cloudy, vision blurrier than that Hennessy he had in his system.

He pulled up to Arlette's crusty ass crib like she was peace in a storm.

And when that front door closed behind him?

I sat in the car and waited. For hours. When I saw the lights go off in her house like it was bedtime? That's when I said, "Oh. Okay."

You wanna play? Cool. Let's really play.

Next morning, I was on a private jet headed to Turks and Caicos, ho.

Sincere had asked me to come chill days ago and I'd said no, but I can show Kendrix better than I can tell him.

While he was laid up in that dusty ass twin-sized bed, inhaling regrets and back shots with a girl who's shaped like every bad decision he's ever made, I was sipping fresh fruit juice in a bikini that probably cost more than your last rent payment.

Feet in the sand.

Phone on *Do Not Disturb*.

And peace wrapped around my body like the sunlight itself said, "You ain't gotta deal with that shit."

See, that's what men don't get. We spin the block with a damn blueprint. We don't just play the game because we built the board. And while they're still fumbling the ball... We're already three power moves ahead.

He thought I was sitting at home mad. No, baby. I was getting rubbed down with hot oil and island breeze while he was getting lied to in polyester sheets. I was in a private villa with ocean views, my own chef, and two security guards stationed at the front gate like I was the daughter of a diplomat.

Sincere hadn't touched me or even tried, because he knew the program.

He knew I was the one who made the moves. The one you present options to... and wait for me to pick the one that benefits me the most.

Every morning, a new delivery came to the villa.

Day one, it was a Cartier bracelet with "MissCommunication" engraved on the inside. Cute. Day two, A black AmEx card with my name on it and a post-it that said,

For convenience. Or chaos.

Day three, a limited-edition fragrance that smelled like secrets and sex appeal.

Only ten bottles were created and in circulation. Number six was mine.

Day four, a silk box from Saks. Inside was a custom dress flown in from Milan.

And still, he didn't lay a hand on me. He knows I'm not impressed by attention, I'm moved by intention.

We'd laughed, we ate, and we would vibe on the beach, drink tequila, and he'd tell me stories that had me forgetting what city I was even from.

But when it was time to go to bed, he went to his and I went to mine.

That's what Kendrix didn't understand.

A nigga could spoil me, worship me, put me in heaven on earth, but unless **I** decide to unlock something more, It's just an offering.

Day five, I finally left.

Not because I wanted to, but because I needed to. Because being a bad bitch also meant being responsible. The same way I can pour champagne into a Baccarat glass and sip on a yacht in silence, I can also get back on a flight and be in mom-mode before the wheels hit the damn tarmac.

Hux and Zejah had a doctor appointments.

The first prenatal for her with a new doctor and some counseling resources I'd lined up for him. I told them I'd be there, and I don't miss when it matters.

Ty held the club down long enough. So yeah, I packed up my lil' designer duffel. Kissed the view goodbye. Gave Sincere a wink and a thank-you smirk... and got the hell on.

Zejah was sitting on the exam table, legs swinging nervously like a child waiting on a shot, and Hux was damn near chewing a hole through his bottom lip. His knee kept bouncing, and he kept checking the clock like it was gonna speed up time.

I sat in the corner chair with my arms crossed, pretending like I was calm and collected. Like it wasn't also my first time in that kind of appointment. I didn't know what the hell was going on, either. I've been to checkups for myself. Annuals. Pap smears. A lil' look under the hood to make sure Ms. Kitty was still purring and premium grade.

But their appointment was about life. About watching two teens who were just learning how to drive now get handed the keys to parenthood. And somehow, I was in the passenger seat of it all.

The nurse came in and smiled at Zejah, asking her a million questions that made her voice tremble when she answered. I could see her hand inching toward Hux's under the thin paper sheet, and he laced their fingers without blinking.

"First pregnancy?" the nurse asked, typing something into the chart.

I wanted to yell, "Hell yeah, and it better be the last!" but I kept it cute.

"Yes, ma'am," Zejah said, barely above a whisper.

The nurse looked at me next.

"Are you mom?"

"No," I said. "I'm the sister-slash-guardian-slash holding this whole damn house down."

The nurse laughed politely. Zejah looked over at me with those big eyes and exhaled like she was finally safe. Like she believed I knew exactly what I was doing. Joke was on her. We were all about to learn together.

A woman stepped in wearing a maternity scrub top stretched over a perfect, round belly. She had the kind of glow people swore pregnancy gave you, even though I knew damn well sometimes it was just highlighter and good moisturizer.

"Hey, y'all," she said with a smile. "I'm Talynn Baldwin, your nurse practitioner." She rested a hand on her stomach. "And this little one in here is Rylan"

Zejah's shoulders loosened just a little.

Talynn walked closer to Zejah. "If it makes you feel any better, this is my first time doing this too. I've assisted plenty of births back when I was an RN. I went back to school to be your provider. My husband's even an ER MD, so technically, I'm surrounded by all the medical advice in the world" She laughed. "But, I still get nervous. Because I've never done this before either."

Something about that honesty cracked Zejah open in a way my pep talks never could. She gave a little half-smile, like maybe she wasn't so alone in it after all.

Talynn kept talking, keeping it light and steady. Asking her about school. About how she was feeling. Then she shifted her attention to Hux, who was still glued to Zejah's side.

"And you," she said, grinning at him. "First time for you too, huh?"

He nodded, awkward, like he wasn't sure if he was supposed to say *thank you* or *help*.

"Let me tell you now, prepare for anything. My husband, Reggie, has more cravings than I do." She laughed. "Last week, he wanted a burger at two in the morning, and he's not even the one carrying the baby."

Even I cracked a smile at that, though I was still side-eyeing my brother like he better soak up every word this woman was saying.

While she kept them talking, her hands worked. She snapped on gloves, squirting gel bottles to the side, and pulled the ultrasound machine closer.

"So," Talynn said looking at Zejah. "You've had one of these before?"

Zejah nodded. "Yeah, but... it just looked like a glob. The doctor said it was really early."

"Well," Talynn said, her tone lifting. "Let's take another look and see what we've got this time."

Talynn squeezed a clear blob of gel onto the ultrasound probe and grinned. "Okay, we'll start abdominal and see what we get. If baby's playing hide-and-seek, we might switch to a transvaginal just to get a clearer look. Totally normal either way."

Zejah's eyes widened a little at *transvaginal*, but Talynn kept talking like she was telling a bedtime story. "Feet here, shirt up just a little, and this might feel cold at first."

She placed the wand on Zejah's belly, moving slow, eyes on the monitor. A black-and-white galaxy swirled into focus until there it was a little bean-shaped figure curled up like it was protecting its own peace.

"There's your baby," Talynn said, tilting the screen so they could all see. "You can see the head right here, tiny arm buds... and that little flutter? That's the heart."

She tapped a few buttons, taking measurements before smiling. "You're measuring right at eleven weeks and two days."

Then she pressed another button and the room filled with a quick, steady rhythm.

thump-thump-thump-thump.

Zejah's hand went over her mouth. Hux leaned in closer, eyes locked on the screen like it was the most important thing he'd ever seen.

"Strong heartbeat," Talynn added. "That's music right there."

I saw both of them smile. I felt it hit me low in my chest before I could stop it. Damn near teared up in that little exam room. Not because I was soft, but because life had been kicking them in the teeth lately, and for once, they looked like they had something worth holding onto.

Talynn wiped the gel from Zejah's belly, printed a couple of pictures, and handed them over before leaving the room. Zejah held them so carefully you'd think they might crack in her hands.

"Alright," I said, sliding my bag strap over my shoulder, "Rules still apply." I gave them both the look, the one that said I meant it. "Separate rooms. Doors open. If I walk in and see y'all playing house, I'm gonna start charging rent and making chore charts."

They both smirked, trying to hide it, but I caught it. "Mmhmm. Laugh now." I pushed the door open and nodded toward the hall. "Rita's outside waiting. She'll take y'all to pick up lunch and home."

Hux frowned. "You're not coming with us?"

"I gotta run to the club, work out some things for tonight. But I'll be back in time to chill and have dinner before I head out again." I pointed at them both. "Don't start acting like fools who don't know what a condom is while I'm gone."

That earned me a real laugh out of Hux, but what caught me off guard was when Zejah stepped forward and hugged me tight.

Then Hux, my *I don't like physical touch,* little brother leaned in and hugged me too.

I played it cool, but inside it felt good.

NETRAANTIONETTE

Ty was leaned over the stage, counting out bills while I checked the bar inventory. "So... you handled everything?" she asked without looking up.

I laughed, low and petty. "Yeah. Its handled."

Kendrix can really be a dumbass sometimes. His little hoe, Arlette, must've gone through his phone and sent herself the nudes I'd sent him, and then tried to threaten him like she had ammo. Cute, right? Kendrix and Kross tried to keep it on the low, handle it before I found out. But Arlette is too loud for her own good. Word travels. The tea hit me and Ty before she even texted him with her little "leak threat."

Whatever Kross said to her made her back off posting them. Hell, I didn't care if she did or not, but my get-back is always better.

I called Khloe. My favorite attorney with the smile of a saint and the mind of a cartel boss. We didn't just make a plan. We made a 48-hour wipeout.

Hour 1

Khloe makes one phone call and Arlette's "forever home"? That big, shiny, Instagram-perfect house? Was never technically in her name. Belonged to a holding company... a holding company managed by one of Khloe's close associates. And when I tell you we surgically snatched that lease-to-own agreement right out from under her.

Hour 6

The power company gets a report of "serious safety hazards." Lights? Gone. AC? Gone. WiFi? Gone. Her "smart home" went dumb as hell. HOA was tipped off about "noncompliance". Her patio furniture ended up on the curb like a yard sale no one wanted to shop at.

Hour 12

While she was out, thinking life was sweet, we had the locks changed. She didn't even know until morning.

Hour 18

She pulls up from her little night out and errand run with a trunk full of groceries and couldn't even get in. Movers were already on-site with instructions to pack everything for "storage only." Not a single box going to a new address.

Hour 24

Oh, and the cherry on top? We slapped a lien on that bottle-girl "business" she was running out her living room. By "business," I mean a couple of dusty hookah hoses and overpriced vodka bottles. Her liquor distributor suddenly had "supply chain issues."

Hour 36

She was on Instagram, selling Gucci slides and tagging it #MovingSale. By the time she goes live, she's sitting on a blow-up mattress in her cousin's den, box fan humming, swearing it's "just a minor setback" while begging people to book bottles with her "new location."

From house to no house in under 48 hours. All without me lifting a manicured finger in her direction.

Arlette had money. But not the kind of money that could replace the lifestyle Kendrix had her living for years. She couldn't even fake that type of upkeep. And the reason she didn't even try to fight us legally was simple. Sis has so much illegal shit going on, she couldn't risk a lawyer poking around her finances without catching her in 30 felonies. She packed, got her shit, and played quiet because she knew one phone call from the wrong person could have her in county orange by the weekend.

Ty bent over, laughing so hard she had to brace herself on the bar. "Bitch! Stop, my stomach! You're telling me by the time she got back from Target, she couldn't even get in the door?"

I was laughing so hard I had tears in my eyes. "Girl, the groceries was sitting on the porch like a delivery she ain't order."

Ty damn near slid down the bar laughing, wiping her eyes. "Niv... you're evil."

"Not evil, baby. Efficient."

I looked up and there was Kendrix, standing in the doorway of the VIP, that unreadable look on his face. The music was still going, Ty was still catching her breath from laughing, but everything in me went still.

He didn't say a word at first, just scanned me up and down like he was trying to decide if he wanted to kiss me or start an argument in the middle of the damn club.

I smiled slow. "Well, look who decided to show up."

Ty caught the vibe immediately. She grabbed her drink and grinned at Kendrix like she hadn't just been laughing about me ruining a woman's life.

"Ima go clean up the private rooms," she said, winking at me. Translation: *Handle your business.*

Kendrix didn't waste a second. "You've been ignoring my calls and texts."

I leaned on the bar, completely unbothered. "I know."

His jaw flexed. "So that's just it? You don't give a fuck?"

I tilted my head, giving him the laziest smile I could manage. "Looks like it."

That muscle in his cheek ticked again. "I love you, Niveah."

For half a second, I froze. Just half. Then I laughed, slow and humorless. "Love don't mean shit, Kendrix, when you're laid up with the next bitch. The same bitch I told you to stop fucking with because of what she did."

His brows pulled tight. "What she—"

"Oh, don't play dumb." I cut him off with a smirk sharp enough to cut glass. "The same bitch who got my pictures out your phone, trying to send my shit out like she runs something."

He blinked like he hadn't seen that one coming.

I chuckled low. "I'm always two steps ahead, Kendrix. Always. I hope your little nightcap was worth it."

I grabbed a clean bar towel, tossed it straight at his chest, and leaned close enough for him to catch the heat in my smile.

"Tonight's gonna be amazing at GivGold," I said sweet as honey. "Now, clean some shit up... and pick your face up while you're at it."

I paused just long enough to let my eyes drag over him, top to bottom. "And next time you wanna play in the dirt... make sure you don't come home tracking mud on my floors."

23

Kendrix

I should've known Niv had some shit up her sleeve. The flyer said *The Highness' Playground.* Cute name, but I knew her. That wasn't just branding, that was a damn motive.

I walked in right before the night started and stopped dead.

She had someone come in and decorate the hell out of GivGold. Not just a theme, but a whole experience. The shit looked like a real seductive playground... except instead of swing sets and monkey bars, there were velvet ropes, glass tables, low couches you could sink into, and shadows that made you wanna sin in them.

Purple. Everywhere.

Purple drapes. Purple lights. Purple on every wall, every corner glowing rich and low. She knew exactly what the fuck she was doing.

She knew what that color meant to me. Why I loved women in it.

Purple is power without having to scream. It's royalty, danger, and sex all in one shade. It isn't loud like red, it's smooth, confident, like a woman who doesn't have to beg for attention. She just walks in, and the room tilts without her saying a word. That was my favorite thing. Always had been. I loved my woman in purple because that let everyone know that she's untouchable.

Every bottle girl, host, bartender, every dancer wore gold. Shiny, glowing gold against that deep purple. I ain't gonna lie, that shit was perfect. Purple pulled you in, but gold made you spend.

The lights dropped lower, and music slid in like it had been poured.

Niv never did opening dances. It wasn't her lane anymore. But I knew that silhouette the second it stepped out from behind the curtain, lit just enough to tease. I could pick that body frame out in a blackout.

It was her, and she wanted to make sure everyone in that club knew exactly who the hell *The Highness* was.

The curtain lifted slowly, like the club knew it needed to pace itself before it passed out.

Niv was in a purple two-piece that left **nothing** to the imagination. Everything was out on display. Not in a cheap way, but in a *'damn, I could ruin my life over this'* way. She has thighs that looked like they could break a man in half. Her shape had always been something you couldn't really hide, no matter what she wore, but she was usually a one-piece, tease-you-but-don't-touch type. But she wasn't teasing. She was flaunting. And it had me going crazy and pissed at the same damn time. She was giving everybody a front-row seat to what I'd been losing sleep over.

The DJ dropped a heavy bassline, but before the track really kicked in, her voice slid over the speakers.

"I let my body speak."

The way she said it had every man in the room ready to empty his account. Then the beat flipped and *Bad Girl* by Usher hit.

Niv moved like the music was hers. Slips, spins, twerks — her heels clapping against the pole in perfect rhythm. She flipped upside down like gravity bent for her, sliding down slow before shooting back up, then climbing all the way to the top just to drop into a split that stopped inches from the floor. And the whole damn time, she was looking dead at me.

Her body was saying every word she didn't. She was telling me she couldn't be fucked with, that she was in control here, and I knew it. And the worst part was that she orchestrated the whole thing to make sure I knew and needed a reminder.

It explained everything and why I'd fallen for somebody like her. She could stand on her own. She could walk me like a dog if she wanted. She knew it, and still refused to drop her crown for anybody. Yeah... that was the problem and why she had me losing my mind.

She didn't just finish the song, she finished me.

Right when the beat hit its peak, she grabbed the pole, lifted herself slow, and wrapped both legs around it like she was holding on to somebody's waist. Then she leaned back, arching so far her hair almost kissed the floor again, and rolled her hips in a motion that was so nasty, so *obvious*, every dude in there started throwing money like they just wanted to pay for a taste.

Her eyes were still locked on me. Not breaking or blinking, and I swear I felt every slow grind in my chest, in my gut, in my bones.

She let go, slid down into a squat right at the edge of the stage, and without looking away, she ran both hands up her own thighs, over her stomach, and cupped her breasts before letting them drop with a bounce that had the whole room yelling. And just when I thought it was over, she leaned forward, stuck her tongue out just enough to make it sinful, and mouthed, *"Fetch."*

Like I was the dog in this game.

She stood, blew me the slowest, most disrespectful kiss I've ever seen, and walked off knowing damn well I was two seconds from clearing the whole damn club just to get to her.

Every muscle in my body was telling me to get up and drag her off that stage. But I knew that's exactly what she wanted.She wanted me foaming at the mouth while she strolled away like she owned me. And she did.

The second she disappeared behind that curtain, I felt my chest tighten. The air in the club felt hot, heavy... suffocating. I tossed back what was left in my glass, stood up, and walked straight out the side door before I did something that made the news.

The cool air hit my face, but it didn't help. My heart was still racing, so I pulled my phone out and hit FaceTime on the brothers.

Kross answered first, screen shaking as he laughed soon as he saw my face. "Oh yeah... she made a believer outta you, huh?"

Kairo popped, grinning wide. "Nigga look like he just lost a custody battle."

I gritted my teeth. "Shut the fuck up."

The third box popped up. Kordai was calm and quiet. Just staring at me like he was waiting for me to say what we both knew I was about to say.

"Put Rivah and Khloe on the phone," I said, leaning back against the wall.

Nobody laughed then.

24

Niveah

From the stage, I could see everything.

The gold lights bouncing off the purple walls, the bills floating through the air like confetti... and Kendrix storming his ass right out the side door.

I smirked mid-spin, because that meant my mission was accomplished.

Men like Kendrix, want you soft, grateful, and waiting for them to "decide" if you're worthy. Nope. I'll make you question your breathing pattern while you're watching me, then I'll leave you outside wondering who the fuck you even are.

By the time the curtain closed, I was in my dressing room with Ty, peeling off my heels and sipping champagne like I'd just clocked out of a board meeting.

"He's mad," she sang, scrolling through her phone.

"Good," I said, leaning back in my chair. "Mad men spend more money."

Truth was, I knew exactly what I was doing. I'd planned that set for days. The outfit, the lighting, the song, the way every move would hit him in the chest like a loaded gun.

The host came barging in, breathless like she'd just sprinted across the damn club.

"Niv, you got at least eight requests for private dances tonight. All big spenders. They're throwing around numbers like it's tax-free day."

I shook my head, grinning. "Tell them it's not happening tonight. But let them know I'm putting together a *Private Playground* night real soon, and may the best price win. Make sure they hear the word *bid*. Men get real stupid when they think they have to compete."

The host nodded like she was about to go start a war and darted back out.

Ty, who'd been lounging in the corner scrolling on her phone, set it down and leaned forward, her eyes soft but serious.

"Real question, Niv. How you feel about Kendrix? For real, not the 'I don't give a fuck' answer you give everybody else."

I gave her the lazy smirk I save for questions I don't feel like answering. "What you mean 'how I feel'? I feel like he fine, he got money, and he knows how to eat coo—"

"Niv."

Her tone was enough to cut me off.

I sighed, eyes drifting to the empty champagne flute in front of me. "Alright. I like him, Ty. More than I've liked anybody in a long time. But I don't... trust that shit. I haven't done serious in years. I'm used to moving how I move, answering to nobody. The last time I let a man in, it cost me damn near everything. I'm not rushing back into that trap."

Ty nodded slowly, her eyes locked on me. "I get it. But you know, at some point, you gotta stop living like everything is a game of survival. You deserve more than this hustle-love. You deserve somebody who makes you feel safe enough to take the armor off."

I tilted my head. "And if taking it off just gives him a better shot at stabbing me in the chest?"

"That's the risk. But it's also how you get the reward."

I let out a humorless laugh. "Ty, I got kids to raise. I'm not tryna be the woman who catches a case because I had to beat my man and the bitch he was playing with. I've been through too much to put myself in that position. And honestly, it's not about softness for me. Softness don't pay tuition, it don't keep Hux out the streets, it don't make sure Heidi has what she needs. Security does. And like I told him, I won't risk security for romance. Not ever."

She leaned back, giving me that look. The one that makes you feel both called out and understood. "You say that like you can't have both. Like maybe he couldn't be both."

"Ty…" I met her eyes. "Men can't even handle me keeping my own damn bag. I asked him for a title. Just one simple thing that would make me feel like I'm not just out here risking my peace for somebody who's keeping their options open. And you know what happened? NOTHING. Like claiming me was too much, but me pouring into him wasn't. I don't rearrange my life for a man who can't even give me the bare minimum of calling me his."

Ty's eyes narrowed, like she was studying me. "So, what? You like him, but you're just gonna pretend you don't?"

I let out a slow exhale. "Ty… I *really* like Kendrix. That man has a way of looking at me like he can read my whole mind. I like the way he talks to me. I like the way he moves for me. But I've worked too hard to build the life I have. You know what it took for me to get here. I'm not about to jeopardize Hux's stability, Heidi's future, or my peace just to see if this man might be worth it. My life runs smooth because I made it that way, and the second a man starts thinking he can dictate it? I'm back in survival mode. And I promised myself I'd never go back there."

I leaned back, shaking my head.

"Ty, I've seen what happens when women let a man's promises become their plan. They end up begging for the same energy they gave for free. I'm not doing that. I've built my life so that noone—not a man, not the market, not the damn weather—can shake it. If he wants me, he's gonna have to step up in a way that makes me feel safe dropping my guard. And until then, I'm not risking what I built for 'potential.'"

Ty tilted her head, half-smiling like she already knew what I was gonna say next. "So, what, you're just gonna keep playing it cool?"

I smirked. "Cool, hot… whatever keeps me in control. Because love don't pay the mortgage, and 'I'm sorry' don't keep the lights on."

She laughed, shaking her head. "Bitch, I know I didn't just give you all that good advice for nothing."

I clinked my glass against hers. "And you gave it for free. That's on you."

We cracked up, but behind my laugh was a truth I'd never say out loud. Kendrix made me feel things I'd locked away. I liked him more than I wanted to. Wanted him more than I should. But until a man proved he could be the anchor and not the storm... I wasn't letting up.

NETRAANTIONETTE

Pulling into the garage felt like crossing the finish line after a marathon. My shoulders dropped. Finally, home.

I half-expected to see a text from Kendrix blowing up my phone about my dance earlier. You know, some half-ass attempt at "putting his foot down," which would've only made me horny, not obedient. But nothing. Not a damn word.

That pissed me off more than him actually saying something.

No long paragraph. No, "we need to talk." No showing up at the club to pull me into the office like he owned the place. He didn't even come back inside after he left. I know, because I had the host keep eyes on the door and tell me if anyone spotted him.

I stepped inside through the kitchen, expecting quiet. Maybe the tick of the clock or my own thoughts finally stretching out. Instead, I heard laughter.

Not just any laughter. Heidi's giggles, Zejah's breathy chuckles, and Hux yelling at the TV like he was trying to coach the players through the screen. My house wasn't usually that loud at night, but those were the kinds of noises that hit me right in the chest. The ones that made all the chaos of my day worth it. So I quickened my pace, eager to join in.

I turned the corner into the living room and stopped dead.

Kendrix. Sitting on my damn couch, controller in his hand, eyes locked on the screen with Hux next to him.

The girls were camped out on the floor, running a full-blown nail salon. Toys, dolls, snacks everywhere, like they'd been at it for hours. Heidi was carefully painting Zejah's toes, both of them in fits of laughter over something I missed.

Kendrix looked comfortable. Too comfortable.

I leaned against the doorway, arms folded.

"What the hell are you doing in my house?"

Kendrix didn't even look my way. Just smirked a little and kept playing the game. Fine. Two could play that game.

I cut my eyes to Hux. "WTF, Hux?"

He barely glanced up from the screen. "He said he was your dude."

My head snapped to Zejah, who was busy watching Heidi apply another coat of glitter polish.

She shrugged like it was nothing. "I've seen him with you a few times. He's the one who helped bring me here, so I thought it was cool."

Cool? COOL? My blood pressure raised up about twenty points.

But just when I was about to light the room up, Heidi ran over to him, wiggling her little fingers in his face. "Look, Kendrix! Gold with sparkles!"

He gave her this big grin and started hyping her up like she just won an award for Best Nail Design in the city. I caught the way her eyes lit up at his attention and... damn it. That stopped me.

Before I could process that, Hux jumped up, hollering, "LET'S GO!" at the top of his lungs. He'd apparently just won the game and turned to dap Kendrix up like they'd been boys for years.

I just stood there, watching all of them like a stranger in my own living room. They weren't used to interacting with people like this. Especially not men. And I wasn't used to seeing them look at someone like that.

"It's late," I finally said, breaking up the cozy little family picture before it went too far. "Y'all have things to do in the morning, so get to bed."

Zejah started gathering up the snack wrappers and nail polish bottles from the floor, but Kendrix stopped her with a shake of his head.

"Don't worry about it, just get some rest. I'll clean and get everything squared away."

That was exactly what Hux wanted to hear. His whole face broke into a grin. He stood, dapped Kendrix up, and said, "Nice to meet you, man. Can't wait to play you again."

"Bet," Kendrix said with that easy smile, like I was the one to personally introduce them.

Zejah gave him a quick hug. "Thanks for the snacks."

He smirked. "Those were for the baby."

She laughed, rolling her eyes before heading toward her room.

Heidi was the last one lingering, dragging her feet like bedtime was the end of the world. She wrapped her little arms around him, face buried in his shoulder.

"Can you come back tomorrow?" she asked in a tiny voice.

"I'll have to ask Niv first," he told her, glancing at me with that smug look like he knew exactly what he was doing. "But if she says yes, then of course, and we can play dolls."

Her eyes lit up instantly. "Yay!"

Then she whipped her head toward me. "Niv, please say yes!"

Before I could even respond, she kissed his cheek, grinned, and skipped off to her room, leaving me standing there with my arms crossed, staring at the man who'd just walked all up into my space and got my people loving him in a matter of hours.

The second Heidi's bedroom door clicked shut, I turned toward Kendrix, ready to start in on him. He was still sitting there on my couch, looking way too comfortable like it was his spot. One arm stretched across the back cushion, legs spread, the faintest smirk pulling at his mouth like he'd just won something.

"What the fuck was that?" I asked, my voice low so the kids wouldn't hear.

He just shrugged. "What was what?"

"Walking in here like you pay bills and getting them all up under you like that?"

"I didn't know I wasn't allowed to meet your family," he said, leaning forward, elbows on his knees. "They like me. You like me. Feels like we're already halfway there."

I laughed once. "Halfway where? You really think you can just show up at my house, charm my people, and that's gonna get you in good with me?"

"Looks like it's working."

The nerve.

I crossed my arms, holding my ground. "Kendrix, you got lucky tonight. That's all. Don't make this into something it's not."

He tilted his head, eyes locked on mine in that way that made my stomach flip, no matter how much I hated it. "See, that's the thing, Niv. You talk like I'm trying to pull something, when all I'm doing is showing you where I fit. And I do fit, here. With them. With you."

For a second, I didn't even have a comeback. I hated that he could do that—slip under my skin and settle in before I even realized it.

I broke eye contact first, walking past him toward the kitchen like I needed a drink, when really I just needed space.

"You should go," I said over my shoulder.

He didn't even flinch. "Come home with me."

My head snapped toward him. "The fuck you just say?"

"I already talked to Rita."

My eyes widened. "Damn... you met Rita too? I thought somebody in this damn house had some sense."

He smirked, slow and unbothered. "I told her to get some rest while I was here, and I stayed up with the kids. I already told her you were coming back to my place with me."

I blinked at him. "I don't know why the fuck you did that, because I'm not going anywhere."

That's when his whole vibe shifted. "You can go willingly, or forcibly. Your choice."

That should've made me take a step back. Instead, every nerve in my body lit up like he'd flipped a damn switch. My thighs pressed together without permission, because if there's one thing I hate and love all at once, it's a man telling me what he's about to do with the kind of certainty that doesn't leave room for a no.

He must've seen the heat in my face because his tone softened as he took a step closer. "You wanna know why I came over here?"

"Please enlighten me."

"I just wanted to take a minute to step inside your world without you being around. Get to know the kids a little. See them for myself, not just through you."

That hit somewhere I wasn't ready to acknowledge. So I threw up a wall. "You mean lie to Heidi about playing dolls?"

He shook his head, no smile this time. "Not a lie. I used to play dolls with my niece all the time. Ain't no shame in it. She loved that shit and so did I."

That... did something to me.

He ran a hand over his jaw. "I never had sisters, but I always wanted one. Being around them tonight—it's right up my alley. And it's easy to see why you go so hard for them."

My chest tightened. Damn him. He was supposed to be the one chasing, but here I was trying not to melt.

Before I could think of another smartass remark, he stepped into my space and wrapped his arms around me. The heat from his body, the weight of his hands at my back. It was ridiculous how fast my shoulders relaxed, like my body decided on its own that it trusted him.

"You can relax, Niv," he murmured.

And I did. Then he kissed me.

It wasn't rushed. It wasn't tentative, either. It was slow enough for me to taste him, deep enough to make my knees weaken. My hands slid up his chest before I even realized they were moving.

"Come home with me," he whispered against my lips.

That time, I kissed him back. Harder. His hands went to my hips, and in one smooth move he picked me up and set me on the counter, his mouth claiming mine again. The heat between us got hot, fast.

"Kendrix—" I broke the kiss, breathless. "The kids."

"I told you to come to my place," he said, brushing his mouth against my ear. "Either that, or the kids are gonna hear you screaming my name."

My pulse slammed against my throat. His grip on my thighs tightened, his eyes holding mine like he already knew what my answer would be.

25

Kendrix

Pulling into my driveway felt different. She'd been there before, but only for me to grab something real quick before we dipped out again.

The headlights swept over the front of the house, all that glass and stone staring back at me like it was trying to prove something. Big. Empty. Expensive. The kind of place people brag about but don't actually live in.

She'd once joked, *"Damn, this big ol' house for just you?"* and I'd laughed it off. But sitting in her living room earlier, listening to her kids laugh, smelling food in the kitchen, hearing the little everyday noises? That shit hit different. Her place wasn't big, but it felt full. Alive. Peaceful.

My house was quiet enough to hear your own thoughts, and sometimes that's the last thing you wanna do. It could swallow a man whole if he wasn't careful.

I cut the engine and looked over at her.

"So..." I started, leaning back in my seat.

Her shoulders relaxed like she was ready for whatever slick shit I was about to say.

"There was this girl..."

Her head turned fast, attitude slipping right out of her face like she hadn't seen that one coming. Those eyes locked on me, sharp and curious.

"My first love. We met in high school. You know, that type of love where you really think you're gone marry each other, grow old together, the whole movie script."

She didn't say anything, but I could feel her watching me.

"We had it all planned out. College, careers, kids. Everything. Then one day she told me she was pregnant. She hadn't told her parents yet, so I hadn't told mine. We were still figuring out how to even be grown enough for that. And before we could... she got in an accident."

I stopped for a second, jaw tightening. "Killed her. And the baby."

The car felt smaller all of a sudden, like the walls were pressing in. "My family... they knew I was grieving her. But they didn't know the whole story. They didn't know I lost both of them that day. I kept that part to myself, because I didn't want the pity or the questions."

I finally turned to look at her. "Since then, I've never given anybody the title of girlfriend. Not because I didn't want to... but because giving it meant letting her go. And I couldn't. Not for a long time."

Her expression softened, but I kept going.

"With Arlette... I ain't like her like that. Not the way you think. But when she had her accident and lost the baby, it hit me in a way I can't explain. It pulled me right back to that night. Made me feel like I had to step up for her in ways I couldn't for my first love, like I was making up for the past. It was fucked up, but it was how my mind worked."

I dragged a hand over my beard. "That's the truth about why I haven't made shit official yet. I'm scared, Niv. Scared of forgetting her. And even more scared of losing you."

Her lips parted, like she was about to say something, but I beat her to it.

"Because the shit I feel for you?" My voice dropped. "I didn't even feel it with her. And if losing her hurt me like it did... I can't imagine what it'll do to me if you ever walk away."

"It's okay. I never want you to forget her... she was a part of you."

She watched me, waiting to see if I'd fold. I didn't. I just shut up and let her talk.

"Since you told me the truth," she said, "I'll tell you why I don't move without a title."

Her eyes went somewhere past the windshield.

"I was sixteen. He was... grown. He kept my lights on, filled my fridge, bought me shoes. I thought I was safe because I was provided for." She huffed. "One night, he put a duffel in my closet. Said it was clothes, and told me don't touch it. So, I didn't."

She swallowed. "A week later, there's banging on the door at six in the morning. Not a knock, banging. Two cops, a third behind them with gloves. Hux is half-asleep in a Ninja Turtles tee, scared. Mama's on the couch half high, acting lost. They said they had a warrant because paperwork ties my name to a storage unit and a P.O. box that wasn't even mine. Guess who set it up? Guess who used my phone number and my mama's address?"

My hand flexed on the steering wheel.

"They went through my underwear drawer. Dumped my backpack out like I was a grown man moving weight. Pulled that duffel from my closet, and it wasn't clothes. It was cash and pills he stashed." She shook her head. "You ever had a cop hold your bra up with two fingers in front of your little brother? You ever had your neighbors watch you get put in handcuffs on your own porch while somebody whispers 'I knew she'd end up like that' like you planned it?"

My stomach went cold.

"Ty's uncle is the only reason I don't have a record. He showed receipts—my school schedule, my timecards, proved I never went near that storage unit. But for three weeks, I was the girl who might be a felon. The guidance counselor wouldn't look me in the eye. My manager at McDonalds 'lost' my hours. CPS did a 'wellness check' because there was another minor in the home." She looked at me. "Do you know what it feels like to have a stranger take pictures of the mold in your shower and the food in your fridge like they're deciding if your family is worth keeping together?"

I didn't breathe.

"That day, I wrote rules," she said. "No man parks anything in my house, my name, or my peace. No situationships. If I can't introduce you with a title, you don't get access to my address. If there's no claim, there's no claim on me. Because when shit hits the fan, the only thing the world recognizes is paper. Titles. Contracts. Accountability with a signature."

She tilted her head, eyes cutting into me. "People think 'titles' are romantic. It's not. It's governance. It's who the hospital calls. Who's on the lease. Who has keys, codes, and obligations on record. No title means plausible deniability. I don't date deniability, Kendrix."

Silence sat heavy between us.

"When a man keeps you in the gray, he keeps you disposable. I survived being disposable once. I'm not gambling my kids' stability on a man's comfort ever again. If you want me, it costs clarity."

I stared at her, and everything in me rearranged. The anger I felt for that man; the respect I felt for her was cold and solid. She wasn't being difficult. She was protecting a life she built brick by brick after somebody almost used her as a blueprint for a charge.

"Now you see why I demand a title," she finished, calm. "It's not a crown. It's a seatbelt."

I nodded slow. "Yeah," I said.. "I see why."

I didn't toss her a pretty promise. Didn't spit out "be my girlfriend" like a bandage in a driveway. I let the weight of what she said settle where it needed to: in my plans.

I reached for her hand. "If my name touches your life, it's gonna mean something on paper and in practice," I told her. "I'm not here to keep you gray."

She shifted in the seat, fingers tracing the seam of her jeans.

"I want to tell you something before we go any further."

My eyes cut over to her.

"I met Sincere when I was eighteen," she started. "He's the one who took me to my first strip club. He taught me the game—not just how to dance, but how to make my intellect cash checks just as easy as my ass could."

I didn't move, just listened.

She leaned back like the memory was playing in front of her. "I already had the body. Already knew how to move. But he sharpened my mind for this shit. I grew up around things that made me wise before my time, and he showed me how to package that wisdom into leverage. And it worked. It's why I've been able to build the life I have."

My jaw tightened. Not because I didn't want to hear it, but because I could hear the truth in every word. The kind that comes from living it, not dressing it up.

"Sincere's never been someone I saw long-term," she said. "He's just... one of those people who was there from the start. Someone I'll always lean on when I need it."

Her eyes found mine and held. "He knows about you. He knows how I feel about you. So when it comes to him, there should never be a question."

There wasn't an ounce of hesitation in her face. No shifting eyes. No nervous smile. Just straight, uncut honesty aimed right at me.

"That's me being honest," she finished. "Giving you everything up front."

I just sat there, taking her in. That wasn't small talk. It was her putting the cards on the table and trusting I wouldn't flip them over to see if they matched. And for some reason, that hit me harder than I thought it would.

Her fingers threaded through mine like a test she decided I'd passed for now.

"Come on," I said, finally exhaling. "Let me get you inside."

We got out the truck and walked up to the house. She still had her hand in mine, so I unlocked the door and let her step in first.

The smell hit her before the sight did. Her head tilted. "Kendrix... what the hell is that smell? Smells like... cinnamon? And... Play-Doh?"

I bit back a grin. "You'll see."

We rounded the corner into the living room, and she stopped.

On my coffee table was the most ridiculous, crooked-ass diorama a grown man had ever made. Colored construction paper, glitter everywhere like a unicorn had a stomach virus, tiny plastic figurines standing on little cardboard cutouts I'd labeled in my own handwriting. At the center was a small cardboard stage I'd built, with a Barbie in a purple two-piece—cut from a piece of felt—standing in front of a crowd of mismatched LEGO men, Hot Wheels, and two GI Joes. Off to the side, I'd glued a Monopoly "title deed" card, but instead of "Boardwalk," I'd written in black Sharpie:

"Official Title: Girlfriend."
- *Applicant must be fine as hell* (checkmark drawn next to it)

- *Must own crown, not borrow it* (checkmark)

- *Must walk me like a dog when necessary* (checkmark)

- *Must be willing to accept bad arts-and-crafts proposals* (pending)

She stared at it for a solid thirty seconds before she looked at me. "You did not just..." Her voice cracked, but she was smiling.

"Hell yeah, I did," I said, keeping it light. "Look, I know you don't like cliche. I could've done roses or a dinner or one of those corny 'will you be mine' cakes. But that's not you. This?" I gestured to the ridiculous display. "This is the most 'you' shit I could think of. A little crazy, a little bold, and way too much glitter for a man my size to be buying at the craft store without people asking questions."

She laughed and I stepped closer.

"Niv, I get it now. Why you need clarity. Why you need a title before you let somebody in your space for real. And I'm telling you... I want to be that title. Not because I like you. Not because I want you. But because I love you."

Her smile faltered in that way where you know the other person's hearing something they've been waiting on without admitting it.

I pulled the crooked Monopoly card off the table and held it out. "So... Niveah Elise, will you be my girlfriend? My official girlfriend? On paper and in practice."

She took it slow, walked over, plucked the card from my fingers, looked at it like it was something worth framing. Her eyes got glassy, and she blinked fast, like she wasn't about to cry but also might.

"You really made a Barbie of me," she whispered, shaking her head.

"Yeah," I said, shrugging. "And I'm keeping it on the table so when people come over, I can say 'That's my girlfriend.'"

She laughed again, but this time it broke a little in the middle. She looked at me, serious. "Yes, Kendrix. And for the record... I love you too."

I didn't wait for her to overthink it. I just pulled her in, kissed her until her hand slid up the back of my neck and her body melted into mine.

Somewhere in the back of my mind, I thought about how a crooked, glitter-covered table in my too-big house just became the most important piece of furniture I owned.

She stepped into my bedroom and stopped dead in the doorway, eyes locking on the sleek chrome pole in the center of the room. The overhead lighting caught it just right, making it gleam like I'd polished it for the occasion.

Her mouth fell open in a slow grin. "Kendrix... you did not put a damn pole in your bedroom."

I leaned against the wall, arms folded. "I did. Just for you."

Her eyes shifted back to the pole, then to me. "If I dance for you... you gone behave?"

I tilted my head toward the bed. "Not a chance. But I'll sit still for now."

She bit her lip, grabbed her phone, and hooked it to my house Bluetooth. A soft static click filled the air before that slow, honey-dripped intro of *Love Language* by SZA floated through the speakers.

I sat back on the bed, leaning against the headboard, watching her move like I had all the time in the world.

Her hand wrapped around the pole, slow, her hips rolling in perfect sync with the beat. She didn't just dance. She told stories with her body, every sway and arch a sentence, every look she threw me a paragraph. That's what got me from the start. Her body spoke louder than most people's mouths, and I understood every damn word.

She let her fingers trail up the pole as she spun, that slow climb like she was measuring my patience. I knew exactly what she needed before she even did. I could tell by the flex of her shoulders, the way her breath hitched when she dipped low, the way her eyes held mine when she flipped upside down, thighs gripping chrome like it was an extension of herself.

Halfway through, I couldn't help it.

"Dance naked for me," I said.

Her eyes glinted in the dim light, but she didn't stop moving. She reached for the tie on her top and let it fall, her breasts spilling free in a way that made my pulse slam against my throat. The bottoms followed, sliding down those hips I'd dreamed about touching without barriers.

And then she was just... her. No layers. No armor. Every inch of her body mine to see. The raw and real version of Niveah Elise—unapologetic, unashamed, and somehow, even more beautiful like that than she was dressed to kill.

The chorus hit, SZA's voice floating.

Nobody put that purpose in me like you do,
Nobody get that work up out me like you do
Nobody get the truth up out me quite like you
You the definition of my right hand
Never mind riding backseat when you lead me...

She closed her eyes for a second like the lyrics were touching her too, then looked right at me. And it hit me, that was her love language. Not flowers, not dinners, not pretty words. *That.* Her body moving for me, speaking to me without a single syllable.

I thought I could only imagine a woman like her, someone who could challenge me, burn me alive, and still make me feel safe in the same breath. But she was real, standing bare in my room, and I was falling in love with her in ways I couldn't stop if I wanted to.

When she slid to the floor, still moving, still telling me things without saying them, I swung my legs off the bed. The second her feet hit the rug, I had her in my arms.

And the way she gasped when my mouth found her neck? That told me everything I needed to know.

The second her bare skin pressed to mine, something in me shifted.

Yeah, I wanted her. Hell, I needed her.

Her breath caught when my hands slid down her back, palms spreading over the curve of her ass. I pulled her closer until every inch of her lined up against me. She was still warm from the dance, skin flushed, heartbeat racing against my chest. I kissed her like I'd been starving for her for years.

I laid her back on the bed, the pole just feet away like a witness to what she'd started. My hands traced the same paths her body had taken during the dance—over her ribs, down the smooth plane of her stomach, around the dip of her hip. I wanted to memorize her the way she'd just told me to without words.

She looked at me, eyes dark, mouth parted. "Kendrix..."

"I'm here," I told her. "All the way."

I kissed down her body, slow enough to make her squirm, tasting her skin, feeling her tremble under my mouth. When I reached her thighs, I didn't rush. I wanted to watch her fall apart, to see the truth she'd never speak out loud.

My tongue slid against her, deliberate, and her hips jumped. She bit her lip hard, probably to keep from moaning, but I wasn't having it. I hooked her legs over my shoulders and went in deeper, flicking my tongue until her breath turned ragged and her hands fisted in the sheets.

"Kendrix..." This time it was almost a cry.

I looked up at her, chin wet, and said, "Say my name again when you cum."

It only took a few more seconds before she broke, hips grinding up into my mouth, that sweet, sharp sound spilling from her like she couldn't hold it in. I kept going, drawing it out until she was shaking, her thighs clamped tight around my head.

When I finally pulled back, she was breathing like she'd just run for her life. I crawled up over her, kissing her hard, letting her taste herself on my tongue.

And then I pushed inside her until we both groaned at the stretch.

Her nails dug into my shoulders, not to hurt but to anchor herself, and I started moving, steady at first, then harder, faster, until the rhythm felt like it matched the pounding in my chest. Every time her eyes met mine, it was like the rest of the world faded, and it was just us. Her body was telling me everything I needed to hear while mine answered back in the only way it knew how.

"Niv..." I rasped, holding her face so she couldn't look anywhere but at me. "I love you."

Her lips trembled, but she didn't look away. "I love you more."

That was it. The match to the gasoline I'd been holding in. I kissed her hard, gripping her like I was afraid she'd disappear, and drove into her until we both came undone.

When it was over, I didn't move right away. Just stayed there, inside her, forehead to forehead, catching my breath while my hands smoothed over her hair.

For the first time in a long time, I didn't feel like I was missing something.

She was everything.

26

Niveah

Three weeks.

Three whole weeks of nothing but *peace*.

Not that fake "we're good for now" peace, but the kind that sinks into your bones. The kind that feels like sunlight through your window on a Sunday morning.

Kendrix had been in my space so much, it was starting to feel like our space. Most nights he was at my house, falling asleep on my couch with Heidi tucked under one arm and Hux yelling at him from across the room during 2K. He swore he wasn't homesick, but I knew better. The man was only going home to feed his dog and make sure his house hadn't burned down.

So I flipped it.

One night, me and the kids surprised him. Showed up at his front door like we owned the place. I thought we'd spend the night, let him sleep in his own bed, eat his food, then head home. But that one night turned into three.

The kids ate like royalty, thanks to his chef. They swam until their fingers pruned up in that heated pool of his. They roamed that big house like it was Disneyland, and the way he looked at them—like they weren't mine, but ours—did something to me I didn't even want to admit out loud.

I even gave Rita a whole week off to go see her family.

And the craziest part was that it didn't feel like a chore. No stress, no weight on my back. Just me, the kids, and Kendrix holding it down without me having to ask.

It was like life decided to give me a break.

Even my mama was doing better. Heidi had seen her for the first time in almost a year, and she swore she was serious about rehab this time. I wanted to believe her. I really did.

Everything just... looked up.

And I knew exactly when it changed.

The moment I finally stepped to the side and let Kendrix in my world.

Not halfway. Not with the door cracked. All the way.

The house was quiet in the kind of way that told me everybody was either gone or settled, and for once, I didn't mind it. No kids running up and down the hall. No Ty calling my phone to ask if I approved the new bottle menu. Just me, my playlist, and the glow from my vanity mirror bouncing off the satin robe wrapped around me.

Kendrix had told me it was a birthday dinner for his mama, but the way everybody had been running around, the calls I'd overheard between him and his brothers, the way Mama G's friends had been moving, it was bigger. I just didn't know how big.

Turns out, they had been planning an event to honor her. Not just a party with cake and balloons, but a whole night dedicated to giving her flowers while she could still smell them. Everybody she loved and everybody who loved her was going to be there.

If I'm being honest, I loved that woman like she was my own. I'd spent hours with her, just listening. She told me her life story. Every high, every heartbreak, and every fight she had to fight. The way she opened up to me was rare. It made sense why those boys loved her like the sun. Mama G wasn't just a mom. She was the blueprint.

So when Kendrix asked me to be his date, it wasn't even a question. I was honored.

Matter fact, if he hadn't asked, I was still going to show up, and slap his ass for even thinking he could leave me out of something that important.

Per his request, we were both wearing purple. He said it was one of his mama's favorite colors. That alone told me it was about to be a night.

I had just stepped into my dress—deep purple silk that hugged in all the right places—when the door opened. Kendrix leaned against the frame for a second like he was taking me in before he walked over and put his hands on my waist.

"You don't even know what you do to me," he whispered, pulling me in until my back hit his chest. "I love you, Niv."

He said it like it was easy. Like it had always been there, sitting on his tongue, waiting for the right moment to fall out.

His lips found the side of my neck, and his hands smoothed over my hips, his reflection in the mirror catching the way I smirked.

"You look perfect," he said, brushing his fingers along the strap of my dress. "Purple looks good on you. Looks good with me."

And even though I'd never admit it out loud, the way we matched, the way it felt to be standing there with him before something so important...

It made me feel like I belonged in his world in a way I didn't even know I wanted.

His lips stayed at my neck, slow and warm. I could feel his smirk against my skin when I tilted my head just a little, letting him in without even meaning to.

"You keep looking at me like that, we're not gonna make it to this party," I teased, watching our reflection in the mirror.

"Maybe I don't want to," he said low, his voice in that tone that always messed with my head. His hands slid lower, catching the fabric of my dress and inching it up my thighs just enough to make my heart kick up.

I tried to stay steady, but my breathing was already changing. "Kendrix..."

He met my eyes in the mirror, that hooded look that said he was already thinking about how to ruin my makeup. "I've been in your space, with the kids, watching you, breathing you in... for three weeks straight. You really think I can stand this close and not touch you?"

I put the lipstick down before I ended up with a streak across my face. "And you really think I can be late to your mama's party because you don't know how to keep your hands to yourself?"

His grin deepened, the kind that meant he was two seconds from ignoring every word I just said. His fingers traced a slow path from my knee to my hip, his other hand locking around my waist. "One kiss. That's all I need."

That was a lie. And we both knew it.

He turned me around, caging me in against the vanity, and kissed me like the whole night didn't matter—just me and him. My hands ended up in his hair before I could think, pulling him closer, his tongue brushing mine in that way that made my knees weaken every time.

It would've been so easy to let him take it further. To let him strip that dress off and make us both late on purpose.

But the buzz of my phone from the vanity broke us apart just enough for reality to sneak back in.

"Kendrix," I said against his lips, breathing heavier than I wanted him to know. "We have to go."

He searched my face for a second, then stepped back with that cocky grin that told me this wasn't over. "Fine. But you're not getting away from me tonight."

I smirked, fixing my lipstick and grabbing my clutch. "I never said I wanted to."

When he held his hand out, I took it without hesitation.

The second we stepped out of the car, I knew Kendrix hadn't been exaggerating. The venue was damn near glowing under chandeliers that looked like they belonged in a movie. Long tables were draped in white linen with centerpieces so big you couldn't see the person across from you without doing that little side-to-side lean. Everything smelled faintly like roses and money, two of my favorite scents.

It was still early, so most of the seats were empty, but the setup alone was enough to make you stop for a second just to appreciate it. The kind of event that made you double-check your lipstick in your phone camera, even though you just did it in the car.

Security stood at the front like they were guarding a bank vault. As soon as we got to the front of the line, one of them gave me that polite-but-serious look before motioning for my bag. I handed it over without fuss, but my eyes followed every move. When they pulled my gun out like it was a rogue chapstick, I smirked.

"Ma'am, I'll have to take this to the car for you," one of Kendrix's men said.

I tilted my head toward Kendrix. "I hate going places unstrapped. My hands work just fine, but you never know."

He looped his arm through mine, smirking. "You're good. It's for safety. We've got a lot of my parents' friends here tonight. People in high positions, so no weapons inside."

I smiled sweetly. "It's okay. I keep someone strapped to my thigh."

He laughed because he knew I wasn't bluffing. I never went anywhere without my knife.

We stepped past the checkpoint and into the main hall, and for a second, I forgot to walk. It was like stepping into a dream you'd never had, but if you had, it would've been exactly that. The lighting was warm and flattering, like it knew its job was to make every Black woman in the building look ten shades richer. Gold accents caught the light just right, and the music floating through the air was soft enough not to drown conversation but smooth enough to make you sway when you walked.

We made our way to the front table where his brothers were already posted up. Kross had his arm draped over Rivah's chair, and Kairo was halfway through clowning Khloe about something she said. It was the kind of loud, easy laughter that made you feel welcome before you even sat down. Kendrix pulled my chair out for me, and the second I sat, Khloe leaned in and whispered, "Girl, you clean up nice. Purple's dangerous on you."

Before I could respond, Mama G walked in.

All white from head to toe, skin glowing like she was lit from within. Her smile was so wide it damn near touched her ears, eyes glistening as she took in the room. You could tell she knew the night was for her, but the way she gasped and put her hand over her chest made it clear she hadn't expected that much.

The woman worked the room like a champ. Hugging, kissing, laughing, talking her shit to old friends and strangers alike. She stopped to tell one couple they hadn't aged a day and another that they had, but "in a cute way."

When she made it to our table, Kendrix pulled her in for a hug. "Where's Dad?"

She rolled her eyes but grinned. "He's coming. Had to run to the restroom. You know how men are when they're tryna make a good impression. He's probably in there giving himself a pep talk in the mirror."

Everyone at the table cracked up.

Kendrix leaned closer, his hand brushing against mine under the table. "You good?"

I turned my head toward him. "Yeah," I said softly. And it was true, or at least it was before my heart started doing that flutter thing. Not because I was nervous, but because it was one of his habits. Always checking on me, even in a room full of people. That kind of care snuck up on you.

Before I could even get lost in that thought, Mama G's face lit up. "Oh, Kendrix, there he is."

Kendrix turned in his chair, then stood. "Dad!" he called, his whole face brightening.

I turned too, catching sight of a tall man in a dark suit making his way toward us. Kendrix put his hand at the small of my back as he said, "Dad, this is my girlfriend, Niveah. Niveah, this is my dad."

"So... we finally meet face-to-face," he said, his voice deep and familiar in a way that made my skin prickle. "No more over-the-phone conversations."

I rose to my feet automatically, smiling as I extended my hand...

...and then I saw him.

The smile slid clean off my face. My stomach dropped so fast it felt like the floor gave out under me. I'd know that face anywhere. Even in my worst nightmares, it was there.

My hand, still hanging in the air, trembled. Then I dropped it before he could touch me.

And in that split second, my mind was racing, clawing at memories I'd tried to bury. Memories that had voices. His voice. It couldn't be the man I'd spoken to over the phone, the one whose laugh I'd gotten used to hearing, the one who'd traded sarcastic little jabs with me until the line between banter and something warmer blurred. This couldn't be the same man—God help me—who kept saying he was glad that his son had me in his life.

The table went quiet, confusion thick in the air. My mouth moved, but no words came.

Kendrix stepped closer. "Baby... what's wrong?"

My chest was tight. I could barely breathe. My voice finally broke through, raw and shaking. "You ruined my life."

The words were out before I could stop them.

Kendrix's brows pulled together. "What?"

"You ruined my life," I said again, louder this time. My voice cracked on the third repeat. "You... ruined my life."

The man, his father, just stood there, looking at me like he didn't know me. Like I was crazy. And that look made it worse.

"You ruined my life!" I screamed it and every head in the room turning toward us. Forks clinked against plates. Conversations stopped mid-sentence.

He put his hands up slightly, his voice low, like he was trying to soothe me. "Alright, let's calm down—"

"Calm down?!" I could taste the blood pounding in my mouth. My vision tunneled. All I could see was red.

He took a step toward me. That was all it took.

Before anyone could register what was happening, I reached down to my thigh, my fingers curling around the cold steel I always kept strapped there.

The rest was a blur... just motion and heat. I lunged, the knife flashing once under the soft lights before it buried into him. I didn't even think about where it landed. I just kept going and stabbing wherever I could reach, my breath ragged, my hand sure.

The sound of people screaming, chairs scraping the floor, someone shouting "Kendrix!" All of it blurred into the background. In that moment, there was no party. No crowd. No music. Just me. Him. And the years of rage that had been waiting for that exact second.

Mama G's scream ripped through the room like glass shattering. She dropped to her knees beside her husband, her white dress instantly stained with the deep red pouring from him. Her hands shook as she tried to press against the wounds, sobbing, her voice cracking, "What did you do? Oh my God, what did you do?!"

Kendrix stood frozen for a moment, his mind refusing to catch up with his eyes. The woman he loved was the one on top of his father with a knife still dripping in my hand. He moved, instinct taking over, but when he grabbed for me, I thrashed so hard that he lost his grip.

He didn't even realize he'd let me go until I was stumbling backward, chest heaving.

His brothers came running. Kross dropped to their mother's side, holding her up as she tried to stop the bleeding. Kairo bent over their father, his hands shaking as he applied pressure, his face twisted between rage and fear.

The rest of the room was chaos. Chairs clattering over, glass shattering, heels pounding the floor as people ran screaming for the exit.

Rivah was the first to reach me. She pushed me back, out of the circle of carnage, her own hands streaking with red as she caught me by the arms. Khloe moved slower, her eyes locked on the knife. "Niv," she said softly, "hand it to me, baby. Just give me the knife."

My chest was heaving, tears streaming down my face, but my eyes... my eyes were locked on *him*.

The man on the floor. The man I'd waited years to see again—not for closure, not for healing, but for this.

My voice shook, but it was steady enough for the whole damn room to hear. "You ruined my life," I said, voice breaking halfway through. "My mama was gonna get better. She was gonna beat it. She just needed time, not drugs. But you—" My whole body was trembling "—you gave her that shit. You put it in her hand and you smiled about it. She's been chasing that first high since I was twelve."

Mama G's head whipped toward me, her face streaked with tears, her voice almost unrecognizable. "Why would you—why would you do this?!"

Kendrix's brothers moved like they might rush me. Kairo's jaw was tight. Kross's hands were curling into fists. But one look at Kendrix stopped them cold. He wasn't even speaking, but the warning was in his face—*don't touch her*.

My grip on the knife loosened just enough for Khloe to slide it from her fingers. Rivah still had me by the shoulders while I cried with my whole body shaking.

Kendrix wanted to come comfort me. God, he wanted to. I could tell by his body language. But his father was on the floor bleeding out, his mother sobbing into his suit jacket, and the sound of EMTs rushing in was loud enough to drown out every thought in his head.

Security swarmed the room. The EMTs went straight to Kendrix's father, cutting his shirt away, calling out vitals. Then two uniformed officers moved toward me.

Rivah stepped in front of me instinctively, but they shoved her aside so hard she hit the ground.

It was like the same story I had told Kendrix just weeks ago—the one about my ex, the one about being cornered at sixteen, manhandled like I was the biggest criminal on the block. That memory slammed into me as they grabbed my arms and forced me to the ground, their knees pressing into my back, their hands forcing my wrists behind me.

This time was different, though.

This time, I'd done something. Something bad.

And I didn't regret a single second of it.

Lying there with my cheek pressed to the cold floor, I could still see him out of the corner of my eye. The man who had played God with my family. The man who destroyed my mother and left her a child to pick up the pieces.

He wasn't untouchable anymore.

And for the first time in years, that made her feel whole.

27

Kendrix

The police were taking her out.

I couldn't hear anything. Not the radios, not the sirens outside, not even the gasps and murmurs still floating through the air from the people who'd stayed behind to watch the train wreck unfold.

All I could hear was my own heartbeat in my ears.

I followed behind the cops, every step feeling like my body wasn't mine. My eyes stayed locked on her. Niv. My Niv.

She wasn't fighting. Wasn't yelling anymore. Just crying. The kind of tears that break you from the inside out. And she was looking at me. Like she wanted me to see her. Like she wanted to say she was sorry without having to form the words.

And I got it.

But God, Niv... why?

Why couldn't you have just told me?

We could've found another way.

I would've found another way.

Now I was walking behind two people I couldn't imagine my life without. The woman I love and the man who brought me into this world, and knowing there was no way my family would ever come back from this.

Hell, I don't even know if *we* could.

My family would hate me for loving her. And I wasn't even sure if loving her would be enough after this.

We made it outside and the night air hit me with a slap full of reality. The flashing lights painted everything red and blue, and the moment felt like something out of a nightmare.

That's when I heard it.

"Niv!"

Hux came running from across the lot, Zejah right behind him. The kid's eyes were wet, his chest heaving like he'd been crying for a while already. But the second he saw her, saw the blood on her hands and shirt, saw her cuffed and flanked by cops, he stopped dead in his tracks.

And Niv, she broke.

Her whole body caved in, her cries turning into full sobs. Because she knew what that sight was doing to him.

All he saw was blood.

All he saw was his sister like that.

I moved fast, cutting across to him before he could get closer.

"What's going on?!" Hux demanded, his voice cracking.

"Don't worry about it," I told him, grabbing his arm. "Just get out of here—"

"No!" he yelled, jerking against my grip. "I need to talk to my sister!"

He was pulling hard, fighting me, his voice getting louder and more desperate, and the last thing I was about to let happen was him running at the cops and getting himself slammed to the ground.

"Hux, stop—"

"What's wrong?!" Niv's voice tore through the chaos. She was crying harder now, twisting to try to see him.

And then it happened.

Hux's knees buckled and he hit the ground, his palms slapping against the cold pavement. His face crumpled like he'd been holding something in and couldn't anymore.

Zejah's scream cut through me like a blade. "We've been trying to call you! My sister said your mom overdosed!"

The words punched the air out of my lungs.

Niv froze. And then I watched it hit her. Every ounce of pain, fear, guilt, and love for her mom, all at once. Her cry was the kind of sound you never forget.

It was like the world just... stopped.

The cops still had her arms, still moving her toward the car, but Niv wasn't walking anymore. She was thrashing, jerking, her voice ripping through the night.

"No! No! No, no, no—"

It wasn't a word anymore, just a sound. A raw, ugly sound that made every head turn.

Her whole body was fighting the air, fighting fate, fighting the truth she'd just been hit with. She was kicking against nothing, twisting like if she just moved hard enough, she could undo it all.

I grabbed Hux and Zejah and pulled them into me. Hux was shaking, his face buried in my shirt, Zejah's sobs rattling through her tiny chest. My arms were tight around them, but my eyes—my eyes never left Niv.

I wanted to go to her.

God, I wanted to run and take her out of their hands, wrap her up and tell her it was going to be okay.

But it wasn't okay.

Not even close.

She'd just put a knife in my father. My father. My flesh and blood. The man I'd looked up to my whole damn life.

And still... still, I looked at her like she was mine.

Because in a matter of minutes, the love of my life had lost everything.

Her freedom.

Her mom.

And those kids she'd risked her whole life to protect.

She caught my eyes through the chaos, through her fight against the cops, and for a split second she wasn't screaming. She was just looking.

Looking at me like I was the last thing tethering her to earth.

And I knew... nothing I could say, nothing I could do, would ever make that moment go away. For either of us.

28

Niveah

The cuffs cut deeper the longer I sat there, metal biting into my wrists with every bump in the road. My skin burned, but I didn't flinch. Pain was nothing compared to the fire in my chest. Compared to the sight of Kendrix's face when I did it.

I stabbed his dad.

And God help me, I wasn't sorry. I loved it.

The second that blade sank in, it was like every memory of my mama spiraling, every night I held Hux and lied that everything would be okay, every demon that man handed to us split wide open. For once, I wasn't helpless. For once, I got to put my hands on the devil instead of him always putting his hands on me.

But, the way Kendrix looked at me... He looked at me like the earth had caved in beneath his feet. That was the part that hurt me. The part I didn't love.

How do you explain to the man you love that his father ruined your life? That the only reason your mama ever started using was because of him. That every past due bill, every night without lights, every time you had to step up and play mama before your time, traced back to the man who created and raised him.

I pressed my forehead to the window, watching the streetlights smear into streaks, and whispered to myself, *"How do I love you, Kendrix, when you come from the man I hate?"*

Zejah's voice kept echoing in my ears. *"Your mom overdosed."*

That one line hit harder than the cuffs, harder than the blood, harder than the screams.

My mama had overdosed while I was in the back of a squad car, fighting with my own mind.

What kind of daughter am I? What kind of woman?

I wanted to laugh, bitter and broken. Women like me don't get happy endings. We get mugshots, court dates, and the kind of love that turns into collateral damage. I finally let someone in and the first thing I did was paint his mama's white dress red with her husband's blood.

And the worst part was that I'd do it again.

I closed my eyes, fighting the tears burning behind them, but Kendrix's face wouldn't leave me. That hurt in his eyes. That confusion. That love still hanging there, even though I didn't deserve it.

I didn't want revenge anymore. I didn't want to be the baddest bitch in the room.

I just wanted him, but I knew I'd lost him.

I whispered a prayer I wasn't even sure I meant.

"God... if nothing else, don't let him forget me. Don't let him forget us. Let him hate me. Let him cuss my name until his tongue bleeds. Let him walk past me one day like I'm a stranger. But don't let him forget the way we loved. The way we laughed. The way we made each other feel alive."

My voice cracked, but I kept whispering.

"Don't let him forget the nights he swore he saw himself in me. Don't let him forget that I tore my walls down for him when I never trusted noone else enough to. Don't let him forget my body in his hands, my mouth on his ear telling him he was mine. Don't let him forget that for one moment in this dirty world, I was his peace and he was mine."

Tears burned but I refused to close my eyes.

"Because if Kendrix forgets us? If what we had turns to dust in his memory? Then what the hell was all this pain for?"

The squad car slowed, pulling into the jail's lot, the flashing red-and-blue lights bouncing off concrete walls and barbed wire like a damn movie scene. My stomach didn't flip, not once.

They opened the door and helped me out. My shoulders rolled back, chin lifted. I wasn't scared. I couldn't be. If somebody tried me on the inside, I'd beat their ass and smile about it. That was the least of my worries.

What ate at me was what I wasn't doing. I wasn't at home, holding my sister while she painted her nails and laughed at youtube videos. I wasn't checking in on Hux, making sure his little hotheaded ass didn't run into trouble. I wasn't at the hospital figuring out if I was about to bury my mama or help plan her rehab.

Every step I took into that building, all I could think was *I should be anywhere but here.*

I should be in somebody's waiting room, demanding to know my mama's condition. I should be whispering a game plan with Rita about possible funeral clothes and phone calls "just in case." I should be figuring out how the hell to hold my family together when all of us were crumbling.

But instead, I was being escorted across dirty-ass jail floors, past women looking just as dirty. They stared like fresh meat had just walked in, and I stared right back.

Let one of y'all try me. Just one.

What scared me was the thought of my siblings' eyes when they realized their big sister wasn't there to keep shit together.

They walked me through intake like I was nothing but a case number. Shoes gone, jewelry gone, fingerprints pressed into some machine like I was buying groceries instead of about to sit behind bars. Then, the mugshot. Bright-ass flash. I tilted my head just right because fuck it, if my face was about to live in the system, it wasn't about to be ugly. My kids weren't gone look me up one day and see me looking like life dragged me. Hell naw.

"Next." They shoved me toward holding. Steel doors buzzed open, and the stank hit me first—sweat, perfume, nerves, and a whole lot of life choices gone wrong.

"Bitch... Niv?"

I squinted. "Toni? Girl, I know the fuck not."

She was sitting there on the bench, hair wild, one lash halfway to glory, the other hanging on for dear life.

"What you in here for?" I asked, sliding onto the bench across from her.

She sniffled. "I cheated on my husband."

The whole cell got quiet.

I rolled my eyes. "That ain't illegal, dumbass."

She sniffled harder. "With his mamma."

The whole cell erupted like Showtime at the Apollo. Even the chick in the corner with her head wrapped in toilet paper looked up and hollered.

Toni kept going, tears streaming. "And when he left me, I trashed her house and keyed his car. That's why I'm in here."

Some chick yelled from the back, "Bitch, you a family terrorist."

Another said, "Not you fucking yo' man mama. You need Jesus and a therapist, hoe."

I shook my head. "Toni, you've been toxic since middle school. Still unhinged, but I'm glad to see consistency, though."

Everybody screamed laughing.

Then another girl with braids down her back jumped in. "Please. My baby daddy married my cousin, so I poured bleach in all his Jordans. That's why I'm here."

The room gasped like it was a horror movie.

"Bitch, not the J's!"

She said, "Yes, the J's. Every pair. Even the Space Jams."

One woman clutched her chest like she'd just been shot. "You going straight to hell for that."

Another chick piped up: "Shit, I'm in here 'cause I fought my boss at Popeyes. Bitch told me I couldn't take a ten-minute break. I said bet. Clocked out and clocked her ass instead."

The cell exploded again. Somebody yelled, "Did she at least give you some chicken to go?"

"Nah, but I grabbed a biscuit on the way out."

By then, my stomach hurt from laughing.

One chick in the corner suddenly spoke up.

"Y'all stories weak. I got y'all beat."

We all looked over at her. She was pale, sweating, sitting next to the trash can like it was her emotional support pet.

"I went on a high-speed chase."

Everybody gasped.

I leaned forward. "Bitch, you WHAT?"

She nodded, dead serious. "Police got behind me, lights flashing. I thought it was a race. Like... NASCAR. I hit 110 down the freeway. Whole time, I'm drunk off Casamigos thinking they tryna see what my car could do."

The whole cell fell out.

I wiped a tear. "So... so what happened?"

She burped, then grabbed the trash can and threw up again before answering. "They... they didn't wanna race. They wanted me to stop."

"NO SHIT!" somebody screamed from the back.

Another chick hollered, "This bitch thought she was in *Fast & Furious*."

The whole room exploded in laughter again. She just sat there looking pitiful, whispering, "I woulda won, too, if I ain't hit that curb." Then she gagged and threw up again.

I couldn't breathe. My stomach hurt from laughing so hard.

I damn near fell off the bench.

It was like group therapy for the ghetto and the unhinged. Women telling war stories like they were in combat, just fighting different enemies.

Toni, the loudest one in the corner with the biggest laugh, wiped her eyes and leaned toward me.

"Okay, Niv. You sitting up here clowning everybody else. What you in for?"

The whole room got quiet, waiting.

I leaned back, smirk tugging at my lips. "I stabbed a man. My man's father. At his mama's birthday event. In front of him, his brothers, their women, the whole family."

Silence.

They all just stared at me like I'd dropped a dead body in the middle of the room.

I laughed, because hell, what else was I supposed to do? "What, y'all quiet now? Don't tell me y'all can laugh about high speed chases and biscuits, but not this."

A skinny chick with braids, pushed off the wall and pointed at my hands. "Oh, girl ... you crazy. You know how men get about they daddies."

I smirked. "Yeah. And you know how daughters get about their mamas."

Another one sucked her teeth. "That ain't no regular fight. That's attempted murder."

Somebody else shouted, "That's why your hands are red, bitch? That's blood!"

The whole room shifted away from me like I had the plague.

I looked down at my hands. Stained and crusted. The blood I'd been too numb to notice. The blood of the man who made my mother an addict, who made my childhood hell, who made me into this.

The women got quiet again, some side-eyeing, some nodding like they understood, others looking at me like they never wanted to be on my bad side.

The holding cell door creaked open. A cop stood there with his clipboard. "Niveah Jones."

I looked up, confused. All the women turned to me like *huh?*

"Come with me. You have a visitor," he said.

The girls started muttering.

"Visitor?" Toni snapped, standing like she was ready to protest. "Hold up—*visitor*? I been in here since this morning, and I can't even get a damn phone call. But she gets a visitor?"

The cop didn't even flinch. "It isn't phone time yet."

Another woman with lashes lifting at the corners rolled her eyes. "Nah, this some bullshit. She got blood still on her hands and she getting company?"

The whole cell started grumbling, women cussing under their breath. One chick banged on the bench. "Yeah, where my visitor at, huh?"

The cop didn't bother turning around, just motioned for me. "Let's go."

They groaned in unison. *"This some bullshit!"*

The walk down that hallway felt longer than the entirety of the day until this moment. I kept my head high, though. Part of me was ready to see Kendrix. Mad, hurt, maybe even disgusted...but at least him showing up meant something. Comfort in the middle of all the chaos. I wouldn't even have been mad if he cussed me out. Him coming would've been enough.

The cop opened the visitation room door and I stepped inside, bracing myself for Kendrix.

But it wasn't him.

It was her.

MammaG.

Sitting stiff in the chair, still in that white dress, the one now ruined with blood stains. She hadn't even changed. Her makeup was smeared down her face like streaks of war paint. Fear, hurt, and rage all in her eyes.

My stomach dropped. "Oh, fuck naw..." I muttered, instinctively stepping back, but the officer pushed me forward and shut the door behind us, locking it with a loud *clank*.

Just us two.

"Sit the fuck down."

It wasn't loud. It wasn't angry. It was calm, measured, and chilling. The kind of calm that made you realize you're not in control anymore. I sat down without another word.

She didn't waste time. Her eyes stayed on me, unblinking. "After everything I've done and been through for that man. I can't wrap my head around the fact that someone else thought they had the right to take him from me?" She leaned forward, her blood-stained dress shifting under the light. "If anyone was going to take him out, it would've been me."

Her words landed like a blade pressed against my throat.

I swallowed hard, trying to form something—anything. "MammaG...he ruined my life. It wasn't towards you, it wasn't towards Kendrix, it was—"

"Shut the fuck up," she snapped.

And I did. That shocked me more than anything—me, quiet. But there was something in her voice, a weight that made me realize I couldn't win this round. So I sat there, staring, my pulse racing, listening.

She leaned back, her voice steady as ever. "My husband is in surgery. There's nothing I can do for him right now except sit with my sons and wait for an update. And I couldn't do that, not yet. I had to handle some business first." Her eyes locked on mine. "You."

I blinked, my throat tight, waiting.

"I don't hate you for what you did," she said finally, and for a moment, I almost believed her. "He did something horrible to your family. He deserved some type of consequence." Her voice dropped. "But what I don't like is that you think you're God. Instead of being an adult, instead of handling it with your mind—you went with your hands. You stabbed a man in broad daylight, in front of his friends and his family. And you think that's strength?"

Her lip curled. "That's not grown, Niveah. That's what dumb asses do. They act off their feet. They think it makes sense. Not realizing they've just ruined their whole damn life."

Her words cracked me open in a way fists never could.

"You talk about those kids so much," she went on, softer now, but it cut even deeper. "How you sacrifice for them. How you're building something better for them. And yet, you did the one thing guaranteed to make it worse. Who's gonna hold them down now? Who's gonna guide them while you sitting in a cage? Tell me that, huh?"

Her stare pinned me in place. I wanted to argue, to spit back something, but all I could do was sit there with my jaw tight, eyes stinging, realizing she wasn't wrong.

Her eyes locked into me like she was reading every thought before I even said it.

"I know about Huxley. About Heidi. About little Zejah," she said. My stomach dropped.

"I'll get you free. But you give me your word that those kids will never, ever, see the inside of a jailhouse because of your temper. You want to protect them?

Then prove it by learning to control yourself. Be their anchor, Niveah. Not their downfall."

It felt like she had her hand wrapped around my soft spot. My weakness. My kids.

She leaned in closer. "The DA will look the other way. The witnesses will forget what they saw. Those cameras? They'll get lost. You'll walk out of here clean."

Mamma G's words didn't just land—they cracked me wide open.

Her voice was calm, her back straight, but her words? They were a sledgehammer.

"I know people who know people. You'll walk out of here like tonight never happened. But in return, you'll also walk away from my son."

For a second, I couldn't breathe. My chest rose and fell, but it felt like no air was reaching me.

Because she was right.

I loved Kendrix. God, I loved him so bad it scared me. But I loved Hux, Heidi, and Zejah. And I couldn't lose them. I couldn't be the reason they stood outside a jailhouse waiting on visits that would never fix the hole left in their hearts. I swore to them I'd make their lives different. And there I was, in jail, facing the reality that with one more wrong move, I'd be the storm that sank us all.

And it killed me because the choice wasn't fair.

I hated Kendrix's father. I hated that bastard with every bone in me. I hated the fact that he'd been allowed to smile and prosper while my mother rotted, chasing the first high he ever handed her. I hated that Kendrix didn't hate him too. That maybe he couldn't. That maybe the same blood that raised him was the same blood I wanted to drain out of a knife wound.

So, what did that make us? Oil and water. Fire and gasoline. Love and poison.

The tears slid down my cheeks before I could catch them. And I never cried. Not in front of anyone. But it was all too much.

How could I love Kendrix now, when every time I looked at him, I'd see the face of the man who destroyed me? How could I ever forgive him for not understanding? For not joining me in my hate?

"You want to protect them? Prove it," Mamma G said, her voice softer now but no less sharp. "Don't make me watch my son choose between the woman he loves and the family that he also loves. If you care about him, you'll let him go. Because this family will destroy you before we let you destroy us."

I bit my lip until it bled. My whole body trembled. Not from fear, but from rage. Rage at her. Rage at him. Rage at the world for forcing me into a choice that would break me, no matter which way I turned.

My freedom for my siblings, or my love for Kendrix.

And the truth was a knife in my throat:

I'd choose them every single time.

But God, it hurt. It hurt so fucking bad.

I shook my head so fast I thought my neck might snap. "I can't. I love him." My voice broke, spilling into a whisper. "I love him, Mamma G."

She didn't flinch. Didn't soften. She just slid her purse over her arm, smoothed her blood-stained dress like she was brushing away wrinkles, and said calmly, "Okay, then. I'll tell my friends there's no deal. Enjoy prison."

Her heels clicked, each step a countdown to the end of my life.

"No!" The word tore out of me, shaking the whole room. "No!" My body collapsed into the chair, sobs tearing through me like glass. I didn't cry pretty. I cried ugly, broken, loud. The type of cry that let you know your whole world just shattered.

Mamma G stopped at the door, turned just slightly, and for the first time I saw sympathy flickering in her eyes. Not pity, not hate. Just... sorrow.

"You are such a strong girl, Niveah. And I really like you. But all actions have consequences."

My throat burned. My heart bled out on the floor between us. "I'll do it," I rasped. My chest heaved like I was suffocating. "I'll walk away from Kendrix."

Her nod was small, sharp. "Good. You should be out later tonight. Lay low for about a week."

She turned again, ready to leave, and panic clawed up my throat.

"Wait." My voice cracked, but I pushed through it. "Can you—can you just be there for him? Please. He won't admit it, but he hates that house. It's too big, too empty. He told me once it feels like it swallows him, like he's drowning in it. He only keeps the lights on for the dog. That's how lonely he is."

I couldn't stop. The words rushed out, soft and desperate. "He doesn't eat right unless someone's in the kitchen talking to him. He'll tell you he likes silence, but he doesn't. Silence kills him. Don't let him sink in it."

Mamma G's eyes softened in a way I'd never seen. She stepped closer, her hand landing on my shoulder. For a second, I felt like a daughter instead of a criminal.

"I'll make sure he's fine," she whispered. "Thank you, Niv. Take care of yourself. And those kids."

Then she was gone, leaving me bleeding inside and more heartbroken than I'd ever been in my life.

29

Kendrix

Five weeks.

Thirty-five days.

Eight hundred and forty hours.

Fifty-thousand, four hundred minutes.

That's how long it'd been since I last saw her face. Since I saw her eyes on me, and even then, they were red and swollen, screaming something I couldn't fix.

I called. I texted. I damn near begged. Every day. Multiple times a day. Nothing. No replies, no call back, no "fuck you" text, no emoji, no cursing me out. Nothing. Silence.

I thought, stupidly, that dropping the charges would mean something. That if I could just get her out, she'd at least talk to me. Even if she cursed me from sun up to sundown, at least she'd be speaking to me. But my mom made me beg for it. Every day, I was at her house, on her phone, in her ear. I begged so much I think she just got tired of hearing me breathe. One day she sighed, rubbed her temples, and said, *"Fine. I'll make some calls. As long as you shut up about it."*

That was a week later.

Which meant, all I could picture was her sitting in that cold-ass cell for seven long days because of me. Because of my dad. Because of everything.

When she finally got out, I thought I'd have a chance. I pulled up to her house the second I got word somebody had seen her around. Rita came outside, arms folded, that firm-ass nanny stare like I was a trespasser. She said Niv didn't wanna see me. Said she didn't want to call the police on me, but she would if she had to. That cut deep.

I just wanted to see her. To touch her. To make sure she was breathing right.

I hit up Hux. He had nothing but short answers. *We're good. She's fine.* That's all I got. No detail. No openings for conversation. Just walls.

I tried to respect it, but how the fuck do you respect distance from someone who owns you?

And through it all, I was still trying to wrap my head around my dad. The shit he did... fucked me up. My father. The man I built my whole damn moral compass from. The man I followed like he was the ultimate hero. And now, I couldn't even say his name without tasting bile.

I kept telling myself I didn't understand why he was in Gun Hill all those years ago. He never had a reason to be there, so what was he doing? I heard my mom on the phone with her best friend one night. She was questioning it too.

And I'm stuck in the middle. Between the woman I love and the family that made me.

I pulled up to *Her Majesty* like I had every damn day I saw her car parked outside. I wasn't about to stop until she faced me.

The second I stepped onto the curb, the bouncer straightened up like he'd been waiting for me.

"Aye, man. I thought I told you. You can't come here no more. Get the fuck off the premises."

I clenched my jaw. "Man, fuck you. I need to get inside and talk to Niv."

He puffed his chest, already motioning for his radio like he wanted to call backup. Before I could swing first, Ty's voice cut through.

"I got this." She slid between us, her eyes sharp and tired.

"Kendrix, chill the fuck out before they shoot or arrest your ass."

"I don't give a fuck," I snapped. My voice cracked with the kind of desperation I couldn't hide. "It's been too fucking long. I told y'all. I'm coming here every damn day that I see her car until she tells me to stop. Until she looks me in the face and explains why."

Ty's eyes softened, just a little. I saw the water build before she blinked it away. "Look, Kendrix. I liked you for her. But please, let this go. She can't come back from all that. She just wants to move forward like nothing's happened. If you weren't out here acting crazy, they wouldn't have banned you. You could at least come watch her dance. But nah... you wanna go all bat-shit crazy."

"Man, fuck this club," I growled, dragging a hand down my face. "She wanna crawl back to this place, fine. I get the loyalty thing. But she's better than this. Way better. The numbers at GivGold been slipping since she left. I'm this close to shutting that bitch down until further notice. I don't wanna run that shit without her."

Ty shook her head, already turning away. "Kendrix... keep your club open. Hire a fire-ass face. Move on."

Her words felt like bricks.

She started walking back to the doors. My blood boiled hotter. I could feel the bouncer smirking at me, like he was enjoying every second of me being shut out.

That was it. I walked up to him and cracked him in the mouth before he could even flinch. His head snapped back, body staggering, and for a second I almost wanted him to swing back, give me a reason to lay him out.

But he just spit blood, smirked wider, and said, "Banned for life now, play-boy."

NETRAANTIONETTE

We were sitting at our parents' dining room table. Kross on my left, Kordai across from me, and Kairo at the head of the table where his ass might as well glue his phone.

I swear, we'd only been there twenty minutes and in that time, he'd made seventeen calls and typed out at least a hundred texts. Every time it buzzed, he picked it up. Didn't matter if it was food in front of him, me clearing my throat, or Kross trying to crack a joke. His phone was his woman, his mistress, and his best friend all in one.

Kross leaned over, elbowing me. "He ain't even here, bro. Just his body."

I laughed, shaking my head, but truth be told, my mind wasn't on Kairo, that table, or even the damn food. If Niv had answered my calls, I'd be somewhere else. Anywhere else. I'd rather be listening to her fuss at me, cussing me out, than watching my brother romance an iPhone.

Kordai sat back, taking a swig from his glass. "Somebody snatch that nigga's SIM card. He act like he about to lose the world if he miss one call. You worse than a woman waiting on a man to text back."

Kairo didn't even look up. He just waved his hand like we were gnats buzzing around his ear.

Kross shook his head. "Man, I don't know why I even bother setting this shit up. Brother dinner my ass."

I leaned back in my chair, arms crossed, forcing a grin. "Be grateful we even here, bro. Between you and Rivah being tied to the hip, Kordai being secretive about his love life, and Kairo over there married to his hustle instead of his actual wife, I'm surprised we can still sit at one table without killing each other."

Kairo pointed his fork at me, grinning. "Correction, you're the one almost got somebody killed. Our dad."

The table went quiet for a beat, the weight of his words sitting there. My jaw clenched.

I could still see Niv's face. Her hands in cuffs. The blood. Her eyes telling me she was sorry and not sorry at the same time.

I forced down the lump in my throat, reaching for my drink, and muttered, "Eat your food, man."

Kairo slammed his fork down, shaking his head like he couldn't believe what he was seeing. "Man, loyalty must not mean shit to you. You sitting here sulking over a woman who almost killed our dad. Our father, Kendrix. Do you even understand that? That one move could've ruined everything—our family, our name, the legacy we've been building."

I clenched my jaw, gripping the edge of the table. "Don't start with that legacy shit, Kairo."

"Nah, fuck that," he snapped, pointing at me. "How do you even know for sure it was Dad who did whatever she said? You ever stop to think maybe she's wrong? Since we were kids, Dad had workers handling that side of town. You think he really went down to Gun Hill himself? Come on, Kendrix. That don't even make sense. You putting pussy over family."

That hit me right in the chest. My chair scraped back hard against the wood floor as I stood. "Say that shit again."

Kairo jumped up just as fast, eyes locked on mine. "Pussy over family. That's exactly what it is."

I leaned across the table, my voice dropping. "You think you know everything, huh? You think because you married Khloe at eighteen and played house, you the moral compass of the family? You don't know shit about your own family that you created because your head is everywhere but there. You don't know what I feel for her. You don't know shit about what Dad really did. So watch your fucking mouth."

The table erupted in noise. Chairs moving, voices raised.

Kross jumped up, hands out like a damn referee. "Yo! Chill the fuck out. Both of you. This ain't it."

But neither one of us was listening. My fists were balled, ready, and Kairo's chest was puffed out like he wanted me to swing first.

That's when Kordai finally snapped. He hit the table hard enough for it to rattle the dishes. "Enough!"

We all froze. Even Kairo.

"You two are brothers," Kordai spat, his voice sharper than we'd heard in years. "And you acting like you at war. For what? To prove who can yell louder? Who loves this family more? Fuck that. I ain't a big fan of what happened either, but it's more to the story that none of us know. So just leave that shit alone. Dad is alive. Thank God. Don't give Mama something else to stress about. She's barely holding it together as it is."

The room went quiet, all of us staring. My chest was still heaving, but his words hit.

Mama walked in, stress written all over her face. She didn't even look at us right away. She just walked straight over to Kordai and kissed him on the cheek.

"Thank you for having some sense," she said, her voice calm but tired. "They're all older than you, but it's obvious they don't act like it."

I glanced at Kairo. He looked like he wanted to say something slick, but even he kept his mouth shut at first.

Kross leaned back, hands up. "Dang, Ma. I ain't in this one. Don't lump me in."

Mama turned to him with a sigh. "You're right, baby. And I appreciate you. You set this dinner up, you tried to get your brothers together. I see that."

Kairo finally muttered under his breath, "Some of us got real shit to do, not just sit around—"

"Shut the fuck up and sit down!" Mama snapped.

Dead silence.

Even the air froze.

Mama never yelled. She didn't have to. Her usual calm voice cut deeper than any scream could. But the fact she raised her voice was lethal. That was the kind of thing that made grown men shrink back like little boys.

We all sat. Nobody said another word. Forks clinked softly against plates, but that was it. No smart comments. No arguments. Just Mama standing at the head of the table, her chest rising and falling as she stared us down like she dared us to test her again.

We were all staring at our plates, waiting for the storm to pass, but Mama wasn't finished. She leaned on the back of Kairo's chair, her eyes burning like she was tired of raising boys who thought they were men.

"I really thought some of my brain lived in you boys," she said low, calm, the way only she could make it sound worse than yelling. "But all I see is your daddy's mistakes running through your veins. You know how long he was out of surgery before he started asking for his damn phone? Not even forty-eight hours. Tubes still in him and he was asking about schedules. About meetings." She shook her head, lips curling. "That's what you call dedication. I call it sickness. And he didn't wanna talk to nobody about what happened—nobody but me. So if you think there wasn't some truth to that girl's pain, you're blind. Your daddy's a retaliation man. He don't explain shit and for him to sit there and even discuss it with me means he knew what that girl was talking about."

She turned her glare to Kairo, and he damn near shrank into his chair. "And you. You get on my fucking nerves with all this work shit. Running around with that phone glued to your hand like it's the Bible. You work so hard trying to prove yourself valuable to your daddy, but guess what? We worked hard so you wouldn't have to work this hard. So you could live, so your kids could live. But your daughter is about to be sixteen, and all you are to her is an ATM. And your wife?" Mama's voice cracked sharp. "She throws herself at you for scraps of attention, and you don't even look up. You wanna be your daddy so bad, but let me tell you something—your daddy never made me fight for attention. Never made me wonder if I was seen. He worked, yes, but he always took care of home. So turn the fucking iPhone off, Kairo. Go see about the family you created before you lose them. Stop being a coward, because I damn sure didn't raise one."

Kairo looked like he wanted to defend himself, but the words died in his throat.

Mama's gaze slid to me. My chest tightened before she even opened her mouth.

"Kendrix, baby..." Her tone softened. "I know love has been heavy on you. You lost young, and I've seen you carry that weight like a ghost chained to your back. Took you forever to bring someone around. But when you did? I saw it. The light came back into you. I liked Niv. I really did. But she walked away. And instead of drowning in your own sadness, you need to pick yourself up and keep going like she did."

She leaned in. "Do you ever think for once that maybe walking away was the hardest decision she's ever made? That maybe, knowing what she knows about this family, she loved you too much to make you choose? Maybe she thought hurting both of you now was better than destroying you later. Maybe that was her love."

My throat burned, but I couldn't speak.

Mama straightened, gathering her purse off the back of her chair. "Pick yourself up, son. Move the fuck on. Don't make me bury you while you're still alive."

She pushed back from the table, her eyes sweeping all of us. "Now, enjoy the rest of your dinner. And before you leave, go check on your daddy in his office."

And with that, she walked out... calm, collected, lethal.

We all sat there, silent. Nobody moved. Nobody breathed too loud.

Because Mama had gutted every single one of us in one sitting.

30

Niveah

I sat on the edge of the tub, elbows digging into my knees, staring at that little white stick like it was the devil itself.

Two lines. Clear as day. No second-guessing, no squinting under bathroom light. Positive.

My hands were shaking so bad I almost dropped it. I wanted to cry—God knows I did—but the tears stayed stuck somewhere behind my eyes, like even my body was too tired to break down.

"Damn, Niv... how the fuck did you let this happen?" I whispered, like the mirror could answer me back.

I wasn't reckless. I wasn't some fool who didn't know better. I'd built my whole life on controlling everything. My money, my body, my moves. And here I was, knocked off balance by a stick with pink lines.

The ache in my chest doubled when his face crossed my mind. Kendrix. His laugh. His stupid beard I liked to tug at when I wanted to piss him off. The way he said my name like it belonged to him.

And I couldn't even tell him. Couldn't call, couldn't text.

I set the test down on the counter, pushing it away like it was a bomb. Wrapped my arms around myself, rocking forward, because the only thing louder than my heartbeat was the voice in my head questioning everything.

How do you raise kids on broken trust? How do you carry a baby with a man who carries his daddy's blood? And worst of all, how do you love somebody who might never forgive you, even if the whole damn world pushed you into this corner?

My stomach flipped and it wasn't nausea. It was fear. Hope. Anger. Love. All rolled into something I couldn't name.

I hated it. I hated the way that little stick made me feel connected to something I didn't even want to touch. I didn't want to talk to it. Didn't want to imagine it. Didn't want to start planning a life around something I never asked for.

Because how the hell could I?

I'd already been raising kids my whole damn life. Carrying my mama when she couldn't carry herself. Wiping Hux's tears when he was too proud to cry in front of anybody else. Making sure Heidi had bows in her hair and lunch in her bag when I was barely eating myself. And Zejah? She was another baby in my care too, and pregnant. Pregnant with my brother's flesh and blood. Another mouth to feed. Another body to care for. Another future I'd have to stretch myself thin to provide for because their parents were too young, still trying to live the lives ahead of them.

And there I was. Adding one more life to my plate with a positive pregnancy test.

I grew up in chaos. Watching my mama slip further into a high, watching our home rot, watching my childhood disappear under the weight of bills and secrets and survival. I promised myself if I ever had kids, it would never be like that. They'd have peace. They'd have a mama and a daddy, not just one exhausted woman fighting the world with her fists and her teeth.

That wasn't in the cards. Not with Kendrix. Not now. Maybe not ever.

Because how was I supposed to look at a child that carried his blood. The man I loved so bad that it hurt, but he also carried his father's blood? The man who ruined my life? The man who ruined my mama?

Every day, I woke up asking myself if I could separate him from that monster. And most days, the answer was no. No matter how much I loved Kendrix, I still hated that his bloodline lived in the veins of the man who destroyed me. And, that same bloodline was inside me.

It wasn't fair. It wasn't what I wanted.

I pressed my hand to my belly, eyes burning. I thought about Mamma G, about the way she looked at me that day in jail. How she'd thrown me a lifeline not for me, but for my siblings. A trade. My freedom for them. And I was a woman of my word. If walking away from Kendrix meant Hux and Heidi and even Zejah got to breathe a little easier, then that's what I had to do.

But sitting there in my bathroom, staring at that stick, all I could think about was how damn heavy the word "choice" felt when it was sitting on your chest like a brick.

I wiped at my face, grabbed my phone off the counter, and stared at the screen like it had all the answers. My thumb hovered for a second before I pressed the contact.

The line clicked.

"Dr. Baldwin," Talynn's voice came through, like always.

Relief spilled out of me. "Oh, thank God it's you. I thought I'd have to leave another message with your secretary to call me back."

Talynn laughed. "You caught me, lucky. I'm just finishing up some charting for now. I'll see you later, right? Unless this is about Zejah needing to reschedule her appointment?"

I swallowed, leaning against the sink. "No. No, I called about me."

Her tone softened. "Niv... you took another test, didn't you?"

I closed my eyes. "Yes. I just had to make sure."

"Yeah, what number was this? Twelve?" she teased. "I hope you've accepted it by now."

"I guess you can say I'm stubborn."

We both laughed.

"Have you made up your mind?" she asked gently, sliding into that steady, nurturing tone I'd come to trust.

I exhaled slow. "Yes. I was wondering... after Zejah leaves, if I could see you."

There was a pause, then I heard papers shuffling. "Let me check... yeahhh. I've got a two-hour break between her and another client. I can slide you in. We can talk."

I was relieved. "Okay. Great."

Just then, Hux's voice spoke from the other side of the bathroom door, rough and impatient. "Niv! We're ready!"

"Okay!" I yelled back, then lowered my voice quickly. "Okay. See you in a bit."

I hung up, shoved my phone in my pocket, and took one more look in the mirror.

"I'm coming!" I hollered again, grabbing the doorknob and plastering on my mask before walking out.

NETRAANTIONETTE

I sat back in the chair, trying to keep my face unreadable while Zejah lay on the table with her shirt lifted and Hux gripping her hand like she was about to sky-dive instead of get an ultrasound.

Talynn's voice was professional, but with that little spark of humor she always had. "Alright, let's see this little peanut. There we go... spine looks strong, head is measuring perfect..." She pointed at the screen and Hux squinted like he was trying to make sense of an alien.

"That's the head?" he asked.

Talynn laughed. "Yes, unless you think your child will be born with a football."

Zejah rolled her eyes. "Boy, that's your head anyway."

I actually laughed at that. Talynn kept calling out body parts, fingers, toes, showing off the little flutters of movement.

And Hux... God, he was smiling. Really smiling. That soft, boyish smile. It tugged at something deep in me.

But at the same time, it hurt. Watching them. A messy, young love forming a family. It made me think about me and Kendrix. About how we could never sit in a room like this, grinning at each other over a blurry black-and-white picture. Not when his father was who he was. Not when I'd promised his mother I'd walk away.

And even if we did... even if I let myself want that? It'd be a cold day in hell before I let his dad put his hands on something that belonged to me. My child. Our child. No.

That thought made my stomach twist harder than morning sickness ever could. Kendrix had already lost two kids. How could I be cruel enough to make him choose between me and his family—between them and his child? I loved him too much to drag him into that kind of pain.

Talynn's voice cut through my thoughts. "Alright, I'm about to take a peek at the gender." She grinned and added, "But I don't want to ruin the surprise just yet. Hux, Zejah, close your eyes."

They did, squeezing each other's hands tight.

Talynn looked at the gender of the baby, typed a few notes into her chart, and then pressed print. The machine whirred before spitting out the glossy photo, and she handed it to me, folded.

"Okay," she said with a smile. "You can open your eyes now."

Hux's head shot up, and his gaze snapped to me. "Tell me," he pressed, all wide eyes and hope.

I laughed, even though my chest felt like it was splitting open. "Nope. You have to wait until the reveal party."

He groaned, Zejah giggled, and even Talynn smiled as she finished wiping down the probe. "Everything looks good," she assured them. "Go up front, and they'll schedule your next visit."

They got up, gathering their things, Hux still side-eyeing me like he thought I'd cave. Before they could leave the room, I said, "Hux, wait for me in the car. I need to talk to Dr. Baldwin for a minute."

He shrugged. "Cool."

The door shut behind them, and Talynn bent back over the machine, cleaning it off with quiet efficiency. The soft squeak of sanitizer on plastic filled the silence until she glanced over her shoulder at me.

"Alright," she said. "Talk. Because I can see it written all over you."

I shifted on the chair, pressing my purse against my lap like it could hide the truth. "What truth?"

Talynn raised a brow. "The one you keep running from. You're not fooling me, Niv."

I tried to laugh it off, but it sounded thin. "I just... I don't know what the hell I'm supposed to do, Talynn. I've already got three kids on my plate—Hux, Heidi, and now Zejah. I'm raising them like they're mine. And now this? A baby I never planned for, with a man I can't even have?"

Talynn leaned back against the counter, arms crossed, belly ready to pop. She was calm, but I could see it in her eyes that she wasn't gonna let me bullshit my way out of it.

"You sound like you already made a decision," she said softly. "You just don't like how it feels in your mouth yet."

Her words cut me deep.

"I hate it. I hate that I even have to think about carrying something that belongs to him. To them. You know what it means if I keep it? That one day his father—*that man*—might want to claim my child as his grandbaby. And it'll be a cold day in hell before I let that happen."

Talynn didn't flinch. Didn't argue. She just nodded, like she already knew.

"And I can't bring a child into the same chaos I was raised in," I pushed on, the words tumbling too fast now. "I promised myself—no chaos, no broken-ness, no begging a man to be around. Two parents, love, stability. And I can't give that. Not now. Not with him."

His name caught in my throat. Burned all the way down.

Talynn walked over, laying a hand on my shoulder, firm and grounding. "Then whatever decision you make, Niv, own it. Don't let guilt raise that baby if you can't. Don't let fear take it away if you can. Either way, stand ten toes on your choice."

I blinked fast, my eyes burning, because she was right. And I hated her for being right.

Talynn dragged the chair closer and sat down right in front of me. Her tone shifted to less doctor, more big sister.

"Niv, listen to me," she said. "Pregnancy isn't just about carrying a baby in your body. It's about carrying it in your mind as well. Every day. Every minute. The crying, the sleepless nights, the bills, the doctor's visits. The way it changes you and everything around you. If you're not mentally ready for that? Then that's something you have to consider. No shame. No judgment. Because forcing yourself into motherhood when you're not prepared is how cycles repeat. That's how trauma passes down."

I didn't realize I was shaking until I felt her squeeze my knee.

"You already know how to be a provider," she continued, her eyes looking into mine. "You've raised Hux, Heidi, and now Zejah. You've held it all together when you should've been falling apart. But this?" She leaned in closer. "This baby and this decision has to be about *you*. Not what anyone else thinks. Not what anyone else says. What can *you* handle? What can *you* live with?"

I swallowed hard, blinking back the tears stinging my eyes.

"Do you know how far along you might be?" she asked gently.

I shook my head. "I don't know. My cycles... they're always all over the place. Sometimes I bleed heavy, sometimes I skip. It's never been consistent."

She nodded. "Okay. A lot of women are like that as well, but it also makes it harder to track. Would you be okay if I took a look? We could do an ultrasound, just to see. It might help give you clarity."

My heart raced. An ultrasound meant proof. An ultrasound meant no more hiding in denial.

"I—" I hesitated, my fingers twisting in my lap. "What if I'm not ready to see it?"

"Then you don't have to look," Talynn said. "You can close your eyes, and I'll tell you what I see. But sometimes... facing what's inside you is the only way to really make a decision."

I let out a long breath. Everything in me screamed to run, to shut it all down and go home, to crawl back into bed and pretend it wasn't happening. But I couldn't.

"Okay," I whispered. "Do it."

Talynn nodded and moved smoothly into motion. She dimmed the lights, pulled the machine back toward me, and told me to lie on the table. I slid onto the paper-covered bed, nerves rattling through me. My skin felt cold against the air.

And in that moment, one thought looped in my mind, over and over:

I can love Kendrix with everything in me. I can hate his father with every breath I have left. But this choice. This choice about this baby, has to be mine.

Talynn angled the screen toward herself, not toward me.

"You're definitely pregnant," she said gently. "Measuring about seven weeks. Still early enough to make whatever decision feels right for you."

I nodded, swallowing hard. My throat was dry, but she kept talking.

"This decision is yours, Niv. No one else's. Not his. Not your siblings. Not even me sitting here. So..." her eyes caught mine, "...what do you want to do?"

The words came out before I could overthink them. "I want to end it." My voice cracked, but I forced myself to keep going. "If motherhood is meant for me, it'll be different. It'll be under better circumstances."

Talynn shook her head quickly, cutting me off. "Stop. You don't have to explain yourself to anyone. Not to me, not to him, not to the world. This can stay right here. No one ever has to know. Put yourself first, for once."

She rolled her stool back, pulled out her prescription pad, and began writing. "There are pills you can take to end this pregnancy safely. You'll cramp. It'll hurt. You might bleed heavier than a normal cycle. But your body will recover. Most women feel back to normal in about a week." She tore the paper free and handed it to me, looking me dead in the eyes. "If anything feels off, or you're scared, call me. We'll get through this together."

Tears burned behind my lids. I blinked them away and whispered, "Thank you. For being here. For dealing with me while you're..." I looked at her round belly, "days away from delivering your own. It can't be easy, talking to a woman who wants to end her pregnancy when you're about to give birth."

Talynn laughed softly, shaking her head. "Oh no, honey. This is exactly why I love my job. My husband, Reggie, is heaven sent. But it took me a long, messy road to get here. And I can't say with certainty that I would've kept a baby with my ex, after everything we went through. So I get it. Truly. Get out of your head. This isn't shame. This is choice. *Your* body. *Your* life. *Your* decision."

"I'll go pick up the pills as soon as I leave here," I told her. "And... thank you. For everything."

"Don't thank me," she said. "Don't thank anyone. Choosing yourself doesn't earn anyone else credit. It's not charity. It's not luck. It's you. You don't owe any apologies for that."

That was the kind of truth you don't argue with.

I felt something. Relief. Not happiness. Not joy. Just relief. Like I'd just loosened a knot that had been choking me since the day that test first showed two pink lines.

I nodded, blinking back tears. "Okay," I whispered.

Talynn stood, rested a hand on my shoulder, and gave it a squeeze before heading for the door. "Put yourself first, Niv. Always. No one else can live in your body. No one else carries what you carry. Don't ever forget that."

31

Kendrix

I pulled up to Kairo's big-ass house, the kind of place you knew looked good on paper but felt empty inside. I wasn't going there for him though. I went to see Khloe and my niece. I missed them, and honestly, I worried about them.

Kairo was still on my bad side, but his dumb ass never listened to our mama anyway. I knew he wouldn't be home. He was probably at the office or glued to a damn laptop somewhere, pretending the world would end if he didn't answer an email in five minutes.

Khloe though... Khloe had always been different. I loved her like a real sister. Since our families grew up close, I damn near knew her my whole life. When Kairo married her, for a minute I was actually happy for him. Thought he finally had something real, someone who balanced him out. But now, every time I looked at Khloe, all I saw was how much better she deserved.

She opened the door before I could knock, hair tied up in a bun, wearing a tee shirt and leggings. She smiled when she saw me and it felt genuine, like she was glad I was there. "Kendrix. You hungry? I just made pasta for me and Kennedi."

"Yeah, I'll take a plate," I said, stepping inside. The house looked nice, like always, but it had that cold Kairo stamp all over it. Expensive, spotless, and damn near lifeless.

We sat at the counter, Kennedi in the living room with her headphones on, wrapped up in TikTok or whatever she was always watching. I watched her for a minute, growing into herself, and it hit me. My brother was missing it. Missing her. Missing Khloe. All because he couldn't stop chasing our daddy's shadow.

"That nigga," I muttered without thinking, shaking my head.

Khloe gave me that look, like she knew exactly who I meant. She sighed and slid a plate in front of me. "Kairo?"

"Yeah." I stabbed at the pasta. "Always been the same. Always fighting for Dad's attention. Always trying to prove he's the workaholic golden child, the one that'll carry the family when Dad's gone. And for what? He look desperate as hell. That's all he does with his life. And the fucked-up part? It's pushing y'all away."

Her eyes softened, but there was pain behind it. She didn't say anything right away, and that silence said enough.

I leaned back, shaking my head again. "Khloe, you deserve better. I don't even know how you deal with it."

She smirked, sad but honest. "Because I love him. And because sometimes... I still hope he remembers to love us back."

That shit hit me hard. Harder than I expected. I looked at her and Kennedi, and I knew Kairo had no clue what he was throwing away.

Khloe leaned her elbows on the counter, staring into her glass like she was trying to read the future. "You know what I miss?" she finally said. "Teenage Kairo. College Kairo. Back then, we were inseparable. He was my best friend. We didn't have sooo much money, we didn't have anything figured out, but God, those were the best years of my life. We laughed, we dreamed. It felt like us against the world."

Her voice cracked a little, and I stayed quiet, letting her get it out.

"I wanted more kids, Kendrix. You know that. I adore Kennedi, but I always pictured a house full of them running around. I kept thinking maybe he was just waiting until she got a little older. Then one day he told me... more kids would stunt his career growth." She let out this bitter little laugh, wiping under her eyes. "Imagine hearing that from the man you love. That your dreams of a family don't fit on his schedule."

"Khloe..." I leaned forward, my voice steady. "Don't ever think that's on you. You've been everything. A wife, mom, the glue. If he's blind to that, that's his failure, not yours. And if Kennedi is all you got, then make damn sure she knows how loved she is. Don't let his tunnel vision make you forget you've already done the most important job."

She breathed out hard. "Thank you, Kendrix. Sometimes I just need somebody to remind me I'm not crazy for wanting more."

Her eyes glossed over, then she smiled weakly. "I miss you and Niv together. You don't see it, but she balanced you the way I used to balance Kairo. When you were with her, it was like... you weren't so heavy. You laughed more. You looked lighter."

I swallowed hard. That ache I'd been carrying for weeks throbbed even worse. She wasn't lying. Niv made me feel like myself. She made me forget the pressure of being a Givelle for a while.

I leaned back in the chair, rubbing my face like I was trying to scrub the ache. "You right, Khloe. I miss her so much. But she's doing everything in her power not to face me. Out of all the ways she could've handled this. Curse me out, throw a bottle at my head, even tell me to fuck off. I didn't think she'd just... ignore me. Like I was nothing. Like we were nothing. I'd rather she look me in my eyes and tell me she's done than have me out here begging to see and talk to her."

I cut my eyes at Khloe. "I know y'all still talk."

She looked guilty immediately, then rolled her eyes. "We do, but—"

"But nothing. What she be saying?" I pushed, leaning forward.

Khloe bit her lip, shaking her head. "Kendrix, don't do this."

"Man, sis, just let me know if I need to give up. Please." My voice cracked on that last word, and I hated it, but it was the truth.

She sighed, leaning against the counter. "She doesn't say much about you. You know how Niv is. She'll replace hurt with jokes, laughter, and sarcasm. But I can see it in her eyes. She's hurting. She just won't show it. That's how she survives."

I sat back, feeling that familiar heaviness in my chest. "Yeahhh... that sounds like her. But I swear, Khloe, these last couple of days, I've felt like I'm grieving. Like I'm losing a piece of myself that I left with her. And I hate that feeling. I just... I just need her. I want her. But I get it. The shit with my dad, the weight of all that, makes it damn near impossible. I just gotta find a way to figure it all out."

Khloe studied me for a long second, her eyes softening. "It's gonna be hard, Kendrix. And it may take time. But I think it's possible. If anybody can fight their way back to each other after all this chaos... it's you and Niv."

Just as Khloe and I got quiet, the sound of footsteps came into the room. Kennedi came strolling in with her phone and thumbs flying over the screen.

"Are y'all in here talking about Ms. Niv almost stabbing Pawpaw to death?" she asked, like it was regular conversation.

Khloe whipped her head around. "Baby, don't say that."

I just shook my head, covering my mouth to hide the laugh pushing through.

Kennedi blinked, unfazed. "What? It's true. I heard Dad on the phone telling somebody what Pawpaw did to her mom. I'm not mad at her. Mama gets on my nerves sometimes, but I'd do the same for her."

I laughed at how bluntly honest my niece was. Khloe threw her hands up. "Well, thank you, Kennedi, for everything except the part where I get on your nerves."

Kennedi smirked. "You're welcome, Mommy." Then she turned to me, grinning. "You know you're my favorite uncle, right?"

I squinted at her. "Uh-huh. You told Kross the same thing last week."

That made Khloe laugh too, because it was true. Kennedi was the only grandchild in the whole damn family, and she knew it. Rotten to the core, spoiled in every way, but we couldn't blame anyone but ourselves.

She dropped down in the chair beside me, all smiles. "So... Mom's meeting with her friends tonight, and I really wanna go to this basketball game. Dad said I can't unless I have an adult that he knows and trusts with me."

I shook my head. "Well, your dad probably doesn't trust me right now."

"Kendrix, stop," Khloe cut in, shooting me a look.

"What? I'm just telling the truth."

"Pleaseeee," Kennedi dragged out, her big eyes pleading. "You might even see Ms. Niv there. Her brother is playing, it's at his school."

That stopped me in my tracks. My whole chest tightened. Hux's game? That meant Niv would definitely be there. She wouldn't make a scene at her brother's school, wouldn't risk embarrassing him. Maybe that was my shot.

But then another thought hit me, and I frowned. "Wait, why the hell do you even wanna go to his school's basketball game? Don't you go to one of the most elite schools in the city? Tuition higher than most people's mortgages?"

She smirked, twirling her phone between her fingers. "Uncle Ken, he's cute."

Khloe busted out laughing.

I damn near came out my seat. "What the hell did you just say? Don't call no lil' nigga cute in front of me again."

"Dang, Uncle Ken," she sighed dramatically. "I'm not tryna marry him. Relax."

"Relax?" I repeated, my blood pressure spiking. "You too young to date. Matter fact, you can never date. He has a situation anyway. Hell naw!"

Kennedi side-eyed me, then turned to Khloe. "See, this is why he's my favorite. He's crazy, but cooler than my parents."

Khloe put her hand to her chest. "Excuse me?"

Kennedi grinned, kissed Khloe's cheek, and skipped toward the door. "I'm lying, Mom. You know I love you."

I shook my head, still heated.

"So is that a yes?"

I groaned, rubbing my forehead. The truth was, she had me. If Kennedi wanted to see that game, I'd take her. And if it put me in the same room as Niv? Even better.

"I guess," I muttered.

She screamed, "YES!" and hugged me so tight I couldn't breathe. "Best uncle ever."

Khloe rolled her eyes, smiling, while I sat there thinking. That game might be the only way I could get close enough to Niv to force her to hear me.

32

Niveah

It had been a little over a week since I took the pills. A week since I curled up on my bathroom floor, clutching my stomach, riding waves of cramps so deep they felt like someone was wringing me out from the inside. Nobody warned you about the sound of your own body expelling what could have been. The blood, the clots, the heat in your thighs, the kind of ache that makes you bite your lip until it bleeds just to keep from screaming.

At first, it was hell. The physical pain, the nausea, the way I couldn't stop shaking. Then came the silence after—the emptiness that sat heavier than the cramps. Every time I went to the bathroom, I stared too long, thinking about what I'd just lost and why I chose it.

But then... it got easier. Each day, I reminded myself: it was what was best for me. For Hux. For Heidi. For Zejah and the baby she was carrying. For the life I'd built clawing my way out of chaos. I couldn't bring a child into a storm. Not when I was still fighting to keep the roof above our heads steady. Not when I wasn't even sure if I'd survive the weight of seeing Kendrix's face in a child every day.

I didn't tell Ty. I didn't tell anyone. At the club, they all thought I had some bug, maybe the flu, so I let them believe it. It was easier than opening my mouth and letting the truth fall out. I spent the week mostly at home, wrapped up in blankets or in the quiet corners of my mind, working through the guilt and the relief like they were two sides of the same blade.

I was back in Gun Hill, leaving the neighborhood behind as I drove with Hux and Zejah in the car. I had to stop by the hospital—Mama needed a few items, and even though I'd spent most of my life angry at her, the sight of her hooked up to machines still punched me in the chest every time. Zejah wanted to see her siblings while I got things out my mom's house, so she rode too.

Hux sat in the back, earbuds dangling around his neck, his face turned toward the window. His game was later that night, and I could tell he was already focused. He'd never say it, but I knew he wanted Mama to see him play. At least just once.

The three of us had become our own unit. Our own broken little tribe, pieced together from scraps and survival. And as much as I hated the hospital walls and the way they smelled, I had to go in there and make sure Mama had everything she needed before I shifted into big sister mode again. Cheering Hux on like nothing in our world was falling apart.

The beeping was the first thing I heard. Then came the sight of Mama lying in that bed, pale, thinner, her arm bruised from all the sticks and needles, a fistful of wires taped to her chest. Tubes running down her arms. A dialysis machine humming beside her, pumping life through her veins.

I used to think my strength was my own. That I was born to claw out of chaos and keep my siblings alive. But seeing her like that, hooked up to machines, still breathing when the doctors swore she wouldn't see sunrise many nights... I knew where I got it from. Mama was stubborn enough to keep fighting when her body gave up.

Her voice was raspy and weak. "I can't wait to get out this place."

I forced a smile. "Me too. I didn't want Hux sharing a room with Zejah, but if you're coming home, looks like I don't have a choice."

Hux started laughing from the corner. "You better not put her in my room, if you—"

"Don't make me slap you," I cut in.

Mama shifted against the pillows. "Maybe you can get rid of that Rita woman and let me take care of my Heidi."

My chest tightened. Same old Mama. Same old deflection. "That won't happen. Rita's been good to us. Heidi needs her. I need her."

Her face twisted. "Well I'm going home then. I'm an adult. I wasn't coming there anyway, whether you keep her or not."

There she went with that bullshit. I exhaled, pressing a kiss to her cheek. "Okay, Mama." No point in arguing.

I leaned back. "Hux has a game tonight, so we just came to see you, spend a little time."

"Where's Heidi?"

"Rita took her to an arts and crafts workshop. She wanted to go."

Mama's eyes sharpened, anger fighting through her tiredness. "You letting some other woman raise my baby?"

That did it. My patience snapped. "Bye, Mama. I'll be back later. Call me if you need anything." I kissed her forehead before she could spit more venom and walked out.

At the nurses' station, I asked, "How's my mom really doing?"

The nurse smiled gently, like she'd had this talk with too many daughters before me. "She's improving daily, but we've got someone working with her mentally. She's up and down. She prefers to be medicated, but we're trying to keep that minimal after... everything. One day at a time."

I nodded, swallowing the lump in my throat. "Call me if anything changes."

NETRAANTIONETTE

The gym was hot, packed wall-to-wall with parents, students, coaches, and a whole lot of folks who came just for the energy. It smelled like popcorn and floor polish. Sneakers squeaked across the wood.

Hux was in his element. My little brother had that focus in his eyes. The same one I'd seen when he practiced in our driveway until the ball's leather peeled. The scoreboard glowed red: his team was down by two. The clock had only seconds to spare.

The crowd was on their feet. Everyone screaming, stomping, clapping. My heart beat against my ribs so hard I swore I could hear it over the noise.

Zejah was clutching my arm, bouncing up and down. "Come on, Hux! Come on!"

The ball was in his hands. He drove past one defender, then another, sneakers sliding across the floor like he was skating. The obvious move was to take it to the net, force the tie. That's what the coach was yelling. That's what half the gym was begging for.

But I knew my brother. Hux never did the obvious. He was the type to risk it all, the type to shut everybody up with something bold.

The clock hit five seconds.

He stepped back to the three-point line.

"No, no—" I whispered, holding my breath.

He launched it. Perfect arc. The gym seemed to freeze with the ball hanging in the air, the whole world suspended in that heartbeat between hope and heartbreak.

The buzzer blared just as the ball swished clean through the net.

The gym exploded.

The sound was crazy. People screaming, stomping, and horns blasting. His teammates lifted him in the air like a hero. Zejah and I lost our minds, jumping up and down like two kids ourselves.

I screamed until my throat burned. That was my little brother. That was Huxley, pulling off the impossible, shutting the whole damn gym down with a shot he probably shouldn't have taken, but did anyway.

And watching him, I felt it. Pride so big it hurt. Love that stretched across every scar life had given us. For one shining moment, chaos didn't matter. Trauma didn't matter. It was just him, his victory, and the reminder that even when life swung hard, we still had reasons to cheer.

Zejah and I made our way down the bleachers, people high-fiving each other, parents hollering like they'd just won the championship. My ears were still ringing from the noise when I heard somebody yell—

"Ms. Niiiv!"

I turned, and there was Kennedi, grinning from ear to ear like she'd been waiting just for me. That little pretty girl had the whole Givelle face stamped on her, but spoiled rotten written all across her aura.

She ran straight into my arms, hugging me tight. "Hey, baby," I laughed, pulling back to get a good look at her. "You look so pretty."

Kennedi twirled in a slow circle like she was on a runway. "I told Mamma this outfit was cute!"

I laughed, shaking my head. "And you were right. Where's your mom, anyway?"

Kennedi pouted. "Oh, she's somewhere at a work dinner." Then she popped right back to grinning like it didn't matter one bit.

"Mm-hmm," I said, filing that away but letting it slide for now. I gestured to Zejah, who was standing stiff beside me. "This is Zejah."

Kennedi's smile got even wider. "Congratulations," she said sweetly, pointing at Zejah's little bump.

"Thank you," Zejah said, her lips tight like she was trying not to show any expression at all.

Then Kennedi tilted her head, eyes scanning around. "Where's Hux?"

The way Zejah's whole face shifted, I had to bite the inside of my cheek not to laugh. She looked like she wanted to fight.

I leaned closer, low enough for only her to hear. "Relax, girl," I whispered. "You live in the same house with him. You're carrying his child. Don't let a little crush ruffle your feathers. This won't be the last time some girl bats her lashes at him."

Zejah side-eyed me so hard.

Aloud, I told Kennedi, "He should be out soon, getting his things out the locker room. When you see him, tell him we'll be waiting in the foyer."

"Okay!" Kennedi said brightly, giving me another big hug. "I sure willlllll."

She stretched out the last word like she wanted to make sure Zejah heard every syllable. Then she bounced away, ponytail swinging.

Beside me, Zejah rolled her eyes so hard.

I just smirked and wrapped an arm around her shoulder. "Come on. Let's go wait."

And we walked off, me holding back a laugh. In the foyer, I had my head down, scrolling through my phone, trying to distract myself until Hux came out.

Then I heard my name.

"Niv."

Not just a voice. The voice.

The one that crept into my dreams and dragged me awake in cold sweats. The one I tried to drown out with liquor, with laughter, with anything loud enough to keep my heart from remembering.

I looked up and there he was. Kendrix.

For half a second, I lost my breath. My knees damn near buckled, but I caught myself. There were too many eyes there. Too many people that knew me, that knew my siblings. I couldn't give them a show.

I whispered. "What are you doing here?"

The way his face lit up...like just hearing me say five words was enough to make his whole night. He looked like a man starved, finally tasting food.

"Kennedi wanted to come," he said softly, almost proud. "She begged me to bring her."

Beside me, Zejah's mouth dropped open like she just walked into the middle of a movie she wasn't supposed to see. She quickly recovered, clearing her throat. "Um... I'll be back, I gotta go to the restroom."

"I'll go with you," I said immediately, ready to escape.

But Kendrix's voice cut through, louder this time, "No!"

Heads turned. A couple parents glanced over.

"Don't make a scene."

"Then talk to me."

The foyer seemed to shrink. All the chatter faded, and it was just him and me standing in the middle of too many people.

I turned to Zejah, forcing a small smile. "Go to the bathroom. I'll be right here waiting on you."

She didn't hesitate, eyes flicking between us like she knew she was leaving me to wrestle with fire. But she nodded slowly and slipped away.

Kendrix's eyes broke me before his words ever could. The kind of eyes that begged for mercy without saying a damn thing.

"I'm sorry," Kendrix whispered. "I'm sorry, Niv. I swear I'm not mad at you. I love you. God, I love you so much. We can get through this."

Every bone in my body screamed yes, but my mouth betrayed me. "We can't."

"Yes, we can." He stepped closer, pleading, his chest heaving like he was carrying the whole world. "Tell me what to do. Please. Just tell me, and I'll do it."

The thing I wanted most. Him, choosing me. Him, begging for me. And I had to kill it with my own hands.

"There's nothing you can do," I choked. "Nothing."

His jaw shook. He blinked hard, but the tears still came. "Then at least... at least let me be your friend. Let me check on you. Unblock me."

"I don't need that."

He cut me off. "I didn't ask if you needed it. I want to. I need to know you're okay."

And that's when I broke. My lips trembled, tears spilling hot and furious down my cheeks. He saw it. He always saw it.

"Okay," I whispered, so soft it almost didn't exist. "I'll unblock you."

Then Zejah reappeared, pretending like she didn't feel the tension. And Hux and Kennedi came skipping in laughing together like they didn't just walk into a warzone.

And then Kennedi shouted. "Uncle Ken, I'm ready to go!"

I thought it would break him. But Kendrix never blinked. His eyes never left me. Not once.

And then he kissed me.

Right there, in the middle of that foyer. In front of kids, parents, teachers, whoever the hell wanted to look. He didn't care. His lips crushed mine, desperate, wet, shaking. He kissed me like I was air and he'd been drowning for weeks.

And God help me, I kissed him back. I let myself have one last taste of him, one last dream, one last home.

When I pulled away, I knew.

That was goodbye.

"I love you," he whispered, his voice breaking into pieces.

And then he turned, grabbed Kennedi's hand, and walked away.

33

Kendrix

I should've known the office would smell like cigars and old money. That's where my Pops lived whenever he was home and not with my mama.

When I pushed the door open, I saw him at his desk, laptop on, paperwork stacked neat. And sitting across from him, arms crossed, was Kairo.

The second I stepped in, the energy shifted. Kairo's eyes cut to me, unforgiving. Pops looked up too, slow, his body still stiff from recovery.

"Son," Pops said, nodding like nothing was wrong. "You're just in time."

Kairo leaned back in the chair and smirked. "Yeah, perfect timing. Maybe you can explain to me how you still think it's okay to be running around after the same woman who almost killed Dad. The same woman who put this family's name on the line."

I walked further in, shutting the door behind me.

"You're really on this again?" I asked. My voice was low, already heated.

Kairo's jaw ticked. "On this? Pops is walking slower, barely traveling, working from home because of her. The love of your fucking life, huh, Ken? And you're still out here acting sad about her going no contact like she's worth everything we built."

The air thickened. I pushed back from the table, heat rushing in my chest.

"Shut the fuck up, Kairo."

He stood, puffed out his chest like we weren't brothers but enemies. "Truth hurts. She didn't have to stab him. She didn't have to—"

Our father's voice boomed from the head of the table, calm but commanding.

"Kairo. Leave."

"Dad—"

"I said leave."

Kairo froze. If there was one man Kairo feared, respected, and wanted to be more than anyone, it was our father. He stormed out, talking under his breath.

My father's fingers were still tapping on his laptop keys. He looked smaller, slower like Kairo said, but his eyes were still the same.

I stared at him. "Did you really give that to her mom?"

He didn't flinch. Didn't deny. He just sighed, eyes still on his screen.

"That was years ago. I don't know. I'm not the man I was then. Possibly, yes. But the charges are dropped. Your mother is fine. Her mother is fine. I'm fine. Let it go."

My jaw clenched. "What were you even doing in Gun Hill, Dad? You don't go there. Not ever. If we need something, we always send someone else."

His voice snapped, louder than before. "Let it go, I said!"

And just like that, he buried himself back into his laptop, his favorite shield.

Then he pivoted like nothing happened.

"You know, I've been thinking. There's a man I've done business with for years. Good man. His daughter is single. Smart girl. Comes from a strong family. Good head on her shoulders."

I cut him off before he could continue. "Respectfully, Dad, I don't need help with my love life. I don't want anything arranged. I'm good."

I stood, slipping my phone in my pocket. "I got a meeting at the club. Just wanted to check on you before I left."

He nodded slowly. "I appreciate that, son. Go handle your business."

We locked eyes for a moment, two stubborn men carrying different weights. Then we both said it, out of habit because no matter what, it was true.

"Love ya."

And I left.

I honestly didn't like going to the club because, without Niv, the vibe didn't hit the same. Numbers had been slipping. Energy too. Without her, the place looked polished, but it didn't feel lived in.

But one thing was for damn sure, without Magnolia, I'd been forced to shut that shit down weeks ago.

Niv was the one who brought her in. Magnolia had been doing admin work at their old club, so Niv brought her in to do the same. She was making sure paperwork stayed clean while Niv handled the day-to-day chaos. When Niv left me, Magnolia was ready to follow her out. Couldn't even blame her. But I begged. I didn't just beg, I threw so much money her way she would've been a fool to say no. I needed her. Hell, I still needed her. Without Niv, the numbers weren't the same, but without Magnolia too? I might as well put a "Closed Forever" sign on the damn door.

I walked in and heard Magnolia's voice before I even made it to the main floor.

"Now, baby, what did I say about them rhinestones? You look like a disco ball at a high school prom, not a grown woman at GivGold."

I damn near choked holding my laugh in. Magnolia. Mississippi-born, sweet tea in human form, voice full of "bless your heart" but words sharp enough to slice. Her name fit her perfectly. Soft and beautiful, but could grow in any damn soil.

She was standing in the middle of the room with her hands on her hips, fussing at two bottle girls who looked like they'd rather roll their eyes than listen.

"I don't care what them girls at that other club let y'all do. Here, we coordinate. That means if the theme is *Midnight Gold*, I don't need to see nobody walking out in neon pink thinking she's Beyoncé. Beyoncé gets billions, sweetheart. You get tips. Learn the difference."

One of the girls said something under her breath. Magnolia turned her head slow, still smiling, and said, "Sugar, I will knock the glitter off them lashes if you say it again."

Magnolia really had a way of telling people "fuck you" and making them thank her for it.

The dancers were the same. Some of them thought Magnolia was too sweet to run the floor, tried to half-ass their practice sets. She clapped her hands at one of them.

"Sweetheart, that move was lazy. Shake yo' ass like they're putting an eviction notice on your door tomorrow. Don't make me call your mama and tell her you ain't using what she gave you right."

The girl actually got back on the pole and did the move properly, mumbling, "yes ma'am."

I shook my head. Only Magnolia could be both a manager and a Southern auntie at the same damn time. She had the whole room laughing, even as she roasted them.

Truth was, the girls couldn't touch Niv, Ty, or any of the ones they pulled in from their old club. There was something different about dancers who danced through struggle. Dancers who had to make rent, feed kids, survive. The hunger hit different. The new ones? They wanted clout, Instagram stories, and a couple of dollars for brunch. Pretty, but not hungry. And Magnolia knew it, even if she never said it out loud.

When she spotted me, she smiled so wide you'd think I was her favorite cousin coming home from college. "Well, look who finally decided to come check on his own club instead of just wiring money and letting me run it."

I smirked. "From what I just saw, it look like you don't need me."

Magnolia laughed, waving her hand like she was shooing a fly. "Boy, please. You know good and well I need someone else to keep these girls from showing up here dressed like a clearance rack."

Then she clapped her hands, like she about to play a church tambourine.

"Alright, sugarplums, keep practicing until you can do this routine in your sleep. And bartenders, run another trial of those signature drinks. I told y'all last week, we want 'em tasting like Kool-Aid with a kick. Something folks can drink back-to-back till the liquor sneaks up and their debit cards stay out. Wreckless spending is the goal, babies."

They scattered and Magnolia wiped her brow with the back of her hand before turning to me. "You. Office. Now."

She didn't wait for me to follow. Just stomped in her stilettos like a Southern auntie who caught you sneaking out after curfew.

Once the door shut, she leaned against it, took the deepest breath I'd ever heard, and let loose.

"Kendrix, baby, I am runnin' 'round here like a chicken with my head cut off, feathers flyin' every damn where. I ain't got no penis in ages 'cause by the time I drag my country ass home, I fall straight into the bed. And when I wake up? I got just enough time to brush my teeth, pray to Jesus, and start game-plannin' for this club. This is too much."

I sat back, trying to hide my laugh because she was so country.

"Look at me, do I look like somebody that approve dance sets and coordinate colors? No. I'm paperwork, baby. Licenses, contracts, making sure the liquor shipments ain't short. That's my lane. Niv handled the glitz. I was just the grease in the machine. And now you got me up here tryna tell grown women that rhinestones ain't a personality trait."

I ran a hand down my beard, finally getting how much weight she was carrying. I thought tossing money at payroll was enough, like that covered everything. But Magnolia wasn't just working, she was holding the whole place up by herself.

She pointed at me, eyes aggravated but voice still sweet. "And you...you sitting back like throwing dollars fixes everything. Let me tell you something my great-grandmamma used to say—'Money don't clean no dirty drawers.' Meaning, baby, it ain't always about the cash. It can't do everything. Sometimes you gotta get down in the mess yourself."

I laughed, but it hit me in my chest. Magnolia was right. She was drowning, and I was letting her.

I sat back in my chair because she was fire and sugar in one breath.

She huffed, fanning herself with a stack of receipts. "Baby, I can't keep doin' this. My people used to say, *'You can't fry the chicken if you still chasin' it.'* And right now, I'm doin' both."

I tried to hold back my grin, but it was useless. "Magnolia..."

She pointed at me. "Niv said I was going to be doing business, not coordinate who twerking in the left corner and who upside down in VIP. Now look at me. No rest, no peace. My rose battery probably think I died."

I choked out a laugh, and she leaned forward, dead serious.

"You need to call Niv."

I shook my head. "She ain't gonna come back. And definitely not if it's me asking."

I ran my hand over my beard and sighed. "Magnolia, listen. I got this deal I'm tryna secure. Big money. I need her. Not just her face on the flyers—her dancing for me. You know how she is. Niv can walk in a room and say absolutely nothing, and still be louder than everybody in there. She got that way of telling you yes or no without ever opening her mouth. These niggas respect that. I need that. If nothing else, I need that."

Magnolia squinted at me like she was trying to see straight through the lie I hadn't told yet. Then she leaned back, crossed her arms, and smirked.

"Mmm-hmm. Sound real good, boss man. All that 'business deal' talk got a nice ring to it. But let's be honest—" she leaned forward, tapping the desk for emphasis. "You just want me to beg that girl for you. You sat here and cooked up a fancy-ass reason."

I rolled my eyes, but she wasn't wrong.

"Magnolia—"

"Don't Magnolia me," she cut in, wagging her finger. "I know a lovesick fool when I see one. I left Mississippi to get away from men begging me. And here you go, sitting in this office with your heart on your sleeve looking pitiful." She shook her head, lips twitching like she was trying not to laugh. "Chile, let me go pour me a drink before I agree to this nonsense."

She threw her hands up and sighed like her spirit was being tested. "Lawd. I'll think about it. But I'm telling you now, if she cuss me out, I'm packing up my purse, catching the first Greyhound back to Mississippi, and leaving you to run this club alone with these Dollar Tree dancers."

Even while clowning me, Magnolia had a way of making me believe she'd get it done. She was sweet enough to sugarcoat a bullet and country enough to fire it anyway.

Out of nowhere, we heard a loud *CRASH* out on the floor. Magnolia jumped like somebody slapped her.

"Lord, have mercy!" she shouted, throwing her hands in the air. "Glass breaking again? These yo' kids in here, Kendrix. I swear I can't leave these babies two damn minutes without them breaking shit. This ain't no damn Chuck E. Cheese! If one more bottle girl knock over one more shelf, I'm sending her back to Hooters where she belong."

She pointed at a folder down on the desk in front of me. "That's some paperwork that needs your John Hancock. If you need something, holler at me. I gotta go before I catch a charge on these heffas."

She left out, her voice already carrying through the hall, fussing like somebody's great-grandma who'd been raised on peppermint and switch whoopings.

I sat back in the chair, ran both hands down my face, and let out a heavy breath. Magnolia talked her shit, but she missed Niv just as much as I did. She'd never admit it, but I heard it in the way she said "yo' kids." Truth was, none of us knew how to handle the club without her. Not really.

I leaned back, pulled out my phone, and stared at the screen. She said at Hux's game she'd unblock me, but that didn't mean she'd actually answer or respond. Still, fuck it.

> Just checking in on you. I have a big meeting coming up to secure a deal. Just thinking about that hoping it all turns out good. I'm thinking about you too. It's weird without my business partner.

Pressed send. Leaned back. Closed my eyes. Prepared myself for the silence that could follow. I had already prepared myself mentally for her not to respond, but a few minutes later, my phone buzzed. My heart jumped like I was fifteen again. I unlocked it fast as hell and instantly regretted it.

All good this way. You got it. You had the hottest club before I came into the picture and that means you'll have it even with me out.

I just sat there, staring at the screen. How the fuck do you even respond to that? Cold but polite. Like she was handing me back my heart in a manila envelope with *Return to Sender* stamped across it.

I shoved the phone in my pocket. Magnolia was right. Without Niv, the whole thing was on life support. And I was sitting there hoping she'd throw me one lifeline.

34

Niveah

By the time the DJ cut the music and announced we were about to start, I was already over it. Over the whole damn party, over the fact that I spent three mortgage payments on balloons, backdrops, catered food, and a cake taller than Zejah's belly.

All because those two little lovers decided to send me fifty damn Pinterest pictures. Fifty. Talking about, *"We want this one."* Then two seconds later, *"Ooo, we want this one too."*

Chile...my debit card was crying like a newborn, but I smiled through it.

We were at the park because hell no, I wasn't mixing Gun Hill cousins with Hux's prep school teammates under my roof. That sounded like a recipe for a drive-by or a PTA meeting gone left, and either way, it wasn't happening at my house. Everyone didn't need to know exactly where I laid my head, anyway.

The balloons started popping in the sun, and baby, I ducked like somebody let shots off. Folks laughed at me, but shit, muscle memory don't lie. Hood trauma don't disappear just because you booked a luxury balloon arch.

I looked around and sighed. Money well spent, I guess. The kids were happy, the grown folks had plates in their laps, and everybody was posted up like this was the Met Gala of the hood and the suburbs colliding.

But real talk? The whole baby reveal culture...scams. Straight scams. Between the custom cake, catered wings, balloon arches, and photographer, I could've put a down payment on a damn duplex. People talk about kids being blessings, but nobody says how expensive the rollout is.

Still, I was proud of them. Proud that Hux was standing tall, even nervous, but taking responsibility. Proud that Zejah was becoming a young woman. But I was tired as hell.

Boss bitch or not, I was tired.

The people from Gun Hill came out heavy...with empty hands. No diapers, no bibs, not even a pack of wipes. They pulled up for the free food, full stop. Like I ain't notice. Baby, I noticed.

But see, I planned for that. I knew my people.

I asked a few girls from the club who knew me and Hux to be hostesses. They were standing at the gift table sharp as security guards. Rule was simple:

Drop off a gift or a card → get a ticket.

No ticket → no plate.

The caterer already knew the deal. One pan of wings could feed a whole hood block, and I wasn't about to let freeloaders run through it.

It got so bad that folks from Gun Hill started clowning me. *"Man Niv, you wild as hell for this."* But funny enough, they started sliding the hostesses $10 and $20 for a ticket. My girls handed the cash right to me. *"Here sis, we putting this towards more pampers."* That's why I keep my circle tight with hustlers who understand the assignment.

Meanwhile, the "privileged prep" kids were standing around looking confused like, *"Why do we need tickets for food?"* And I wanted to yell, *"Welcome to the hood, baby. Nothing free but stress."*

You can take the girl out of Gun Hill, but that hood mentality never leaves.

When it was time, everybody crowded around. Hux and Zejah looked so happy, holding hands like they were about to announce the winner of a Grammy. For a moment, I forgot how much the whole thing drained my pockets. Seeing them smile like that...was worth it.

We counted down. Three...two...one—

POP!

Pink confetti rained down everywhere. The park erupted. Screaming, clapping, hollering, phones out recording like it was the BET Awards.

Zejah was crying, Hux was cheesing like he just hit another game-winning three, and me? I was standing there with confetti in my wig, laughing at all the chaos and thinking, *Damn, this baby already expensive as hell and she ain't even born yet.*

We were just a family celebrating new life, so it didn't take long for that gender reveal to turn straight into a grown folks' party.

Soon as the pink confetti hit the grass, the old heads started dragging folding tables out their trunks like they had 'em on standby. Somebody yelled, *"Aye, bring the spades cards!"* And before I knew it, decks were slapping, dice were rolling, and the whole thing turned into a block cookout.

They even pooled money together to send somebody's cousin to the corner store for beer, wine coolers, and juices for the kids. My eyes rolled because I already dropped racks on that fancy-ass sweet table and those kids had enough sugar to power a spaceship. But hey, at least the grown folks were happy and the babies were busy.

The kids were tearing up the swingset and jungle gym, mouths sticky from candy and cake, while the DJ switched it up. Next thing I know, "Before I Let Go" came on and everybody's auntie instinct kicked in. You know what that means… the electric slide.

And when I say everybody? I mean everybody. Gun Hill, private school preps, church folk, cousins, random plus-ones…we were all lined up like we'd been rehearsing. I was tired as hell, feet hurting from being cute all day, but it had been a long time since I'd let myself just enjoy a Gun Hill hood party. Laughing, sweating, singing off-key.

For a minute, it didn't feel like stress. Didn't feel like bills, or taking care of the whole house, or heartbreak. It just felt good. A party in Gun Hill, like old times. Except that time, I was the one who'd paid for everything.

I looked around at all the chaos and couldn't help but smile. Then I caught Magnolia's hand waving from the parking lot. She passed Ty a pink gift bag and then started pointing toward her truck like she was going to unload groceries.

I walked over, curious. "Magnolia, what you over there plotting?"

She grinned wide and said, "Hey, baby. I just gave Ty my little bag but listen. My whole damn truck is full of shit. Crib, playpen, walker, that expensive swing everybody swear rocks babies straight to sleep, oh, and I got some breast pumps too. But if she don't breast pump, I got that bougie machine that makes the bottles for her. Don't play with me, I cleared out half of Target."

Ty's eyes got big. "Damn, Magnolia, GivGold paying you like that?"

Just hearing the name *GivGold* made my stomach flip. I swallowed back the knot in my throat before it showed. Thinking about Kendrix was the last thing I wanted to do.

Magnolia hugged Ty like she always did and then turned her attention on me. "Girl, you know who that from."

I rolled my eyes because I knew. "Tell him I said thank you, but he ain't have to do all that."

Magnolia put her hand on her hip and gave me that look only a Southern woman could give. "Now look here, Niv. You gon' take this shit. Because I don't have the time, patience, or gas money to haul this back to him, let him beg me to bring it again, only for you to get mad and send it back. Uh-uh. I'm already running around that club like a chicken with its head cut off. I'm not about to add baby gift relay service to my job description."

I burst out laughing. "Send back what? A shidddd. I didn't even know how expensive baby stuff was until I helped Zejah with her registry. He can send more if he want."

Magnolia wagged a finger at me. "Mhm, I bet you'll let him."

"Damn right," I said with a smirk. "Just follow me home after we leave, and we'll unload it all in the house."

Magnolia grinned, shaking her head. "Lord, y'all gone stress me into wrinkles before my time."

I cut my eyes at her. "Hold up. There ain't no y'all. It's a Niv and it's a Kendrix. Not no y'all."

She sucked her teeth so loud the cousins nearby turned their heads. "Oh whatever. I'm sick of this shit. It's forever a y'all. Both of y'all act like you slow.

Meanwhile, both of y'all only think about y'all and want us to pretend like we don't notice, when really? We all know y'all some in love dumbasses."

I blinked, deadpan. "...Damn."

Magnolia shrugged, throwing her hands up. "Well, I'm just saying. Y'all doing the most, and it's affecting everybody around here."

That made me straighten up. My attention sharpened. "What you mean, affecting everybody?"

"Don't worry about it." She waved me off and started to walk, but I stepped in front of her.

"No. Say it."

Magnolia sighed, dramatic as hell. "Okay. Shit just ain't been the same since you left. I ain't good with all the shit you did with the crew. I don't have the mind to plan themes, coordinate routines, or approve drinks, plus keep up with paperwork, contracts, licenses, and all that admin stuff I do. Kendrix's mind so gone about you not being there. He barely shows up. Numbers ain't good at all, baby. That place about to be closed down soon. And if it does, plenty of people gone be without jobs. It used to be the hottest spot in Antionette, and now we might as well start paying folks to come in and post like they having a good time just to get traffic up."

I swallowed hard. Damn. I hadn't thought about it like that. I knew Kendrix loved that club, but Magnolia was right. He wasn't the type who could function in chaos. If something was wrong, he couldn't just shove it in a corner. He let it eat at him until it spilled everywhere else.

Magnolia's voice softened. "He got this big meeting coming up with vendors, upgrades, hookahs, all that extra stuff that could save us financially. But his mind so messed up over you, I don't even know if he can focus." She went quiet for a second, then blurted out: "How about you come dance in the VIP room for that meeting?"

I damn near choked. "Hell no."

Magnolia put her hands together like she was praying in church. "Please, baby. That would help us out so much."

I squinted at her. "How you even know he wants me there?"

She smirked. "Uh, because he said—*and I quote*—'I can't get this deal without her.'"

That shut me right up.

Magnolia leaned in, country as cornbread. "Don't make me beg, girl. Don't do me like this. We talking about jobs on the line. Folks got kids, bills, car notes. I'm already running around like I'm crazy. You wanna add me explaining foreclosure to the bartender crew? Please."

Her pitiful begging made me laugh, but it also hit me in my chest. Even with everything going on between me and Kendrix, I wasn't about to let him lose his club. That was his baby. And truth be told, I loved him too much for that.

I sighed, crossing my arms. "Fine. Only this one time."

Magnolia clapped her hands and shouted like she was at Sunday service. "Thank you, Jesus! God is so good. My God, never fails!"

35

Kendrix

The club was packed wall-to-wall. I wanted to lie to myself, say it was Magnolia's promo crew and all the staged social media posts that pulled folks in, but I knew better.

Word must've spread about Her Majesty closing for a few days over a busted pipe. And if Her Majesty was closed, that meant everyone needed somewhere to go. All it took was a whisper of her name possibly being at the club and bodies came running. Everybody knew when MissCommunication touched a stage, it wasn't a night. It was an experience.

I moved through the crowd, dapping up old heads, nodding at familiar faces, pretending like my chest wasn't tight. The music, the lights, the smell of liquor and perfume should've felt like my domain, but it felt like hers.

Magnolia spotted me before I even got halfway across the floor. "Well, look at you," she teased. "All sharp in that black suit and purple tie. Lord, you trying to make these girls weak in the knees?"

She gave me a look up and down, shaking her head. "Mm-mm-mm. You and Niv... y'all something else. Coordinating colors. That's good marketing, baby. Real good idea for the business meeting."

Her words caught me off guard because I hadn't told Niv what I was wearing. Hell, we hadn't talked about colors at all. But knowing she had on purple? After everything? My heart jumped.

Magnolia leaned in a little, her tone softening. "She's been back there about fifteen minutes now. Dancing and working the room like she never left."

I nodded, jaw tight, pulse thudding in my ears. "Good timing," was all I could manage.

My hands damn near shook knowing she would be moving her body in ways I hadn't seen in weeks. While probably looking dead at me just to remind me what I lost.

When I stepped into the room, she was already on the pole twirling. Every slow spin of her thighs and arch of her back pulled the men forward like they were hypnotized, their eyes wide like she was the next damn ticket into heaven.

The door shut behind me, muffling the bass from the main floor, and the men snapped their attention my way. They broke from their trance and came over, grinning, hands extended. The setup was clean. A low glass table with contracts already laid out, couches circling like a private king's court.

It was the first time meeting them in person. They'd been chasing me for weeks with big promises—new vendors, upgraded experiences, ways to take GivGold even higher. They had the energy, the money, the vision. Everything about them screamed opportunity.

We shook hands, and I sat down with them. And then the music shifted.

The song ended, replaced by *Body Language*—Big Sean. My head jerked up. That was our song. One of the ones we used to ride to late nights, her legs stretched across my lap, both of us vibing to the words like they were written about us. She never played it in the club. Not once.

And then, almost instantly, she flipped the LED lights to red.

The men lit up like it was Christmas. "A red light special? She tryna spoil us tonight!" one laughed, leaning back, eyes glued to her. Another rubbed his hands together like he'd just been served a feast.

My chest tightened. Niv had walked in wearing purple, her crown color. She would never wear that color and mix red lights with it. That wasn't her. Red meant something else.

I stayed alert.

They started talking. Contracts, percentages, future collabs, but I couldn't focus. Out the corner of my eye, I saw her, and I knew her. It wasn't her normal sway, that soft hypnotic seduction she had mastered. It was harder. Every move looked like it was pulled out of anger. She bent low and snapped up fast, heels slamming the stage, pole swinging under her grip like she was fighting it.

It was beautiful, yeah. The men thought they were getting the show of their lives, but my stomach dropped. I knew that body better than anyone else, and her body was screaming something else.

Everything sounded good on paper. Too good, maybe. Contracts lined out clean, percentages adding up. Still, something in me was twitching. With my pen in my hand, my eyes flicking back and forth between the paperwork and her.

She didn't look at me. Not once.

Niv always talked to me with her eyes too. Even when her mouth was spitting venom, her body, her eyes, always told me the truth too. But she gave me no eye contact. Just hard, sharp movements. Heels smacking against the stage like gunfire, her body cutting through the music with anger.

It pissed me off, her not giving me that one look. Maybe she thought if she did, it'd give us away. But fuck that, I needed it. I needed her to say with her eyes that she was okay. That I was okay.

Instead, I felt my chest tighten. That familiar pressure I hadn't felt since my first shootout. I just signed the papers, telling myself it was nerves. Telling myself it was all business.

The men smiled wide like I'd just handed them the kingdom. One scooped up the folder with a slick *thank you*, while the other reached under the table. He dragged out a black briefcase smiling as he set it on the glass.

"All of this is for you," he said.

My focus snapped between them and the briefcase, and then I realized something: only one of them was standing at the table. The other was moving slowly towards Niv.

Towards *my* woman.

My pulse slammed. Before I could even push back my chair, Niv dropped low, snapping into a split so fast the floor shook as her palm smacked against it. Not sexy. Not seductive. A *signal*.

My hand went to my strap before my brain caught up.

The briefcase man snapped it open—no money. A gun. Extra clips. My aim was already set, my heart hammering in my throat. He lifted the piece, but I pulled first. One round dead-center through his forehead. His head snapped back, body collapsing into the table like dead weight.

Before the other fool could even blink, I swung and fired again. Straight through his chest as his hand reached for his waistband. He stumbled back, crumpled near the base of the stage, a pistol falling from his grip and sliding across the polished floor.

Silence, except the bass from the other side of the walls and the sound of my own blood rushing in my ears.

Niv didn't scream or flinch. She froze on the stage, fear in her eyes but not weakness. She was too smart to scare the clients outside, but I saw it. That flicker of terror she tried to bury.

I stood, breathing hard, gun still raised.

The briefcase lay open in front of me. A setup. A straight-up execution plan.

I flipped the body nearest her, pressing my boot down until he rolled. Sure enough, another weapon tucked in his pants.

Niv's voice cracked, low but panicked. "Were they going to kill you... and then me?"

I didn't look at her, just kept my eyes moving, scanning the corners of the room like my father drilled into me. But my voice came out calm, too calm. "Looks like it, Niv."

Calm was a mask. Inside, I was shaking.

Her eyes weren't focused. They were glassy, locked somewhere far away, like she wasn't even in the damn room anymore.

Blood smeared across the stage, across my shoes, the smell of metal heavy in the air, and she just sat there frozen.

"Hey. Niv. Hey."

I crouched in front of her, grabbing her face with both hands, forcing her chin up. Her skin was cold, her lashes wet, but her body wouldn't move.

"You gotta snap out of it. Right now. Look at me."

Her lips parted, but no words came out. Just shallow breaths. The silence scared me more than the two dead men on the floor.

I pressed my forehead to hers. Controlled, like my father taught me when panic set in. "I had a silencer, Niv. You didn't hear the shots. Be thankful for that. But I need you now. I need you to tell me everything. Every word they said."

Finally, her eyes flicked to mine, and when she opened her mouth, her voice cracked. "They... they kept saying shit. Seductive, creepy. 'Save the last dance.' 'Dance like it's my last.' And then—" Her throat worked hard as her tears came faster. "They kept asking each other if they were ready. Over and over. Not business-ready. Ready-ready. Like... ready to do some shit they couldn't take back."

She shook her head violently, her hands going to her face. "I knew it. I knew something was wrong. I wanted to look at you, to warn you, but—" Her sob cut her sentence in half. "I know what these eyes do to us, Ken. We can't even look at each other without everything we felt coming back. I thought if I kept it in, maybe... maybe you'd see it in my body. I thought I was protecting you."

Her voice broke completely then, her shoulders collapsing forward as she cried. "I was so stupid. I should've just looked at you. You would've known sooner. I almost got us both killed."

That broke me.

I pulled her off the stage and into my arms, holding her so tight my chest ached. For weeks, I hadn't touched her. For weeks, I'd craved that and of all nights, it was killing me that it happened like that.

Her body trembled against mine, her tears soaking through my shirt. My own eyes burned until the first one fell, and then another, and I couldn't stop them.

"I love you," I whispered into her hair, pressing kisses across her temple, her cheek, anywhere I could. "I fucking love you. I've missed you every second, Niv. You hear me? Every second."

She pulled back just enough for me to see her face, raw and red. I cupped her cheeks again, speaking into her, giving her everything I had.

"You are not stupid. You are not weak. You're the strongest woman I've ever seen. You didn't almost get us killed, you helped me save us. You saved me tonight."

I didn't let her go. Couldn't. My arms were locked around her like if I eased up even a little, she'd vanish again and leave me in that hollow place I'd been stuck in.

"I been lost without you, Niv." My voice cracked, and I didn't care. "I ain't slept in my bed since you left. Not once. You know where I sleep? My damn car. Because it's easier to pass out in the driver's seat than it is to lay in that big-ass bed and reach over for you and come up empty."

Her lips trembled, her eyes wet and wide. I brushed my thumb across her cheek, swallowing the lump in my throat. "I swear, I'd rather break my back in that car than face how cold that house feels without you."

She sucked in a breath, and for the first time in forever, she didn't hold back. "You think you the only one? You think I've been fine, Ken?" Her voice cracked on my name, and it damn near split me open. "I been dying, every day, pretending like I don't miss you. Pretending like I don't wanna answer when your number pop up. But I don't... because if I do, I fall all the way back in, and I don't know if either one of us survives that."

I closed my eyes, forehead pressed to hers. Her breath hitched, her body still shaking.

"You don't get it," I whispered. "I don't care if it kills me, Niv. I'd rather die with you than live without you."

Her sob was sharp, raw. "Don't say that. Don't you put that on me. I already feel like loving me is poison for you. Look at your family. Look at your father. Look at what I did."

I shook my head hard, refusing to let her spin it. "You didn't ruin me. You didn't ruin us. We're here because life keeps throwing shit at us that we didn't ask for. But you're the only thing that's ever made me want to fight through it."

Her tears slid hot against my skin. "And what happens when fighting for me means losing everything else you love?"

That one gutted me. I didn't have an answer. My throat burned. My chest hurt. And still, I clung to her.

"I can't promise it'll be easy," I said finally, voice breaking. "But being apart is already killing me. So either way, I lose. I just don't want to lose you."

She shook her head, crying harder, whispering against my lips. "Why you make it sound so simple?"

"Because it is," I said, desperate now. "You love me. I love you. That's the truth. Everything else is noise."

Her hand lifted and pressed flat to my chest, right over my heart. She stayed there, feeling the rhythm under her palm, like she was trying to decide if she could risk it beating for her again. I wished like hell I could freeze us right there. Her in my arms. My lips on hers. Her tears soaking into me like proof she still loved me. If time would've stopped, I could've stayed in that moment forever. But I couldn't. Reality was clawing at the door.

I leaned back, grabbed her face, kissed her one last time, then gave her that look. The look that told her it was time to stop crying and listen.

She looked anxious. "What?"

"Listen to me and listen close." I said.

She blinked fast, chest rising and falling like she was already bracing herself.

"You're gonna walk out of here," I said steady. "Go find Magnolia. Tell her CodeGold. Shut the club down immediately. Say somebody's got a weapon if you gotta. Whatever it takes. Get every single body out of this building. I'll keep this door locked, but get my security to stand in front of it. No one comes in. Nobody."

She shook her head but I pressed my thumb under her chin, forcing her eyes on me. "After that, go to your dressing room. Strip. Everything. Put it all in a bag. Clothes, heels, earrings, everything." My eyes swept over her face. "You're beautiful as hell, Niv. That lace front looks fire, I know it's fresh. But take that shit off too. Put it in the bag. Hand it to Magnolia. She'll know what to do with it."

Her lip trembled. "Okay... but once it's done, I'm coming back."

I cut her off. "No. You're going home."

She jerked back like I slapped her. "Nooo, Kendrix, I'm not leaving you! I can't—" her voice broke, "—I can't leave you."

Her tears broke me, but I had to steel myself. I grabbed her tighter, forced her to hear me. "You have to. This ain't about you or me right now. And there's only one person I can call to handle this... to make sure it looks like this never happened."

Her eyes widened in disbelief. "Who?"

I swallowed hard, the weight of it pressing on my chest. "My dad."

She froze, shaking her head instantly.

I leaned in, voice low, cold, because I had no choice. "It's gotta be him. He's the only one who can make this disappear. The only one who knows how to clean up something this dirty and keep the Feds, cops, *everyone* off my back. I don't want you here when he comes."

Her tears continued harder. I squeezed her face gently. "So please, baby. Don't fight me on this. Go. Do what I said. And trust me to handle the rest."

36

Niveah

I sat in my car outside my house, hands still shaking. Kendrix's face was burned into my memory. The way he looked at me, the way his arms felt when I finally let myself collapse into him. His kiss. God, that kiss. If I wasn't careful, it'd pull me all the way back.

I wanted to call him so bad. I kept looking at his name on my phone, but I stopped myself. No. He told me to go home. I needed to stay out of it. And if there was one thing Kendrix was good at, it was handling shit. That was his world.

So instead, I scrolled until I landed on Magnolia's name.

She picked up on the first ring.

"Magnolia," I breathed.

"Chile, why you sound like you just seen the Grim Reaper? Calm your nerves before you give yourself high blood pressure."

I exhaled hard. "Magnolia, is he okay? Please just tell me he's okay."

She didn't even hesitate. "He fine, baby. I saw with my own two eyes. His daddy came in there with his people like he was not new to this but true to this. They had everything sparkling quicker than a Waffle House after a fight. Lord, I knew I shoulda stayed my ass working over there waiting tables when I moved to Antionette. Y'all got me living a *P-Valley* episode forreal."

"Magnolia..." I said, finally catching my breath. "You're the only person who can make me laugh when I feel like I'm losing my mind."

"Well, good, 'cause you know laughter keep you young. Stress'll age you faster than bad makeup. And we can't have that, baby."

I laughed before I could stop it, but my chest still felt heavy. "So... did you go in the room?"

Magnolia sucked her teeth. "Hell naw. I stayed my ass out the way. Don't you tell me what was in that room neither, 'cause I don't wanna be tied to nothing. I just know what I saw. He walked out alive, cool as ever, and took a couple shots before he left with his daddy and brothers. So quit panicking, he's good. Question is, are you good?"

I swallowed, throat tight. "Yeah... I just feel so stupid for caring about him this much after everything."

Her voice softened, losing some of that sharp edge. "You ain't stupid, baby. You love him. It ain't his fault he came from that man and it doesn't mean he's the same. Don't mean he don't love you back just as hard."

My eyes burned, and I pressed my palm to my face before she could hear me crack. "Magnolia—"

"Don't even," she cut in, her voice quick and warm. "Take a breath, wipe them tears, and remember who you are. The strongest woman I know, and I love you for it. I gotta go, but call me if you need me."

I hung up before I could fall apart completely, the sound of her words still replaying in my head.

My phone buzzed and for half a second, my heart leapt.

Kendrix.

Damn, Niv. Really? You almost died next to this man, and here you are grinning at a text like a teenager with her first crush. I had to remind myself to calm down and breathe.

> Just checking on you. You good?

I chewed my lip, staring at the screen for a while before I finally typed back:

> Home. Fine.

Three dots appeared, disappeared, came back again. Then his reply hit:

> I can come by after I leave from my dad and my brothers.

And that's when a wave of emotions hit me. Anger and hurt all rolled into one. I knew it wasn't fair, but damn, it stung. After everything, he was with them. His flesh. His blood. The same man who ruined my mama and ruined me. The same brothers who looked at me like I was poison.

And what else was he supposed to do? That was his family. His people. The ones who'd been there before me and would be there long after. Still, knowing that didn't make it hurt less.

I typed slow, each word like swallowing glass.

> Don't worry about it. I'm fine.

Then I tossed the phone on the passenger seat, but my hand reached for it again, scrolling past his name and straight into another thread.

Sincere.

I scrolled back through our thread, months of messages from him stacked on top of each other with nothing from me in between. Messages I ignored because Kendrix was my whole damn world.

> Mornin, Princess.

> This bag made me think of yuh today.

> Yuh slipping, rude girl.

And then one from two days ago:

> Yuh not responding. A guy come lay eyes, so I know yuh fine. But just want to let yuh know in town.

My stomach flipped. Without thinking, I pressed call. One ring. Two rings. By the third, I figured he'd ignore me, then—

"Look who finally decide fi call," his Jamaican accent smooth as always. "As if ghosting mi for months wasn't childish behavior."

I bit my lip. "I can explain, if you let me."

"Explain?" he drawled, voice low. "Maybe mi deh wid somebody else. Maybe mi busy."

"I don't care," I said. "She can be excused."

That made him laugh. "That's crazy, coming from somebody who couldn't be woman enough to tell me she was committed to someone else."

I smirked, even though he couldn't see me. "Sincere, are you going to excuse the hoe so I can come meet you or not?"

I heard a muffled voice in the background: "Hoe? Who the fuck—"

I laughed because I realized that he had me on speaker. That man did not give a single fuck.

Sincere laughed too, unbothered. "Your services are no longer needed," he told whoever she was, like he was firing an employee. Then, back to me: "I'm at the usual hotel. Room 734. Security will escort you up."

The girl in the background went off again, cursing. That only made me laugh harder. "See you soon," I said, hanging up, not caring to hear her finish her rant.

I tossed my phone on the passenger seat, shifted my car into reverse, and shook my head, *"Damn, Niv... you ain't shit."*

NETRAANTIONETTE

The elevator dinged at the seventh floor, and Sincere's security guard walked me down the plush hallway. He opened the door without a word.

Sincere was leaned back in a chair, phone in one hand, glass of Hennessy sweating in the other. He grinned the second his eyes caught mine.

"Well, look at who finally crawled out the shadows. Took long enough."

I smirked, stepping in. "Had to make sure your nightcap cleared out first. Didn't want any confusion. I'm not in the mood to be whooping ass."

He laughed. "Oh, I made sure of that. Woman is still cussing me out in the parking lot. So you better have a good explanation for ghosting me."

I dropped my purse on the bed and kicked off my heels. "Long night. I need to shower it all off."

He raised an eyebrow, following me toward the bathroom. "So you washing your boyfriend's fluids off you?"

I laughed, shaking my head. "That man hasn't touched me in a while. Truth is, after what my body's been through these last few weeks, I've been scared to get touched at all."

His eyes narrowed, testing me. "You lying. You love being touched."

"I am," I admitted with a half-smile. "But still."

What I didn't say was how traumatic taking those abortion pills was. Talynn drilled in me that it was my business. My choice. My body. So just like everyone else, he didn't need a detailed explanation.

I cut the shower on and steam filled the room. He sat on the toilet, casual as ever, while I stepped under the spray. Like the best friend he'd been for years, he just let me talk.

I told him everything. How Kendrix had finally been the man to break through me, and how I let myself fall. How I found out his dad was the very devil who gave my mother her first high. How it gutted me to love a man tied to the monster who ruined us.

My voice broke under the water, but I didn't stop. "I feel so stupid, Sin. Stupid for loving him. Stupid for hating him. Stupid for sitting in silence these past weeks, just drowning in myself."

When I turned the water off, he was already there. A towel in his hands. He crouched down, wrapping it around me with a gentleness that damn near broke me open.

"Come," he murmured, drying me off like I was fragile when he knew damn well I wasn't. "You not stupid. You human. You hurt. And mi gon' tell you this. Love don't make you weak."

I just looked at him, spilling my hurt to the one man who never judged me for the chaos I came from. I didn't bother with clothes. Not a robe. Not even the towel he'd just wrapped me in. I walked straight to the bed, my skin still damp from the shower. He watched me the whole way, but I kept talking like he wasn't staring.

I flopped onto the bed, stretched out naked, staring at the ceiling.

He didn't move at first. Then he stood, slow, and made his way over. He didn't touch me. Just looked down with that mix of disappointment and patience he'd perfected over the years.

"You know what hurts me?" His voice was calm. "For years, yuh and me had one unspoken agreement. When either of us calls, we answer. Period. Don't matter if we in another country, don't matter if we laid up, don't matter if we tired. That's our rule." He shook his head. "And you broke it. Like it meant nothing."

The shame burned hot in my chest. "I know." My voice was small. "I know, and I'm sorry. So much was going on, Sin. I didn't handle it right. I wish I would've done better."

He sat down on the edge of the bed, finally, close enough that his presence pressed against me without a single touch. "Our friendship ain't built on sex, Niv. Never was. You should know that. We've been around each other a hundred times, and sex wasn't involved. It don't have to be that, for us to be real."

"I know," I whispered again, softer, like saying it enough times would make him believe me. "And Kendrix...he knows about you. About us. About this."

I stopped there. My throat closed.

He didn't buy it. He turned to face me fully, his eyes catching mine, reading me like he always did. "You ain't telling me something."

"What do you mean?" I tried to sound annoyed, but the crack in my voice betrayed me.

He leaned down, close enough that I felt his breath graze my lips, but he didn't kiss me. His voice dropped, low, steady, pulling the truth out of me without force.

"I know yuh body language, Niv. Always hav. Yuh carrying somethin else. And yuh not leavin until yuh say it."

I sucked in a breath. "You know when I told you Kendrix's mom dropped the charges? It wasn't just because she liked me." My throat tightened. "She made me agree to stay away from him. Said she didn't want to see her son hurt. She didn't want him having to choose between his family and me. And I had to do it. She was my only way out. My siblings needed me."

Sincere's head dropped, and when it came back up, his jaw was tight. He shook his head slow, like he was annoyed, like he'd heard enough.

"Why you looking like that?" I snapped, my chest already hot.

"Because you coulda fuckin call me." His voice shot through the room, loud and echoing against the hotel walls.

My voice went up to match his. "For what? So you could do what? You don't have those type of connections, Sin. They know people."

He shot up from the bed, chest heaving. "They know people, and I know people. They have money, and I have money. What makes them different?" His finger jabbed the air. "Now look at you. Feelin like yuh owe somebody for a deed they did, when you could've relied on the person who's been there from day one. Me."

The words cracked something inside me and I broke. Tears rushed fast, my throat burning. Because he was right.

He'd always been right.

Over the years, I'd picked up so much from him, his older friends, his game, his way of thinking. He'd schooled me on survival and strategy, but somehow, I was still always in survival mode. Always bracing. Always preparing for the bottom to fall out. Even with him, I couldn't let myself rest or depend.

"Sin..." My voice trembled. "I don't know how to stop. I don't know how to let somebody carry me. I just...don't."

He just looked at me, eyes softer than they had any right to be. And the silence that filled the room was heavier than any scream.

"Yuh know wah mi nuh like, Niv?" His voice dropped low. "Mi nuh like di fact dat yuh let yuh crown tilt. Since when yuh ever let people tell yuh what fi do? Since when?"

I opened my mouth, but he didn't give me a chance.

"Dat's him mom, yeah, but she nah run shit inna yuh life. She cyaan tell yuh who to love, who yuh talk to. Wah she gon' do if yuh tek Kendrix call? Put yuh back in jail? Risk mashin' up di whole relationship wid her own son? Stop playin' dumb, woman. Yuh know she nah do dat."

His words cut deep, too logical, too true. My chest burned.

He jabbed his finger toward me, eyes sharp. "Yuh so deep in love yuh lose yuh head. Lose yuh mentality. An mi hate it. If yuh gon' love him, love him. Stand up in it. But nuh let it break yuh down, nuh let it twist yuh into something weak. Because hear mi now, di man fall for strong Niv. Fierce Niv. Not dis broken-up shadow sittin' inna mi bed."

Tears welled in my eyes, but not just from hurt. Because it was like he held up a mirror I couldn't avoid. He wasn't letting me excuse my pain or letting me sink in it.

The tears burned hot as they slid down my face, and before I could pull away, Sincere caught my hand.

"I went..." My voice cracked, my chest tightening as the words forced their way out. "I went and danced for a business meeting Kendrix had at the club earlier today. I knew something wasn't right. I felt it in my bones. I tried to send him signals through my dancing, but I wouldn't give him eye contact. I refused. And that refusal almost got us killed."

The sobs came harder, heavier, shaking through me. "I watched him... I watched him kill two men before they killed us. I've seen bodies before, seen death before. But it was... It was never me. Never almost me. This was the first time I felt like the victim. And I wanted to stay with him, I swear I did, but then he said he had to call his dad."

My voice broke through my sobs with rage. "And that's when I realized... he depends on the devil to fix shit for him."

Sincere leaned back, let out a laugh, the kind that said he was annoyed but amused by my blindness. "Yuh hate dat man so much, Niv, yuh cyan even see straight. Yuh nuh even hear yuhself. He did everything. *Everything* to protect you, and yuh still boiling up over his father. Yuh mad because he handled it clean, without yuh hands getting dirty."

I wanted to argue, but his words were cutting straight through me.

Sincere leaned in, kissed my cheek softly, then whispered against my ear, with truth that stung. "Baby girl... yuh more mad than di person he gave di drugs to inna di first place. Y*uh mother.*"

That hit me so hard I gasped, my body curling in on itself as the sob tore loose. I never even thought about it like that. I'd been too busy hating, too busy clutching onto anger like it kept me alive.

"I want to love him..." My voice broke again, trembling. "God, I want to love him. But I know I can't."

Sincere pulled back just enough to look me dead in the eyes, shaking his head like I was the dumbest woman alive. "Yuh see? Yuh know yuh can, but yuh keep telling yuhself yuh cyan. Convincing yuh own self of a lie. But mi know better. We both know yuh can love dat man. Yuh want to love dat man. So stop frontin', Niv. Stop frontin' on him, and worse, on yuhself."

I wiped my face, but the tears kept coming anyway. "Maybe one day I'll get there," I whispered. "But not today. Not right now."

Sincere tilted his head. "So what yuh want me to do den, Niv? Hmm? Two men almost kill yuh. I need names. Faces. I want to know who di fuck dem is."

I shook my head quickly, because I knew exactly what that meant. If I gave him even half a name, bodies would start dropping by sunrise. "No, Kendrix is handling it," I told him firmly. "All I want from you... is to fuck me so good I don't feel hurt anymore."

He leaned back and laughed, like I just said the most predictable thing in the world. "Baby..." He shook his head. "I can do dat. But it's only temporary. When mi done, di pain gon' come right back. Mi gon' do as yuh command, only if yuh fix dis." His eyes narrowed, piercing into mine. "Because mi don't like dis Niv. Dis Niv no better than any average female. And yuh not average."

The moment his lips touched mine, I already knew what it was. It wasn't just sex. It wasn't even about release. It was goodbye. The kind of goodbye you don't say out loud because words aren't strong enough to hold it.

Sincere took his time with me, like he had all the patience in the world. Like he'd been waiting months for me to let him close again. His hands traced every inch of me, like he was reminding me who I was beneath all the weight I'd been carrying. Every kiss, every stroke, felt like him putting my crown back on my head piece by piece.

"Look at me," he whispered in that accent that always made my knees weak. And I did. His eyes stayed locked on mine as he slid into me, filling me so completely that tears slipped down my cheeks without permission. He didn't tease or rush. He gave me every inch like he was trying to stitch me back together from the inside out.

It was deep, unhurried, every movement a vow, every thrust a reminder. He angled his hips, pressing into that place that made me cry out, and still...he never broke eye contact. The tears in his eyes matched mine, even though neither of us said a word about them.

I wrapped my legs tighter around him, pulling him deeper, needing him to take everything I couldn't say out loud. The hurt. The fear. The love I had for a man I felt I shouldn't have. And Sincere gave it all back. Harder thrusts when my voice broke, softer when my nails dug into his back, kissing me until I almost forgot why my chest ached.

It felt endless and fleeting all at once. His body speaking to mine, saying goodbye in the only language we'd ever trusted between us. His pace built, each stroke rougher, more desperate, until he buried himself inside me with a groan that felt like both surrender and release. I came undone beneath him, clinging like if I held on tight enough, it wouldn't have to end.

But when it was over, when the room was nothing but silence and ragged breathing, I knew. We both knew. The tears still clung to his lashes, just like mine. We wouldn't speak on them. We wouldn't call it what it was.

Our friendship would always be ours. But the intimacy and the crossing of that line? We both understood it had just died in that bed. Because no matter how much we loved each other, my heart already belonged to someone else.

37

Kendrix

The smell of biscuits and bacon was the only reason I dragged myself out of my old bedroom. Mama insisted I stay the night and how she'd sleep better knowing all her boys were under one roof while things cooled down. So there I was, sitting at her kitchen table in sweats, trying to pretend like I wanted to be bothered with anyone but Niv.

My mama slid a plate in front of me, smiling. That was her way of saying she was worried without saying it out loud. "Eat, baby. I made your favorite." she whispered before turning back to the stove.

I was halfway through my eggs when the door opened and in came my dad, cane tapping slow against the floor, Kross right behind him with folders in hand, and Kordai looked like he was ready to go just as much as I was. Kairo followed, phone glued to his ear, saying something about contracts before Mama snatched it out of his hand and pointed at the table.

"Sit down. Family business first," she snapped.

Dad eased himself into the head chair.

"Kendrix. Until we know more, I want that club of yours closed for a few days. No exceptions."

I nodded, but I was pissed. Like shutting GivGold down even temporarily was an admission that I couldn't protect what was mine.

Kross opened his folders, sliding papers across the table like he was about to teach a class. "A few friends and I have been up all night gathering info. Credit cards, license plates, business ties, everything. From everything I pulled, these guys weren't connected to any organization we know of. No families, no crews. Just free agents. Looks like they'd been watching you, plotting for a while."

The tension in my chest eased, just a little. Until Kairo opened his mouth.

"Or," he said, leaning back in his chair, "it's connected to those stupid-ass poker games you keep running. Maybe somebody lost big, came back for payback. You never think about the way your little hobbies put the rest of us at risk."

I slammed my fork down. "Man, get the fuck out my business. You don't know what I do or don't do."

"Don't I?" Kairo shot back, smirking. "Seems like every time some shit goes left, it's your name in the middle."

Tired of all the back and forth, Kordai started talking.

"You checked on Niv?" he asked.

I sighed in relief. *Bout time somebody asked something that actually made sense.*

"Yeah," I said. "She's good. She went home."

Both my mom and dad said *"Good"* at the same time, like they'd rehearsed it. Mamma immediately tried to change the subject, though.

"Kross, the event planner says the ceremony setup is almost done for tomorrow. I'm so excited to see Rivah's face—"

Kairo cut her off because he couldn't help himself.

"Nah, see, that's the problem. We keep breezing over this Niv stuff."

Mamma's voice snapped. "Kairo, would you shut up, please—"

But before she could finish, my dad's cane tapped against the floor, hard enough to make the table vibrate.

"You got one more time to think I'm gone let you sit here and disrespect my wife. One more time, Kairo. And all them teeth I paid good money for? Gone be down your motherfucking throat."

Silence. Nobody laughed, even though we wanted to. Kairo's hands shot up like he was a guilty kid caught red-handed.

"I don't know what's wrong with this family. She literally almost killed you! You know what? I don't gotta deal with this. I'm going home."

He stormed out, dramatic as hell. And nobody moved because nobody cared.

I pulled my phone out under the table and shot Niv a text.

> Can I see you?

It took a minute, but she finally responded.

> Her Majesty is open tonight. I'll make sure you're off the unwanted list.

I smirked.

> Haha, real funny. Ima beat that bouncer's ass if he tries me again.

> Just come see me then. And hush.

> Bet. I'll be there.

NETRAANTIONETTE

Walking up to *Her Majesty* felt different. It wasn't GivGold, but I couldn't deny the place had a soul. The neon lights, the line outside was long, and the bouncer at the door already had a stupid-ass look on his face when he saw me.

"Didn't I tell you—" he started, but Ty came storming up behind him.

"He good," she said and the bouncer's lip curled with a stank face.

I leaned in, fake-jumped like I was gone swing just to watch him flinch. "Yeah, keep playing."

He straightened up quick, trying to act unbothered, but I caught that little shake in his chest.

Inside, the vibe hit me. It wasn't polished like GivGold, but it had history in its walls. You could tell it was the stomping ground where half the city's best dancers sharpened their hustle before moving up. The floors creaked, the paint was chipped, but the crowd was thick. And with GivGold closed, I spotted plenty of familiar faces who usually threw money at my bar.

Ty gave me a look and motioned for me to follow. She pushed through the noise, weaving me to the back, then to a small hallway lined with dressing rooms. She opened one door without knocking.

Niv was on the pole, butt-ass naked, flipping and twisting. Sweat gleamed down her back, her body poetry in motion. She thought it was just Ty walking in, but when her eyes caught mine, her whole face changed.

"Damn, Ty!" She scrambled, snatching her robe from a chair and wrapping it around her.

Ty laughed so loud the walls shook. "Girl, it ain't like he ain't never seen you before." She smirked, glancing between us. "Anyway, it's time for me to hit the stage. Just wanted to bring him in here first."

She shut the door behind her, leaving me standing there with Niv still clutching her robe like it could protect her from me.

"You really covering up now?" I asked. "After all the times I've seen every inch of you. That robe ain't saving you from me."

"Maybe I don't want saving," she shot back, chin high. But the tremble underneath it betrayed her.

"Yeah?" I stepped closer, low voice. "Or maybe you scared. Scared because the second you let me look at you too long, it's over. You know it. I know it."

Her lips moved, like she wanted to argue, but she didn't. Instead, she sighed, sinking down onto the little stool by the vanity.

I leaned against the wall, eyes locked on her. "My people checked those guys and nothing came up. Just some clowns plotting, freelancing. But I'm keeping a low radar for a minute. Just in case."

"Good," she said softly. But her face told another story.

"What's wrong?"

"Nothing," she whispered.

"Bullshit. Your 'nothing' look like everything, Niv."

She shook her head slow. "Last night just made me realize how much I still care. And I hate it. I hate caring about you when I know I shouldn't."

I pushed off the wall, stepped in close until she had no choice but to look up at me. My voice cracked a little, but I didn't care.

"Niv... I never stopped caring. Not for one day. Not one damn second. You been in my head, in my chest, everywhere. And I don't want out. Fuck my dad. Fuck what he did. Fuck all of it. We'll figure it out. We can figure it out. Don't let him or anyone else win by being the reason we don't make it."

Her lips trembled, and I pressed a hand to her cheek.

"You hear me? I don't need perfect. I just need you. Broken, stubborn, scarred, whatever, just you."

She closed her eyes, a tear slipping out, and whispered back, "And what if I can't give you all of me?"

I kissed her forehead. "Then give me whatever part you can."

Her tears caught the light, and I swear they burned holes straight through me.

"Kendrix," she whispered. "I don't want to face your dad. Or your mom. I can't sit across from the man that ruined my life and pretend I don't feel hate in my chest. I can't be the girl at Sunday dinner when they're looking at me like I'm poison."

I cupped her face, thumb brushing her cheek. "Then don't. You don't have to be anything but mine. You hear me? You ain't never been scary, Niv. Not once. You walked through fire your whole life and came out crowned. Don't start doubting yourself now."

She shook her head. "You don't get it... I can't breathe when I think about it. I don't want to put myself in a position to break all over again. I love you, but loving you feels like standing in front of a firing squad."

I leaned closer, forehead pressed to hers.

"Then let me take the bullets with you. I don't give a fuck about what my dad thinks. I don't care what my mom whispers when the lights are off. I choose you. I'll choose you every time, even if it makes me the black sheep of my own damn family."

"But how do we live like that? How do we love each other knowing the room gets colder every time I walk in?"

"Easy," I said, not blinking. "We stop letting the room matter. I didn't fall in love with their approval. I fell in love with you. And I'd rather spend a lifetime fighting beside you than a second pretending I could live without you."

"You don't know what you're asking for," she whispered.

I kissed her hair. "I know exactly what I'm asking for. I'm asking for you. All of you. Even the pieces that don't fit. Even the scars. Even the rage. Especially the rage. That's the woman I love."

She wiped her tears.

I smirked, trying to lighten the mood. "So... you rehearsing butt-ass naked now? That a new Her Majesty policy?"

Her head lifted, laughing. "You interrupted. I was two spins away from a full set."

"Bet. Then finish it. Do it while I'm sitting in the audience tonight."

She rolled her eyes, trying to act hard. "You really think I'm about to dance for you?"

"Nah, not for me. For the crowd. I'll just be the only one in the room who knows every little twitch in your body language ain't for them. It's for me."

She bit her lip, caught between laughing and cursing me out. "You sound real delusional, you know that? Thinking I'm gonna be out there sending you signals when I could just be sending you to hell."

I laughed, brushing my knuckles under her chin. "Baby, if hell looks like you on a pole in purple with the lights low? Send me."

NETRAANTIONETTE

The bass dropped, and the crowd got loud. "Thuggish Ruggish Bone" poured out the speakers, that heavy 90s vibe, and when the spotlight hit her, I swear the whole room held its breath.

Pretty stepped out like she owned the damn decade—baggy, low-rise cargos slung tight on her hips, a cropped jersey knotted in the front, and her hair styled in that old-school half-up, half-down with baby hairs laid sharp. It was retro, hood, and sexy as hell all at once.

She grabbed the pole, swung around, and landed in a squat so clean the men in the front row damn near lost their voices. She slid up slow, that curve in her back so deep I clenched my fists just watching. Then she hit that heel-toe move, dropped low, and clapped her thighs so loud it cut right through the beat.

The crowd lost it.

And through all that, her eyes locked on me. Not the money-throwing dudes with their mouths wide open. Not the women in the back recording like they'd never seen art before. Just me.

Out the corner of my eye, though, something snagged me. A familiar smirk. A tilt of the head I knew too well. Arlette. Sitting in the lap of some older dude, whispering in his ear like she was selling him heaven for the night. I almost laughed out loud. She wasn't even watching the stage, too busy running her same tired game.

Hell, I was fucking happy and relieved that she was somebody else's problem. I just prayed she wasn't on no bullshit. I'd saved her ass before, but shit, I wasn't stepping in again. I was gone sit my ass right there and watch Pretty drag her ass by that lace front.

And that old head she was sitting on? He could get it too if he even thought about puffing his chest out. I'd fold him so quick his ass would be back in 1993 wondering why his pager was buzzing.

I forced myself not to look too long, because I didn't want Pretty to catch it and fall off her rhythm. And she was in her zone. She climbed high, spun, and slid down the pole into a split. Men were standing on couches and women yelling like it was church.

The crowd saw a dancer. I saw my undoing. And I knew right then, I'd let the whole damn club burn before I'd let her be done with me.

38

Niveah

I shut the dressing room door behind me, still out of breath from that set. My body was sweating, sore, alive but the ache felt good. I couldn't even lie to myself: being around Kendrix made life feel... lighter. Like my smiles weren't staged. Like my laughter wasn't something I had to practice. Around him, I felt like I didn't have to hold the damn world together on my back every second.

Sincere's words echoed in my head. *If yuh gon' love him, love him. Stand up in it. But nuh let it break yuh down, nuh let it twist yuh into something weak. Because hear mi now, di man fall for strong Niv. Fierce Niv. Not dis broken-up shadow.* He was right. I wasn't some fragile woman. Yeah, his mama gave me a lifeline, but who the hell said I had to keep living in chains? I could've told Kendrix the truth about her little "agreement," but why toss more gasoline on family fire? No. I'd try to figure out how to manage it all. Only problem was, my feelings were unmanageable.

Because if it wasn't for his father, me and Kendrix? We'd be damn near perfect.

I was mid-swipe fixing my lipstick when Ty pushed the door open, eyes sharp.

"How you doing?" she asked.

I smirked, suspicious. "I'm good. Why?"

She leaned on the doorframe, arms crossed, a look on her face like she was holding something back. "I know Kendrix was out there. And judging by that little smirk you got, I already know how you doing."

I laughed, caught red-handed. "I'm good. We're good."

But Ty wasn't smiling back. Not really.

I put my compact down. "What's wrong?"

She shifted. "Well... somebody is here. And I was about to kick them out, but then I thought, nah. Last thing I need is you saying I treated you like some weak ass bitch."

That had me laughing. "Ty, who the hell is it? That Arlette bitch?"

Ty's lips twisted. "Yeahhh, and—"

But I didn't let her finish. I was already on my feet, walking out. "Arlette is the least of my damn concern."

I stormed out, Ty hustling behind me, still trying to talk. The bass from the main floor hit me in the chest as soon as we rounded the corner. And like some twisted sixth sense, Kendrix's head snapped up. Our eyes locked. His smile was instant like he'd been waiting for me. And that smile damn near buckled me.

Ty tugged at my arm. "Niv, wait, listen—"

But I wasn't listening. My eyes flicked past Kendrix, across the floor. And there she was. Arlette. Perched in the lap of some older man like she was auditioning for a cheap porno, whispering in his ear.

Cute. *Real cute.* She thought that would get to me? Thought she could sit in a man's lap and make me sweat? Please. If she wanted a show, I could give her one better.

I was already plotting how I'd own her little stunt. Maybe a kiss planted right on Kendrix in front of everyone, maybe another set on stage with his eyes on nothing but me. My blood was hot with the thought of showing her who the fuck I was.

But then—

She shifted. Tilted her head. And I caught the man's face.

My world froze.

My breath left my chest like someone had socked me. My hands shook. My vision blurred. I started hyperventilating right there in the middle of the damn club.

It was him.

My father.

The deadbeat bastard who walked out on his wife and kids with no explanation. The man who left my mama drowning and forced me into the water just to keep afloat. The coward who lit the fuse on every struggle I'd been through since I was twelve years old.

And Arlette was sitting in his lap like some fucking trophy.

My knees almost buckled. Kendrix's smile dropped, and he was already moving toward me, fast. He saw my face, saw me stop cold. But before he could reach me, Ty rushed up, her arms sliding around me, guiding me back toward the dressing room.

"I tried to tell you," she whispered urgently against my ear. "I tried, Niv. You're gonna be okay. You're gonna be okay."

But nothing about that was okay.

The second the door shut behind us, my legs gave out. I crumpled to the floor, curling into myself like a child. Fetal position. Shaking. My sobs came out ugly and violent, the kind that ripped straight out of the chest no matter how hard you tried to swallow them back.

I hadn't seen that man in years. Not since the day he walked out. But I knew that face. God help me, I knew it. And now, older, heavier, with more gray around his mouth. He looked like an older version of Huxley. My baby brother.

The thought made my stomach turn.

Ty bent down, tugging at my arm. "Niv... come on, Please, get up. You're gonna be okay, you hear me? You're gonna be okay."

But I couldn't move. My body wouldn't listen. All I could do was cry harder, my nails digging into my own skin as if I could claw the memory of his face out of my mind.

The door burst open.

Kendrix stood there, confusion all over his face. His eyes swept the room, then locked on me curled on the floor. Concern hit him like a blow, softening his whole expression.

"What's wrong?" His voice was scared but urgent.

I didn't answer. Couldn't. My sobs drowned out everything.

"What's wrong?" he repeated, louder this time, stepping closer.

Still nothing.

"What the fuck is going on?" he snapped, voice breaking with frustration.

Ty's lips parted, her eyes darting between the two of us. She hesitated, then whispered, "It's... it's Arlette. She's with her dad."

Kendrix's eyes went wide. Shock, then fury, then something else I couldn't name. He looked back down at me. Still shaking, still crying like I'd never cried before.

Slowly, he dropped to his knees beside me. His big hand slid gently into my hair, his thumb rubbing slow circles against my temple like he was trying to soothe me back to life.

"Ty," he said quietly, never looking away from me. "Give us the room."

She started to protest. "Ken—"

"Respectfully," he cut her off, his tone sharp but steady, "get the fuck out. Let me handle this. I promise... I got her."

Ty lingered for a second, her eyes soft with worry. But she knew better than to argue with that tone. With one last look at me, she slipped out, shutting the door.

And then it was just me and him.

Kendrix didn't hesitate. He lowered himself to the floor beside me, his big body curling around mine like a shield. His arms wrapped tight, so tight I could feel his heartbeat pounding into my back. It wasn't sweet. It wasn't soft. It was desperate, protective, like he was holding together the pieces of me that kept trying to scatter across the floor.

His voice broke the silence, steady against my ear.

"Listen to me, Pretty. I know after all this time, seeing him is hard. That man might've given you blood, but he didn't give you shit else. No love, no wisdom, no blueprint. He left you to figure out life with scraps. But look at you. You took scraps and turned them into gold. You built a home. You kept kids alive and thriving. You became what he couldn't, what he wouldn't."

I shook my head, sobbing harder, but he pulled me tighter, refusing to let me slip away into the pain.

"You're not broken because he left. His absence doesn't make you weak. Nah, baby. You're proof that even when a parent leaves, God don't. You're the example so many girls need. The ones sitting in their rooms right now thinking they can't do it because their daddy ain't there, or their mama's too broken. You show them it's possible. You turned struggle into a crown and dared the world to knock it off your head. That's not broken, Pretty. That's brilliance."

My breath hitched. His words cut straight through my chest.

"I know you wanted a blueprint from your parents. Fuck a blueprint. You *became* the blueprint. You taught yourself how to survive, and you didn't just survive. You flourished. You created a life out of scraps, and you made it look like silk. You should be proud of you, because I'm proud of you."

The tears wouldn't stop.

He shifted, pressing his forehead to mine so I had no choice but to look at him. His eyes were wet too, but steady.

"The little girl inside of you wanted her parents. That's understandable. That little girl wanted to be tucked in. Wanted her daddy to clap for her dance recitals, wanted her mama sober and cooking Sunday dinner. She didn't get that. And that shit hurts. But she should be proud of who she grew up to be. Because that little girl grew up into a woman who didn't fold. A woman who turned pain into power."

My lip trembled. His hand slid across my face, his thumb catching every tear.

"You want to know how you handle a man like him? You don't fold in front of him. Don't you dare let him see you sweat. If anything, make *him* sweat. Let him choke on the truth when he sees what you became without him. Let him see the crown he walked away from."

I closed my eyes, the words lodging in my chest.

"You ain't gotta carry that weight no more, Niv. Not by yourself. Not with me here. You hear me? *Not with me here.*"

The words sat in the air like a vow.

"We gone sit here for a minute. You get it all out, every tear, every scream if you need to. But when we walk out of this room, Pretty, it's gone be with our heads lifted high. You hear me? No more folding. No more shrinking. You don't cower for nobody, not even the man who left you bleeding long ago. You face him, not as his daughter, but as the woman who made it without him."

He kissed my forehead, firm, grounding.

"Because broken girls stay here and cry on the floor. But women rise. And you've already done that over and over again."

I swallowed hard, chest burning, but the strength in his words cracked something open inside me.

"Okay," I whispered.

NETRAANTIONETTE

I touched up my lipstick, wiped away the last trace of tears, and stole a few kisses from Kendrix like I was charging myself with him. I swear, I loved him in ways words could never pin down. The way he held me, the way he made me feel like I wasn't broken, even when I felt like nothing but pieces, I'd never forget that.

But low was low, and that night had cut me deeper than I thought possible. I had laid eyes on the two men who had ruined my life in a matter of months. One gave my mama her first taste of hell. The other was the reason I couldn't breathe without choking on love for his son and hate for him at the same time. And my dad was playing house with a hoe I couldn't stand while Kendrix was standing behind me like the only man I'd ever trust to catch me when I fell.

I'd played out every version in my head of how I'd confront my dad if I ever saw him again. I thought I'd scream, or cry, or ask him why he left. But seeing him leaned back like a certified sugar daddy with Arlette perched in his lap? That shit flipped something ugly in me.

I walked with my head high, Kendrix right behind me like my shadow and my shield.

Arlette's ugly ass turned just in time. And no, she wasn't ugly for real but when your soul was nasty, it automatically stained your face. She smiled that greasy smile because she knew exactly what she was doing.

"Ohhhh hey, Kendrix," she dragged out, like I wasn't standing in plain sight. Then, with fake sweetness dripping like spoiled syrup: "Oh, and hey, girl."

I smirked. *Girl.* That was cute.

Then she turned to the man holding her like she was worth something, not even looking at me hard enough to recognize who I was. "Baby, this is my ex. And his... well, I don't even know what she is."

The man—my father—extended his hand, casual as hell, and said, "Nice to meet you."

Neither me nor Kendrix moved an inch. We didn't shake. We didn't blink. I just stared at that outstretched hand, the same hand that built my hell, until the weight of my silence made it drop.

I didn't even spare Arlette another glance. She could rot right there in his lap for all I cared. My eyes locked on him. The man who gave me his blood and nothing else.

I stepped closer. "You know, you're a great sugar daddy. Look at you, dressed sharp, paying for bitches who don't even respect themselves. Wine, dine, and whisper sweet nothings to women half your age." My voice rose, cutting sharper with every word. "But when it came to being a daddy to your actual kids? The ones with your last name? You were garbage. Trash. A ghost."

His brows furrowed, confused, but not enough. He tried to look unbothered until I tilted my head, really stared at him, let my eyes cut into him the way he deserved. Until he recognized who I was and filled himself with shame.

"Niveah..." he breathed, like the name got stuck in his throat.

Hearing it come from his mouth almost made me sick. But it didn't stop me. If anything, it made it worst.

"Yeah. Niveah. The little girl you left behind with a broken mama and a baby boy who had to figure shit out without you. The one who watched her mama crumble and thought maybe—just maybe—her daddy would come back and fix it all. But you never did, did you?" My voice cracked, but I didn't let it soften. "You went and built another life like we were nothing. Like I was nothing."

He opened his mouth, but I cut him off, stepping even closer, close enough to see every wrinkle, every line life had carved into his face. "Don't you dare look shocked. You know exactly who I am. You left me. You left *us*. And now you sit here playing house with this... this bottom-feeding bitch like you ain't got kids who carry your damn DNA walking this earth."

Gasps echoed from the tables nearby, but I didn't care. My voice was shaking, but my rage made it steady. "You ruined my mama's life when you left. You ruined mine before I even had a chance to build one."

Arlette was sitting there grinning like she was center stage in some cheap-ass production, still perched on his lap, eating it up.

But then, as I kept going, I saw it hit. His eyes flickered. His shoulders slumped. And without saying a word, he shoved Arlette right off his lap like she was nothing but dead weight.

She stumbled on the floor. "What the fuck—?" She looked between us, trying to grab his attention again, but he didn't so much as glance her way.

All his focus was on me.

I didn't even break stride. "Oh, so now you recognize me? Now you want to act like something clicked? You're years too late."

Arlette was still on the floor, fuming, brushing herself off and mumbling something about how both of us were crazy. But nobody paid her any mind. The air in the room was thick as hell, all eyes bouncing between me and him.

I leaned in just enough to let him know I meant every word: "You can push off every woman in this world, but you'll never push off the guilt of abandoning your kids. That shit stays with you forever."

His mouth opened, desperate to form some defense. "Niveah, it wasn't—"

I cut him off. "I don't wanna hear shit about any of those excuses." My lips curled into a smile that felt like fire spreading across my face. "And the best part? I made it happen without you. Hux is great. He's gonna be much better than the man who created him."

A laugh burst out of me, bitter and loud, until it shook the room. "And my mom? She turned to drugs after you left, to cope with the hurt. She drowned in what you did to her."

His voice cracked as he cut in. "She didn't turn to drugs because of me! That was one of the reasons I left."

The admission cracked something in me. For a split second, the air thinned and I couldn't breathe. My chest caved in, confusion rattling every bone. What the fuck? That wasn't the focus. He still left. He still abandoned us.

"You still should've protected us," I said. "You still should've been there."

His face fell, the weight of years sinking into the wrinkles around his eyes. "You're right," he whispered. "I should've come back. At least to make sure you and Huxley were straight. I didn't...and I'm sorry for that."

Sorry. A word too small for the damage done.

I straightened my shoulders, my smile returning. "Go to hell. That's where you've been in my mind all these years, and that's where you'll stay."

When he reached out, I recoiled like his touch was poison. My voice dropped low. "You see this man behind me?" I tilted my head toward Kendrix, his presence solid as a wall of iron. "All I have to do is say one word, and your ass is grass. So it's best if you don't fucking touch me."

Silence. Then he nodded once, shame heavy in his eyes, and turned to leave.

Arlette was still standing there, dumbfounded, her mouth open like she'd just lost the script. Whatever stunt she thought she pulled? It crumbled to dust right in her hands.

I turned, locking eyes with her.

"Now you, bitch."

Arlette laughed, her head thrown back. "It didn't take long for me to understand why you're such a hoe. Your daddy didn't want you, so chasing after men who belong to other people is what you do to cope."

"Bitch, who belongs to you?" Kendrix snapped before I lifted my hand. That one gesture was enough. The man stood back like I pressed a mute button. I needed to handle her.

My voice was calm, maybe too calm. The kind of calm that meant danger.

"I've been so nice because I could see you're not all the way there. Mentally? You're dumb as fuck. Ain't nothing in that head but a rock rattling around where your brain should be. I felt sorry for you. But I'm done wasting my words, because clearly, you don't understand them. You don't need anymore talking. You need me to lay hands on you so you'll finally learn to stop fucking with me."

Her mouth twisted, and she started with, "Try me. You'll catch a charge, I'll—"

Before she could finish, my fist met her face with every ounce of generational rage sitting in my chest. The sound cracked through the club louder than the bass, her head snapping back like a rag doll.

Arlette staggered back, clutching her face, but her mouth was still running. "Bitch, you gon'—"

I lunged before she could finish, tackling her clean out that chair. The crowd scattered like roaches, screams bouncing off the walls. Chairs scraped, glasses shattered, feet stomped for the door.

Arlette swung wild, sloppy punches cutting through the air. None of them touched me. I was ducking, weaving, talking the whole time.

"Swing harder, hoe! You been chasing for my attention all this time and can't even land a hit?"

Her acrylic nails scratched the air, desperate, but I grabbed her wrist and bent it back. She hollered, and I popped her in the mouth again.

"Ugly ass! You thought sitting on my sperm donors lap was gone break me? You dumb as hell."

Another swing and she missed. I slammed her head into the floor once, twice, her wig sliding off like it wanted no part of her either.

"Look at you! Can't keep a man, can't keep a wig, can't even keep your damn balance."

The crowd gasped, phones out, some too scared to record, others bolting for the exits. The DJ had killed the music, leaving nothing but the sound of me dragging that bitch like laundry day.

She clawed weakly at my clothes, and I smacked her hand away. "Don't touch me! You diseased-by-choice-ass hoe!"

Her lip was busted, her nose leaking, her cries drowned out by me laughing. Yeah, laughing. It felt that good to let every ounce of rage go.

And Kendrix stood back just watching. Just letting me handle what needed to be handled.

When I finally stood up, hair wild, breathing heavy, Arlette laid flat on the floor, half-conscious, looking like roadkill. I wiped blood off my knuckles with her shirt and looked around the room.

Everybody was gone. Silent. Empty. Except me, her, and the man behind me who never flinched while I showed the world exactly why nobody fucks with Niveah Jones.

39

Kendrix

I had to damn near bite the inside of my cheek to keep from laughing.

The way Pretty had just dog-walked Arlette across that sticky-ass club floor was legendary. But she was still so heated that if I let even a smirk slip, she might turn around and start throwing them same hands at me.

She was stuffing her heels and makeup bag into a duffel when the club owner waddled in, old man belly first, barking like he really ran shit.

"Get all your shit. You can't come back here," he snapped, like he'd been waiting years to say it.

The look on Niv's face said it all. If looks could kill, he'd be laid out right next to Arlette.

Before she could let loose, Ty popped off.

"Excuse you? We the only reason this club still got a pulse. We recruit the girls. We keep your lights on."

He tried puffing up, talking about, "And the same reason I'ma get shut down. Y'all bring too much drama, too much fighting in here!"

Niv just laughed before putting a hand on Ty's shoulder.

"Nah. Let him talk. We don't need to be here. Everybody know this club has always been just a stepping stone."

But I could still see the fury, the hurt, the kind of hollow in her eyes that said she was bracing for the next blow before it even landed.

I hated that. I hated how much life had trained her to expect bad shit to stack on top of more bad shit.

I stepped forward. "Did you drive?"

She shook her head. "Nah. Rode with Ty."

I turned to Ty. "She's riding with me."

Ty gave me that look but kept grabbing her bag.

We slipped out the back door into the alley. The cold air hit, and I tried to lighten her mood, cracked a couple jokes, tried to tease her into saying something.

Nothing.

She just walked, eyes fixed ahead, breathing shallow, like her mind was in a place way darker than the alley. Like she wasn't even there with me.

The whole ride felt like I was talking to a ghost.

I tried everything.

Jokes. Stories. Reminders of the way she used to light up when we'd clown on each other.

But all I got back were one-word answers.

"You hungry?"

"No."

"You cold?"

"Fine."

"You wanna put on some music?"

"Don't care."

Every time, I tried to laugh it off, tried to push past the wall she was building brick by brick. But that shit cut me deep.

Because it was her. The woman who could shut down a whole room with her words, or make me feel like I was flying just off her laugh. She was sitting next to me, staring out the window, locked inside her head. And I hated that.

I hated that life, or my family, or Arlette, or her no-good-ass daddy had done enough damage to make her shut down like that.

So I kept talking, even if I sounded like a damn fool.

"Remember when we argued about who was better, Jill Scott or Floetry, and you damn near threw my phone out the window?"

Nothing. Just the faintest twitch at the corner of her mouth.

"I was right though. Floetry."

That earned me a little side-eye, but it was something.

So I kept going.

"Or what about when you told me you could cook better than me? You remember that, Pretty? How your ass almost set the kitchen on fire?"

That time, I swore I saw her lip curl, just a little. She tried to hide it, but I caught it.

"See, I knew you remembered," I said softly, leaning back into the seat. "And I know you're hurting. I know it feels like everything hit you at once tonight, because it did. But I got you. I always do."

If I had to talk the whole damn ride just to remind her who she was, I would've.

When we pulled into her driveway, she finally turned to me.

"Thank you... for everything tonight. For not letting me drown."

I just nodded, because what else was there to say? She had no idea how much I needed her.

"I love you, Kendrix," she whispered. "God, I love you so much. I want you so bad it hurts. And I heard everything you said tonight, every word. I just... I need time. Time to see if I'm ready for everything that comes with you."

It wasn't the answer I wanted. But it was better than goodbye.

So when she leaned in and kissed me, I kissed her back like I could lock her there with me forever. Her lips tasted like salt from old tears and promises I wasn't sure I deserved.

Then her phone started ringing.

She hit decline and kissed me again.

It rang again, vibrating against her thigh. She declined it again.

I pulled back, frowning. "What's wrong?"

"Nothing," she said quickly, breathless. "It's Khloe."

She leaned in again, but I put my hand on her chin, making her look at me.

"What's going on?"

"Nothing. She's just... dealing with Kairo."

I sucked my teeth, leaning back against the headrest. "That dumbass. Always something with him."

She tried to shrug it off. "I'll call her back when I get back to the house."

My brow wrinkled. "Back to the house? It's late as hell, where are you going?"

Her eyes flicked away. "I need to see my mom. My mind's running a hundred miles an hour and it won't stop unless I get answers. I can't rest until then."

I already knew this was a bad idea.

"Pretty, can you please just get some rest and handle it in the morning?"

She was already shaking her head. "No."

That's when I snapped. My voice got sharper than I meant, but I needed her to hear me.

"You just had one of the roughest nights of your damn life. A night most people would be drowning in liquor and crying themselves to sleep over. Sleep that shit off. Try to clear your head, and then talk to your mom in the morning."

Her eyes narrowed, but I pressed on.

"Right now, all you see is red. And when you're like this? You don't talk *to* people, Niv. You talk *at* them. You're too angry to listen, too wound up to make sense. If you really want answers, don't walk in there tonight ready for war. Go when you can actually hear her... instead of just swinging with your words."

She just sat there, staring out the windshield, chewing her lip like she was trying to bite back a war.

I could see her mind spinning, trying to find something to throw at me just to prove I was wrong, but the fight wasn't there. Not that night.

Her shoulders sagged. I leaned in, brushing my thumb along her jaw until her eyes finally flicked to mine.

"Pretty," I whispered. "you're tired. Not just tonight-tired. Soul tired. You've been carrying too much, and I'm not letting you carry one more thing tonight."

Her eyes glossed over, but she didn't say a word. No smartass comeback, no deflection.

So I kissed her. Gentle, like I was kissing the chaos off her lips.

"I'm staying," I whispered against her mouth. "Tonight, I'm staying. Just to make sure you get some real sleep."

Normally, she would've hit me with a *you don't have to* or *I'm fine.* That was her favorite armor... pretending she didn't need anyone.

But she just nodded, silent.

That's when I knew my girl was done—mentally, emotionally, physically.

And if the only thing I could give her tonight was rest, then that's what the hell I was going to do.

NETRAANTIONETTE

Jill Scott's voice floated through the air like warm honey, the kind that sticks to your soul.

Her room smelled like vanilla and the soft lavender she always spritzed on her sheets because it was her safe place.

Our safe place, that night.

Niv was curled against me in her bed, the comforter tangled around her legs.

Her breaths had slowed and her lashes brushed her cheeks like they were too heavy to hold open any longer.

I thought she was asleep. The words sitting in my chest were too heavy for her waking ears, but too real to keep buried.

So I whispered them into her hair like confessions meant for her dreams.

"You make me feel like I'm not wandering anymore...like home isn't a place, it's you."

She stayed still, but her fingers twitched lightly against my ribs.

"I thought I knew what love was...but this? This is deeper. It's like my soul found its match and refuses to let go, even when it hurts."

I brushed my lips across her temple.

"Even after all the chaos...my heart never left. It stayed right here, in this bed, with you."

Her breathing hitched.

"You're the strongest thing I've ever seen. I've watched empires rise and crumble, but nothing compares to the way you survived what should've shattered you."

My throat burned, but I didn't stop.

"If you ever forget who you are...remember who I see. I see the girl who rose from scraps, the woman who built a world from rubble. You're proof that broken beginnings can birth the most unbreakable endings."

I closed my eyes and held her tighter, breathing her in.

"And if you ever lose your crown...I'll always be here to put it back on you."

"I love you so much," she whispered, breath warm on my chest. "No one will ever have me the way you do."

I grinned.

"So you were faking sleep," I said, kissing her hair. "Got me out here spilling my heart like a damn simp."

She laughed like she only does when she's tired and soft.

"Go to sleep," I said.

"Can't," she said, eyes still closed. "Too busy thinking about how much I want you."

"Then think about this—" I brushed my thumb over her cheek, tilting her face up to me. "I want you to come somewhere with me tomorrow."

Her lashes lifted just enough to meet my eyes. "Where?"

"A surprise ceremony Kross is doing for Rivah."

She blinked. "Oh yeah... Khloe told me about it. But Kendrix... I don't know. All your family will be there."

"Good." I slid my hand down her spine, pulling her closer. "Because you are my family. And I'm gonna be with you. You're gonna be a part of my life whether they like it or not."

She exhaled, her face burying into my neck like she was trying to hide her smile.

"Khloe will be there," I added gently, "and more than anything, I know you'd want to support your girls."

"I'll think about it," she said quietly. "But I'm going to visit my mom first. After I get some rest."

"Yeah, I know." I pressed a kiss to her temple. "So I'll be back to pick you up around five."

Her head tilted up. "I never said I was going."

"I know," I said, smirking as I tucked her under my chin. "But I said you were. Now get some sleep."

Before she could argue, I wrapped my arm tight around her waist until her breath fell slow and even. And she let herself rest in me.

She was out.

I knew it the second her soft little snores turned into full-blown sloppy mouth-breathing. I grinned, kissing her forehead. "Tired ass," I whispered.

I tried to lay there with her, but my mouth was dry as sandpaper. I needed water bad. Carefully, I slid out of her bed, eased my arm from under her waist, and blew out the candles flickering across her room before heading to the kitchen.

I heard movement down the hall. At first, I thought, Hux probably snuck into Zejah's room. I wasn't finna say shit. Hell, if my mama had ever let a girl move in back when I was in high school, I'd have been doing worse than sneaking around. Damage was done.

But then the back door clicked open.

I froze, listening as it creaked shut again. My chest tightened.

I stepped to the kitchen window and looked out. Huxley was sitting on the patio furniture, hood up, hunched forward. Then I saw him pull something from his pocket.

I eased the door open and stepped outside quietly, letting the night air hit me. The cicadas were humming, but my focus was on him.

"What you doing out here, man?" I asked, voice calm.

Hux's head jerked up, surprised. He palmed whatever was in his hand real quick, but I'd already seen enough. A lighter. A blunt.

He damn near dropped the lighter trying to shove both it and the blunt back in his pocket.

"I—I just needed some air," he stuttered. I sat down right next to him, calm as hell.

"It's cool, man. I know what I seen. And I already smell it."

He froze, shoulders slumping. That guilty-as-hell look hit his face, like a kid caught red-handed sneaking out of class.

"Please don't tell my sister."

I leaned back in the chair, exhaling. That wasn't my business. Hell, I was just glad it was weed and not something harder.

"Why you smoking though, Hux?" I asked, looking straight at him.

For a second, he didn't answer. Just rubbed at his face, jaw tight like he was fighting whether to tell me the truth.

"When I first found out about Zejah being pregnant... my mind was everywhere. I couldn't sleep, couldn't stop thinking. My boy had some, told me to try it, and for the first time my body felt... quiet. Like my brain just stopped running laps."

He shook his head, looking down at the blunt still in his hand.

"But after my mom overdosed..." his voice cracked, "I started smoking heavy. Just to think less, feel less. 'Cause all I keep doing is thinking about how fucked up my life been. How nothing ever makes sense."

I leaned forward, elbows on my knees.

"Listen, lil' bro... I ain't been through everything you been through, so I won't sit here and lie like I understand it all. But what I will say is this.. everything you survived? That shit is shaping you into an even stronger man than you realize. You seen struggle at a young age, when most people don't see it until adulthood. So in life, a lot of shit gone feel like small shit to a giant because you already know what heartache and heartbreak looks like."

His eyes lifted to mine, watery but still trying to be tough.

"I ain't gone hit you with that 'stop smoking' lecture either, because I know at your age, when somebody told me not to do something, that just made me wanna do it more. So here's what I'm gone say... if you ever feel like you need something to smoke, you come to me. Don't get it from anybody else. I don't care if it's your boy, your teammate, your cousin. Too much shit out here laced and dirty. You don't trust nobody with your life. You hear me?"

He nodded quick. "Yeah... yeah, I got you."

I slapped his back. "Nah, say it like you mean it."

"I got you, Ken," he said, stronger this time.

"Bet. But one more thing. We gone lay off too, because you're an athlete first. Weed ain't gone cost you your future. Once a day? Cool, I'll take that. But you gotta keep your head straight. You got too much potential to drown yourself."

Hux exhaled like I had just lifted a brick off his chest. "I understand... I said I was gone go down to once a day anyway."

"That's a bet. It's gone be alright, young bull. You been the man of the house since you were a boy. You're strong. And whatever you battling? You gone get through it."

He didn't say anything back right away, just nodded.

"Ken... I like having you around, man. It feels easier. Like... like I ain't the only one watching over the castle no more."

That hit me deep. He'd been holding all that weight so long, trying to be protector, brother, son, and now a father on the way.

I couldn't help but laugh a little, shaking my head before I reached over and pulled him into a brotherly hug.

"Lil' bro, I always got you. Always. And your sister? You already know. I love that girl. That means whatever comes with her, comes with me too."

He nodded against my shoulder, trying to play it tough but I could feel the relief in the way he let that breath go.

We sat there for a minute longer, two men from different worlds but bound by the same woman.

40

Niveah

When I finally opened my eyes the next morning, the first thing I noticed was the faint scent of Kendrix still lingering on my sheets. His cologne. His warmth. His damn energy. It was everywhere, wrapped around me like a hug I wasn't ready to let go of.

For the first time in weeks, I hadn't woken up in the middle of the night overthinking. I hadn't rolled over to stare at the ceiling until my mind ran me into exhaustion. I actually slept. Deep, heavy, drooling and snoring.

But with the sun slipping through my blinds, reality crept back in. Every single thing I'd been through started pressing on me again. It was like my heart didn't know whether to beat faster because of the chaos or slower because of the peace I felt from the night with him holding me.

I sat up and caught myself smiling. Smiling because even after all the bullshit, Kendrix had a way of making me feel like the world wasn't ending. Like I wasn't drowning. And that scared me more than anything. Because how could the same man tied to everything that ruined me also be the one giving me breath?

I dragged myself into the bathroom, splashing water on my face, whispering to my reflection:

"Get it together, Niveah. You got too many people counting on you."

Zejah was already knocking on my door talking about she needed to iron something for school, and Hux was yelling down the hallway about practice later. The chaos of my life didn't pause just because my heart wanted to.

Kendrix pressed a soft kiss to my temple, then my lips, lingering for a moment like he didn't want to let go.

"I gotta head out for a bit, Pretty," he said, brushing his thumb across my cheek. "But I'll be back later. If you need me... anything... call me, alright? I know you're planning to go see your mom."

I gave him a small smile, the kind I only give when I'm trying not to melt.

"I'll be fine," I lied gently, because if I told him the truth—about how much I needed him just to breathe straight right now—he'd never leave. "See you later."

He nodded like he wanted to say something else but thought better of it. As soon as he opened my bedroom door, though, he didn't get two steps.

Because there they were.

Hux. Zejah. Heidi.

All lined up like they were plotting something but instead, they swarmed him.

"Ken!" Heidi squealed, launching herself at him like she was half his size again.

Hux grinned and gave him one of those strong teenage back-slapping hugs, and even Zejah smiled, wrapping her arms around him.

It was... a sight.

They were just as happy to see him as I was to have him back in my space. And that realization tugged at something deep in me because maybe that's what safety was supposed to look like.

Zejah slipped past us and grabbed the iron from my vanity like she had a whole fashion show to run. Heidi stood at my full-length mirror, twirling like a tiny model, glancing at me out the corner of her eye, hoping I'd look away long enough for her to steal some of my lip gloss.

And Hux—

Lord.

He plopped down on the edge of my bed. "I got Friday practice, and after that I'm hanging with Kennedi, but I'll be home after."

I paused, slowly narrowing my eyes.

Boy. Don't play with me.

He knew it too, because he said it low like he didn't want Zejah to hear. The way she was fanning her belly with that "I'm glowing and hormonal" energy, I knew she'd burn the house down if she even suspected something.

"Just be home before nine," I said, giving him the *I'm not playing* look.

"I will," he promised, like I was a parole officer.

I started grabbing my purse and keys. "I'm about to go see Mama."

"Oh, okay," he said, uninterested, like he wouldn't go even if he wanted to.

"Can you tell her I said hello?" Heidi asked sweetly, still making kissy faces at herself in the mirror.

It stung, a little. How she looked at me and Rita as her mothers more than the woman who birthed her. But it was better this way. Safer.

"I will," I promised, bending down to kiss her forehead.

Right on cue, Rita's voice yelled through the halls. "Let's goooo, y'all gon' be late!"

The place smelled like bleach and loneliness.

Even the sunlight sneaking through the tall windows looked tired.

I signed in at the front desk, the pen on the chain clicking against the counter as I wrote her name. *Patient: Heaven Jones.*

Just seeing it there still didn't feel real. My mama. In a place they called a "short-term rehab facility." It felt like a place you went to disappear quietly while the world kept going without you.

Her room was halfway down the hall, and I could hear the faint beeping of machines before I even opened the door.

She was sitting in a recliner by the window, feet propped up, eyes half-lidded like she'd been fighting sleep and still hadn't won. The dialysis machine sat beside her. Tubes taped to her arm, the blood filtering through the clear lines, circling out and back in, like her life was on a loop.

She looked over when I walked in.

"Hey," she said, like I was just coming in from school.

Like she wasn't months removed from overdosing and almost dying.

"Hey," I whispered back, shutting the door quietly.

She went right back to staring at the window.

"They keep asking me if I want to see a therapist. I tell 'em no. What's a therapist gone say? Don't do drugs'? Already heard it. Find better coping skills'? I know that too. I just... don't want to be here, Niv."

My chest tightened.

"I know."

"No, you don't."

Her eyes finally shifted to me.

"You think this place is saving me, but it's just... pausing me. I'm sober, but my brain's louder now. You think getting clean makes you feel better, but it don't. It just makes you feel everything."

She tapped her temple lightly.

"And my mind... it don't know how to be quiet."

I swallowed, because I did understand. I'd just never heard her say it out loud.

"You scared you'll use again?" I asked softly.

She didn't answer at first.

"I'm scared I won't want to... but will anyway."

She laughed.

"You would think after almost dying, I'd be different. That I'd wake up grateful or religious or something. But I just woke up mad I didn't finish the job."

I didn't know what to say.

There wasn't a response for that kind of pain.

So I just sat beside her, silent, until the machine beeped and the nurse walked in to disconnect her lines.

My mama grimaced, rubbed her arm, and muttered, "I'm going home soon."

"Not until the doctors say you're ready," the nurse said.

Mama rolled her eyes.

I hated how part of me was praying the doctors would keep her there longer. Because as much as Mama hated it, that place forced her to live.

There... the drugs couldn't get to her. The nurses made sure she got her dialysis. She was safe. But once she went home, it would be on her.

And I knew my mama.

She wanted to be strong, but I'd watched her choose chaos over care too many times to trust it wouldn't happen again. Sleep had been hard enough knowing she was there. I couldn't imagine the kind of panic that would eat me alive if she was home, in that little house, alone with her thoughts and her cravings.

I sat on the edge of her bed, picking at the thread on the hem of the blanket.

"Mama... can we talk about something?"

She kept her eyes on the muted TV, where some soap opera couple was kissing like the world was ending.

"What else I got to do?"

"No, Mama," I said softer. "Like... really talk. About stuff I've wanted to ask for years, but didn't know how to."

That got her attention. She turned her head slow, her eyes narrowing like she was sizing me up.

"Niv... where else I'm gone go? Talk."

My throat tightened.

"What happened between you and Daddy?"

Her face didn't change at first, but her eyes closed like I'd cut her somewhere deep. Her voice came quick though like she'd rehearsed it.

"He was a coward. Had a family, life got hard, and he left. Left me to do it all alone."

Her jaw clenched.

"The end."

It wasn't. I knew it wasn't.

But I also knew my mama didn't hand out pieces of herself easy.

So I didn't push.

Instead, I said quietly, "I saw him."

Her head snapped toward me so fast, I flinched.

Her eyes went wide, like I'd just said I'd seen a ghost walk past the window.

And for the first time in years... my unshakable, unbothered mama looked scared.

"Hux looks like him," I whispered.

"Mm," she hummed. "He does."

"I was so angry," I said, voice trembling. "I just... went off. He didn't even recognize me until I said something. Like he just forgot all about us and moved on with a new life."

My mama let out a bitter "hmph" and shook her head.

"As you should've. He deserved it."

"Ma... one day I saw you go outside and a man handed you something. And I know it was drugs."

My throat burned.

"I've hated that man since I was twelve for ruining your life. I blamed Daddy because I thought he had hurt you so bad that you turned to drugs... until he told me that one of the reasons he left was because of you using."

A slow, cold laugh slipped out of her like she'd been holding it for years.

"I bet you he did."

The way she said it... half mockery, half heartbreak, sent confusion through my mind. Her eyes locked on mine like she was about to rip the stitches out of old wounds.

"You want the truth?" she rasped.

I nodded.

"I was pregnant with Hux," she said.. "And your daddy's first cousin... his best friend... came into the guest room while everyone was outside grilling. I thought he came to check on me. Instead, he... he took from me."

I froze.

"I told your father," she said, her eyes flooding, "and he told me I probably smiled at him... said that's why he told me not to wear clothes that showed my figure. Said if you put it out there, men gone think it's for them to take."

My chest cracked open. I couldn't breathe.

"I felt so disgusting. So... dirty. But I had to keep showing up. Kept seeing him at cookouts and holidays. And after Hux was born, the postpartum just..." She shook her head like she could rattle the memories loose. "It swallowed me. So I started using. Just a little. Enough to make my brain go quiet."

Her voice trembled.

"He caught me and said if I didn't stop, he'd leave. And I tried. God, I tried. But one night he invited that same cousin over. They got drunk. Your dad passed out on the couch, and I was in the bedroom breastfeeding Hux."

Her breath hitched.

"He came in. And he did it again."

Tears blurred everything. My ears rang.

"I didn't say a word," she said. "Because what was the point? He would've had another excuse to use against me. He would've just said I wanted it. So I used more. Because nothing hurt when I was high. Nothing felt real."

She stared at the ceiling like it was the only thing holding her together.

"And then... your dad left. Said he couldn't watch me kill myself. He took care of the bills, and when he stopped... we got kicked out. Ended up in Gun Hill. And by then, I was too far gone to care."

My throat burned. My hands shook.

"I never did it in front of y'all," she whispered, like she needed me to know. "Always waited until you were at school or asleep. You deserved a mother... even if you didn't get one."

I couldn't hold it in.

My body moved before my mind could catch up. I leaned in and wrapped my arms around her. Her frame felt so small. Fragile.

How could someone carry that much pain and still be here?

Her tears soaked through my shirt, and I didn't care. I held her tighter.

I didn't want her to think for a second that I hated her. I could never hate her... not knowing that.

"I can't imagine," I whispered, voice cracking. "Mama... I can't even imagine that kind of pain."

For so long, I thought she was just... cold. Distant. I remembered those days after he left, when the phone rang and Grandma's name flashed on the screen.

How Mama would slam it shut, saying, *Tell them to leave us alone* before locking herself in her room.

I thought she was just bitter. Angry that they didn't make their son stay for his family.

I pulled back enough to look her in the eyes.

"Is this why you didn't want us around his family?" I asked softly.

She stared at me for a long moment... then nodded, slow.

"He left and never looked back," she said. "You and Hux... y'all were his only kids. They knew we got kicked out. Knew we ended up in low-income housing. They told him. And he still didn't care."

She swallowed hard, like even the words burned coming out.

"I didn't trust his people around you," she admitted. "His parents knew what his cousin did to me. They knew. Nobody flinched. Nobody cared. So I thought... maybe they're all like him. Maybe the whole family's sick."

She blinked, and a fresh tear slid down her cheek.

"I didn't want them to ruin you the way they ruined me."

Her breath hitched.

"But I know now... turning to drugs ruined you anyway."

The air went still. My heart ached like it was cracking in my chest. I wanted to tell her she hadn't ruined me. That I turned out fine. But the truth was that we were both just survivors pretending we were okay.

"I'm sorry, Ma."

Her brows knit together like she didn't understand, but I kept going.

"I'm sorry for... for how I looked at you. For how angry I was. I thought you chose the drugs over us. Over me. But now I know... you were just trying to survive something nobody should have had to."

Tears blurred my vision as I cupped her hands in mine.

"You didn't deserve that. Any of it. You were so strong just to stay. And you kept showing up, even when you were falling apart inside."

Her bottom lip trembled. I could see the war in her eyes—the part of her that wanted to believe me and the part that had been told she wasn't enough for so long.

"I see you now," I whispered. "Not just my mom... but the woman who lived through hell and still tried to raise heaven."

For the first time in years, she leaned forward and kissed my cheek.

It wasn't the absent-minded peck she gave when I was rushing out the door as a teenager.

It meant something.

For the first time in forever... she felt like my mom. Not a child I'd been raising, not a ghost of who she could've been... just my mom.

Her tears slowed, and a small smile spread her lips.

"You know... Heidi's daddy saved me for a while," she said quietly.

"I met him in rehab. He knew everything. And he didn't flinch. He helped me breathe again. Helped me want to be better for you and Hux. Y'all were older, but I still had plans. I wanted to make up for all the lost time."

Her eyes softened, lighting with something I hadn't seen in years.

"We were perfect," she whispered. "I was so happy my whole pregnancy with Heidi. He was such an amazing man. Life was... finally starting to look up. He had a good job. I was getting back on my feet."

Her smile faltered, cracked at the edges.

"But he wasn't strong enough to be around the drugs at that job. It got to him again. And it killed him."

Her voice crumbled on that last word.

My chest tightened.

"That... killed the little hope I had left," she whispered. "I went back in that hole, deeper than before. I loved him so much. I felt like... God didn't love me. Because why keep letting me meet love, only to snatch it away?"

Her tears fell silently now, like even they were too tired to make a scene.

"I didn't understand why God would let me meet someone so amazing... just to take him away."

I pressed my forehead to hers, holding her face gently in my palms.

My forehead pressed against hers, and the second our skin touched, the dam inside me cracked wide open.

Tears came hot and fast, slipping down my cheeks, dripping onto her gown.

"I know, Mama..." I sobbed.

"I know exactly what you mean by that. Wanting someone so bad... knowing it's damn near impossible to have them after everything."

She pulled back just enough to see my face, her frail fingers brushing my tears away.

Her eyes were still cloudy with pain but so sharp with mother's instinct narrowed just a little.

"Kendrix?" she whispered.

I froze, then nodded.

And then it all came spilling out. About how finding out his daddy was the one who gave her that poison all those years ago broke me in half. How my rage took over and I stabbed him right there in front of everyone while she was fighting for her life in a hospital bed. How his mama had come to me in that jailhouse, not as some emotional mother-in-law type, but like a CEO making a deal with her rival. How she told me if I wanted my freedom and wanted to protect my siblings... I had to walk away from him.

Her lips parted in shock, but she stayed quiet.

"I thought I was doing what was best," I whispered. "But Mama... it's been killing me."

Her mouth curved into the softest smile.

"Don't let me... or his mama... keep you away from happiness."

My head jerked up. "Mama—"

"I know G," she interrupted, and actually laughed.

"I know exactly who you're talking about."

That stunned me. She shook her head, almost like she was reminiscing on something private.

"G is a good man. He used to come to Gun Hill from time to time. He knew my situation. And he always told me I had to show up for y'all. Said I couldn't keep letting the world chew me up."

She chuckled sadly, shaking her head at herself.

"I was so broke, I used to get it from whoever had it, not even thinking about how dangerous it was. Back then, bad batches were taking people out left and right. G... he saved my life more times than I can count. Made sure if I was gonna use, I didn't end up dead or laced. He gave it to me so I wouldn't get it from the streets."

Her voice dropped to a whisper.

"He wasn't trying to ruin me, baby. He was trying to protect me the only way he knew how."

Then her eyes locked on mine, piercing through all the hate I'd been carrying.

"Baby... you hate the wrong person."

I blinked through tears as Mama reached out, her hands trembling, and cupped my face like I was still her baby girl.

"I'm so sorry you had to be strong for me.

"You were just a child, Niveah... but I made you carry the weight of the world like you were already grown."

Her thumbs brushed away my tears like she could erase the years of pain written across my skin.

"You became the protector when I was supposed to be the safe place.

"You've been everybody's anchor... while drowning quietly yourself."

I swallowed the lump in my throat until it burned.

"Baby... it's your turn now. Your turn to be soft. To be loved on instead of used up.

"Stop surviving. Start living."

I sobbed. Ugly, gut-wrenching sobs.

And she kept going, her voice stronger like she'd finally found her way back to herself too.

"Love that man if he makes you breathe easier.

"Don't let my fears, or his mama's past, cheat you out of joy.

"You deserve good things, even if they come from complicated places."

Something cracked deep inside me. Not the kind of crack that breaks you. The kind that makes room for light to get in.

"You've held everyone else together for so long... Now let someone hold you."

I melted into her arms. It felt like I was being hugged by my mother and not a broken woman.

41

Kendrix

I pulled up at five on the dot, like I told her I would. My nerves had been on edge all damn day, but the second I saw her step out that house, my chest eased up.

We both wore purple. Our color. She knew what the fuck she was doing. Kross said some dumb shit about everybody wearing "girly flowery colors" for Rivah's ceremony, since they were wearing white. Purple only made sense for us.

I got out and opened her door before she could. I didn't even let my hand brush her waist, because if I touched her... we weren't leaving that house. I needed her by my side, not under me.

She was in the passenger seat, and she looked... lighter. Like something heavy finally got up off her shoulders.

"What's up with you, Pretty? You smiling like you hiding something."

She looked at me, and her eyes got wet. Then she told me everything.

About her dad and what her mom went through. About my pops and how apologetic she was for everything that happened for hating a man who was innocent all along.

I had already forgiven Pretty for that, but I won't lie and say I didn't feel relieved finally knowing why my dad moved on with life like it was okay. For so long, I thought he was heartless, but if he had nothing else, he had a heart of gold. Just like he'd always taught us to have.

She cried so hard, I reached over, grabbing her hand. "Pretty, it's okay." But she shook her head, still crying.

So I cracked a smile to try and lighten the mood. "Stop crying before you fuck up that makeup. Then my hating-ass brother Kairo gone clown you all night. His jokes already lame as hell so I don't want to embarrass his ass too much tonight."

She laughed through her tears and smacked my arm. That laugh made my heart feel damn good. All I ever wanted with Niv was to be the one who held her when she fell apart and the one who made her laugh in the same breath.

I looked over at her again. She was looking out the window, probably thinking about how the night would go with everyone being there.

"You want me to have a convo with my parents about all of it first?" I asked. "Kinda ease the room for you?"

She didn't even hesitate snapping her head toward me.

"No. I want to have the conversation with them... both of them. Myself. And it'll happen, even if it's not tonight."

"Tonight is about Rivah," she added. "She deserves that."

"You're right," I said, because she was. "You always are."

I brought her hand to my lips and kissed her knuckles.

We pulled up to the venue, and even from outside, I could tell Kross had done his big one.

Inside... man. It looked like something out a damn magazine. Purple, pink, yellow, and orange flowers draped across white linen tables, soft lights glowing, a live violinist tucked in the corner. You could tell Mamma, Kross, and Rivah's best friend Vane had poured their whole hearts into it.

We hadn't even made it five feet before we walked up on my parents. They both looked... surprised, seeing her. But they didn't say shit. If my parents were anything, they were professionals, and it wasn't the time to give guests another scene. They told me hello and simply nodded their heads at Niv. Mamma gave her a look though. One of those tight smiles that really said, *"We'll talk later."*

I slid my hand against the small of Pretty's back. A silent "I got you."

Then in walked Khloe and Kairo.

Khloe ran straight for Niv, hugging her like they hadn't seen each other in forever. And Kairo... of course had that 'what the fuck' look on his face like I'd brought a loaded weapon instead of the woman I love.

Before his mouth could open, I cut him off.

"Lay off all that back-and-forth talking shit. Some stuff came out, and we know the truth. I'll explain later, but now ain't that time."

Shockingly... he just nodded, sipped his champagne, and kept it pushing. That caught me off guard. If Kairo had nothing else, he had opinions. Loud ones. So the fact that he didn't pop off? Yeah... whatever was going on between him and Khloe had him moving different.

I turned to Khloe, trying to change the subject. "Where's my favorite niece at?"

Khloe smirked. "She begged to stay home with her friend. She's hanging out with Hux."

I damn near choked on air.

Niv tried to hide her laugh, but it was too late. I was caught confused as fuck. Yeah, me and Hux were gonna have a long talk. Kennedi had always been my baby, and hopefully it was innocent, especially with Hux's situation with Zejah. But my niece? Yeah... that's one girl I don't wanna have to strangle the woman I love's brother about.

Mamma's voice cut the chatter, making the people listen.

"Alright, everyone... quiet down. Get in place."

The violist's bow glided across the strings, and the band eased into *"Know That You Are Loved"* by Cleo Sol.

And just like that, the air changed. It was like everyone could feel what was about to happen.

Then came my brother. Kross walked in with that familiar slow stride, like he was trying to play it cool, but the grin on his face gave him away. He wasn't just happy. He was whole.

But Rivah... she froze. Her eyes widened, her lips trembled, and her hands flew to her mouth. It was like her heart was trying to outrun her body.

Kross reached out and gently took her hand. She let out this shaky laugh that sounded like a sob trying to pretend it was brave. He led her to the stage and took the mic.

His voice cracked on the first word.

"A few weeks ago, we were in bed talking... and my parents called, just to check on me before they went to sleep. When I hung up, you grabbed my hand and whispered, *'Sometimes it hurts... knowing I'm no one's daughter.'*"

He paused and everyone was silent.

"You said it like it was just a passing thought, but it broke something in me. Because you are everything. And you deserve to know—without question, without conditions—that you are everything to others."

Rivah's shoulders shook. Kross swallowed hard and kept going.

"I dream about spending forever with you as my partner. But more than anything... my best friend. And you probably think this is a proposal."

He smiled, tears running down his face now.

"But it's not. This is an adoption ceremony. The only thing that will ever separate us... is death. You have changed my life. And now, you are part of my family forever."

The room broke.

Mama and Pops walked up first, hugging her like she was flesh of their flesh. Our grandparents followed, their old hands trembling as they placed delicate jewelry around her wrists and neck pieces that had passed through generations of Givelle women.

You could see it hit her. It wasn't just sentiment. It was legacy.

Rivah sobbed openly as Mama clasped a gold chain at her neck and kissed her forehead.

Then came the framed document, sealed and signed, declaring her an official part of the Givelle family.

Mamma took the mic, holding Rivah's hand tight.

"Never again will you feel like you have no one or wonder if you belong. Because you do here. You are ours. You are family. You are home."

Everyone was crying. Even me. Even Pretty, who gripped my hand so tight.

For weeks, it had felt like our whole world was burning down. It felt good to watch Kross and Rivah and how their love rebuilt something from ashes.

42

Niveah

Everyone was mingling. They were talking, laughing, and loading up on little finger foods that cost too damn much to be that small.

Somewhere across the room, someone pulled Khloe off to the side for a chat. The photographer started grabbing Kendrix and his brothers, telling them to take a few pictures. They all groaned but went anyway, because if their mama said smile, they smiled.

I sipped my champagne and scanned the room.

And that's when I saw Mr. Givelle standing off to the side. Glass of champagne in his hand, wearing a perfectly pressed suit.

We locked eyes.

My chest squeezed. I didn't want to do it there... not in a room full of people, but I was tired of the awkward tension lingering. People were already sneaking glances at me like they were watching the prequel to a fight. They'd seen me almost kill him last time, so I was sure they were shocked to see me there with Kendrix... and still alive.

So I moved.

My heels clicked against the floor as I crossed to him. I didn't speak. Just stood beside him, staring out at the crowd like I was part of the decor. He didn't look at me. Just raised his glass and took a slow sip.

I mirrored him.

We swallowed our champagne like we were trying to wash the past off our tongues.

Finally, he broke the silence.

"I'm sorry about your mom. I've known her a long time. A good woman. Always has been. She just... had some demons she wasn't strong enough to fight alone."

I clenched my jaw.

Demons. That's what people always called pain they didn't want to understand.

I turned my glass in my hand, watching the bubbles rise and burst like tiny ghosts.

"You knew everything all along.. the real truth," I said softly, "and never said anything to Kendrix... or your wife."

He didn't flinch. Just swirled the champagne in his glass like we were discussing the weather.

"Because it was never my story to tell. Your mother told me what happened to her in confidence...and no matter what her child or anyone else may think about me or her, her trauma and scars were safe with me until she decided she was ready to reveal them to you."

Something in me cracked. All these years, I imagined him as this heartless man who could walk away without looking back.

But standing there, I realized—

He wasn't heartless. He was just a man of integrity. A man with a heart... who chose silence to protect someone who'd been broken enough.

My throat tightened.

"I... I apologize," I whispered. "For attacking you—"

He stopped me with a small shake of his head.

"Don't apologize," he said. "I've done many other things in my life... and every man reaps what he sows. Karma doesn't have a time limit or a certain way it comes back. I was just getting what was owed. Don't apologize for something I've already given to God... and moved on from."

I swallowed hard, staring down into my glass. It felt lighter... like maybe so was I.

Movement caught my eye. Kendrix. He was scanning the room until he landed on me, concern pulling his eyebrows together like he was ready to come rescue me from my own storm.

I gave him a small nod. *I'm okay.* His shoulders eased. He nodded back, then turned to hug Rivah and pull Khloe into a laugh, letting me have my moment— the moment I finally let go of hating the man who gave me half my face.

He cleared his throat softly, like he was about to say had been sitting on for years.

"My time in Gun Hill..." he started, voice low, "exposed wounds I buried so deep, even my family forgot they existed. They know nothing about why I was there, and if I can help it, they never will. I'd rather they keep their image of me intact and let us all move forward."

I stayed silent.

"I apologize," he said, "for giving your mother what she wanted. I knew she would find a way to get it regardless. And because of the two kids she had inside her home... I wanted to make sure it wasn't something that would kill her and leave you both in the system, motherless."

He paused, sipping his champagne like it burned.

"I thought I was helping her cope... helping her suppress pain she couldn't name. I never meant to ruin the life of a young girl. But God... God works in mysterious ways."

Finally, he turned his head, just enough for our eyes to meet.

"Because through everything... I'm grateful my son has a woman as strong as you and one who loves him as fiercely as you do."

Something in me cracked. He wasn't a monster. Just a man who made a choice and had to live with its echo. I wanted to be angry. But the way he said it... it didn't sound like a man defending himself. It sounded like a man who had carried the ghost of a choice for decades.

My mind spun.

All those years, I'd poured her hate into his silhouette. I'd let him become the villain, the shadow I could blame when life cut her too deep to name where it bled.

But He wasn't trying to destroy us... He was trying to save us from something worse.

And I hated that realization. Where the hell was I supposed to put all that pain now? Pain that had become my compass, my armor, my excuse.

My throat tightened.

If he wasn't the monster...then maybe there never was one. Maybe it was just life being cruel, and me trying to find something—someone—to fight back at. That was the day that I no longer saw Kendrix's father as the villain in my story.

Mamma G glided across the room like the world belonged to her. Even in heels, she didn't walk... she arrived. Heads tilted as she passed, like they all felt it too. The air of quiet power she carried, the kind you can't fake, the kind life has to carve into you.

She stopped right in front of us, and her husband's face instantly softened, that grin tugging at his lips like it always did when she was near.

"Baby, can I steal you for a minute?" Mamma G's voice was soft.

He turned toward her. "I would love to be stolen by the prettiest woman in the room," he said, and the way he said it... it wasn't even cheesy. It was devotion.

You could see it on them... years wrapped into smiles, into the way their fingers naturally found each other. That kind of love people pray for but rarely get. The kind that bends with life, but never breaks. He would burn the world down if it meant keeping her warm, and everyone knew it.

She gave me a small nod, one of those subtle, regal Mamma G nods that said '*I see*' you and '*remember who I am*' all at once.

"Niveah," she said, smooth and poised.

"Mamma G," I replied, holding her gaze and lifting my chin just a little higher, even though my heart was doing backflips. She had given me strict instructions. Rules meant to protect her son. And there I was, standing in defiance of them with love written all over my damn face.

This was my life. My choice. My heart.

"We'll talk later," she said simply, like a promise and a warning all in one.

Then she turned, slipped her hand into his, and they walked off together.

Khloe and Rivah came strutting up to me with champagne in their hands and trouble in their eyes.

I hugged Rivah first, squeezing her tight.

"Congrats on making it into the family that'll probably never accept me," I joked.

Rivah rolled her eyes, grinning. "Girl, please. Ken brought you, so it's clear he doesn't give a damn who accepts you because he does."

Khloe sipped her drink and chimed in, "I mean, I've been in since I was eighteen, and it ain't all it's cracked up to be. Maybe you're dodging a bullet."

We both stared at her.

She blinked, then burst out laughing. "I'm just joking! I'm joking!"

Rivah tilted her head at me. "So... how was that chat?"

Khloe leaned in like she was sharing gossip. "Yeah, because I was talking to a family friend, and I ain't hear shit she said. I was too busy trying to read y'all lips."

We all cracked up.

"It went good," I said. "I'll catch y'all up later. But now...the real convo's gonna be with Mamma G."

They both groaned. If anyone had the power to shake the earth under your feet, it was her.

Khloe fanned herself with her clutch. "I'm going out this way by the little pool area. I don't think anyone even knows it's out there. I was trying to find the bathroom and spotted it. I just need some time to breathe and not look at Kairo and pretend like I enjoy being in his presence right now."

"I'll come," I offered instantly.

"Me too," Rivah said.

We both side-eyed her. "This celebration is for you."

She waved a hand. "I don't give a damn. I'll text Kross and let him know I snuck off with y'all. He knows I get overstimulated fast."

We laughed, heels clicking softly as we slipped through the side door like we were escaping prison making sure no one saw.

We found a little fire pit tucked away on the far end of the pool area. All three of us groaned in unison as we sank into the cushioned chairs. Khloe kicked off her heels with a dramatic sigh and started rubbing her feet.

Rivah snorted. "Only a couple more hours until you can go home and get them rubbed. Kross already knows once these heels come off, his hands better be ready."

Khloe rolled her eyes, lips twitching like she wanted to laugh but couldn't quite make it there. "That sounds way too romantic for something Kairo would do. He'll be in bed snoring before I finish undressing."

You could hear the tiredness in her voice. The way exhaustion sometimes doesn't make you cry, it just makes you... flat.

"I'm sorry for missing your calls," I said softly. "I was with Kendrix. He wanted me to get some rest after the day that I had."

Khloe waved it off. "Oh, it's okay. I was just really upset and needed someone to talk to."

She stared at the flames for a second, voice low. "Whenever Kairo used to piss me off, I'd just go spend time with Kennedi or go tend to her. But she's so independent now that I'm stuck... just facing things with no outlet."

Rivah and I went quiet, letting the crackle of the fire fill the space, because neither of us knew that kind of lonely.

Rivah reached over and rubbed Khloe's knee, her voice soft.

"Hey... We're here if you wanna talk."

Khloe shook her head, blinking fast like she was trying to hold herself together.

"No. This is your day, Rivah. It's about you. We can worry about me tomorrow."

Rivah smiled. "Kross is very much a man and I love him for everything he's done tonight... but my night here is over. I'm not worried about nothing but getting that man home. I haven't taken my pill in a few days and I'm about ready to risk it all. So in my mind, my night here is over."

We all burst out laughing, the tension cracking for a second.

"I know people would die for the careers and the money Kairo and I have," she said. "And I get it... after college we worked so damn hard to get here. We even sacrificed time with Kennedi to build all of this. Outside of love, she was our reason. Our driving force.

"I just... miss the man I fell in love with. We used to spend nights talking about dreams, about what we wanted to accomplish. I never knew that through it all, it would be the thing that came between us."

I reached out, stopping her. "Khloe... where is all this coming from?"

She took a shaky breath.

"We had this week-long, all-inclusive trip to Greece planned. For almost two years. We were supposed to leave in a few months. It's my dream trip. My dream destination.

"I was just trying to tell him about the updated itinerary, and he said he couldn't go because of work."

Rivah and I went still, and Khloe's shoulders sagged.

"He knew how important it was to me. We've never celebrated our union, never taken a real vacation in years. Sixteen years of marriage, and nothing. That's all I wanted. One trip. One week. With his undivided attention."

Rivah wrapped her arms around her and said, "Fuck him. We can make it a girls' trip."

That pulled a watery laugh out of Khloe, but her voice shook when she spoke again.

"I just... lost it. I went crazy. I went off for every time I've felt pushed to the side... which has been more years than I can count."

I reached over and patted Khloe's tears back before they could ruin her makeup.

"Everybody expects me to just be so damn happy," she whispered. "I don't want for anything. To my knowledge, he doesn't cheat, he's never given me a reason to think he does... but money and love isn't enough. And every time I try to say that, people look at me like I'm ungrateful. Like I'm crazy. I need time and affection too."

Rivah leaned forward.

"Bitch, who the fuck you be talking to? It must be those Real Housewives of Antionette hoes you hang around because you ain't never heard us say no dumbass shit like that."

I snapped my fingers in agreement.

"Right. Don't lump us in with them hoes. They ain't your friends anyway and they're in those marriages for the money."

That made Khloe cry harder, shoulders shaking.

"I'm just so depressed, y'all. Kairo... he's so bad about sweeping shit under the rug. We'll argue all night, and by morning, he's up moving like it never happened. No resolution. No compromise. Nothing. Just the next day, same cycle."

"And then he wanna touch all on my back and kiss my cheek here tonight like he's the perfect man. Like he's the whole package. But I'm standing right next to him secretly lonely as fuck. Drowning. I'm tired of faking like I'm okay."

Then she dropped her head into her hands and whispered.

"I feel like I'm over the edge. One simple thing... just one more little thing... could really be my 13th reason. The thing that sends me over for good."

Me and Rivah just stared at her like she'd lost her whole damn mind.

Rivah's eyes were wide. "Hold up, bitch."

I sat up straighter. "Khloe, don't piss me off. I don't have time for this shit. I just got fired from my old faithful club and my rent due next week. I got too many goddamn bills to be planning a funeral. I'm just telling you now if I gotta pay for it, that shit is gone be trash because I have two trips out the country planned."

Rivah screamed laughing, because she could see it all over my face that I was dead serious. Her laugh made Khloe laugh, even through her tears.

"Bitch," Khloe choked out between laughs, "that is not what you say to somebody when they're telling you they're going through it!"

"Well, excuse me for being honest. I know how luxury you are and nothing about it will be luxurious, so don't even try it." I shrugged, sipping my drink like it was communion.

Rivah nodded hard. "Facts."

Khloe sniffled, wiping her face. "Damn. All I was gone ask was for y'all to watch out for my little girl. Make sure she was good."

Rivah side-eyed her so fast. "Don't tell me that. I barely handle them kids at school. You tryna add yours too?"

I locked eyes with Khloe.

"Oh hell naw. You spoiled her too damn much and ain't nobody got time to be feeding into her name-brand addictions. You created that monster, sis, so you gotta stay and deal with it."

Khloe's mouth dropped open, then she started laughing.

"I already got three kids plus a newborn coming," I went on, shaking my head, serious as hell. "Hell naw, this is not Daddy Daycare. You better calm your bougie ass down and keep raising the little diva you birthed."

Rivah clapped her hands, hollering, "Not Daddy Daycare!"

Khloe was wiping her face, crying-laughing so hard. "Bitch, y'all are not right."

"Duh. We know that, so don't try and leave us," I shot back, smirking. "We are in this together so that means you gotta stay."

The door creaked open, and all three of us snapped our heads around like kids caught sneaking candy.

It was Kross and his eyes softened the second he spotted Rivah. "Baby, I been looking everywhere for you."

She covered her mouth, laughing. "Damn, I said I was gonna text you to tell you I was slipping away but... I forgot."

Before I could even gag at how sweet they were, Kendrix and Kairo walked in behind him.

Kairo's eyes landed on me with a stank face like he was tolerating my existence and nothing more. Honestly, I couldn't blame him. But he might as well get comfortable because whether he liked it or not... I wasn't going anywhere.

(*I cant believe I just said that shit. Ew. It's giving simp.*)

Kendrix didn't miss a beat. He reached for my hand, tugging me up out of my seat.

"Afterparty at GivGold if y'all down. Magnolia took care of extra security so we could open tonight."

Kross and Kairo lit up immediately. "Hell yeah."

Khloe groaned but stood anyway. "That's fine. I'll go ask Kordai, but I'm sure he'll be down."

Rivah rolled her eyes. "Y'all got one hour. One. I got other plans with my Mandingo."

The whole group gagged at once, groaning, "Ewwww, what the fuck!"

But that was Rivah for you. Only she would say some shit like that with a straight face.

We all started grabbing our things, talking about rides and shots and who was riding with who.

Then the door opened.

Mamma G stepped in with that soft-but-deadly presence she carried that made everyone's voices drop mid-sentence.

"Can I have a moment alone with Niveah?" she asked.

Everyone went silent. Eyes flicking from her... to me... back to her. *Oop.*

"Yes, you can," I said. My voice didn't shake, even though my stomach flipped

Kendrix cleared his throat beside me, that little warning sound like he wanted to intercept. I could feel him gearing up to tell his mom maybe we could talk later, but I cut him off with just a look.

I'm okay.

He stared at me, wondering if I was sure, but I knew I was. He then nodded once before stepping back.

Everyone else caught on without saying a word. One by one, they filed out. The door closed behind Kendrix last. The room suddenly felt five sizes smaller.

"I had one rule," she said. "One. Walk away from my son. So he would never have to choose between the woman he loved and the family that raised him."

Her eyes sharpened.

"And here you are. Which tells me either you're not a woman of your word... or you're not a woman I can trust."

I stayed exactly where I was, shoulders back, chin lifted, heart punching at my ribs.

I smiled. "With all due respect, Mamma G... I did everything I could to uphold that agreement. I tried to cut him off clean. I pushed him away until it broke me."

Her brow arched.

"But for some reason," I went on, "the stars kept aligning anyway. Even when I ran, he came back. Every time."

"I apologize," I said lightly, "for being addictive. The same kind of woman you told me, the very first day we met, that I'd have to be... because that was who your son fell in love with."

Mamma G tilted her head like she'd found something unexpected, something she couldn't quite label.

"Addictive women burn bright, Niveah," she said slowly. "But they burn everything around them too."

I leaned in just enough to let her know I wasn't folding. "Then maybe the problem isn't the fire, Mamma G. Maybe it's the people who don't know how to stand close without getting scared of the heat."

Her eyes softened. She masked it quick, but I saw it.

"You really love him," she said, almost to herself. "That much is clear."

I lifted my chin. "Enough to fight for him. Enough to walk away when I had to. And enough to stand in front of you right now letting you know that I'm not spending another minute without him."

Finally, she nodded. "It was clear from the start that my son made his choice, and from the way you speak..." She let out a laugh, shaking her head. "Looks like you've made yours too."

I smiled. Not sweet. Confident. "I'm not here to break your son, Mamma G. I'm here to build with him. Whether anyone approves or not."

Mamma G lifted her chin just a little. "Does my son know about our arrangement?"

"No. This family has been through enough. I felt it was best to keep that to myself."

Her eyes narrowed, but not in anger. More like... evaluation.

"You kept it to yourself," she repeated, almost like she was testing the words on her tongue. "That tells me something. Plenty of women would've used it as leverage. A card to play. You didn't."

She tilted her head, a slow smile creeping across her face like she was satisfied. "You know... I always liked you. Even when I acted like I didn't. I was just waiting."

"Waiting for what?" I asked.

"For you to show me who you really are," she said plainly. "To stand on your own two feet. To prove you'd fight for his love no matter how cold I came across. That you weren't just here for a season, or for the shine of his last name, but because you really loved him."

Her words settled heavy, but not in a bad way. Almost like she was laying down a crown she'd been holding.

"You passed the test," she said finally, a little smirk tugging at her mouth. Then she shook her head, almost laughing. "But Lord... it took you long enough."

I couldn't help it so I smirked back, chin lifted. "Worth the wait though, wasn't it?"

For the first time since I'd known her, Mamma G actually laughed. Not a polite chuckle, not a cruel one. A real laugh.

And just like that, the power between us shifted. Not equal, not yet. But damn sure closer than it had ever been.

Mamma G's gaze softened, just a flicker, before she spoke again.

"Every woman who's been serious about one of my boys... there's always been something about her that made me see myself."

She looked out toward the garden.

"Khloe—she's got the kindest heart. Been by Kairo's side since they were teens, even when he didn't deserve it. She put her own wants on hold and put her husband and child first. That reminded me of me. She's proven her love and loyalty time and time again. And every time life knocks her down, she gets up swinging even when nothing changes. I love her deeply, and I pray for her true happiness... even if it's not with my son. I hope it is, but..." she chuckled dryly, "...we're talking about men. The most unpredictable species God ever made.

"And Rivah? Lord, that girl is pure fire. Empowering. Unapologetic. She makes her own rules and doesn't give a damn who disagrees. She reminds me of the version of myself I had to fight to become. She teaches women not to be ashamed of their past but to scream it from the mountain tops because every wrong turn and every man they survived shaped the powerhouse standing there today."

Then her gaze slid back to me, sharp and unwavering.

"And then... there's you."

My breath caught.

"I've watched you make a way out of no way," she said softly. "I've watched you choose yourself, even when it broke your own heart. You had every reason to crumble and you didn't. You stood. You survived. You built. That takes a kind of strength most people will never understand."

Her eyes flicked down, just briefly, to my stomach. My throat tightened.

"You had the perfect excuse to claw your way back in with an agenda," she said gently. "But instead, you chose peace. I pray every day that you made that decision for you and you alone."

I opened my mouth to speak, but she lifted a finger.

"Dr. Baldwin is trustworthy," she said, voice low and deliberate. "But I had someone watching your every move for weeks. The dollar store pregnancy test runs. The appointment. The pharmacy run after. The following days you stayed home... it didn't take long to know what was happening."

My tears burned hot.

She reached up, cupped my face in both hands, and her voice softened into something maternal.

"Don't worry. You kept my hands clean with my son by never telling him about our arrangement. Your secret is safe with me."

Then she leaned in, pressed a kiss to my cheek, and whispered against my ear:

"But you're family now. So don't do it again. I want more grandbabies and you have no reason to think you'll struggle. We are your village now."

That broke me. I smiled through my tears, nodding.

She patted my cheek like I was one of her own. "Now, go find my hardheaded son and enjoy your night out."

And just like that, Mamma G turned and walked away. She left me standing there, heart in pieces and whole all at once, like she'd just stamped her approval on my soul and dared me not to rise to it.

43

Kendrix

Everybody knew the unspoken rule. If you went home to "change," you weren't coming back. So we rolled into GivGold still dressed like Rivah's damn flower girl squad, ceremony clothes and all.

The bass thumped through the floor. Lights spun. The whole section looked like royalty had pulled up for bottle service. Khloe had her heels half off already. Rivah was curled in Kross's lap like she'd been glued there.

We were on our third round of shots when someone walked by.

A woman none of us knew—at least, I didn't. But Kordai did.

His whole body stiffened like she'd called him by his full government name. Her eyes lingered on him the way people stare at old scars.

"Sorry to interrupt," she said sweetly, eyes never leaving him. "Kordai... can I talk to you for a second?"

Nobody got a chance to speak before he was already standing, sliding out the section like his seat was on fire. He didn't even grab his drink. Just... left with her.

We all stared after them, blinking.

"Welp," Kairo said, leaning back with his drink. "Guess that solves that mystery. Thought prison done turned him celibate or worst."

I snorted. "Celibate ain't even in that nigga vocabulary."

"Man, me and Kross been trying to hook him up for months," Kairo went on. "Thought something was broke. Guess it still works."

Khloe rolled her eyes so hard I thought they might get stuck.

"You trying to be a matchmaker is wild. You can't even—"

"IT'S SHOT O'CLOCK!" Rivah cut her off like a damn foghorn. She shot up from her seat and flagged down the bartender, shaking her empty shot glass like maracas.

The bartender hustled over because Rivah scared every damn body. Magnolia came strolling up behind them, hair stacked to the heavens, dress flowing like she was fresh out a Sunday revival, bag in her hand like it held the Ten Commandments.

She looked at me and Pretty, eyes shining like she was proud of us for finally getting it together. The type of look mamas give their kids on graduation day.

Magnolia grinned wide, country as hell.

"Lord, look at my babies. Don't they look good? I swear, if y'all don't make it this time, I'm gone have to whoop both y'all asses myself."

I couldn't help but laugh. Magnolia wagged her finger at us.

"Kendrix, you got that look like you about to mess up this girl's lipstick. Don't start no shit in here. Wait 'til y'all get home."

"Nah... if we make it farther than our favorite VIP room, it'll be a miracle."

Magnolia clapped her hands loud enough to startle the bartender.

"Uh-uh, not on my watch. That can wait till *after* the dance."

Pretty smiled slow, devilish, and I swear my pulse jumped.

"You didn't think I came here just to watch, did you?" Magnolia grinned like a proud stage mom.

"Outfit's already ready in the back."

Pretty gave me one last look before Magnolia took her hand to lead her away. She leaned down, lips brushing my ear as she whispered,

"I can't wait to speak to you through my body language... make sure you keep up."

NETRAANTIONETTE

The lights dimmed, and the DJ cut the chatter with a soft crackle from the speakers.

Then she walked out and my heart damn near stopped.

Pretty wore a purple sparkly tutu and matching ballet slippers—the kind of outfit I'd only ever seen her admire from a distance. It was like someone had cracked open her soul and sewn it into fabric. No sex appeal, no seduction.. just power cloaked in grace.

I'd never seen her like that. I'd seen her fire. But that... that was her light. She didn't look like she was coming to tempt us. She looked like she was about to set the world on fire just by showing us what she survived.

The beat dropped— *"It's Getting Late"* by Floetry—and I sat up straight.

That was one of our songs. The one that played on late nights. She picked it on purpose. I knew it.

She moved toward the pole like it was an extension of her body. Then she spun—one clean, perfect turn that bled into a hard ballet pirouette. Her legs cut through the air with razor-sharp elegance, then melted into a slow, aching back arch as she wrapped herself around the pole.

The whole room gasped. And I just stared.

When the song hit the line— *"I'm afraid..."*

—her body crumbled low to the floor, folding in on itself like she was whispering secrets to her own bones.

Then as the lyrics said *"Don't be"*, she rose, spinning again—stronger and faster like she was answering herself. Like she was healing in front of us all.

Every twirl, every extension of her arm told a story: of fear, of survival, of choosing love anyway.

She wasn't performing. She was testifying.

The second her eyes found mine, the rest of the world blurred.

She spun and the glitter of her tutu caught he soft lights like stardust. Her ankle wrapped the pole in a perfect climb, then she lifted into an jade split.

The song wrapped around us.

Time was slipping by, but we were suspended in our own world, like maybe if we held our breath long enough, the clock would never stop for us.

She slid down the pole in a slow spiral, toes pointed, every inch of her controlled. The second her feet touched the stage again, she launched into a clean fouetté turn, tutu flaring, then dropped to her knees in a soft spin.

She pushed up into a backbend, hair brushing the stage, eyes still on me. The shift was like watching her pull herself out of darkness and into light. Her legs hooked the pole again.

It was intimate. Not sexual. Vulnerable. Not fragile.

Like she was saying:

"We've been through hell, but here we are... and I'm still choosing you."

Each move melted into the next.. Her dance told a story of soft urgency, of two souls trying to stretch their moment before reality could intrude and her body told it louder than the music ever could.

I sat there, without words, knowing it wasn't just a dance.

It was love... timeless and suspended. A bubble only we existed in.

And God, I never wanted it to end.

44

Niveah

I was still floating.

The music was gone, the lights were dim again, and yet my body buzzed like I was still on that pole, still spinning with every ounce of my soul spilling out of me.

I'd barely made it out of my dressing room. My heart was set on one thing—Kendrix.

Ty caught me halfway down the hallway.

"Your boo in y'all's regular VIP room," she said, wagging her brows like a nosy auntie.

I laughed, shaking my head, but my feet picked up pace anyway. That man was about to be smothered in kisses and whatever else he asked for.

But then—I hit the main floor.

And froze.

Walking through the door like sin wrapped in cologne and custom-tailored trouble... was Sincere.

Same powerful confidence, same faint smirk that said he always knew something you didn't.

I walked straight toward him. "Mi gyal," he said, that smooth Jamaican accent rolling off his tongue. "Still as dangerous as the day you got rid of me."

I laughed under my breath, shaking my head.

"I didn't get rid of you."

"You did," he countered with a sly grin, eyes dragging over my face like he was cataloging every change. "But mi not vex. Mi business ran over, and word reach me that di club open back. So mi sed to meself... she follow mi advice, eh? She go believe in love and tek back what is hers. Mi had to come see it wid mi own eyes."

I slipped my hands into his without thinking, squeezing them.

Some people would never understand us and they didn't need to. There was never, and would never be, a world where our hearts beat for each other. But there was love here. The kind rooted in survival and the joy of seeing someone rise.

"I'm happy you're happy that I'm happy," I said softly, and he smirked like he knew exactly what I meant.

Before the moment could get too sentimental, Magnolia's scent touched us both.

She floated behind us like the Southern storm she was. Hips swaying, earrings swinging, that bright laugh. She was all curves and chaos wrapped in a silk dress, and still somehow managed to make everybody feel like her favorite cousin.

I caught Sincere's gaze flick toward her... then stay. He didn't even try to be subtle. His head tilted slightly, eyes narrowing like he was trying to solve a puzzle, or maybe just take in all of her at once.

Magnolia was everything.

And judging by the way Sincere's expression softened, the lightbulb had just flicked on for him too. Sincere's eyes never left her.

"My black queen," he said low, like it wasn't meant for me to hear and slipped straight out his soul.

Then he tilted his head, still watching Magnolia as she floated through the room like she owned it.

"Niv... who is that?"

I turned, already smiling.

"Oh, that's Magnolia," I said, letting the syllables roll slow just to mess with him. "Yeah... she's something."

He repeated it, soft, like he was trying to taste it on his tongue.

"Magnolia... Magnolia."

"From Magnolia, Mississippi," I added, reading his face like a book.

His lips curved.

"A southern goddess. Just like I like them."

I smirked, because I knew then he was done for.

"Magnolia!" I called.

She spun on her heel, hips swaying like she had a drumbeat only she could hear. She made her way over, her usual mix of grace and chaos bottled up in one honey-coated hurricane.

"This is Sincere," I said. "Sincere... Magnolia."

Magnolia's eyes flicked over him, curiosity brightening her face. She reached out to shake his hand, but Sincere caught her fingers instead, bowing just enough to kiss her knuckles.

Magnolia's cheeks flushed that soft rose color she tried to hide.

"Sincere is one of my very good friends," I said lightly. "But I think you'd do a much better job entertaining him... make sure his night is great."

Magnolia shot me a *bitch, what?* look, but I saw the little spark of interest she thought she was hiding.

"Will do," she said sweetly, slipping back into hostess mode.

Sincere gave me one last warm hug before turning and following Magnolia into the crowd. His eyes were locked on her like he'd just spotted his favorite song in human form.

And knowing Magnolia... she was about to make him dance.

NETRAANTIONETTE

I pushed open the door to our regular VIP room, already grinning just ready to melt into him after everything.

But the second I stepped in, my feet stopped. It didn't look like our regular room anymore. The entire space glowed in rich, layered shades of purple—lavender lights along the ceiling, dark purple couches tucked against the walls, velvet drapes brushing the floor. Soft gold accents caught the light like flickers of flame.

The chandelier. Gold, dripping in crystals, scattering light like falling stars. And a gold pole gleaming in the center of the room like it had been waiting... just for me.

Kendrix was leaning back, lips curved into that slow smile that always undid me.

"This is our room," he said simply.. "Only designed for us."

Something fluttered deep in my chest.

I crossed the room and sank onto his lap. For a long moment, we just stared at each other, eyes locked, like we were both replaying every heartbreak, every near-ending, every impossible thing we'd survived.

And then—we laughed.

Big, real, from-the-belly laughter.

"Kendrix... we have been through some shit," I said, shaking my head.

He grinned, brushing his thumb along my jaw.

"I was just thinking the same thing... but look at us now."

He leaned in, forehead against mine.

"Sitting here. Together."

"Ready to conquer the world," I whispered.

"Together," he finished.

He stood slow and the purple lights pained his skin.

"Take your clothes off," he said.

I blinked, half-laughing. "Huh?"

"Take your clothes off, Pretty."

His voice was soft but commanding, and something about the way he said it—like he was asking me to shed everything, not just fabric—made my pulse trip over itself.

So I stood. And piece by piece, I let every layer fall.

He did the same. Until it was just us. Bare. Breathing. Seeing.

We didn't move. Just looked at each other, like maybe this was the first time we'd really seen one another without all the wreckage between us.

His eyes traced every inch of me. Reverent.

"I love your body," he said, voice low. "But not because it's perfect, because it's yours. The same body that carried you through storms, through hell, through heartbreak you didn't deserve... and still walks in rooms like this."

He stepped closer, his hand brushing my cheek.

"I love your mind. The way it never stops fighting for everyone else, even when it's breaking. I love your mouth... not just how it feels, but how it speaks life into people who don't even know they need it. I love your hands, how they've built whole empires while wiping tears off other people's faces."

He kissed my shoulder, my collarbone, my heart.

"I love... every version of you. The real. The raw. The raging. The soft. The broken. The rebuilding."

His lips touched mine, and he whispered—

"I'm not just in love with your body, Pretty... I'm in love with your *body language*. The way every part of you speaks, even when you don't say a word."

Tears burned the back of my eyes as he pulled me closer, pressing his forehead to mine.

"No one will ever have me the way you do," he murmured. "And no one will ever have *you* the way I do. We've survived it all. Now it's just us."

Just us. Naked. And understood.

I stayed standing, staring at him.

He sat back on the plush purple couch, golden light glinting off his skin, and his erection stood tall like it knew I belonged to it.

"This," he said, voice dripping with hunger, eyes dropping to his length, "...is your kingdom. Your throne to ride."

The words alone made my knees weak, my core clenching as if my body understood him before my mind could catch up.

I leaned forward, my lips brushing the warm skin of his neck, and whispered,

"We've said so much with our mouths... but it's our bodies that have never lied."

I climbed into his lap, his hands settling possessively on my hips as I sank down onto him with a gasp. The world blurred. Just us, skin to skin, soul to soul.

"You feel that?" I breathed against his lips as I moved slow, rolling my hips to match the deep rhythm of his thrusts.

"This is my body language... telling you how much I love you."

He groaned, head tipping back, gripping my waist tighter like he was anchoring himself to me.

"I understand every word of it, Pretty," he rasped. "Every clench, every tremble... you're screaming I'm yours."

I rode him deeper, harder, tears slipping down my cheeks as pleasure and love tangled inside me.

"Tell me you hear it," I cried softly, hips crashing down with desperate devotion. "Tell me you hear my body saying I need you."

His hands slid up my spine, holding me flush against his chest as he met every roll of my hips.

"I hear it, baby. And mine's saying it back—I need you. I love you. You're my everything."

The room disappeared. The past disappeared. Everything disappeared.

All that remained... was us.

Two bodies speaking one language.

Our language.

Body Language.

Epilogue

It's been three months of love and happiness.

Three months of waking up without my chest feeling heavy, of not bracing myself for the next disaster. Some mornings, I still have to pinch myself, because part of me is always waiting for something bad to snatch it all away.

But Kendrix... Kendrix has me living my soft life. I've finally entered that era.

I was on a lounge chair near the pool, sunbathing with Rivah. We were at the Givelle Estates for Mamma G's sacred Sunday dinner that she didn't play about. If you were invited, your ass better be here, or she was gonna let your ass have it.

I stretched, letting the sun soak my skin, sipping on a frozen cocktail. Meanwhile, Kendrix was in the pool with his brothers, glistening, giving me those sexy eyes like he'd forgotten we were surrounded by family. Kennedi was on the pool deck bossing them around like a tiny CEO, arms crossed and sunglasses on, making sure nobody splashed her hair.

Mama was still on dialysis, but she was starting to take her health seriously. We'd made an agreement: if she showed me she was really trying, I'd start letting Heidi come around more. And it worked. My little sister was in heaven because what's better than two mother figures spoiling you?

The surprise was that Mama and Rita had actually grown close. They'd sit up on the phone, talking like old girlfriends, cackling about the soap operas they watched together every week. Hearing my mama laugh like that again? That shit healed something in me I didn't even know was still bleeding.

I was still riding that high when Mama told Rita she was ready to try rehab again. For real this time. And I believe her. I'm praying this round she finds not just sobriety, but peace and maybe even a man to confide in. She's been lonely for so long, and after everything she's endured, she deserves a love that feels safe, steady, and hers.

Zejah and Hux were curled up at home, just days away from delivering my niece Kensley.

Yep... Kensley.

Over the last few months, Kendrix and Huxley have grown ridiculously close, and I love everything about it. And the way he'd completely won Zejah over was crazy. He catered to her cravings like it was a sport. From late-night fries dipped in strawberry milkshakes to mango snowcones at two in the morning.

Zejah always said she didn't have her dad, but she was just grateful her daughter would have two strong men in her life, so she named her after them both.

Kensley.

Kendrix and Huxley.

Her village, built in blood and love.

I smiled to myself as Kendrix caught me staring and mouthed, *"Fine Ass."*

Rivah was side-eyeing her drink like it personally offended her.

"This virgin piña colada is nasty as hell," she said, smacking her lips. Yeah, Kross had took her out the damn game. And I'm mad as hell because I was planning so much bald-head hoe shit for us to do together just to make them mad.

I burst out laughing, nearly spilling my drink. She was almost out of her first trimester, and already showing the tiniest bump. Mamma G was floating around grinning like she'd just won the grandma lottery, and honestly, I was excited too. Rivah had always had this soft underlayer beneath her savage mouth. Kross had already started pulling it out of her, and I couldn't wait to see what a baby would do.

"You gone be a good mama," I said, smiling at her.

She tossed her hair and grinned. "I pray every night that I am. Everything in life has just been better. OH! Girl, the sex has gotten better too. I always had a waterpark... but now?" She lowered her sunglasses. "It's the whole damn ocean. And Kross loves to swim."

I choked on my straw. "Rivah!"

She was dead serious. "No, for real. But this morning sickness? This shit for the birds."

Before I could even respond, Khloe came and sat down beside me like she was auditioning for a tragic soap opera scene. She didn't say a word. Just sat there, still and dramatic, like life had snatched her soul.

Rivah and I both stared at her.

"Uh... what the hell wrong with you?" I asked.

"Yeah," Rivah added, tilting her shades down. "Bringing all that bad ass energy over here."

Khloe sighed, sinking deeper into the chair.

"The only reason I came was to see y'all," she admitted. "If it wasn't for y'all, I'd be at home. I'm just... tired. Tired of faking it with Kairo. Tired of arguing about the same damn things and telling him what I need."

Rivah gave her a soft look. Normally, she'd be the first one to snap and call somebody out, but pregnancy had her wrapped in feelings lately. Instead of cutting her eyes and cussing, she just rubbed Khloe's arm.

Khloe scrolled on her phone casually, like she was just reading the weather, while she casually dropped bombs.

"All I wanted was some intimate alone time. Just us. But it's like he's a damn machine. He wants to schedule sex." She paused and looked at us. "Schedule. Sex. I don't want to schedule dinner or dates, so what the hell makes him think I wanna schedule sex?"

Me and Rivah both made the same face like, girl, what?

She kept going. "He just lets his career control everything. I'm sick of it. I've got a career too, a whole law degree, but I've never put it before him or Kennedi. He said..." she stopped, biting her lip.

"What?" Rivah pressed.

"He said maybe... he's not enough for me."

"I know tf he didn't." I sat up, eyes wide.

"Right?" she said. "Said I want a lot of quality time and sex he just doesn't have the capacity for."

"So what the fuck does that mean?" Rivah shot back.

Khloe exhaled like the words burned. "He asked me how I felt about an open marriage."

"OH SHIT!" we both yelled so loud everybody turned.

We waved them off quick. "It's nothing!"

I turned back, whispering harsh. "So what are you gonna do? Are there... rules?"

Khloe rolled her eyes. "He says he doesn't even want to see anyone else. And honestly, I believe him. I've been watching him for years just waiting for signs and there's never been any. He's just... married to his damn career."

Rivah leaned forward, blunt as ever. "So what do you want to do?"

Khloe... smiled. Like full teeth, dimples, and eyes sparkling.

"I'ma do it," she said.

Me and Rivah damn near choked on our drinks.

Khloe nodded, calm as ever. "Kairo is my first and the only man I've ever been with. I'm almost thirty-four. I think he said it because he really doesn't believe I'll do it."

"Me either," Rivah and I both said at the same time.

"Exactly." She laughed, leaning back. "See, that's the problem. I'm done being the good girl that does everything for everyone else and thinks about everyone but myself and what I really want. I'm ready to be adventurous. To learn what I really like... and what I really don't like."

I looked at her, grinning. "Bihhhhhh."

Rivah threw her hands up. "You would wait until I become a whole Givelle incubator."

"Right," I said. "You wanna wait to do this shit when I'm locked down."

Khloe snorted. "What y'all have is amazing. Seeing y'all happy lets me know that I'll be there one day. Hopefully, everything about this lights a fire under Kairo and shit changes. Don't ask for something you're not ready for.. because since he wants me to do it... I'ma go all out."

We all hollered laughing. Then she got quiet, twirling her straw in her drink.

"...but I just don't know how to date," she admitted. "Hell, I don't even know where to start."

I smiled slow and pulled out my phone.

"Don't worry about it. I gotcha. And I have the perfect person. If you wanna have a good time, this man is a great time."

Khloe and Rivah leaned over as I scrolled through my camera roll and held up the photo.

Whewwww.

Stacks.

Chocolate, fine, broad shoulders, locs pulled up into a bun, and a smile that could ruin lives.

Khloe's eyes went wide. "He is fine."

Rivah's jaw literally dropped. "Hell yeah... who is that?"

"Stacks," I said, trying not to grin. "He's like the older brother I never had. We grew up together in Gun Hill."

Khloe was still staring at the screen. "I mean... he is fine as fuck."

Rivah laughed. "Niv... you gone fuck her up."

Khloe blinked, confused. "What you mean?"

I turned to her like I was about to preach a serious sermon to her.

"Because, Khloe... you come from money and so does your husband. Stacks comes from the hood. The straight ghetto. Everything he has, he built with his own blood, sweat, and tears. Ain't nothing like that ghetto love. Those niggas from the hood... they just love different."

Rivah raised her glass like she was testifying in church.

"Once you go hood, ain't no coming back."

Khloe rolled her eyes like we didn't know what the hell we were talking about.

"Set it up, Niv." she said, still staring out at the pool. "But it stays between us three."

"Okay," I said, already typing away on my phone.

Khloe slid on her oversized shades, crossed her legs, and leaned back like a woman who had already made peace with the chaos she was about to cause.

"Kairo will get some act right soon," she said. "He thinks this is about games, but I don't have time to play mind games. I crave mental stimulation... real connection, passion, romance—not just another Birkin or another luxury car."

She uncrossed her legs and looked at us with a face that only came when she'd made up her mind.

"He gives me the world, but I'm starving in it.

I need someone who feeds my mind, not just funds my lifestyle. He wants to test me—fine. Let's see how he handles this."

Rivah's mouth fell open. "Whew. You sound like a woman who just decided to stop surviving and start scheming."

Khloe smirked. "I'm done begging for love in a language he doesn't speak. If he can't meet me where I am, I'll stop waiting on him to catch up... and let him watch what it looks like when someone else does."

The End

45

Netra's Notebook

The book may end here, but my storytelling doesn't. On my Patreon, you'll find:

Exclusive stories & bonus scenes that will *never* hit the shelves

Behind-the-scenes peeks at my writing life & upcoming projects

First looks at covers, titles & secret announcements

Stories too bold, too raw, or too personal to release anywhere else

If you love being first, love getting the tea before the world does, and want to keep this creative journey alive, join me there. Your support helps me write more, dream bigger, and give you the stories you can't stop thinking about.

Discussion Questions

1. If you grew up like Niv (parentified, abandoned, forced to raise siblings) would you use your mouth, mind, or body the same way she did to survive? What's your line between "finessing" and "manipulating"? It's one thing to say, "I'd just get a job," but imagine working a regular 9–5 when you have to worry about two kids, bills stacked like bricks, and a mom who's one phone call away from crashing out and burning everything you've worked for. Would a paycheck stretch far enough? Would patience? Or would desperation push you into different choices?

2. Do you think people who've lived through cycles of addiction, betrayal, or abandonment deserve redemption from the people they've hurt, or is walking away the only path to peace?

3. Is it wrong to take advantage of someone's vulnerability (like Niv does with men who crave attention), if you're doing it to survive and provide? Or is it just smart economics in an unfair world?

4. Could you separate the son from the sins of the father? Could you keep loving a man knowing that the person he loves and respects is the same one who fed your family's destruction? Would the love you built outweigh the rage in your blood?

5. If you found out the person you love blames your father for their deepest wounds, could you still love them the same? Could you defend

your father and love them simultaneously, or would you feel forced to choose? Is it even possible to separate loyalty to blood from loyalty to your heart?

Discussion Questions

1. Kendrix says he loves "the real, the raw, the naked versions" of Niv. What does being seen and loved in your most vulnerable state mean to you?

2. This book peels back the layers of Niv's family history of addiction, assault, abandonment. How does learning her mother's truth shift Niv's own identity and anger?

3. If someone hurt you indirectly (like Mr. Givelle supplying drugs to Niv's mom), could you forgive once you understood their intentions? Why or why not?

4. The deal Niv made with Mamma G was to protect Kendrix, but she broke it out of love. Would you have kept the secret or told him? Why?

5. How does the book challenge the stereotype of women using sex or dance for validation versus using it as power and healing?

6. How do you feel about the quiet hope the story gives for Niv's mom while trying again at rehab, finding friendship, maybe love later in life?

7. Khloe admits she's done "being the good girl." What do you think will happen as she steps into power and explores what she really wants?

About The Author

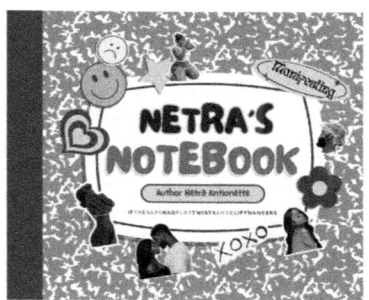

Netra Antionette writes with a heart rooted in Black stories that honor softness, strength, survival, and above all, our power to choose love on our own terms. Whether it's the ache of generational wounds or the joy of hard-earned healing, her stories are a celebration of resilience, a reclamation of tenderness, and a mirror for the kind of love Black women—and all those who've ever been told they're too much or not enough—deserve. Netra Antoinette holds a bachelor's in public health and a master's in business administration; a degree she pursued to support her creative vision to navigate the literary world with intention. When she's not writing, she's embracing her most cherished role: being a wife and mother, grounding her work in the same love and resilience she writes about.

Want more?

Visit her website at www.netraantionette.com to shop signed books, bundles, and exclusive goodies.

Join Netra's Notebook

https://www.facebook.com/share/g/1Y7ENSNY21/?mibextid=wwXIfr

www.ingramcontent.com/pod-product-compliance
Lightning Source LLC
Chambersburg PA
CBHW070204120726
47909CB00001B/251